CHANGING
MARRIAGE

Books by Susan Kietzman

THE GOOD LIFE

A CHANGING MARRIAGE

Published by Kensington Publishing Corporation

A
CHANGING
MARRIAGE

SUSAN KIETZMAN

KENSINGTON BOOKS
www.kensingtonbooks.com

ISBN-13: 978-0-7582-8134-0
ISBN-10: 0-7582-8134-X
First Kensington Trade Paperback Printing: March 2014

eISBN-13: 978-0-7582-8135-7
eISBN-10: 0-7582-8135-8
First Kensington Electronic Edition: March 2014

10 9 8 7 6 5 4 3 2 1

Printed in the United States of America

To Ted, who changes with me

ACKNOWLEDGMENTS

I thank my agent, Loretta Weingel-Fidel, and my editor, John Scognamiglio, for their knowledge and patience. And I thank my family and friends for their continuous support.

CHAPTER 1

NOVEMBER 1988

He had never seen her before, even though he walked that same route from his dorm through the student center to class three times a week. She was sitting in the reception area next to the café, in an upholstered armchair. Lit from behind by the morning sunlight blasting through a wall-sized window, she looked more vision than human. Bob stopped walking. She read a book she held in her lap, as if she were alone in her dorm room or sequestered in the library, with nothing but silence for company. Bob took a step closer, and, as if on cue, she looked up at him. A second later, he was jostled by a passing student's overloaded backpack, momentarily dislodging his focus. Bumped a second time, Bob looked around, again aware of the moving people, of the noise, of the sense of urgency. He looked at the large analog clock on the wall behind him and discovered he had just five minutes to make it to his marketing class. As he cut through the lane of scurrying students, he glanced back, but the girl was gone.

Bob took his assigned seat in Mark Gladwin's class just as the professor entered the room. Gladwin, a short, trim man with wiry black hair and matching bifocals, glanced up at the auditorium rows of students on the way to his desk. He set his briefcase down and ushered his worn cardboard folder of notes to the podium. Bob opened his notebook and took a pen from his back pocket. Less than a minute later, it was as if both of them had been there for hours, Gladwin talking and Bob taking notes. He was a long-distance runner, Gladwin, and carried that unusual combination of drive and patience into the classroom. And he lived up to his reputation as a storyteller, offering a relevant case for just about every question that had arisen in class. He was different, certainly, from most of the professors at the mid-Michigan community college Bob attended for two years before transferring into the state university system. But, unlike those other professors, Gladwin appeared to have no concept of transition: He didn't say good morning; he didn't take roll; he never wasted time. He talked quickly, so that even the serious students had to strain forward in their seats to keep up. Bob knew all this; he had been Gladwin's student for more than two months now. But he still allowed his thoughts to wander. Who was that girl?

He had seen her for only a moment, but a picture of her encompassed his entire brain like an image projected onto a movie theater screen. He looked back at the professor and tried to reengage with him, but Gladwin had become like a word Bob couldn't remember, available but inaccessible. Instead, Bob's mind had become her prisoner, entangled by her auburn hair. The stillness of her pose juxtaposed with the atmospheric chaos of the student center was noteworthy. How could anyone read quietly and utterly without movement in the midst of madness? And the light from the window behind her had been white, unfiltered. Its intensity creating an aura, he mused, an aura of goodness, of serenity, of something intangible and uncommon in busy twentieth-century life.

Bob shifted his weight in his chair in an effort to change gears, to rid his mind of fantastical thoughts and to return to Gladwin, who had turned from the podium to write on the blackboard that covered the front wall of the classroom. Bob wrote in his notebook what Gladwin wrote on the board, even though it made little sense. Maybe his roommate, Evan, knew her. Maybe, if Bob explained where and when he had seen her and what she looked like, Evan would tell him her name. What was her name? Bob jotted down several possibilities in the margin of his notes: *Sarah, Jennifer, Catherine, Christine . . .* Annette? Bob liked Annette. It was different enough to warrant her outstanding qualities. He wrote *Annette* below the list of other names and then wrote *Parsons,* his last name, after it.

Not by chance, Bob found his roommate in the library that evening. Evan Blackhurst, who referred to himself as a book nerd, always sat on the third floor in the northeast corner carrel, walled in by heavy physics books, shed clothing, and assorted caffeinated beverages he smuggled into the building in his oversized pockets. The third floor was the designated quiet floor with absolutely no talking, nothing but the occasional rumble from the heating and air-conditioning ducts for distraction. The third floor, according to Evan, was for the student who went to the library to study rather than socialize. Yet, didn't Bob find Evan every time he looked for him? Didn't they have a quick conversation every time Bob hung over the top of Evan's carrel? And hadn't Bob convinced Evan twice already that semester to quit studying and go to the bar?

"How's it going?" said Bob, popping his head over the top of the carrel. Evan didn't respond, didn't even look up. "You about done?"

"No."

"So, how much time do you need? Thirty minutes?"

Evan looked at his watch. "More like ninety."

An annoyed "Sssshhhhhhh!" emanated from a nearby carrel.

"That's too bad," said Bob, whispering. "There's a party at the complex."

Evan laid his twice-read-already copy of *A Brief History of Time* on the crowded tabletop in front of him. This was Evan's go-to book when he needed a quick break from studying but still wanted to stimulate his brain. Most walked to the student center for coffee when they sought diversion; Evan turned to Stephen Hawking, his idol. Evan gave Bob his best disinterested look, a challenge for a boy whose thick blond hair, although cut in the traditional men's style, grew out instead of down. And because he hadn't made time for a haircut in several weeks, he looked like someone out of the 1970s rather than the late 1980s. "Didn't we go to a function last night?"

Bob nodded his head. "It was a good function."

"I'll grant you that," said Evan, returning to his book.

Taking Evan's concurrence as an opening, Bob pulled up a chair paired with a vacant carrel. Evan sighed, putting his head in his hands for dramatic effect. "Let's go for an hour," began Bob. "I'll let you tell me, again, why Mike Dukakis should be our president. Then you can come back here and continue studying."

"After I've had a couple of beers?"

"You don't have to drink."

Evan raised his head and looked at Bob. "Then why do I want to go to this party?"

"Go to the party and leave us in peace," said the voice from the other carrel.

"I want to see if you know someone," said Bob, lowering his voice that he had inadvertently raised. "I met this girl today; actually I only saw her, in the student center on my way to class. I have to find her."

Evan removed his glasses, which Bob took as a good sign. "Since when have you needed me to meet girls?"

"This is different. She's different. She's absolutely radiant, and I don't want to mess things up. I thought if you knew her, you could introduce us or something."

"Tell me you have a crush," said Evan, the beginnings of a smile around his mouth and eyes for the first time since Bob's arrival.

"Does anyone out of elementary school use that term?"

"I just did."

"Then yes, I do." Evan looked at his watch. "Ev, you've been here all day. One hour. It will be good for you."

"Okay," said Evan, pushing back in his chair. "I'll go for one hour. But not because it will be good for me."

"Thank God," said the voice.

* * *

Harrison Complex was a cluster of dorms connected by glass hallways at the north end of campus. While not the most attractive or desirable place to live—it was a good ten-minute walk from everywhere else—it housed the perfect location for parties. Shay, the northern dining hall, was large enough so that when the tables and chairs were stacked at the perimeter, there was ample room for a couple hundred college students to socialize. It was built in the 1970s, when the energy conservation effort dictated low ceilings, an architectural feature that created an air of intimacy in utilitarian spaces like Shay, which, with support columns, was able to stretch the length of a basketball court. The setup was always the same: admission tables at one end, beer tables in the middle, and whatever the Alternative Club was promoting—chess, Pictionary, card games—at the far end.

As Bob paid the two-dollar entrance fee and had his hand stamped, he began to scan the room. Twenty-four hours ago, when he and Evan had wandered into the Delta Phi keg party on their way back from the library, Bob's sole focus had been a beer blitz on his stress level, heightened by recent midterm exams and finals in a month. Tonight, he was focused on her, the adrenaline rush from his chance meeting with her resurfacing and prompting his heart to beat faster. This could be the night he talked to her. This could be the night he put the lingering unpleasantness of an impromptu, two-week romance with a girl in his dorm to rest. God, he hoped she and her pleading looks didn't show up. He and Evan walked to the beer table and stood in line. Evan looked at his watch. "We've been here five minutes," said Bob.

"Ten."

"You walked here on your own legs. No second thoughts now."

"Fine," said Evan, which is what he always said when it wasn't.

Bob reasoned that the chances of seeing the girl at the party far outweighed those of another chance sighting somewhere else on campus. Large universities were funny that way. On his way to a class, Bob could see the same person every day for a week and then not at all the following week. An extra minute in the shower or a room scan for a missing glove was all it took to change the faces on his trip across campus. It was so unlike life at Winslow Community College, where Bob saw the same people every Monday through Friday. They parked their cars in the same spots. They walked the same wide cement sidewalks to the classroom buildings. They ate the same reheated food in the cafeteria. They sat under the same trees, smoking and drinking coffee, in the courtyard in good weather. While these were comforting features when Bob was first starting out and knew nothing about college life, they quickly turned stale. So much so that Bob had wanted to transfer to the big school after his first semester. It was his parents, citing financial constraints, who kept him home until he completed his sophomore year.

On the other side of the beer table, Evan's friend Matthew, a senior, ignored the red underage ink on their hands and handed them each two twelve-ounce plastic cups of draft beer. Cups in hand, Bob and Evan slowly walked the length of the dimly lit room, sipping as they strolled. There were so many people; it was an effort to distinguish one face from another. Strangely nervous and already discouraged, Bob chugged the second half of his first beer. "I didn't think there would be so many people here," he shouted over his shoulder and the dance music to Evan, two steps behind him.

"There are always this many people here," Evan yelled back. "This is the reason you wanted to come!"

"I'll never find her here!"

"What?" shouted Evan. Bob pointed to a set of doors and walked in their direction. They walked through them and out into the long hallway that ran the length of the dining hall, the party noise fading with a click. "What is your problem?" asked Evan. "We are now on the wrong side of locked doors. If we want to get back into the party, we have to go all the way around and through the line again."

"I couldn't hear in there; I couldn't think. How am I ever going to find this girl?"

"What," asked Evan, taking the last sip from his first cup, "is so special about this girl?"

Bob ran his hand through his short, dark brown hair, a habit more than a style correction. His older brothers had called him Brillo since junior high, a cruel but apt nickname. "I don't know. I don't even know her. It was just something I felt when I saw her today. I haven't been able to stop thinking about her."

"What does she look like?"

"She's got brilliant reddish hair," said Bob, "that goes past her shoulders. And she's got a pretty face, although it was hard to see all of it because she glanced at me for just a moment. I think I told you she was reading a book. Oh, and she's got great posture."

"Great posture?"

"Yeah. She was sitting in a chair and her back was straight, not curved and sloppy like most people's backs."

Evan started walking down the hallway, and Bob followed. "So, I'm looking for a girl with good posture?"

"Yes."

Evan took a sip from his second beer. "We're not going to find her."

"I know."

"Do you want to go back in?"

"You go in," said Bob. "I'm out of here."

Evan watched his roommate walk up the set of stairs at the end of the hallway, then looked at his watch. He decided to go back into the party for another thirty minutes before returning to the library. Maybe he'd meet a girl, a girl with nice eyes, a broad smile, and a lithesome body—good posture optional.

Bob walked back to the library, quiet and bright after the party, and up the stairs to the second floor. His books lay undisturbed in the exact position he had left them almost an hour before. Leave stuff anywhere else and it wouldn't be there an hour later; most unattended things wouldn't last ten minutes. School libraries, it seemed, were one of the last trustworthy places left. Bob breathed in, hesitated, then sat, picked up his market strategy book, and began rereading the first page of "Chapter Eight: Making Your Product Available to the Global Customer." Halfway through the second paragraph, Bob set the book down. He stood, packed all of his belongings into his backpack, and quickly descended the stairs to the first floor. What he needed, he decided on his way out the door, was a couple hours of mindless television in his room. With Evan sure to return to the library after the party, Bob could watch whatever he wanted.

Bob took his usual route through the student center on his way back to the dorm. It was a little longer than going directly to his room—and this was a consideration in mid-November, when the first snowfall was already a week old—but it provided the opportunity to enjoy light conversation as well as forced-air heat on the long walk between the library and John Adams Hall, one of six smaller dorms named after early U.S. presidents at the eastern end of campus. He opened the glass door to the café and was welcomed by sounds of relaxation. Bob wove his way around people and tables that had been moved to accommodate them and into a line of more people waiting to buy food. He reached into his back pocket for his wallet, taking out three singles for a root beer and a large bag of chips. He smiled as he paid the cashier, a cute girl with enormous brown eyes. He had seen her somewhere before, his economics lecture maybe. Bob meandered through another crowd of people gathered just outside the reception area where he had seen the girl that morning. Several games of euchre were in process. Bob stopped for a moment and looked at the chair where she had been reading. It was empty now, and he was tempted for a second to place his hand on the cushion to see if it still held the heat from her body.

The far end of the building housed one of the three campus bars. The Intellectual Grape was a mellow wine bar that attracted girls and guys trying to impress girls on dates. It was not, as Bob had learned, a good place to start a conversation with a stranger. People at The Grape walked in with the company they wanted to keep that evening. Was she in there with another guy? Bob resisted the urge to walk in and have a look around, instead heading for the doors at the far end of the hallway. As he was about to walk back out into the cold night air, she appeared on the other side of the glass. Bob froze, unable for a few seconds to even breathe. Was she real, or was she a product of his longings? She smiled at him; Bob thought he smiled in return. He wanted to speak to her, but the glass was in the way. It separated them, a transparent but formidable wall, and Bob had no idea how to reach her. He pushed against it, but it wouldn't move. Perhaps he could scale it. If only he could find a rope. He checked the ground, but found nothing. When he looked up, she was still there, only now she was reaching for something, and before Bob knew exactly what was happening, the door was opening, as if released by incantation. "How did you do that?" Bob asked, transfixed.

"I pulled on the handle," said the girl, facing him from less than three feet away. "Your side's locked."

"Ah," said Bob, still submerged in fantasy, but swimming toward the surface.

"Are you okay?"

"Yes, most definitely."

"Okay then," she said, turning to leave.

"Wait!" said Bob, breaking through. "Don't go." She stopped and looked back at him over her shoulder. "I'm sorry. I was lost in thought."

She laughed. "Yes, you were."

He held out his hand. "My name's Bob. Bob Parsons."

"And I'm Karen." She took his hand in hers. Bob noticed that it fit perfectly, as if the two had once been molded together. "Karen Spears."

Now what, thought Bob, desperately wanting to say something that would make her laugh again, that would keep her near him. "Where are you headed?"

"To get coffee. I have a huge test tomorrow, and I'm sleepy already."

"I know the feeling."

"Caffeine is so tricky, though. Not enough and I fall asleep; too much and I'm too wired to study."

"A medium should do it. A large will keep you up for a couple of days." She laughed again. "Do you want company?"

"I'm just getting it to go."

Bob hesitated, his banging heart too big for his chest. "I could walk with you, if you'd like."

Karen narrowed her eyes. "Are you a nice person, Bob Parsons?"

"I carry character references for just this kind of chance meeting."

Karen smiled. "Okay. Come on then."

They walked back down the hall Bob had just traveled, back past The Grape, past the student lounge, and into the cafeteria. It was all as it had been, and yet it looked new, as if in the last five minutes a different paint color had been rolled on the walls. They walked in tandem, Karen in front, the thick crowd prohibiting a side-by-side stroll. He should have guessed her name; it suited her perfectly. The radiance he had seen that morning still shone from her hair and, just minutes ago, from her face, which was even prettier than he remembered. She wore little makeup, just mascara, from what Bob quickly gathered, and had the natural kind of looks his mother would call lovely. Her lips were closer to pink than red, with a healthy, lip-balmed look. They would be soft when he kissed them; they would pull, slightly, at his lips when they parted. He would not scare her away by trying to kiss her that night. He would follow the standard dating protocol and ask her out for a movie or dinner off campus. If she accepted and they went out together, then he would have the option of kissing her good night.

Bob observed her as she purchased a medium coffee and then added cream and sugar as if he were watching an arcane procedure seldom practiced. Her hands, soft and steady, poured just the right amount. No drips. And only one teaspoon of sugar: moderation. They walked out of the café and stood for a minute, outside the reception area, talking about her art history test the next day and sipping their drinks. Bob was fascinated that she was in the middle of memorizing more than two hundred paintings and the artists who created them. He liked the sound of her voice, which was both confident and melodic. Had she been able to say nothing but her name over and over, Bob would have listened attentively.

They walked back to the far end of the building, where they had met just fifteen minutes before. Bob pushed opened the same door she had opened for him, and they moved into the night, still talking. It wasn't until they were through the parking lot and into the street that they discovered they had grown up in the same town. They both stopped and looked at each other. "You're kidding," said Bob. "Manchester?"

"Manchester."

"Where do you live?"

"Sealy Street, near the high school."

"Near Ward High School?"

"The only reputable high school in town."

"Oh no!" said Bob, in mock horror. "If you went to Ward High School, I shouldn't even be talking to you!"

Karen laughed. "That can only mean you went to Handley! And if that's true, I *definitely* shouldn't be talking to you!" She walked several steps away from him, stopped, and turned her back to him. Bob approached her, set his drink and chips on the snowy pavement, and put his arm around her shoulders. He bent down and put his mouth next to her ear and whispered, "I won't tell if you won't tell."

She turned to face him, her light green eyes looking into his. "Deal," she whispered back.

Their ensuing kiss seemed right, expected even, as a means to seal their agreement, a handshake too formal. As they drew apart, Bob felt warm and relaxed, not agitated like he had been with other girls. With other girls, he had wanted to go further, to keep kissing them, to touch them, to take them to a place where they wouldn't be disturbed. Not this time. He wanted everyone to see him with Karen, lit by the angled glow of the halogen streetlamp but otherwise surrounded by darkness, and he wanted this very moment to last minutes, hours even, instead of seconds. If they had been the stars in a movie, the director would have shot the kiss full circle, with a beginning, middle, and slow but deliberate end; it was a perfect kiss. Afterward, they stood frozen, Karen with her medium foam cup of coffee in her hands, and Bob with his root beer and chips at his feet and his arms casually draped over her shoulders. He opened his mouth to speak.

"Don't." Karen put her fingers, warmed by the coffee, lightly over his lips. "Don't talk." She picked up his cup and chip bag and handed them to him, then led him out of the street and onto the frozen grass. They crossed the central green in silence, walked around the bookstore, and down a short hill to Karen's dorm. They stopped at the front door and faced each other.

"Can I talk now?"

"Go right ahead."

"What are you doing tomorrow?"

"Going to my classes."

"After that," said Bob. "What are you doing for dinner?"

"Eating whatever the dining hall has to offer."

"Let's go out for dinner. Can I pick you up at six?"

"You may. I live on the third floor of this very building, room three twelve."

"Great." Bob leaned in and kissed Karen's cheek. "I'll see you then."

Karen watched him walk back up the hill and then disappear around the corner of the bookstore. She let out a tiny squeal, then pulled open the heavy wood door and ran up two flights of stairs, taking them two at a time. She jogged down the hallway to her room, opened the door, set her half-consumed coffee down on her desk, and blissfully collapsed onto her bed.

"Uh-oh," said her roommate, Allison Pilsky, lying on her bed on the other side of the room. "I've seen that look before."

"Not on my face," sang Karen, looking at the ceiling. "I have positively never felt this way before in my entire life."

Allison shut her book, sat up, crossed her legs in front of her, and leaned back against the wall. "Tell me everything." Propping herself with one elbow, Karen told her roommate the whole story—from their awkward conversation at the glass door, to their slow walk to get coffee, to their shock about discovering they lived in the same town, to their glorious kiss in the middle of the road. "What kind of kiss was it?" asked Allison, squinting and tilting her head slightly to the side. "Did he put his tongue in your mouth?"

Karen frowned. "Of course not. It was soft and sweet, and I felt it everywhere. It traveled from my lips to my fingertips, to my earlobes, right down to my ankles. It was pure and noble. It was the most beautiful kiss I've ever had."

"Did he touch you?" Allison was eager in her inquiry.

"You are so gross. I'm telling you about the most chaste kiss in the history of the world, and all you can think about is whether he tried to put his hand under my jacket."

"Well, did he?"

"No! This is not the beginning of a two-week physical relationship. This is the beginning of something different."

Allison raised her plucked black eyebrows. "You're in love?"

Karen thought for a moment. "Since I just met him, no. But there's a strong possibility I could be there twenty-four hours from now."

Allison reached for her book. "Go slowly, Miss Spears," she said, eyes back on the war novel she was reading for history class. "As you already know, some of the Romeos out there are pretty smooth operators."

Karen closed her eyes and inhaled before saying, "His name isn't Romeo. It's Bob. Bob Parsons."

After Bob rounded the corner of the bookstore, he started running. He ran all the way to the library, through the glass doors, and up the stairs to the third floor. Evan was sitting at his carrel with his head bent over a large textbook with colored pictures. Bob stood next to Evan's chair. "Guess what?"

Evan shifted his gaze slowly from the book to Bob's face. "I'm not going back to the party. It was a nice break. I drank one beer. I'm relaxed, but still able to study, and I've got a test tomorrow. I'm not going back, no matter what you say."

"Go to the lounge," said the same reprimanding voice from before. "You can talk there and not bother absolutely everyone on this entire floor."

"Good idea," said Bob, holding up the index finger of his right hand. "This will take one minute, Ev, and I promise it's worth it."

Evan took his time standing, stretched, put his socked feet back into his worn sneakers, and then followed Bob down the carpeted hallway to the empty glassed-in lounge. Bob was talking before the heavy door shut behind them. "I met her."

Evan gave him his best blank look. "Met who?"

"The girl. The girl I dragged you to the party to meet. The girl I saw in the student center this morning. The girl I've been thinking about all day."

Evan crossed his arms in front of his chest. "You have got to be kidding."

"I am most definitely not kidding. I cut through the student center to grab some chips, and I'm about to walk out the doors near The Grape, and there she was."

"Did you talk to her?"

Bob laughed. "Man, after I found my tongue, yeah. I was so blown away when I first saw her, I couldn't say anything."

"How awkward was that?"

"Very," said Bob. "But she was totally cool with it."

"So, does this mystery girl have a name?"

"Karen Spears."

"I know Karen. She's in my art history class."

"You know her?"

"Well, I know who she is. She sits in front of me."

"I didn't even know you took art history. She has a test tomorrow."

"As do I." Evan pointed at his watch.

"What's she like, other than perfect?"

Evan shrugged. "She seems nice."

"Isn't she gorgeous?"

"She is, in a very natural kind of way."

"I like that in a girl. Those made-up faces scare me. You know? Like clowns. You never really know what's going on underneath."

"I guess."

"What else do you know about her?"

"Not much. She's there every time and seems to be a pretty good student. She laughs easily."

"She and I grew up in the same town. How crazy is that?"

"That is pretty crazy."

"And what are the chances of meeting her the very day I discover her?"

"Slim. It must be fate."

"I know it's fate. I'm going to marry her."

Evan laughed as he moved toward the door. "How about a date first?"

"Already booked," said Bob. "Tomorrow night is the official beginning."

Evan reached for the doorknob. "No pressure, right?"

"You know me." Bob followed him out the door. "I thrive on pressure."

CHAPTER 2

~~

Karen stood in front of her closet, looking at the jumble of clothes within. She took a couple of steps closer and examined her skirts clipped to a hanging rack, but she was not inspired to remove any of them. She wanted to look mature, in control, not like a schoolgirl. That thought led her to the leggings she routinely wore on the weekends. She pulled her favorite pair off their hanger and inspected them. She had worn them only once since they had been washed, to the basketball game last Saturday and, afterward, Anthony's Pub. Remembering how smoky it had been, she held them to her nose. Nothing but the faint aroma of her laundry detergent. Karen took off her jeans and pulled on the pants. She crossed the room to her dresser and took her thigh-length, fuzzy orange V-neck sweater out of the bottom drawer and pulled it over her head. She put big silver hoops in her ears and a silver chain hosting a clear crystal pendant around her neck; she brushed her hair, and then stood in front of the full-length mirror hung on the exterior side of the closet door. When she glanced at the clock next to her bed, she was disappointed that she had another fifteen minutes to wait. Grabbing a short story she had to read for her English class, she sat on her bed. When she had read the first paragraph three times, she set the packet of paper next to her and leaned back against the wall. Allison charged through the door a minute later. "What a day. Next semester, I am definitely not signing up for four classes on Tuesdays and Thursdays." She dropped her backpack on the floor and extracted her arms from the sleeves of a black quilted coat. "All I want is a long Vitabath and a large hot chocolate." She looked at Karen. "Wow, you look awesome."

"Thank you." Karen was off the bed and lacing up her black boots.

"Oh my gosh!" said Allison, her small brown eyes big with excitement. "You have your date with Bob tonight. Are you nervous?"

"Completely."

"Turn around."

When Karen did, Allison said, "Bodacious bod," which made Karen laugh. "Where are you going?"

"I have no idea." Karen sat back down on her bed. "He's picking me up at six. Do you think I should wait downstairs?"

"No way." Allison made a baseball umpire's safe signal with her hands. "Make him come and get you. Plus, I want to meet him."

When they heard the knock on the door, both girls closed their mouths and faced the door. Then, motioning for Karen to stay seated, Allison pinched her cheeks, a beauty tip her grandmother told her about when she was in junior high, and walked slowly to the door. She opened it and smiled at Bob, who stood in the hallway dressed in a brown leather jacket over a plaid flannel shirt, khaki pants, and black Converse sneakers. His hair, still wet from the shower, was parted, but the sides were already moving toward the middle, like bramble bushes growing over a dirt path. "I'm Allison," she said, extending her hand. "Karen's roommate."

Bob took her hand and shook it. "And I'm Bob, Karen's date."

Allison opened the door wide. Karen, who had decided in the ten seconds it took Allison to open the door that she should look busy, was standing at her desk, looking through a notebook. When

Bob walked into the room, she turned to face him. "Hi," she said, tucking her hair behind an ear.

"Hi." He smiled at her. "Are you ready?"

"Yes." Karen grabbed Allison's black quilted coat from the back of her desk chair.

He waited until Karen took a few steps toward the door, then walked out behind her. "It was nice to meet you," he said to Allison, who had moved forward, as if she were the one going out to dinner on a first date with a handsome college boy. "Maybe we'll see you later."

"I hope so," she said, more to herself than to him.

Bob held the door to the stairway open for Karen. He waited for her to begin descending the stairs, then followed her. "Do you like Italian food?"

"I love Italian food." Karen was pleased they weren't going to the Chi-Chi's down the street, the unofficial State dining hall on Friday nights and the official cheap dinner date location on Saturdays.

"Evan, my roommate, told me about a place in Sterling. He's from around here and said it was worth the fifteen-minute drive."

"Is that Evan Blackhurst?"

"Yeah. I hear you have art history together."

"Have you been checking up on me?"

Bob laughed. "How did your test go?"

"It's over."

At the bottom of the stairs, they crossed the hallway to the front entrance. Outside, they crossed the street to where Bob had parked his blue Ford Tempo. Bob unlocked the passenger side and opened the door for Karen. She sat and exhaled as she drew the seat belt across her shoulder and lap. Her nerves were beginning to settle now that he had shown up, the date had started, and she was in his car. On the way to the restaurant, they chatted about home, about all the places they could have seen each other: football games, the town pool (where Karen lifeguarded during her high school summers), Joe's Pizza (the best in town), the mall (where Bob worked at Foot Locker for two years), and the town park (which hosted an enormous July fourth celebration every year with fireworks). Karen suggested they must have seen each other some-where; Bob said he didn't think so. "I would know if I had seen you."

"Maybe not when you were eight and I was seven," said Karen, using their new common knowledge that he was a year older than she, pleased with the progress of their conversation.

"That's true. All girls that age have cooties."

They took back roads to Sterling, a town whose main street was lined with independent businesses. La Trattoria, a house-like stucco building with white lace curtains hanging in the paneled windows, was at the end of the street on the left. Bob drove into the parking lot and then escorted Karen through the heavy wood front door. Inside were vibrant plaster walls the color of sunshine, a wide-plank wood floor, and several square tables that sat four, covered with red linen tablecloths. Karen wondered if restaurants in Europe looked like this, tucked into the countryside, a welcome sight to hungry travelers. Restaurants in malls, like Chi-Chi's, were all about quick food, whereas this place that Bob had chosen was all about ambience, seclusion, and solitude. Had she been aware of its existence, she would have hoped ahead of time that he would have selected it for this first dinner. The hostess seated them at one of two window tables for two, lit the yellow pillar candle between them, and handed them leather-bound menus.

"I can't believe I'm sitting here with you," said Bob, the candle-light illuminating his freshly shaven chin.

"I was just thinking the same thing," said Karen, even though it was only partly true. She was also thinking about her freshman-year boyfriend, Peter Hopper, or Hop, as his football friends called him. He was a nice enough guy, but after their first couple of dates, he no longer put any effort into their relationship. He didn't take her anywhere, even though he often found time to fill his car with guys needing a 2 a.m. Meat Lovers pie at the Pizza and Sub Palace. He never asked her what she was doing on the weekend, instead expecting her to meet him at a party, where they would drink cheap beer from the keg for a couple of hours, and then go back to his room for a make-out session. Even if they happened to arrive at the party at the same time, he never paid for her to get in. Two lousy dollars is all it would have cost him to get his girlfriend into the party—and be assured of that make-out session—but he never came through. He would walk in ahead of Karen, pay his two dollars, and then head directly to the beer table while she, hopeful that he'd pay for her this time, dug her wallet out of the back pocket of her jeans. When she grew tired of being treated like a weekend roommate and broke up with him, he'd been mystified.

Too soon after Peter came Roger Gordon. Karen knew it was too soon, but she was so affection starved from her relationship with Peter that she plowed ahead. Plus, Roger was charming. They met in an art history class and seemed from the start to have a lot in common: love of art, love of the outdoors, good study habits, pizza a must at least once a week, coffee with cream and sugar. What Karen realized later was that Roger had a lot in common with every girl he met, simply because he thought nothing of making up his life as he went along. Every word, every move was carefully crafted to ensnare Karen's affections. He was incredibly attentive, always wanting to hold her hand or drape his arm around her shoulder. She was taken in.

One night after a party, they went back to his room, where they had made out on several occasions. Roger turned on his bedside lamp, and popping out of the darkness was a girl in her underwear sitting on his bed. "This is Ginger," said Roger as he peeled off his coat. "She lives down the hall and wants to join us tonight." Wishing she'd had two beers instead of three so she could fully process what he was saying, Karen stood still, wondering if she'd heard him wrong, wondering if she'd misconstrued his words. Taking her lack of protest as a green light, Roger moved to unbutton Karen's shirt, jolting her and then prompting her to slap his face. She dashed out of his room, out of his dorm, and changed her daily schedule for the next three weeks so she would not run into him on campus.

Karen looked into Bob's blue-gray eyes. He had touched her several times already that evening, but his touches while not fraternal were not sexual. He placed his hand, ever so lightly, on her lower back when they walked through the door of the restaurant. He touched her shoulder after she sat in the chair he had pulled out from under the table for her. Was it guardianship? Is that what it was? Karen tucked her hair behind her ears, showing Bob her new hoop earrings threaded through holes in the very center of her earlobes. On Karen's thirteenth birthday, her mother, Shelley, drew the ink dots herself at the ear-piercing station at the mall near their house. Shelley, who still wore clip-on earrings, had seen some off-center piercings, which she thought looked cheap.

Bob ordered a bottle of sparking water after their waiter described the evening's specials. Classy, thought Karen, who decided ordering a ginger ale would appear juvenile. When their dinners arrived, Bob suggested they share their entrées, and Karen willingly agreed. Peter hadn't been willing to share a single French fry. She watched as Bob transferred half of his beef tenderloin to her plate and put half of her chicken piccata onto his. He worked slowly and methodically, dribbling some béarnaise sauce over Karen's piece of meat, creating a photo-ready turf-and-turf selection worthy of a gourmet magazine.

As they ate their first bites, her mind jumped ahead several years to when they were out of college and living in an apartment. They would both have jobs and work long hours. During the week, their dinners would be simple: soups and salads, oven-roasted chickens from a deli down the street, grilled hamburgers during the summer. On Fridays, Bob would finish work early and stop at the market to buy fresh ingredients for their dinner that night. When Karen arrived home, Bob would take the soft leather briefcase out of her hand and shoo her into the bedroom to change into casual clothing. When she emerged in jeans, he would hand her a glass of white wine. And then they would sit on the couch and tell each other about their respective days as whatever delicacy he prepared simmered happily on the stove.

"What are you thinking?" He put his fork down and looked at her.

"You don't want to know."

"I do. I want to know everything about you."

"All tonight?"

Bob looked at his watch. "I want it all in the next fifteen minutes."

They talked easily after that, sharing childhood memories and wondering again where they could have met before. They talked about their families and were surprised to learn they both had two brothers. Bob's brothers were older and out of the house. They both moved to the West Coast after college, where they worked day and night, if you asked his mother, on computer technology. They were fully engaged in their lives there and rarely came home, citing work obligations as an excuse to miss another Christmas holiday. Because Jonathan and Mark had never treated Bob as anything but a kid, he felt he had a name-only relationship with them and consequently didn't miss them much.

Karen had twin brothers who were seven years younger. Because there were two of them, they demanded more attention than Karen did from their parents. When Kevin and Kyle were born, Karen's pampered life changed dramatically. Within twenty-four hours of returning from the hospital, Shelley began treating Karen as an assistant instead of a child. There were no more mother-daughter tuna sandwich lunches at the kitchen table. No more chocolate chip cookie baking sessions. No more bedtime stories. Her father had volunteered to read to her for a while, but only on nights when sports weren't on the television. He, Phil, was an ardent hockey fan and, like the rest of the men and boys in the country, closely monitored Wayne Gretzky's dazzling career on the ice.

During her pregnancy, Shelley had taught Karen how to sew. But the partly finished corduroy jumper they were working on sat folded and, eventually, dust-covered on Karen's bureau after the twins were born. Her mother's calm and patient sewing instructions were overthrown by a steady stream of orders: *Karen, run and get me another diaper. Karen, hold your brother while I cook dinner. Karen, watch the boys while I take a shower.* At seven, Karen's childhood was effectively over. And while Karen at first felt very grown up in her new role, she soon resented it and all the responsibility it entailed. She routinely begged her friends to invite her over after school so she could get out of whatever job her mother had planned and have some fun for a while. At her friends' houses she could play board games and run around outside like everyone else her age. By the time her mother fully comprehended the kind of pressure she had exerted upon her daughter, the boys were seven and still could do very little for themselves, and Karen, at fourteen, could have lived in her own apartment. When the boys finally did get it together (when Shelley learned to let them make mistakes and do things on their own), Shelley tried to spend more time with her daughter. She took Karen shopping and out to lunch, which Karen appreciated. After all, her mother was guilty of little more than being overwhelmed, and Karen accepted her mother's apologies. But she didn't turn to her for affection or advice or sympathy like she had before her brothers were born. And her father, who had started his own insurance agency when the boys were four, worked long hours and was tired when he got home. Karen solved her own problems.

Bob told Karen his experience of being the youngest was very different from that of her brothers. His parents' time was spent on the older boys. One of them was struggling in school; the other had acne. One of them was getting his license; the other smashed up the car. One of them had a raunchy girlfriend; the other was grounded for a month. Bob spent a good deal of his childhood playing alone with toys in his room. Occasionally he had friends over, but because his brothers often teased them, most of Bob's friends wanted to play elsewhere. Bob didn't feel particularly neglected; he liked being alone. But one night he overheard his parents talking when they thought Bob, who was at the kitchen table eating his nightly snack of Oreos and milk, was already in bed. They were lamenting about how much longer Bob would be in the house. His brothers were off to college, and if it weren't for that unplanned night of passion after the O'Hearns' cocktail party, they would have the house—and their lives—to themselves. Devastated, Bob packed a small duffel bag and walked into the living room to announce his imminent departure. His mother, Janet, smothered him with kisses and hugs and told him she hadn't meant what she said, that she loved him dearly. But Bob never forgot that night.

"Wow." Bob sat back in his chair, the front two legs an inch off the floor. "What happened to our light, first-date conversation?"

"I hear Gretzky just scored his six hundredth goal." Karen used both hands to push her hair away from her center part.

"He did indeed."

"My dad tells me he's the best player the game has ever seen."

"Your dad's probably right."

Karen nodded. Bob sipped his water. "That's enough," he said. "Let's get back to the good stuff."

After dinner Bob paid the check, refusing Karen's polite offer of splitting the cost, then drove slowly back to campus. The dark serpentine road again gave Karen the sensation of being in another country. The two of them were traveling hundreds of miles from one city to another on a secret middle-of-the-night mission. They had been entrusted with documents that would guarantee the national security of their homeland; their failure would mean international disaster on an unprecedented level. No one knew where they were or what they were doing; they were alone. Looking over at Bob, Karen pushed the fantasy out of her head. He reached over and brushed her cheek with the back of his hand.

Unlike the narrow winding roads to Sterling, the campus was lit up like a small city. Instead of taking Karen directly to her dorm, Bob decided to loop around and see what was happening on campus, a means to prolong the date. As they drove past the various buildings, they commented on the people they could see through windows lit from the inside. In Franklin Hall, a mid-campus dorm, people were dancing in the downstairs common room, their surrealistic body shadows filling the floor-to-ceiling windows. A small group was outside the party, standing on and around the steps, and Bob knew what they were up to before he could see the glowing orange ember they passed amongst themselves. He hadn't smoked pot since high school, when he smoked with enough regularity to buy it instead of merely hope for it at a party. When one of those buys had almost turned into a bust, Bob quit altogether. Now there's a reason, he thought, why he and Karen hadn't met. While she was doing wholesome things like going out for pizza and ice cream, he was going into the woods to get high.

Bob pulled up in front of Karen's dorm and stopped the car. Neither one of them moved. Finally, Bob opened his door, breaking the vacuum seal of their time alone in the car, letting the outside world in. Karen opened her door and pushed herself off the seat. Bob took her hand and slowly led her up the steps to the front door, where they stood facing each other. And, although Bob had thought about this moment, he was suddenly unsure how to proceed. He knew he wanted to kiss her, but he didn't want to alarm her by kissing her too hard or too long. He didn't want to give her a brief, dismissive kiss either. Then she might think the date had been a mistake, even though they both knew it hadn't. He reached up and cupped her chin in his right hand, then slowly lowered his head. He looked at her just before placing his lips on hers and saw her eyes gently close. He kissed her three times before releasing his hand. He heard her inhale. "Thank you for coming out with me tonight."

"I had an amazing time," she said. "I like you, Bob Parsons."

After promising to call her the next day, Bob descended the steps and got back into his car. He looked out the passenger side window and, finding her still standing on the landing, lifted his arm and waved before restarting the car and pulling away from the curb.

CHAPTER 3

By the beginning of the next school year, everything seemed to be as it should be in a relationship. Karen and Bob spent most of their time together, but they also spent time apart, with friends. They trusted each other without having to talk about it. When Bob went off campus one weekend for a marketing seminar at another college and Karen stayed behind, he knew she wasn't kissing someone else at a fraternity party and she knew he wasn't hitting on the female business students. If Karen declined his offer of an evening out, it really was because she had a lot of work to do or was simply overtired. Bob knew he would not run into her at a campus function later that night dancing with the captain of the rugby team. They appeared to have a completely honest relationship, one that friends described as extraordinary.

Bob's housemates were more surprised than Karen's dorm mates. Most college relationships, they told Bob whenever the topic surfaced, lasted weeks, maybe months. Hardly any lasted a year or more. And when they did, someone was cheating. There was good reason for that. All any guy had to do was take a quick look at what was available. There were a lot of pretty girls on campus, as well as a fair number of girls who had the reputation of being easy to bed. This is the time, the guys said, to experiment, to go a little wild before the responsibilities of the adult world faced them after graduation. And they didn't consider themselves unfaithful to Karen for suggesting such things. They all liked Karen; everyone did. But if Bob spent his entire senior year dating the girl he was going to marry, he might regret it later.

Bob listened, half convinced by their propositions. This *was* the time to do whatever he pleased. He was technically beholden to no one. He could stay out all night. He could skip classes. He could drink excessively. He could be with a different girl every night for a couple of weeks before anyone would notice. This could be the most selfish time of his life. Some of the guys advocating this lifestyle lived like that; Bob, an early riser, even after a late night with too much beer, would see their conquests slink past the kitchen on their way out the back door in the morning, dressed in what they had been wearing the night before, hair askew, mascara smeared. Bob admitted to himself and to the guys that their philosophy was certainly intriguing, and that if he hadn't met Karen, he might champion their cause. But his relationship with Karen, he told them, was unusual. It didn't fit in with today's standards of dating for convenience or temporary euphoria. It was out of another era, he said, when faithfulness was commonplace, when a person's word actually meant something more than the air it took up when spoken. The guys dismissed his logic with a waved hand, which Bob routinely met with a shoulder shrug. They didn't understand and wouldn't understand until they met someone like Karen. Some of them would never understand because there were not many girls like Karen. Bob had known this the minute he saw her. His outlook on women and on relationships changed when he became involved with her. She didn't force him to change or impose restrictive rules on him; he wanted to change. His seven housemates couldn't say, specifically, what was different about him—except that he didn't date more than one girl—and yet they knew he was not the same person he had been a year before. Even though some of the guys spent time with just one girl, they weren't committed like Bob. He had an air of responsibility that left them nonplussed. He still occasionally drank too much beer or played touch football in the driving rain.

But he also lived his life in a more measured way at a time when none of his friends wanted to measure anything except how often they got their own way.

Karen's dorm mates wanted what she had, a good relationship. While they liked flirting and dating different guys, a lot of the guys turned out to be immature bozos. They, the boys—Karen and her friends never referred to them as men—were attentive at first, always. Some even paid for a date or two. But most had one thing on their minds. So the girls fooled around, but put off saying yes because they had learned, some more than once, that this was the turning point in the relationship. Any manners the guys had or pretended to have vanished after sex. Their wallets stayed in their back pockets except when they were buying something for themselves, and the inevitable knock on the dorm room door at two o'clock on a Saturday morning was not for meaningful conversation.

Being treated like a queen was every woman's goal—and that included the feminists, who didn't necessarily want to be revered by men, but they certainly wanted the respect and admiration of the men they would one day be supervising. No woman, no matter how independent, was unaware or unaffected by the presence of men. What Karen's friends liked best about Bob, in addition to his good looks, trim body, and attentiveness to Karen, what they envied most, was his willingness to talk to her, that they had so much to talk about.

And Karen and Bob did talk a lot. Often, what started as a comment about a certain class lecture or event on campus turned into a thirty-minute conversation or even a philosophical discussion. And they agreed on so many things, almost as if they had been raised in the same household and taught by the same teachers. Every day, they agreed, had the possibility of being productive and satisfying; if they did what they were supposed to do, worked hard at it, and spent time with each other, they couldn't fail one another or themselves.

That Christmas break, Bob's father, Tucker, began asking the question that had been on Bob's mind for months: When are you going to propose to that girl? Bob had just one more semester at school before graduation. After that, he would be out in the world, out of Karen's everyday life. He wanted her with him, but he knew she wanted to finish her education. And that was almost as important to him as it was to her. Should he put an engagement ring on her finger when it would have to sit without companion for eighteen months? Tucker said Bob would have to do that if he wanted Karen to stay with him. She's too much of a catch, he said, to leave on a state university campus bare-handed. Still, Bob hesitated, wondering if Karen would want to wear his ring for such an extended period of time. He decided he would give it to her the summer after her junior year, when they would have to wait just twelve months to get married. By the end of March, he had changed his mind.

Ray McNamara transferred to the university in January from Salzburger University in Georgia. He was an immediate presence on campus because he was touted as having the potential to be the best baseball player the school had ever seen, which was saying something for a Division Two team that had won the championship four times in the last seven years. Before transferring, Ray played shortstop for the Salzburger Bulldogs, and they were very sorry to see him go. He could throw the ball to first base as fast as the pitcher could across the plate. At State, just like at Salzburger, everyone wanted to get a personal, up-close look at him, and when he or she did, the women, in particular, talked about little else. He was six feet, six inches tall, with sandy blond hair that just brushed the top of his shoulders, and a tanned face with enough fat covering his jawbone to give him a nice guy rather than a tough guy look. His blue eyes were distinct enough to be seen and admired from a distance. If the baseball team held a Meet Ray night, a thousand girls would have stood in line. He had his pick of hundreds, but out of randomness and chance, he found Karen.

They met in an art history class, Ray being one of the few people who majored in the subject with the idea of someday opening an art museum after he was finished with a fifteen-year career in professional baseball. Ray's parents were his most fervent supporters, not only of his interest in baseball, but also of his devotion to the study of the history of art. They wanted him to use his mind as well as his arms and legs; it was their idea that he seek temporary refuge in the north, far away from Georgia and the inexorable pursuit by the Atlanta Braves. If Ray was going to play for them, fine, but he was going to do it with an art history diploma taped to the inside of his locker door.

Like everyone who looked at him, Karen considered Ray to be magazine advertisement–quality handsome. Karen had been told all her life how pretty she was, so she was comfortable around attractive boys. She was comfortable around Ray for another reason, too: She was secure in her relationship with Bob; she wasn't searching for a boyfriend. So she was relaxed in Ray's presence rather than flustered and nervous like the other girls. She was flirtatious, but that was her nature rather than something she turned on for Ray. She talked to him without stumbling over her words, and, even more important in Ray's eyes, she talked to him about art. They sat next to each other in class and, between the two of them, answered half of the questions asked by the professor. This shared interest made them fast friends. They often walked after class to the student center for a quick cup of coffee and more discussion, before heading off in separate ways to their next classes.

It wasn't long before Evan Blackhurst shared the news about their friendship, their coffee breaks with his housemate. Bob was not immediately alarmed, but he didn't like the big deal Evan and the other guys he lived with made out of it. How can you allow this guy unrestricted access to your girlfriend? How trustworthy is Karen? How long do you think it will take her to compare the two of you and realize being with a major-league baseball player might be a more lucrative long-term choice than being with a marketing manager, or whatever it is you think you're going to do? All of their suspicions eventually worked their way into Bob's mind, invading warriors over the wall, and he became, for the first time in his relationship with Karen, intensely jealous. He told Karen to break off her friendship with Ray if she wanted to continue dating him. When Karen dutifully told Ray the next day at the end of their class, he looked at her strangely. "What?" she asked.

He hesitated a moment. "I don't know how you can let a guy treat you like that," he said softly, before slowly exhaling through barely open lips as he often did when he was thinking about something.

"Treat me like what?"

"Like his property. I mean, as far as I know, you two are boyfriend and girlfriend. I'm not looking to change that. I'm just looking to be your friend."

Karen shrugged. "I guess he's jealous. I can see that. I mean, if he were spending as much time with another girl as I am with you, I wouldn't like it either."

"Meaning you don't trust each other."

"Of course we trust each other."

"It doesn't sound like it to me. If you trusted each other, you'd allow friendships with other people, regardless of gender."

"But those are precisely the friendships that can get in the way of a good relationship."

Ray leaned over in his chair, moving a little closer to Karen. "If they get in the way, well, then maybe the relationship isn't as good as you thought it was." And then he slid out of his seat, scooped up his books, and walked out of the room.

What followed was Karen and Bob's first real fight. They had minor disagreements every now and again, but nothing like the discussion that evening in the parking lot behind Karen's dorm. Karen had told Bob at lunch that she needed to talk to him about Ray. And because she wasn't through thinking about it and didn't want to make a scene in the dining hall, she suggested they meet after dinner. Bob went to Karen's room that night with the intention of taking a short walk and talking about Ray in a calm, incidental manner. He assumed Karen had followed his advice and told Ray she would no longer be spending time with him. So, when he ushered Karen outside and asked her what was on her mind, he didn't expect her accusatory tone. "Ray thinks you don't trust me, and I think he's right."

"What?" Bob stopped walking and turned to face Karen.

"You heard what I said." Karen was now facing him, arms folded across her chest.

"Since when does Ray's opinion hold any stock with you?"

"Ray's opinion of art has always been important to me."

"We're not talking about art, Karen," said Bob, hoping to quickly clear up their misunderstanding. "We're talking about us."

Karen looked off to one side, away from Bob's confused expression. "I know we're talking about us. We're talking about you not trusting me because I have a friendship with another guy."

"That friendship is taking up a tremendous amount of your time."

"And?"

"And since Ray McNamara has come to campus, I think you've had a shift in your perspective on our relationship."

Karen turned to face him again. "Maybe it's a healthy shift."

"And maybe I could shift my perspective in a healthy way by spending more time with your roommate."

"Allison?"

"Absolutely. We're good friends. I think the world of her; she thinks the world of me. In fact, one night when she'd had a couple of wine coolers after her shift at The Grape, she told me to consider her if things didn't work out between us."

"Allison wouldn't say that."

"Ask her. She might deny it, but just look at her eyes when she does. She won't be able to look at you because it's true."

"I don't believe you." Karen's stomach was telling a different story.

"Fine. I'll turn my friendship with Allison up a notch, and we'll see what happens."

"Is that a threat, Bob Parsons?"

"Oh no," he said, folding his arms across his chest, creating a mirror image of Karen's pose. "I fully intend on following through."

Karen's lower eyelashes flooded with tears. "That's the meanest thing you've ever said to me. I had no idea you could be so cruel and find enjoyment in it."

"And I had no idea you could delude yourself into thinking your so-called friendship with Ray McNamara wouldn't hurt me."

"We haven't done anything, Bob," said Karen defensively.

"Finish the sentence, Karen. You haven't done anything *yet.*

You think people don't notice the way he looks at you? You think I don't see what's happening?"

Karen gathered her hair into a ponytail and then, not finding an elastic around her wrist, let it fall back onto her shoulders. "Well, I don't see it."

"Then you're a fool."

Karen looked into Bob's eyes. "Perhaps I have been a fool." She turned and started up the sidewalk, back to the dorm.

Bob watched her until she was halfway, waiting to see if she'd turn around, before calling her name. When he did, she turned. "I don't want to talk to you anymore tonight," she announced. She walked the rest of the way, opened the heavy wood door, and was gone. Bob stood looking at the door for another minute, hoping she would come back out, but knowing she wouldn't. His very next thought was to find a jewelry store as soon as morning came.

Karen started to cry on the other side of the door. She dragged herself up the two flights to her floor, opened the door to her room, and lay down on her bed. Allison, who was on her bed reading a novel for her Contemporary American Authors class, got up, crossed the room, and sat down beside Karen. "Do you want to talk about it?"

"Not to you."

"What's going on?"

Karen sat up on her bed. "Are you trying to steal my boyfriend?"

Allison blushed. "No," she said.

"Then why did he just tell me you told him you were interested in him."

Allison looked at the floor. "Look," she said. "It was that night you were with Ray at that gallery opening downtown. Bob was coming home from a bar with his friends when I walked out of The Grape with Maryanne. She ditched me when she saw Terry, so I struck up a conversation with Bob. We joked around. I guess I ended up telling him, kidding around, Karen, to look me up if he ever broke up with you. It wasn't a big deal, but I'm sorry. You were out with Ray, though, and I didn't know what you were thinking. And hey, as you say all the time, Bob's a great catch. Still, I was being more funny than serious."

"I don't think that's funny."

"Tell me you've never had a few white wines and flirted with someone else's boyfriend."

"Don't blame it on the wine."

"Fine. You're perfect. I'm not."

"I am not perfect," said Karen. "I'm confused."

"Okay," said Allison. "Now do you want to talk about it?"

Karen grabbed a tissue from the box on the old steamer trunk that served as her bedside table. "I don't know why Bob is so angry with me."

"He's angry with you because he's jealous. Karen, he loves you."

"How can I be sure? If he loves me, why doesn't he trust me?"

Allison smiled slightly. "Because Ray McNamara is like a Roman god. He's the hottest thing on campus, and he's spending his free time with you. What would you think if you were in Bob's shoes?"

"That's why Bob doesn't trust me?"

"Yes," said Allison. "Now that we've established that you're not perfect, that means you're human."

"He's human, and I trust him."

"That's because he hasn't tested you. You might not feel the same way if he started hanging with an adorable marketing student."

"Or you."

"Look, I said I was sorry."

"That doesn't mean it's over."

Allison stood. "What do you want me to do here?"

"Nothing," said Karen, reaching for another tissue. She blew her nose. "Do you think Ray likes me as more than a friend?"

"Yes. Now what you have to decide is if you like him as more than a friend."

They both turned their heads toward the door when they heard a knock. Allison opened the door and found Ray standing in the hallway. "Hey, Allison. I'm here to see Karen." Allison turned around and looked at Karen, who nodded her head. Allison opened the door wide. He stepped into the room and looked at Karen. "Do you have time to take a walk with me?"

"Sure." Karen stood and put on her coat, still warm on the inside from her ten minutes outside with Bob. Without saying another word, she walked out of the room and into the hallway. Ray followed her, shutting the door behind them.

"Are you okay?" he asked, putting his arm around her like he sometimes did when they were alone together.

"Yes. I've had a long day."

"Me too."

Outside, Karen wrapped her coat tightly around her. In the twenty minutes she had been inside, she had forgotten how cold it was. She had no hat and no gloves and was suddenly not sure she wanted to walk and talk with Ray. She needed time, not more data, to figure out what was going on with Bob. When she turned to tell Ray she wanted to go back inside, he said, "You're cold. I know somewhere we can go where it's warm."

"You're not used to this weather. You must be freezing."

"Honestly, I'm kind of numb right now." Again, he wrapped his arm around her shoulders. "We don't have far to go."

They walked across the street to an older section of campus with century-old granite buildings. Ray walked Karen to the far side of the closest one and opened the door. They walked inside, where it was darker than it was outside. "Why isn't this building locked?"

"The lock doesn't work." Ray took Karen's hand and led her up a short flight of stairs. "I have a government class in here. It's a great place to come when I get distracted in the library or when I have some thinking to do." They walked down the hallway, stopping at another unlocked door. The light from the streetlamp outside shone through the small windows near the ceiling of the classroom, helping them make their way to a large desk at the front. When they reached it, Ray bent down and switched on the small lamp that sat on the corner. The room, Karen could see now, was large enough for only twelve or so desks and chairs. Three sides of the room were lined with neatly stacked books on shelves.

"Whose room is this?"

"Ed Frasure's," said Ray, sitting on his professor's desk. "Nice, right?" Karen walked to the closest stack of books and then brushed the back of her fingers along their worn cloth spines. "When I'm in this class, I feel like one of the founding fathers we discuss," Ray said. "That sounds kind of dumb, doesn't it?"

"No. It's what should happen in a room like this."

"It would be a shame to leave it." Karen turned around and looked at him. "The Braves have made me another offer. I don't know if I can turn this one down."

Keeping her eyes on Ray, Karen sat down in the chair closest to her. He was, as was often said, an outstanding specimen of the human race. His facial features, while well defined, were muted, as if carved out of soft stone. His body was massive, but flexible enough to appear like a contained liquid, masculine *and* graceful. It occurred to Karen, as she studied him, that his interest in art history made sense; he was like a living sculpture, exuding beauty and intensity with every breath.

And he was right about the Braves—it was a very good offer: millions of dollars a year for several years. Car, house, endorsements, everything was in place. All he had to do was sign the contract a Braves representative was flying north next week and pack his bags. This is what, he told Karen, he had been dreaming about since he was seven years old. He had known since then that he wanted to play baseball. It had never been his wish to be a fireman, or a policeman, or an astronaut; he had always wanted to be a major league baseball player. And yet, here he was, attending university instead, waiting for an arbitrary "right time." Some of that hesitation was out of respect for his father. Even though Tom McNamara knew the professional sports game (Ray had, after all, been looked at by scouts since he was fourteen years old), Tom wanted his only son to finish school. Perhaps this was because he hadn't finished. Or perhaps it was because one year really didn't matter that much. But offers like the one on the table were not typical, and when they surfaced, they had a very short shelf life. Plus, Ray said he could finish his degree on the road.

"What do your baseball buddies say?"

Ray laughed. "They tell me I'd be crazy not to take it, every last one of them."

"How does their opinion affect yours?"

"Not in any great way."

"No?"

Ray walked from the professor's desk to the chair next to Karen. He sat down, then leaned back, stretching his long legs out in front of him. "They're baseball players, Karen," he said, arms up over his shoulders, hands cradling his head. "That's what they're supposed to say."

"So, ask someone whose opinion matters to you."

"I am." Ray looked at Karen. "And there's one thing you could say that would make it easy for me."

"What's that?" She smiled, thinking the answer would be easy.

Ray moved his hands to his lap, and sat up, and leaned toward her. "That you'd go with me, as my wife." Karen's smile faded as quickly as it had appeared. Ray moved his head closer to hers so that their faces were inches apart. "You didn't expect this."

"No," Karen managed to whisper.

"Because I never told you how I felt."

"I don't know." Karen closed her eyes.

Before she opened them, Ray kissed her lips. It was a long, slow kiss that she immediately responded to without thinking—a fresh, new kiss, the kind that disappeared after time in a long-term relationship. It stirred up her insides. And when it was over and Ray slowly moved his head away, Karen put her hand around the back of his head, drew him to her, and kissed him. He wrapped his arms around her and they kissed over and over, oblivious to everything except each other. Finally, Karen broke away, inhaling deeply. Ray smiled at her. "I should have done that a long time ago." Karen looked down, away from his eyes. The guilty feelings about Bob exploded in her head. Ray took her chin in his hand and turned her face to his. "It's okay. I know what you're thinking."

"I'm not sure you do."

"Let's not talk about that," he said, getting up and reaching for her hand. "I'm going to walk you back to your dorm, and you can sleep on what I just told you." Karen took his hand and stood, already knowing that sleep would not be possible.

* * *

"I can't believe this," is what Allison said, again and again, until Karen finished the story. It was a long story that started with Ray's offer from the Braves, moved through their friendship to the kiss and his marriage proposal, and ended with Bob. "God, Karen, this is like every woman's fantasy. You are facing choices we all want to make." Allison explained that no matter what Karen chose, she couldn't lose. If she chose Ray, she would move to Georgia and finish her education there while he made thousands of dollars an hour throwing a baseball. She would lead a celebrity life, filled with clothes, cars, mansions, and expensive vacations. They would have adorable children, who would be looked after by a trustworthy nanny while Karen pursued whatever line of interest occurred to her. Maybe she would run their museum, and Ray would join her in the off-season. And they would be deliriously happy. Who wouldn't be happy married to a gorgeous money-making machine like Ray?

And if Karen chose Bob, fine. He was the kindest, most considerate guy Allison knew, and he would give Karen a good life. As a married couple, which was exactly where they were headed before Ray arrived on campus, they would be more than comfortable financially. Because Karen was motivated, she would undoubtedly work—but only before the children were born, and then possibly after they were full-time elementary school students. It was Karen's hard-working conscience, Allison said, that was giving Karen such trouble now. She was in agony when she should have been dancing around the room.

"I can't believe this is happening." Karen was sitting on her bed, her legs folded up underneath her.

"Tell me about it. How does it feel to be the luckiest girl on the planet?"

"I don't feel lucky. I feel miserable."

"Miserable?" Allison got up from the bed. "How can you be miserable?"

Karen closed her eyes. When she opened them, the tears from earlier in the evening had returned. "Because I don't know what to do. I have to choose between the two most important men in my life."

"You are right about that. You can't have them both."

Karen blew her nose, raw from its contact with too many tissues. "What would you do?"

Allison sat back down on the bed. "What does your heart tell you to do?"

Karen rocked her upper body back and forth several times, a soothing method she had employed in stressful times since childhood, since her brothers were born. "My heart tells me to stay with Bob."

"Then let Ray go. Whether he goes to Georgia or not, let him go."

By morning, Karen knew Allison was right. She took a walk with Ray after art history and told him she cared deeply about him, but couldn't continue to spend time with him. Ray told her he admired her integrity, making it even harder for Karen. He also said he had spoken with his parents after his talk with her, and they had given him their blessing on returning to Georgia, where he would start with the Braves and finish his education on the side. He would be leaving in the next week.

After lunch, Karen found Bob in the library. She pulled a chair up to his carrel and laid her head on his arm. "I'm so sorry," she whispered. Bob wrapped his arms about her. "I'm so sorry."

"I know. I know you are."

"Will you forgive me?" She lifted her head to face him.

"That depends," said Bob, reaching into the pocket of his jacket hanging on the back of his chair.

"Depends on what?"

He presented her with the small royal blue velvet box given him by the jeweler an hour earlier. "Will you marry me, Karen Spears?"

Karen opened the box and saw the one-carat diamond inside. After she kissed her answer, Bob took the ring from the box and put it on her finger.

CHAPTER 4

JUNE 1991

Karen and Bob got married three weeks after her graduation from State. Their wedding day was breezy but warm, fitting into the specifications of what Shelley Spears had for fifteen months been hoping for. Most described Karen, dressed in Shelley's dress that had been rescued from a flat cardboard box filled with loosely crumpled balls of white tissue paper sitting in the attic waiting for this day, as a vision. As a new wife, Karen was confident and peaceful, as if she and Bob had already been married many years and had slid into a comfort level known to aluminum anniversary couples. And Bob couldn't stop talking about his bride, repeatedly telling the guests the story about seeing Karen in the student center and knowing that day would lead to this one.

They exchanged the vows Karen had written, which included the word *honor,* but omitted the word *obey,* and the gold rings they had custom made for each other. On the inside of both rings, the words MY ONE TRUE LOVE were inscribed with the date. Allison, who was working at State that summer and going into the master's degree program of English literature in the fall, was Karen's maid of honor, and Evan, with whom Bob had kept in touch via e-mail and occasional phone calls since Evan's move to Texas the previous year, served as best man. The ceremony in the Congregational church was short and simple, followed by a lavish cocktail reception at the Town and Country Club, featuring polished silver trays with gourmet hors d'oeuvres, cut-glass bowls overflowing with shrimp, and a seemingly limitless supply of champagne served in crystal flutes. The band Karen and Shelley had selected made good on their promise to get the old folks out of their chairs with some big band tunes and to rock the house for the younger generation. When it came time for Karen and Bob to leave, the guests enthusiastically threw rose petals at Mr. and Mrs. Robert Parsons as they ran hand in hand through the crowded club entranceway to a decorated limousine in the parking lot.

The weather in the Virgin Islands was just as it was pictured on the postcards. Even though Bob's travel agent had warned him about the possibility of excessive temperatures, Bob and Karen easily adjusted to eighty-five-degree days after a cold, wet spring. They spent their ten days leisurely, reading in the shade, swimming, shopping, and eating exquisitely prepared local food. With a wedding band on her finger and the headiness of a new wife, Karen freely gave her body to her husband, pleasing him and making him especially thankful for their permanent union.

Only once on their honeymoon did Karen think about Ray McNamara. She and Bob were shopping in town when she saw a tall man with blond hair standing on a street corner holding several large shopping bags. Karen knew it wasn't him, but the man looked enough like him from a distance to hold her attention, to send her thoughts back to school, back to that intense night in the classroom when she and Ray kissed. She tried not to think about Ray, and she was mostly successful. She had been engaged for more than a year and was now married to another man. But occasionally she allowed herself a few moments of unrestrained fantasy about Ray. And it was always about that kiss.

Karen repeatedly told herself that Ray's kiss was not as extraordinary as it had felt that night. It had simply been a different kiss, a new kiss. She had been kissing no one but Bob for more than a year. Any new kiss, she reasoned, would feel magical because it emanated from someone else's mouth. And that mouth, Ray McNamara's mouth, was perfectly sized to hers. He had written Karen letters for several months after he left school. They were full of news about baseball—as if Karen didn't devour every Braves story carried in the sports sections of the *Atlanta Journal-Constitution* provided to the university library by an alumnus—and art history. Ray was, indeed, pursuing his degree and finding he had a lot of time to study when the team was traveling. Since leaving school, he had developed a liking for modern art and was toying with the idea of opening a museum for kids. They would appreciate the vibrant colors and geometric shapes and patterns, he wrote, and perhaps as a result develop a taste for art earlier in life.

Karen occasionally reread his letters, which she had kept in the bottom drawer of her State-issued desk, underneath a couple of notebooks filled with information relevant to classes she had already completed. She couldn't name what she was looking for or even why she held on to the letters, but she guessed it had something to do with her interest in the *what if* question. What if she had married Ray and moved to Georgia? What if she had talked her parents into letting her attend a small liberal arts college instead of State? What if, many more years ago, her mother's rocky pregnancy with the twins had resulted in miscarriage? She rarely discussed these thoughts with Bob, who preferred to make choices and live with them, good and bad, and not turn back, not waste time wondering about other options. There were, in his opinion, too many shades of gray. Ray didn't engage in the hypothetical either. In his letters, he did mention their relationship, but he always called it a friendship and told her how much he missed talking to her. He invited her to Atlanta, as a friend, to watch him play. Karen didn't mention this to Bob, however. He would never let her go. He never talked about Ray, or the Braves, treating both as if they didn't exist.

And they existed for Karen only when she wanted them to. Ray didn't creep into her thoughts uninvited. At school, she read about Ray's team, but she had rationalized her interest, telling herself she would follow the news about any famous friend. She wore Bob's ring proudly and directed her attention to him when he visited on the weekends. Only a few times had she slipped, confessing her doubts to Allison or writing back to Ray, and she had chastised herself. Supportive of Karen, as Karen was of her, Allison assuaged her friend's fears, telling her being tempted was a normal part of life. What really mattered was how Karen dealt with it, and in Allison's eyes, the maid of honor's view, Karen did a better job than most young women in her situation.

The man on the street corner was joined by a woman, whom he bent down to kiss just after she appeared at his side. Did Ray have a girlfriend? Was he married? Karen didn't know because Ray had stopped writing to her several months before graduation. She had thought about calling him late one night in mid-April. But Allison had talked her out of it, a decision Karen had been happy about in the morning. Since then, she had not written, e-mailed from the library, or made any other attempts to contact him. And she had forgotten about him completely during the frenzied weeks of wedding preparation.

When Karen and Bob got back from their honeymoon, they set up house in the apartment Bob had been living in since his graduation the previous year. A little less than an hour from their hometown, Canton was a small city on the banks of the Joseph River. Karen had chosen the apartment with Bob, knowing she would be joining him twelve months later. They had the sunny half of the ground floor of a historic house that had been recently remodeled and updated into four apartments just a mile and a half from downtown. In addition to their large master bedroom, they had an eat-in kitchen, a roomy living room, a full bathroom, and a smaller bedroom both Bob and Karen agreed that, when the time was right, would make a perfect nursery.

Karen didn't start her job until August first, leaving her plenty of time to fuss with her new living space. With her mother's help, she sewed new sets of curtains for the living room, kitchen, and bedroom, as well as a new comforter for the queen-size bed she and Bob would be sharing for the rest of their lives. It was a four-post, mahogany rice bed they had ordered from a supplier in North Carolina, easily the grandest piece of furniture Karen had ever owned. It was the bed, more than the pots and pans in their cupboards or their matching coffee mugs, that reminded Karen she was married.

People in less serious relationships slept on mattresses in metal frames, pickup trucked from their college dormitories, or on futons that turned back into living room couches in the morning.

Living in an apartment and calling it home was as much of an adjustment for Karen as being referred to as Mrs. Parsons. Throughout college, Karen had considered the state university campus her home. It was where she had met Bob and they had spent almost two years together. It was where she had met Allison, her best friend. It was where she had decided to make communications her career. Her parents' house, her childhood home, during those years had simply been a place for good food, rest, and occasional social interaction with high school friends. Those visits, most of them brief, were a vacation, a diversion from her real life at the university. Apartment living was for grown-ups, with its electric bills and fridge that needed food and floors that required sweeping. It was quiet, too. With Bob at work all day, Karen, for the first time in many years, was grateful for her mother's company.

And Shelley was happy to have her daughter within driving distance. A good number of her friends' children had moved far away after graduation. Those friends justified this separation, over enthusiastically in Shelley's opinion, with what they called Eternal Truths. The pull of distant cities was strong, they told her. After living in a one-horse town in the Midwest, the children needed some adventure in their lives. It would be good for them to throw themselves into the busyness of city life. Where else could they learn the survival skills needed to be responsible? And Shelley had nodded her head in agreement over the years, mostly because she wondered if Karen would follow the same path. However, when her daughter met Bob, Shelley knew she had a chance of keeping Karen close to home. No matter what her friends said about living a thousand miles from a son or daughter, Shelley knew they were kidding themselves. All parents wanted their children close to home. And for that reason alone, Bob was a godsend.

The first month of married life for Karen and Bob was almost perfect, marred only by small, insignificant events that should have been expected, but weren't. The day Bob had left the door open and Karen had walked into the bathroom and found him cutting his toenails was off-putting, as was the first time Bob emptied the bathroom trash can when Karen had her period. Bob's habit of letting the dinner dishes sit overnight in the sink bothered Karen, who liked a clean, orderly living space. Karen's insistence on pulling out the vacuum cleaner every Saturday morning, interrupting Bob's newspaper time, seemed controlling to him. She had all week to vacuum. But they talked about most things, both wanting to immediately resolve any issues. In fact, making time for conversation was something they did every night before dinner. Karen started with tales of domesticity, as she called them, and then Bob talked about work

Bob had been working for Forester Paper for just over a year, starting the week after his graduation. It was a family-owned and -operated business with its headquarters and largest plant twenty miles from Karen and Bob's apartment. Bob rented a storage unit on the outskirts of town to hold his various corrugated packaging samples and spent a good amount of his time driving from customer to customer to see to their needs. His territory, which at first comprised the middle of the state, had grown over the months. He was now responsible for half the state, with the other half on the horizon. His sales manager was pleased with his performance, for which Bob was rewarded with money and staff. With two sales reps working for him after just one year, Bob traveled more to grow the business than to hawk cardboard. He knew he'd still have to "pay his dues," as his boss liked to put it, but Todd Martin was ten years away from retirement, and Bob could already picture himself sitting in that office.

Karen was newly impressed with Bob's performance and prospects for the future, even though his work habits had been evident in college. A conscientious, focused student at school, Bob had goals and direction, qualities that had separated him from a good percentage of the university's student body. He went to parties, drank beer, and goofed around like everyone else, but he did those things after his work was done. He typically had a plan he diligently followed until its completion before he let his mind and body wander. He was mature for his age, responsible, and Karen loved that about him. So she was an eager listener, nodding her head in encouragement when Bob told her about securing a new account or handling a special delivery.

After they talked for thirty minutes or so, they would walk back into the kitchen, where Bob would sit down at the table Karen set before he got home. He continued talking while she served him and then served herself. They usually drank a glass of red wine with their meal, Bob having decided beer was for the weekends, and the conversation continued. Karen's dinners were always nutritional as well as delicious, and Bob was pleased he had chosen such a versatile bride. He had not known the extent of her capabilities when he first saw her that day in the student center, but he told himself he must have sensed her potential as well as her beauty. There were a lot of pretty girls at the university, but few of them, Bob had decided long ago, measured up to Karen's level of competence.

When August first arrived, Karen dressed in the light gray business suit her parents had given her for graduation (along with the wedding, her father had joked) and drove the seven-minute route she had mapped out to Clear Communication, a small public relations firm in town. Thirty-five-year-old Jennifer Clear had started the company after working for a decade in the regional medical center's communications department, the last three years without raises and with nothing more than promises about promotions. At first, Jennifer had run the business out of her apartment. And because she was as adept at pleasing clients as she was at writing, she had been successful from the start, earning enough in the first year to move into an outside office space and, in the second year, to hire two associates. Karen was the third full-time hire and the reason Jennifer had recently signed a lease for a larger space across the hall from her current office.

Karen had her own office, a small room with a window that had no view, but brought in natural daylight. Her metal desk had an oak writing surface, which held her new desktop computer monitor and keyboard, a phone with her own extension number, and an earthenware lamp as supplement to the fluorescent lights on the ceiling. Her desk drawers had been stocked with legal pads, pens, pencils, highlighters, a stapler, a calculator, a pair of scissors, even her own mug sporting the company logo, and a box of assorted tea bags. The other Clear employees were Mary Bates, who was twenty-four, a Canton native, and Patty Klein, twenty-six, who had returned to town after a relationship breakup had driven her from a job up north. The day Karen moved in, they helped her choose which three of Jennifer's small stock of framed prints to hang on her walls (to tone down the starkness until she found her own art). As they measured and hammered, they told Karen inspiring stories about their boss, whom they described as fair, generous, and a good teacher. Their reservations about working for an independent boss had been eradicated within the first few months of their employment. And there was plenty of work. A number of small businesses in town were happy to use Jennifer's services rather than support their own communications/marketing departments. Dazzled by their stories, Karen couldn't wait to feel like a member of this all-woman, professional team. Until now, men had always served as Karen's role models, from her father to her favorite communications professor.

Jennifer's professionalism was evident to Karen from her very first staff meeting, when Jennifer talked about business strategy and laid out six-month goals. She was looking to secure ten new clients by Christmas and needed Mary, Patty, and Karen to help ferret them out, beat the bushes, she said. As an incentive, she offered them ten percent of the amount of the new contract. "You bring in five thousand dollars' worth of business," Jennifer explained, "I'll cut you a check for five hundred dollars." After work, Karen rushed home to tell Bob about her day, about her work assignments, and to ask him who Forester used for communications. He didn't know, but promised he would find out after Karen told him about Jennifer's offer. He was pleased Karen was working. She had completed a number of household projects and was making incredible meals she found the recipes for in various women's magazines, but Bob could tell she was restless. She needed something other than sewing projects and dinner preparation to fill her days.

And while her days were full, Karen still found time to cook dinner three or four times a week, and to clean the apartment and shop for groceries on Saturday, her wifely duties, according to her mom. Bob made enough money for their everyday needs, so they banked Karen's salary. Socking money away had always been a priority for Bob, who helped his parents with his state university tuition and board expenses, and bought his own car. Karen was interested in purchasing new living room furniture for the apartment and buying nice work clothes, and Bob indulged those desires, as looking good was increasingly important for him at work. But there were a number of ancillary things—like Karen's idea to buy two kayaks so they could paddle along the river on weekends—Bob refused to buy. They had to save, he continually reminded Karen, for their children, so they would not have to juggle jobs during high school or pay for their college education as Bob had done.

Bob's refusal to budge on certain items, extravagances he called them, sometimes annoyed Karen. Of course she and Bob would have children one day (they had agreed upon two before they got married), and of course they would need hundreds of thousands of dollars to raise them and send them to good colleges. Yes, yes, yes. But that was in the future. Karen, on birth control pills, was resolved to remain childless for at least two to three years. There was no pressure from her mother, whose child-rearing stories replete with words like *sacrifice, exhaustion,* and *worthlessness* resounded in Karen's head. And Bob was willing to wait for a while, although he was more anxious than she was to start a family.

So, they occasionally bickered about money, but Karen was quick to discover an effective way to avoid confrontation. If she thought she had crossed Bob's tolerance line with one of her purchases, she simply hid it. She couldn't hide large items, of course, but she could certain easily conceal expensive clothing in her closet. Since Bob had a longer commute and left the apartment before Karen in the morning, he had no idea what she wore to work. And by the time he got home, she had changed into more casual clothing. If they met at a restaurant instead, Karen was careful not to wear something she had recently purchased in secret. She justified this covert activity with the desire and need to keep up with her coworkers, all of whom were nattily attired. Jennifer set the tone with tailored, natural-fiber business suits and imported shoes.

Karen had embraced her boss as her new role model and would rather quit than disappoint her. It wasn't a big deal, Karen told herself, when she hung new clothing in the back of her closet. She and Bob did not have to know every single thing about one another. Plus, with only minor exceptions, she and Bob were still putting her salary in the bank.

A new restaurant called Rascals opened on Main Street the following summer, housed in a long, skinny, clapboard-sided building that had formerly hosted a hardware store. Inside, on the street level, where customers used to find hammers, nails, measuring tapes, brooms, and other workroom staples were high-top tables and stools crafted out of recycled metal. Down a few steps and into the main area that once featured small power tools and other electronic devices was a shiny parquet wood floor big enough for a dozen slow-dancing couples and the bar, the main event. It was a mammoth U-shaped wooden structure, solid on the outside with a brass foot railing, and hollow on the inside to store glassware. Behind the bar, at the rear of the building, was the main eating area with square-topped dining tables and six booths lining the back wall. Those who remembered the building as it had been before claimed that, smoking section aside, it still had that musty, mulchy, slightly sour hardware store smell.

Karen and Bob met there after work one Friday night. Sidestepping through the overcrowded front section of people sitting on every stool and others standing behind them, they made their way across the dance floor and into the bar area. Billy Joel was singing through the oversized speakers, but Karen didn't hear him as clearly as the dissonant sound of a hundred simultaneous conversations. They found Jennifer, Mary, and Patty, who had come at Karen's insistence, and a salesman Bob worked with named Billy Townsend, the Forester party boy. After they shouted their greetings, Billy took their drink orders to the bar. When he returned to the group, who had been briefly engaged in loud small talk but were now content to smile at one another, he beckoned for them to follow him. He led them to the back section, which, with the speakers directed at the front, was quieter. Five minutes after that, a booth cleared, so they all clambered in, feeling grateful and lucky. Perhaps it was this feeling or another euphoric sensation often associated with Friday nights that led them to drink the shots of Southern Comfort Billy ordered. After another round of shots, they all joined Billy on the back deck, took puffs of his cigar, and sang Bruce Springsteen songs in honor of The Boss's world tour and Billy's plans to travel to New Jersey to see him live. When they went back inside, they ate fried calamari, danced, drank another round of shots, and then went home, where all, with the exception of Billy, vomited. Jennifer couldn't stop talking about it Monday. She hadn't lost control like that since she was eighteen years old and, frankly, hadn't thought she was still capable of it. "I'm still recovering today," she told Karen, who nodded in agreement.

And so the following Friday night was more reserved. No one drank shots. No one smoked, except Billy, who joined his friends in the smoking section a half dozen times over the course of the evening. And no one danced. Billy was their entertainment. He seemed to know everyone in the bar and kept calling people over to their table. Some brought chairs with them; others stood and listened to one or two of Billy's work stories, and then blended back into the crowd. At Billy's urging, they drank draft beer and ate club sandwiches, which Jennifer announced was decadently incongruous with her linen suit and pearls, and they laughed about how stuffy and responsible they had all become since graduating from college. Everyone chatted easily, but Billy dominated the discussion. He appeared to listen when others talked, but was quick to interrupt, to steer the conversation back to where he wanted it.

By the third consecutive Friday at Rascals, Jennifer had bowed out, and Karen decided she'd had enough of Billy. They were all sitting at a round table on the outside deck, sipping pink lemonade and vodka drinks and watching the sunset. Billy had already been regaling them with what he called Tattle Tales for half an hour, but he gave the impression he was just getting started. As usual people came and went from the table. Karen pulled on Bob's sleeve to get his attention. When he inclined his head toward hers, she told him it was time to go. Within five minutes, they had said their goodbyes and were on the front sidewalk. "What was that all about?"

Karen looped her arm through his. "I don't know. I just felt like getting out of there."

"Weren't you having fun?"

"Sort of. Were you?"

"Yeah," said Bob, smiling. "Billy's a riot."

"A self-serving riot."

"What do you mean?"

"It's all about him, Bob. For the third week in a row, it's all about Billy."

"You must admit there's a lot of Billy to be shared."

"I do," said Karen, as they crossed the street. "I just don't need it every Friday."

Bob shrugged. "I can understand that. I don't see him every day at work, and that's probably a good thing. I wouldn't get any work done."

"I like him. I'd just prefer to have him in smaller doses."

"He's a salesman. That goes without saying."

The next Friday, Karen and Bob stayed home. Bob cooked rib-eye steaks on their new Weber grill, and Karen made rice pilaf, Caesar salad, and brownies for dessert. They drank a reasonable amount of wine and went to bed early. So Karen did not expect to feel sick the next morning. She didn't eat breakfast and she lay in bed until almost noon, when the nausea subsided. Bob heated a can of chicken broth and encouraged her to rest. She was overtired, he said.

When her sickness continued, Karen, thinking she had a stomach virus, went to the doctor, who told Karen she was not overtired, although she undoubtedly would be in the future, because she was pregnant. Karen's shocked look prompted the doctor to ask if she was happy about the news, and Karen told her she was, but was too sick to feel truly excited about her condition. The doctor reassured her that morning sickness was temporary, lasting three to four months at the most, and that the rest of the pregnancy would be much more pleasant. Karen walked out of the office feeling worse than ever, but knowing that Bob would be pleased with the news. He had talked her into going off the pill earlier than she would have chosen; he wanted a baby.

Bob cried when she told him. (The only other time Karen had seen tears in his eyes was on their wedding day.) He wrapped his arms around her and then gently touched her stomach. He kissed her face again and again and then led her to the living room couch, sat her down, and made her some tea, the only liquid other than water that she had been able to keep down in the last week. He sat down next to her and began to talk—about the nursery, about baby names, about being a parent and all the things he wanted for this child. And Karen was caught up in his enthusiasm. It was evening and she was tired, but she had stopped getting sick in the early afternoon and was receptive to baby talk. For the first time in the several hours she had known she was going to have a baby, Karen was content.

That sense of well-being disappeared the following morning with the reappearance of her nausea. By nine o'clock, Karen had made four trips to the bathroom. Bob decided to stay home with his wife for the morning and work in the afternoon. Karen, who had been out of the office all week with what everyone thought was a bug, decided it was time to call her boss and break the news. After a three-second pause, Jennifer told Karen she was thrilled. She then called Mary and Patty into her office, where they all offered their congratulatory remarks via speaker phone. They told Karen she could count on them for an over-the-top baby shower. When Mary and Patty had returned to their offices, Karen asked Jennifer about work. Jennifer told her to take the following week off, that Mary and Patty could cover for her. After that, after Karen got used to the idea of being pregnant, they would talk about a potential schedule shift.

The hardest part was being in the apartment alone. Even though Karen was glad when Bob stopped fussing over her and left for work, the ensuing silence proved more challenging than Bob's doting presence. There were things to do, like tidying the apartment, reading the newspaper and books, and watching daytime television. (Her mother, Shelley, was addicted to *General Hospital*.) Karen was happy with any distraction from running to the bathroom and growing a baby. She had the time, at least temporarily, to cook and bake, but she could bring herself to do neither very often; just looking at food made her sick. Plus, she missed work.

The next Friday, she called Bob at work and asked him to pick up more Jell-O, tea, and chicken broth at the grocery store. She also asked him to eat something on the way home. Bob hung up the phone and called Billy. He left a message that he had changed his mind and would meet him at Rascals at five o'clock. It would give Bob a chance to tell his friend about Karen, and it would also give him a chance to eat a decent meal. He had eaten Stouffer's frozen entrées for dinner several days in a row.

Rascals was pulsing with activity. Bob worked his way through the crowded bar area to the deck, where he found Billy sitting at a round table with two pitchers of beer in front of him and a cigarette hanging out of his mouth. Three guys in suits Bob didn't recognize were listening to Billy talk, and Bob, ready for some conversation that had nothing to do with puking, eagerly sat down. Billy poured Bob a beer, which he drank down quickly. Billy refilled Bob's glass while Bob ordered a cheeseburger and fries from a waitress shouldering a large tray holding empty bar glasses. When Bob's food arrived, their AT&T salesmen companions said their farewells. "You're not eating, Billy?" asked Bob, biting into his burger.

"And kill this buzz? I'll eat something at home later. Where's Karen?"

"At home," said Bob, chewing.

Billy raised his eyebrows. "You in trouble with the Mrs.?"

"No." Bob wiped his mouth with his napkin. "Quite the opposite."

"That's why you're eating here with me?"

"Yes. She's pregnant."

Billy whooped and shook Bob's hand. "Good job, buddy. That's great news."

"Thanks. We're pretty excited."

"That still doesn't explain why you're here and she's not." Billy poured himself another beer.

"She's sick. She can't keep anything down."

"Morning sickness."

"More like all-day sickness. She's got it bad."

"Doesn't cook anymore?"

"Exactly," said Bob, shoving two fries into his mouth.

"Probably doesn't let you near her, either."

"It will pass."

Billy sipped his beer. "But will it pass before your withered Willy falls clean off?"

Bob laughed. "God, I hope so."

But it didn't pass, at least not as quickly as Karen hoped or Bob calculated. And when Karen reached the end of her first trimester and was still getting sick, her fears about the baby turned into panic. What if something was wrong? Healthy babies wouldn't start out like this. Karen's doctor had reassured her in person and over the phone several times. And Shelley reminded Karen how ill she had been with the twins, but Karen didn't think they realized how sick she was. She was fourteen weeks pregnant and had gained only three pounds. At this point, according to the articles Karen had read, many women had gained close to ten pounds. Something wasn't right.

Nothing Bob did was right, either. The soup he brought her nightly was too creamy, or too watery, or too hot, or too cold. Sometimes he accidentally rolled into her at night when they were sleeping, which Karen found inexcusable. She despised having the baby's sleep disturbed. It was only in the middle of the night, when Karen was completely at rest, that she thought the baby had a chance for survival, that it was growing after all, if only infinitesimally.

It was Karen's boss who came up with the Save Your Sanity work plan. Instead of accepting Karen's reluctant resignation—she was exhausted from trying to rally herself every morning just to meet with failure—Jennifer told her she could work from home. Mary and Patty could do the legwork, if required, for Karen's stories, and Karen could simply write them. The few phone calls Karen would have to make from home could be done in a quiet house. The client would never know Karen wasn't sitting in an office. Even if the client found out, Karen could simply say she was working from home that day. No big deal. And it was a good plan. Bob was happy to buy his wife a home computer, which he set up in the corner of their living room, so Karen could feel productive again. She went into the office every Monday afternoon, when the nausea had passed and she had the energy to shower and dress, for a meeting with Jennifer about the week's assignments, and sent her work to Jennifer via e-mail attachments on Friday afternoons. They then discussed, by phone, the details: what Karen had been able to accomplish, what to do about any unfinished work, and tentative plans for the following week.

Shelley, too, tried to help her daughter temporarily forget about her pregnancy issues by visiting most Thursdays, the only day in the week, what with her bridge games, tennis, walking group, her luncheon circuit, and volunteering at the library that she could block off three or four hours. She brought Karen homemade soups and retold her own pregnancy stories, thinking they might help Karen see that she was not the only one with discomfort and inconvenience. Sympathy was what Karen wanted, but her mother thought empathy was the same thing. Shelley found it uncanny that their symptoms were so similar: nausea throughout the morning and into the afternoon, loss of appetite, no interest in S-E-X, and a general resentment toward people who tried to help. It was this final symptom that eventually prompted Shelley to stop coming. Karen was tired of trying to act cheerful when she was miserable. Plus, miserable people depressed Shelley. So instead, they visited by phone a couple of times a week. "Until this unpleasantness is over," Shelley said.

When, exactly, the unpleasantness would end was a mystery. Even though Bob understood Karen's need for sympathy, he was losing patience with her. Women all over the world get pregnant, he told her one night after an especially long day on the road. Did their lives get turned upside down? Were no meals made? Did their homes look like national disaster areas? "What else, Bob?" Karen shouted. "What else is missing?" And even though he hadn't planned on fighting, he was in it now and told her that yes, he did miss the sex. "God, you're such a selfish prick!" yelled Karen.

"You wanted this baby, damn you, but I'm the one paying the price!" She started throwing things at him; whatever was on the bed was suddenly moving in Bob's direction: a tissue box, an empty mug, a yellow legal pad, a folder full of work papers that came apart in the air and floated to the floor. And then for a moment, all was quiet. "Oh God." Karen covered her mouth with her hands.

"Is this what we've come to?"

"I don't know," she said, breaking down. "I'm so sorry."

Bob sat down on the edge of the bed, and Karen leaned in to hug him, something she hadn't done in weeks. Bob took her in his arms and held her, softly stroking the hair he was still enamored with. "I don't want to fight anymore."

"No," she said, tears running down her face now. "And I don't want to feel like this anymore. I hate everything about this pregnancy. It's ruining our lives."

"For now. But I know it will eventually enhance our lives. We just have to be patient."

"I've been patient, Bob." She was sobbing. "It's brought me nothing but misery."

Bob kissed Karen's forehead and then her cheeks. "Just a little while longer."

Karen looked at him. "Are you sure?" she asked, wanting to believe him.

"I promise."

Bob tucked his wife back into bed and then picked up the room. He made himself a grilled cheese sandwich and read the newspaper in the living room. He watched *North by Northwest,* one of his favorite Hitchcock films. Bob had been watching them with his father since his teenage years, when Tucker introduced his son to the esteemed director by insisting they watch *Psycho* with all the lights out. After the movie, Bob ever so gently got into bed beside his wife and slept soundly. It wasn't until Karen woke him that he opened his eyes, even though it was well past seven o'clock. She was standing over him, smiling. "What?" he asked sleepily.

"You, Bob Parsons, make good on your promises."

Bob sat up in bed. "You feel better?"

"I feel terrific."

CHAPTER 5

MAY 1993

Rebecca Spears Parsons was born at 3:46 p.m. on the fifth of May, just one day late, weighing seven pounds, ten ounces, and measuring twenty inches, statistics that Karen, like many mothers, would reflect on in her child's teenage years. She would call them to mind, often when she was angry or frustrated with her daughter, as a reminder of how fragile and silent she had once been. On that unusually warm May afternoon, Rebecca looked very much like the old-fashioned doll Karen had played with as a child. Her grandmother had given it to her right after her twin brothers were born, and Karen toted it around with her for almost two years. Rachel was the name she had given the doll, and Rebecca had her brown hair and blue eyes, as well as long enough eyelashes to draw comments from the maternity nurses. And even though Karen guessed the nurses said encouraging words to every new mother, each drinking in the compliments like an overdue glass of water, she thought Rebecca was exceptionally beautiful.

When Karen got pregnant again, she was sick, but not nearly as sick as when she carried Rebecca. She had just enough energy, she told Bob, to look at houses. Karen and Bob loved their apartment, but it was too small to house a family of four. The spare room, which Karen and her mother had transformed into a nursery by stenciling colorful kites on the walls, would not house a two-year-old and a baby. It took just under a month for Karen and her mother to find and fall in love with a Cape Cod expanded to twice its original size, sitting on a half-acre lot surrounded by mature maple and oak trees. Shelley proclaimed it perfect the minute Karen stopped the car at the curb out front. Bob liked the house as much as Karen did, so they bought it, putting thirty percent down. This was possible, Bob pointed out at the closing, only because they had been so frugal.

OCTOBER 1995

It took just over seventeen hours of labor on the twelfth of October to push out an eight pound, eleven ounce boy. Robert looked swollen and bruised when he finally emerged, an infant prize fighter. The nurses told Karen he would be strong and handsome, like his dad. Bob was thrilled to have a son, a namesake. His daughter was lovely and intelligent, everyone said, for a two-and-a-half-year-old, but only a son could provide another generation of Parsonses. As Bob held his son in the hospital, he fantasized about playing football with him in the backyard on cool fall days. Karen and Rebecca would watch from lawn chairs on the sideline and serve them hot chocolate with mini marshmallows at the half.

Bob bought Robert a plush football for his first birthday, which Robert stuffed in his mouth. When his son turned two, Bob bought him a Nerf football, thinking it would be easy for him to catch. But whenever Bob tossed the ball to his son, from as little as one foot away, he dropped it. And not only did he drop it, he laughed when he did so, as if dropping the ball had been the intention of the game. Karen told Bob to lower his expectations. *Just let Robert hold the football in his hands and run around the house with it. Chase him.* But Bob refused to give in, to baby him. The kid was supposed to be able to catch a ball without hours of training. Anyone knew that. Bob was so tired when he got home from work; it was a relief actually not to have to give another twenty-minute pep talk—this one about the old pigskin instead of paper and card-board—in an effort to get his uncoordinated son to catch a ball. Karen urged him to continue, like she urged him to occasionally do the dishes or read bedtime stories, but he ignored many of her requests. After a twelve-hour day, he was bushed.

Increasingly, Karen cared for the children and Bob cared for himself. It made good sense to Bob, since he was traveling more and had just been made responsible for the largest sales area in the country. His hard work and devotion to the company were paying off. His name carried clout and suggested a can-do attitude. Customers expected the very best out of Bob Parsons, and they were rarely if ever disappointed. If a shipment was delayed or an order not filled, Bob had the good sense to send expensive gifts or theater tickets to sold-out performances and dinner vouchers to popular pricey restaurants in its place. He was the man everyone wanted to work with, and nobody knew that better than Bob.

Karen, with two children, had lost the short-lived professional status she gained when she officially stopped working for Clear Communication the day before Rebecca was born. She and Bob had agreed when she got pregnant that she would stay home with their children, at least for the first year. Jennifer told her to holler if she ever wanted to work again. And for a while, Jennifer kept in touch, as did Mary and Patty. They invited Karen to birthday lunches and other informal office gatherings, but as time passed and Jennifer hired two additional writers Karen didn't know, the get-togethers became awkward. Minus the commonality of a shared working environment, they had little to link them together. Jennifer, who had recently married her boyfriend of eight years at her parents' house in Naples, Florida, and Mary, and Patty, recently engaged, were all professional women without children. The two new hires were right out of college. Child-rearing stories, Karen quickly realized, were best understood and appreciated by other mothers. And because Karen was no longer in the office, and had not been in the office for more than two years, she had become an interloper, too far out of the loop to know which client was doing what.

What she missed more than the work itself was interaction with other adults. She had Bob, of course, when he was in town. But their conversations were often interrupted by Rebecca and Robert, who seemed to need something at the exact moment Bob was leading up to the crescendo of another work story. He repeatedly told Karen to ignore them, that they were just vying for her attention and that whatever they wanted could certainly wait. But Karen had a hard time ignoring the children, who had perfected whining, crying, biting one another, and shrieking at an early age. What mother could ignore that?

Bob seemed content to kiss their cheeks and pat their heads when he left for work in the morning, and to do the same thing when he got home in the evening, meaning their day-to-day, hour-to-hour, minute-by-minute care fell to Karen. Robert awoke at six o'clock, and Rebecca went to bed at eight o'clock, and the fourteen hours that stood between those defining quotidian occurrences belonged to the three of them. Their long days together were remarkably repetitive. Robert and Karen read books and played with toys until six thirty, when Rebecca got up. Karen then made breakfast for the family. Bob left the house by six forty-five. The television went on at seven. The children watched educational shows for two hours while Karen showered, dressed, tidied the house, and made lists, fueled by coffee. On the days Rebecca didn't have preschool, the three of them then ran errands for an hour. At ten o'clock, weather permitting, they drove to a playground, where Karen sat on a bench and watched her children play. If other kids were there, Karen shared the bench with other mothers. Oftentimes her conversations with the *stay at homes,* as she referred to them, were far less satisfying for Karen than flipping through a magazine.

JUNE 1998

Not ready for summer, for the end of Rebecca's three-day a week preschool schedule, tired of their regular play areas, and desperate for stimulating conversation and company, Karen decided to try a new location. Carson Park was a twenty-minute drive from Karen's house, twice the distance she usually drove for a swing set.

It was a small park with antiquated equipment, nothing special. The only reason Karen knew it existed was because it sat across the street from where she had her hair trimmed every three months. But Karen remembered it as a nicely appointed park, with a grassy area, several picnic tables, a large sandbox (which is all Robert cared about), a climbing and sliding apparatus, and a swing set, which would satisfy Rebecca.

When Karen pulled up to the curb the following morning, the park was empty. The four U-shaped swings hung motionless, which made Rebecca squeal with delight. She ran from the car, as did Robert, who lumbered across the grass carrying an oversized red and yellow plastic dump truck with both hands. Once Karen delivered a pail and a shovel to her son and gave her daughter a starter push, she sat down on one of two wood benches with her travel mug of coffee. It was just after ten, so she would let the children play for an hour before calling them over for a snack. She had packed animal crackers and grape juice; Robert would be pleased.

Several minutes later, another car joined Karen's at the curb. When the doors opened, Karen saw a little girl step out and run to the swings. Karen watched Rebecca's face register casual interest. The girl chose the swing next to Rebecca's and immediately started pumping on her own. At the car, the mother was helping the little boy choose toys from a large plastic laundry basket. Two colorful motorcycles in hand, the boy dashed to the sandbox and sat down a few feet from Robert. Like the girls, they looked very close in age. Karen took a sip of coffee as she looked back at the mother, who was now carrying the basket and a canvas bag. She smiled at Karen then sat on an adjacent bench.

"Britney," she called out to the girl on the swings, "we'll have a snack at eleven." They were on the same schedule. The woman then took a travel mug and a thick novel out of her canvas bag and started reading. Perfect, thought Karen, who went back to the food magazine in her lap. She made an effort to try one new recipe a week, but had fallen behind and was hoping to find something today she could make on the weekend. Bob had been dropping hints for salmon, a miracle for a steak-lover, and Karen had just found what she thought might work. The marinade was simple, even though it called for ingredients she didn't have at home. The pasta salad pictured with the fish looked good, too. While Bob preferred potatoes or rice with his main dish, he didn't object to pasta, especially in the summer. Karen looked up from the glossy pages. She could also make a Caesar salad, Bob's favorite. Karen glanced over at the other woman, who now looked familiar. She wasn't anyone from the neighborhood, or from Rebecca's nursery school. Perhaps Karen had seen her at the grocery store or at one of a dozen regular errand locations around town. The woman looked up from her book and met Karen's gaze. They both smiled and suddenly Karen knew; it was Sarah Kelly from high school.

"Sarah?"

"Karen," Sarah replied, closing her book and setting it down next to her. "I thought I knew you." Karen stood and approached Sarah's bench. "Have a seat and tell me what you do to keep your sanity."

"From the looks of it," said Karen, sitting, "about the same thing as you do."

Both women, relieved to find someone in a situation similar, talked easily. Karen had no nearby girlfriends, now that she no longer saw Jennifer, Mary, and Patty. Her college roommate, Allison, had married a rancher and moved to Montana, and her good friends from high school were scattered, many of them single and working in big cities. The few that were still in Karen's hometown were too busy with their own lives to make the fifty-minute commute to visit. Karen was inundated, too. Using exhaustion as an excuse, Karen didn't try hard enough to keep in touch. She sent Christmas cards and occasionally called, but mostly she did nothing but care for her family.

Sarah's friends, some of whom Karen remembered, were also busy or elsewhere. Since Sarah had ventured out to the East Coast for college, many of those friends had settled in New England. She, too, would have stayed, in Boston, if she hadn't met Vincent Keyworth, her husband of nine years. They met when she was a sophomore in college and he was a junior. Like an idiot, Sarah said, she dropped out at the end of her junior year to get married. Vincent was going to spend a year studying in London, and he wanted

Sarah to go with him. And Sarah's parents wouldn't allow her to do so unless she was Mrs. Vincent Keyworth. "Can you believe that? They wouldn't let me go without a ring on my finger, but they had no trouble with my dropping out of college."

"I was right there with you. Bob graduated a year ahead of me and at times we both thought it was silly to wait."

"Yeah, but you did, didn't you? I honestly don't know what I was thinking. I could have gone to school in London and graduated with my class in the spring."

"But at the time you were in love."

"Oh yes. Plus, my mom thought I should put all my energies into being a good wife."

"Ah, there's nothing like maternal advice."

"Especially when it's misguided and unwelcome."

Karen laughed. "Do you ever think about going back to school?"

"All the time," said Sarah. "I have just two things in my way."

"Time and energy?"

"Britney and Jeremy."

As it turned out, Britney was eight months older than Rebecca, and Jeremy was just two months older than Robert. It was easy to tell they were contemporaries because they played nicely together. Rebecca and Britney had stopped swinging and were lying in the grass pointing up at the clouds. And Robert and Jeremy were pushing trucks around in the sand. Moments like this one, when her children were serenely occupied and Karen could simply sit and watch them, made motherhood enjoyable.

"Mom!" called Rebecca. "I'm starving!"

"Me too," said Britney, getting up from the ground. "Let's get a snack."

The girls raced to their mothers. "And I'm thirsty," Rebecca said. "I want some juice."

"Please," said Karen.

"Please," parroted Rebecca.

Karen poured Rebecca's juice into a plastic cup. She gave her a plastic bag with animal crackers and told her to sit back down on the grass with her new friend. Britney, holding a juice box and cheese crackers, said, "Let's go!" The women then readied the snacks for their sons. Robert needed a lid on his cup so he wouldn't spill it all over himself and just a few crackers at a time, or they would end up in the sand.

"Spills everything?" asked Sarah.

"Absolutely everything."

"Don't worry; there's hope. Jeremy was like that six weeks ago, and now he's much better. He can actually drink a cup of juice without spilling a drop."

"I can't wait."

"I can't wait until they're in college." Both women laughed. "I have an idea," Sarah said, looking at her watch. "What would you think about taking the kids to McDonald's for lunch?"

"My kids would be absolutely thrilled. Robert will do anything for French fries."

"Jeremy, too. He'll pee on the potty if I stand over him with a couple of fries in my hand."

Karen groaned. "Don't get me going on the potty thing. We're not having a lot of success."

"They're young. We've got time."

"That's not what my husband thinks. Bob says there's no reason for Robert to be wearing diapers, now that he's going on three."

"Jeremy's just starting to get the hang of it." Karen nodded her head. "Vincent's impatient, too. He hates hearing about Jeremy's accidents, so I don't tell him anymore. Not that it should matter to him one way or the other, since he's at the lab twelve hours a day."

"You, too?"

"Oh yes," said Sarah. "And then he comes home exhausted. Guess who's in charge of the children for the evening?"

Karen sipped her tepid coffee. "You're telling the story of my life."

"That's just chapter one. So, are you game for lunch?"

"We're in."

Bob stopped for a quick burger on the road between meetings. The first meeting had gone as planned; Tasty Apple had been receptive to his suggestion of increasing inventory to match the boost in production. Bob, who personally researched their numbers, had put together an impressive PowerPoint presentation, citing why an increase in their standard order by seven percent would yield them the cushion they needed. Since Tasty anticipated a five percent growth in product that year, Bob pointed out, the extra two percent in packaging would give them the ability to immediately ship out a bumper crop. If the fall harvest did not turn out as expected, a marginal increase in packaging would not be problematic to store. As everyone in the room already knew, the Tasty Apple container, when collapsed, took up just slightly more space than a couple of flattened cereal boxes. The people at Tasty were good customers and had been for years, so Bob was not surprised by the positive outcome of the meeting. The next one would be more difficult.

The Gallant brothers owned a regional chain of high-end grocery stores and were considering pushing paper bags instead of plastic. It seemed at first like a backward idea in a world where plastic bags were king. But, as John Gallant had said on the phone to Bob the week before, their college-educated customers were beginning to question the use of plastic bags, according to the Gallants' latest survey. While customers certainly knew paper came from trees and were quick to indicate their distaste for overzealous deforestation, they were equally quick to proclaim an inherent and growing distrust of chemical companies and the effect the manufacture and disposal of plastic bags had on the environment. Plus, Gallant said, if they could print their logo onto the paper bags with a vegetable-based dye, their customers could compost the bags. The call had taken Bob by surprise; Ed Felder usually handled the five-pound grocery sack accounts in the western part of the state. Ed was on vacation, which meant that Gerry Osbourne usually filled in. Instead, Bob was asked to handle it. Perhaps, Bob thought as he wiped ketchup from his upper lip with a napkin, this was a test.

He stopped at a mini-mart a few miles from the Gallants' office building to use the men's room, where he brushed his hair and his teeth and washed his hands and face. He changed his shirt and retied his tie. There was nothing he could do about the wrinkles in his suit, yet they could have spawned as easily from an office chair as a car seat. Bob didn't like to give the impression that he was going from one meeting to another, marketing his wares like a door-to-door salesman. The image of the traveling salesman had been tarnished over the years by sordid stories, most prominently of expense report padding and quick stays with questionable company in roadside motels. Bob did everything in his power to portray himself as a clean and honest sales representative; his image was as important as his product.

John and Arron Gallant had done their homework. They knew what kind of bags they needed. They knew how to print their logo on the bags. They knew how long it would take Forester to get the bags to them, and they knew precisely how much they should cost. They also knew what two of Forester's competitors would charge them, which was a little less than what Bob had calculated the night before. Had they called James at River Paper? James was their top salesman and would have told them anything to strike a deal. Had they already met with James? Rather than ask, Bob told the Gallants he would meet the competitors' prices and beat their deadline. The paper bag inventory at Forester was piled to the ceiling; Bob knew they could ship out by the end of the week. The printing was the only issue, but Bob figured he could push it through. Tammy still owed him a favor for misspelling a customer's name on ten thousand cardboard boxes. (Bob had spent almost two thousand Forester dollars in dinner reservations and theater tickets to right that wrong.) What Bob didn't know was John Gallant had also researched sales reps. Bob had an unblemished reputation for service as well as sales, which is why Todd Martin had waited until Ed was on vacation to request a meeting. If anyone at Forester could make it happen, it was Bob Parsons. The deal was sealed with a handshake.

Bob waited until he was outside of the building to allow the huge grin he had been stifling to take over his face. This was just the kind of deal he needed in his portfolio to jump up another notch. He couldn't wait to tell Todd the details. He also couldn't wait to tell Karen. He knew it would be difficult to tell the whole story with the children talking and needing Karen to do things for them. Maybe they could go out. Bob took his Forester cell phone from his briefcase and called home. He smiled when he heard his wife's voice. "Hi. It's me."

"Hi, honey. Where are you?"

"On the way back to my office. I just scored a big deal."

"That's great," said Karen, wondering if the telephone ring had woken Robert. She'd meant to turn off the receiver in the master bedroom upstairs.

"It's really, really great, and I want to tell you all about it when I get home. But I know it can be crazy with the kids."

"Tell me about it." Karen put her hand to stomach. She wished she'd had the sensible cheeseburger that Sarah had chosen instead of the Quarter Pounder with cheese.

"Let's go out to dinner, just the two of us."

"Tonight?" asked Karen, responding to Robert's call by walking up the stairs to his room.

"Yeah, why not? Let's be spontaneous."

"Easier for you than for me." Karen opened her son's bedroom door. Robert was sitting on his bed smiling at her, his eyes still sleepy. She smiled back. "It's almost three in the afternoon. Where am I going to get a sitter?"

"Call your mother."

Karen picked Robert up and set him down on her hip. "She has a life, Bob."

Bob slowed for a red light. "Call someone else. There has to be a high school or college student out there who wants to make some money. Offer to pay double."

Karen kissed Robert's cheek. "I'll see what I can do."

"Great. I'll take care of the dinner reservations, and I'll pick you up at six."

Karen was able to find a sitter on her first try. Jamie Carle, who lived at the other end of the street, was able to come at five thirty, so Karen could get ready for the evening without simultaneously tending to Rebecca and Robert. Late afternoons were the worst. The children were tired, hungry, and moaned at the slightest discomfort. Karen turned the television on at four thirty more often than not. Yet, even when they were sitting on the couch in front of it, they needed her. Could she sit with them? Could she get them some juice and a snack? What was for dinner? When was dinner? Why did Robert have more crackers in his bowl than Rebecca? Rebecca was pretty good to Robert most of the time, but the never-ending late afternoons temporarily turned all three of them into ogres. Karen often dealt with her poor mood by snacking on cinnamon graham crackers and drinking a pot of tea.

When Jamie arrived, Robert, who was going through a stage of stranger anxiety, burst into tears, even though Jamie had already babysat several times. Karen scooped him up, kissed him on the cheek, and told him the macaroni and cheese was ready. At that, Robert brightened. Karen set him down at the kitchen table and told Rebecca, who slid in next to him, that she could have dessert when she finished her broccoli. "I hate broccoli," she announced.

"I know," said Karen, who kissed her head. "But one day you will like it." Karen then turned her back, jogged through the living room, and dashed up the stairs. She quickly undressed and got into the shower, where the warm water instantly relaxed her.

Being in her house without a child at her side (and knowing that the children were cared for) was for Karen an unusual luxury. She felt free. Because she couldn't hear them with the water running, it was like they didn't exist. She fantasized that she and Bob were just married and they were going out to dinner, as they had on many weekends. She pretended she was still working, and that Jennifer had just given her a plum assignment, one that would give her a name in the business. She pretended Bob was going to ask her to go away that weekend, and of course she would say yes. What would keep them home? Karen stepped out of the shower, dried herself, and walked into her bedroom. Even with the door closed, she could hear the commotion downstairs. She walked to her bedside table and turned on the radio. She sat on the bed, closed her eyes, and listened to a National Public Radio reporter tell a story about two brothers who planted trees in California. They were foresters, who prided themselves on accountability and responsibility. They planted trees for the future of mankind as well as the future of their business. The three of them, the reporter and the two men, walked through the woods while they talked; twigs snapped and leaves crunched beneath their feet. It was quiet in the forest, except for their voices and their footfalls, as if the trees were enveloped by a soundproof dome; it was the kind of quiet absent from a house with small children. The reporter finished her story, and Karen looked at the clock. She had ten minutes to dry her hair and dress.

As promised, Bob arrived at six. He said hello to Jamie and the kids, then called for Karen on his way up the stairs. She was in the closet looking at shoes. She chose a soft leather pair she hadn't worn since Robert was born. She slid them onto her feet just as Bob walked through the bedroom door. "Are you ready?"

She smiled at him. "More than you'll ever know."

On the way to the restaurant, Bob started his story. He told it chronologically as he always did, this time beginning with his successful call to Tasty Apple, a customer Karen had been briefed on before. He included names and numbers and dates, diving into the minutiae like an accountant into a tax return, deeply explaining what each percentage and decimal point meant for the customer and, more important, what the statistics meant for him. He had just started talking about the new Gallant account when he drove his new 3 Series BMW into the restaurant parking lot. He turned off the car, leaned over, and kissed Karen on the cheek. Then he reached beyond her to the door handle and pushed the door open from the inside. "Let's get inside. We're a little late."

Karen got out of the car slowly, as if the physical weight of each number she had heard for the last fifteen minutes had settled onto her lap. She shut the door behind her and followed Bob into their favorite Italian restaurant, where they were seated at a side table next to a window. The hostess lit the glass globe-enclosed votive between them and handed them laminated menus. Karen set hers down and looked at Bob. "It feels so good to be out," she said, refreshed by the quiet surroundings and the prospect of a fresh pasta dish prepared by others. "I'm so glad you called."

"Me too. I couldn't be in a better mood."

The Gallant story continued. When the waitress returned five minutes later and filled their water glasses, Bob was not ready to order. And when she returned five minutes after that, Bob was at the story's crescendo, running through the numbers with the speed and persistence of an auctioneer. He was just about to spring the amount of his commission check on his wife and was, therefore, still not ready to focus on anything but his story. Karen looked up wearily at their server. "I'll have a glass of Chardonnay."

"And I'll have a Heineken."

After the server left, Bob smiled at Karen and asked if she was ready. "Ready for what? More numbers that mean nothing to me?"

Bob's smile faded. "What do you mean by that?"

"What do you think I mean by that? You asked me out to a nice dinner and have been doing nothing but spewing obscure figures at me since we drove out the driveway." Karen looked at her watch. "Twenty minutes ago. I know these margins are important to you, Bob. But they mean very little to me."

"I thought you'd be interested in the numbers. They represent what pays our bills and feeds our family."

"I'm very aware of your salary and how hard you work for it."

Bob picked up the menu and looked at it. "Meaning we talk about it too much."

"Sometimes," said Karen, softening.

Bob put down his menu and looked at her. "What are we supposed to talk about?"

Karen took a sip of water. "We could talk about me. We could talk about my day."

"Your day?"

"Yes. You used to be interested in me and what I was doing."

The waitress brought their drinks and didn't even ask them about dinner. Bob waited until she was gone, then reached across the table and took his wife's hand. "Of course I'm interested in what you're doing."

"Well, it doesn't feel like it. It feels like you've lost interest in everything but your career."

Bob sat back in his chair. "Do you really mean that?"

"I'm frustrated, Bob. I have the most difficult, boring, underappreciated job in the world, and nine times out of ten you don't really want to hear about it when you walk through the door at the end of the day."

"I always ask you how your day went."

"With the same level of sincerity and interest as the supermarket cashier who says, 'Have a nice day.' "

Bob took a sip of beer. "I think I'm a little more invested than the cashier at the grocery store." Karen shrugged. "Look. You're so bored and unappreciated, go back to work."

Karen picked up her wineglass. "That's so easy for you to say."

"It's easy for me to say because it would be easy for you to do."

"And just put the kids in daycare, right?"

"Absolutely," said Bob, glancing at the menu. "They wouldn't know the difference."

Karen put her glass down. "That is perhaps the most insensitive thing you've ever said to me."

Bob put the menu back down on the table. "I didn't mean it that way, and you know it."

"No, I don't know it, Bob. You appear to have no idea, no grasp of the numbers—the minutes, the hours, the days—behind caring for and raising our children. You continue along the same path you were on when we were first married. My life, on the other hand, is drastically different, and not necessarily in a good way. And it's a life you don't seem to want to participate in, until the children are asleep and you're lying next to me in bed."

"Oh here we go," said Bob, lifting his Heineken. "Let's talk about how I want sex all the time and you don't."

"No, let's talk about how you used to cater to my every need and how now you only cater to yours."

Bob sipped his beer. "You sure know how to spoil a nice night out."

"Ditto."

They were quiet. The waitress returned and stood next to their table, black leather encased pad in hand. Bob looked at Karen. "Are we staying?"

"We sure are. I'm going to eat a dinner I didn't make, and someone else is doing the dishes."

Bob put his napkin in his lap. Karen ordered the ravioli with pesto, and Bob ordered a New York strip, medium rare, with a side of fettuccini Alfredo. Bob looked at Karen as soon as the waitress left. "I'm sorry. I have definitely been preoccupied lately at work. There's a lot going on, and I want to be a part of it."

"I know, honey. And I want you to be a part of it, too. I just want you to be a part of our lives, too. I really need your support, and the kids need an involved dad. Robert actually picked up that blue football yesterday and tried to play catch with Rebecca."

"No kidding," said Bob, smiling.

"She had no interest in playing with him. He was disappointed."

"Well, I can play with him. I'll make a point of doing that this weekend."

"That sounds good," said Karen, taking a sip of wine. "He needs you, Bob. We all need you."

Bob reached across the table and squeezed Karen's hand twice. "I need you, too."

CHAPTER 6

JULY 1998

Shelley called Karen Thursday morning, just after Bob left for work, and said she needed a grandchildren fix. Karen looked around the kitchen. Eight cereal boxes, all open, sat on the counter. (Robert wanted a little bit of each.) Robert's bowl, half filled with milk, was on the table. The rest of the milk was on the floor, where Robert poured it, mimicking something he had seen on *Magic School Bus,* according to Rebecca. Last night's dinner dishes were still sitting in the sink in water that was now cold enough to have reversed the initial benefits of the hot water soak. Karen intended to get back to them, but had fallen asleep on Robert's bed instead. "What time?" Karen walked with the phone through the dining room and into the living room.

"Oh, I don't know," said Shelley. "What time's good for you?"

Robert and Rebecca, still in their pajamas, were sitting on the couch watching TV. Rebecca's Barbies had taken over the armchair, where they sunned themselves at a pool party most of the previous afternoon. After dinner, Rebecca had told her mother she couldn't put them away because the Barbies were responsible for cleaning up after themselves. It didn't look like they had made much progress. Robert's U Clean It car wash stood in the middle of the area rug with twenty-seven cars lined up. Karen knew there were twenty-seven cars because that was what Rebecca had told her last night. There was no way they could send their customers away, even though it was well past closing time, because she and Robert didn't want to disappoint them. They had offered a special that day and had an overwhelming response. Rebecca had made the decision after dinner to shuttle the customers home so they wouldn't have to lose their places in line. "It doesn't matter," said Karen, hoping Shelley would suggest later on in the day, when Robert got up from his nap.

"Well, I've got a few things to do this morning. How about lunchtime?"

Karen walked back into the kitchen and opened the refrigerator door. She had half a pitcher of iced tea she'd made for Sarah's visit yesterday, and some grapes she could re-rinse and put in a pretty bowl. She could make tuna; her mother loved it. And, she thought, walking to the cupboard, she had some pretzels, somewhere. Bob had taken a liking to them recently, proclaiming them the ultimate snack food: crunchy, salty, and low in fat. Karen found half a bag next to the unopened chips she was saving for the weekend. "Sure."

"One o'clock?"

Karen closed her eyes. Her mother knew the kids ate early, Robert in particular. Since he was up at dawn, he was ready to sleep by twelve thirty. And if she didn't get him down by then, he got overtired and didn't sleep at all, which meant she had a cranky toddler for company all afternoon. How many times had she complained about this to her mother? "You can come at one, but you won't get to see Robert."

"Really?"

"He's up at six, Mom, which means I'm up at six. By noon, we both need a break."

"Okay. If I push myself, I should be able to get there by twelve thirty. Why don't you feed him first, and then put him in for a nap after I arrive? Maybe then just the girls can have a nice lunch together."

Rebecca, Karen thought, would not want to wait until one to eat a tuna sandwich with her grandmother. If Karen made a big enough deal about it, however, and allowed Rebecca to help with the preparations, it might work. "Okay," said Karen. "I'll see you at twelve thirty."

"Can I bring anything?"

What Karen wished was that her mother would simply offer to bring something if she wanted to bring something, cookies for the children or a bottle of mineral water from her basement, or not ask. If Shelley asked and Karen said no, Shelley was covered and could expect lunch or dinner at Karen's house without contributing toward the meal. Ironically, it was Shelley who had taught Karen to bring something to the hostess. "I'm all set," said Karen, listening to Robert and Rebecca arguing in the other room.

"Perfect. I'll see you at twelve thirty then."

Karen set the phone down on the kitchen counter and walked into the living room. Robert was on the floor kicking and fussing, and Rebecca was holding the television remote control in her hand above her head as she sat on the couch. "What is going on here?"

"He doesn't like this show," said Rebecca calmly.

Karen glanced at the TV and saw animated figures. "Why not?"

"I have no idea. It's *Reading Rainbow.*" Rebecca's eyes never left the TV.

Karen picked Robert up off the floor and held him to her. "Is Levar reading a scary book, Rebecca?"

"Where the Wild Things Are."

Karen sat down on the couch with Robert on her lap. "They are a little scary."

"Not to me," said Rebecca, "and not to Max."

Karen told Robert the monsters were nice; they just looked scary. Robert watched for a moment, then started crying again. Karen lifted him and herself off the couch. "I'm going to get him dressed. The TV goes off after this show."

"Are we going to the park today?"

"Grandma's coming."

Rebecca hesitated, absorbing, and then asked, "Does that mean we can't go to the park?"

Karen raised her eyebrows at her daughter. "That depends on how fast we can clean up this house, your room included."

As always, cleaning the house took longer than Karen expected. The children were pretty good at putting their toys into their painted wood chests in their rooms if Karen offered an incentive, like an ice cream from the truck at the park. It was the dusting and vacuuming and general cleaning that was most onerous. She resented doing it; it was constant, and Bob didn't help. If there was clutter on the floor, he walked over and around it. And he hadn't picked up a broom since they left the apartment, instead ignoring the snap and pop of snack crumbs when he walked into the kitchen after work.

Dressed in a pair of tired shorts with an elastic waistband and a stained cotton T-shirt, Karen attacked the kitchen. She cleared the counters, table, and floor, and then scrubbed all three. She did the dishes, then wiped the fingerprints from the lower cupboards. When Rebecca walked into the room and asked if she and Robert could watch one more show, Karen acquiesced, but said they had to put away their toys while doing so. When she was done in the kitchen, Karen joined her children in the living room and dusted around them. In the bathroom, she wiped the dried out, spat toothpaste from the sink and the urine pools from around the base of the toilet with disinfectant cloths. She returned the bath toys to their mesh bag, hung it from the hook next to the showerhead, and then pulled the curtain across. When the TV show ended, Karen turned the set off and told the kids to sit on the couch while she vacuumed. Rebecca, already moping, already knowing they would not make it to the park, sat with her arms across her chest. Whenever her grandmother came to visit, her mother always ran out of time. She asked anyway. Karen looked at her watch. "Let me make the tuna first. Do you want to help?" Rebecca's response was a dark look.

When Karen turned her back and walked into the kitchen, Robert followed her, announcing that he was hungry. She lifted him into his blue wood chair and put some Cheerios in a plastic bowl in front of him. The first few hit the floor before she closed the box. She walked away from him, willing herself not to get out the broom. There would be more, and she would deal with it later. She grabbed two cans of tuna from the cupboard and drained them, then minced a small amount of onion and added it to the tuna before putting in a generous amount of mayonnaise, exactly how her mother liked it. She turned and opened the bread drawer and found nothing but stale bagels. She walked to the fridge and opened the freezer section. "Shit."

"Shit," said Robert.

Karen put plastic wrap over the tuna and put it into the fridge. She grabbed Robert from his chair and strode into the living room, where she caught Rebecca watching TV with no volume. "That television is supposed to be off." Karen stood in front of Rebecca with Robert on her hip.

"And we're supposed to be at the park."

Karen turned off the TV. "And you need to watch what you say, young lady."

Rebecca slid off the couch. "Are we going now?"

"We have to go to the store first. We're out of bread."

"Great," said Rebecca in the sarcastic tone she had picked up from Bob. Karen ignored her; they didn't have time for a time-out.

"Let's go. The sooner we go, the sooner we can get back."

"That's obvious," sassed Rebecca.

Karen took two giant steps toward her daughter and swatted her bottom. Rebecca immediately began to cry. And even though Karen immediately felt like she had done the wrong thing, handled the situation like a stressed-out babysitter instead of a reasonable, rational parent, she said, "You deserved that." Rebecca wiped the tears from her eyes. "No more monkey business. No more fresh mouth. And we might just have a chance of getting to the park."

They walked out to the driveway. Karen secured Robert into his booster seat, while Rebecca, still moping, belted herself. Karen started the car and realized, for the fourth or fifth time in two days, that she had no gas; only now she *really* had no gas, which meant they would have to get some before going to the store. Maybe she could buy bread there. She drove to the Shell station/Food Mart, pumped gas into the car, and ran into the store to check out their bread. Soft&Tasty white filled the bread shelf. Her mother ate nothing but whole wheat. Karen ran back to the car, where she had a brilliant idea: She would get bread at the bakery! She drove to the other side of town to Freshly Baked, where she bought a loaf of sliced whole wheat, six poppy-seed sandwich rolls, six brownies, and six lemon bars. Still feeling guilty about giving Rebecca a spank, she also bought two frosted sugar cookies, which she let the children eat in the car.

Back home, Karen listened to her messages as she put everything on the kitchen counter. Bob would be late that night, and Sarah, who was at the park, was wondering where they were. It was eleven fifteen, which meant it was too late to go. If they left now, Robert would fall asleep in the car on the way back. Karen left a message for Sarah on her home phone and then called Bob, who had an important dinner meeting after work. He would be home by nine. She then told Rebecca they couldn't go to the park, which made her daughter cry for the second time that morning. Karen apologized and then turned on the TV. Rebecca sat on the couch. Karen sat Robert down next to her.

Robert had logged three hours of television by noon and was barely able to stay awake during lunch. Karen sat next to him while he ate a peanut butter and grape jelly sandwich and drank chocolate milk, a special treat for being such a good boy and staying on the couch in a TV-induced stupor while Karen reswept the kitchen floor and folded two loads of laundry. Karen had just finished putting the children's clothing into their bureaus when the doorbell rang. Rebecca, apprised of the girls' lunch that would exclude her baby brother, ran to the door. "Hi, sweetie," said Shelley, bending down to give Rebecca a hug.

"Hi, Grandma. Robert's about to go down."

"I'd better hurry then. Are they upstairs?"

"In the kitchen. What's in the bag?"

"Cookies. I bought them at the bakery."

"So did we."

"Oh," said Shelley. She walked through the dining room, leaving footprints in the freshly vacuumed carpeting, and into the kitchen. Robert, sitting on his mother's hip, smiled. "Hello, big boy! Are you ready for a sleep? Come to Grandma." She held out her arms. "Take the bag, honey," she said to Karen. "I understand we've both been to the bakery this morning. I also got some rolls. I know how you love sandwiches on fresh kaisers."

"Thanks," said Karen, deciding she would freeze the whole wheat bread and use her mother's rolls.

"Shall we take our young friend up?"

"After you." Karen gestured with an open palm.

They walked through the living room, where Rebecca was dressing one of her Barbies in a denim skirt and cowboy boots. "I'm hungry," she said as soon as she saw her mother.

"Me too." Karen accepted Robert from her mother. "We'll be right down."

Shelley started up the stairs, her cordovan tasseled loafers announcing each step. She wore khaki pants and a white cotton T-shirt, both freshly pressed, a belt around her middle, and short, graying chestnut-colored hair that she coaxed with mousse into the casual style she had been sporting for forty years. She no longer wore shorts or sleeveless tops, even on the hottest of summer days, claiming women over fifty should hide their flabby arm wings and double knees. She was even more disdainful of older women with hair that fell past their shoulders, and had told Karen more than once that she would have to change her hairstyle at some point. There was little less attractive, Shelley proclaimed, than a cascade of flowing hair surrounding a wizened face. What she had never said, never admitted, was that growing her hair, which was fine rather than thick like Karen's, had not been an option.

"What a morning I've had," Shelley said. "I've never played worse tennis; I couldn't get anything over the net. Of course, all the girls said I was playing fine, and they meant well, but positive comments in a negative situation can actually do more harm than good. Then I ran over to the dress shop on Main—I think I told you your father and I have a wedding on Saturday and I have absolutely nothing to wear that isn't half a century old. I must have tried on every dress in my size. No luck. The woman there—you know, the attractive one with the short blond hair and the charming smile— told me about a dress shop at the mall. She said it might be a tad youthful, but that I should not be discouraged by that. If I'm patient, she told me, I will surely find something. I'm going to try to scoot over there on the way home, so I want to eat a light lunch. And then, of course, I drove like a teenage boy to the bakery, because I had nothing at home for the children, and come to find out when I get here that you've been there, too. Karen, we really should talk about these things. I almost got a speeding ticket."

Karen said nothing. If she opened her mouth, words that stung, that she could not take back would fly out of her mouth, bees from a downed hive. She laid Robert on his bed and covered him with a fleece throw.

"What kind of cookies did you buy?"

"I bought lemon bars and brownies." Karen kissed his cheek.

Shelley held up her hands. "None for me. I've gained five pounds since the beginning of summer."

Karen nodded, but didn't pursue the subject. She, too, had gained weight. Everything she owned with a fixed waistband was tight. But the more she thought about dieting, the more she ate. Bob had said nothing until the other day when he suggested they go on a diet together. It was a gentle hint rather than a direct statement, but it hit the mark just the same. She knew he was right, but she had become mentally addicted to graham crackers in the afternoon and ice cream after dinner. She was around food all day now and ate out of boredom or as a reward instead of only when she was hungry. And she didn't get much exercise. Karen had never been heavy—even through her pregnancies the doctor complimented her on staying the course. But since then, she paid less attention to her figure, opting for comfort over style. She wore sweatpants and large cotton turtlenecks in the winter and shapeless shorts and oversized tops in the summer. She had a closet full of beautiful things she didn't wear, except when Bob took her out. Over the last several months, she had moved away from the tailored pieces in favor of Empire-style dresses. Bob told her he would gladly eat whatever low-fat, low-calorie dinners she prepared, and Karen knew he was trying to be helpful. But it made her angry rather than grateful. He didn't need to lose weight, because he was busy and engaged and out in the world doing relevant things. Hard-working, important people never got fat.

"Nice to see you, honey," called Shelley to Robert over her shoulder.

Karen followed her mother into the hallway, where she turned and said, "Sleep tight, big boy," before closing the door behind her. They descended the carpeted stairs quickly and quietly before stopping in the living room, where Rebecca was sitting in a circle of Barbies. "Are you still hungry?" asked Karen.

"Starving. Can my friends come to lunch?"

"You can set them up on the counter. Only breathing people get to sit at the table."

Rebecca nodded and picked up the six dolls in her group. They all walked into the kitchen, where Rebecca reassembled the circle on the counter and Shelley sat at the table. "Can I do anything?"

Karen reached into the fridge for the tuna and iced tea. "No, Mom. I'll have lunch ready in a minute."

"Remember, no bread for me."

"No bread? I thought you just didn't want dessert."

"Carbs, honey. I'm trying to cut down on carbs."

"What do you want me to do with your tuna?"

"Just put it on a plate. And if you have a hunk of cheese, I'd like that on the side."

"Iced tea?" asked Karen, turning around with the pitcher in her hand and facing her mother.

"Water," said Shelley, "with ice please."

Rebecca sat next to her grandmother as soon as the Barbies were situated. Shelley asked what she thought about going to kindergarten soon, and Rebecca grinned. Karen had told her mother to ask about school; it was what Rebecca talked about most. Sarah's daughter, Britney, had already completed her kinder-garten year; Rebecca couldn't wait to catch up. Karen made the lunch plates while Shelley and Rebecca talked. The children had an easy relationship with Karen's parents, seeing them frequently enough that all of them were comfortable. They were not comfortable with Bob's parents, who had moved to Florida just after Rebecca was born and had become the kind of grandparents that long distance and absence created. Tucker and Janet sent gifts and called Rebecca and Robert on their birthdays and on major holidays. And they welcomed them, along with Karen and Bob, into their beachside condominium for a week every winter. But they were so worried the kids would ding the walls or spill on their pristine floors that the visits were just barely worth the effort and the relief from February's snow and ice. They never offered to babysit—even though they talked incessantly about the fabulous restaurants in town—and they didn't spend more than five minutes at a time chatting with Rebecca or Robert. Tucker and Janet seemed happiest at the end of the day, when it was cocktail hour and the kids were in their glassed-in sitting room, in front of a movie that Janet had selected at Blockbuster.

Shelley and Phil did babysit. In fact, Shelley urged Karen to call her whenever she and Bob wanted to go out to dinner or the movies. But, it was such a production. Karen had to pack up everything and drive fifty minutes to their house. Shelley often offered to take the kids for the night, but she wanted them picked up by ten o'clock the next morning. It was much easier on everyone to get a sitter at home. Plus, it was usually easy for Karen to find a sitter in the evening. What Karen really wanted from her mother was a genuine offer to stay with the kids during the day. Teenagers didn't get home from school until three or so. And while that would have been a fine time for Karen to get a break, most of the girls in the neighborhood were involved in after-school activities or had homework. Their weekdays were often booked. Summer was different. Several of the thirteen- and fourteen-year-old girls were eager to work because they were too young to get jobs elsewhere. And sometimes Karen called them. But it was the thought of leaving her children with a thirteen-year-old kid that often made her stop. Karen knew the younger sitters were up to the task of watching television in her living room while Rebecca and Robert slept upstairs, but she wasn't sure they were responsible enough to watch two fully awake kids run around the backyard or inside the house. Robert was ripe for a trip to the emergency room, and how would

Karen feel if he hit a doorjamb and needed six stitches in his head when a seventh grader was in charge?

Unbeknownst to Karen, it was this very prospect that stopped Shelley from offering daytime sitting. It had been such a long time since Karen and her brothers were small and demanded that kind of vigil. Shelley had never been comfortable during the toddler years and was grateful when her kids were finally under the auspices of the local elementary school. The few times Karen had asked her to babysit during the day, Shelley had simply said she was busy. Eventually, Karen stopped asking, and the matter took care of itself. Evening babysitting was different, and Shelley was happy to have the kids. They were calmer in the evening, happy with sedentary activities like playing a card game or listening to a story. And, Phil was home. Shelley knew he would be able to adeptly handle any emergency thrown at him. His calm demeanor was a good balance for her excitability, just one set of opposites in what Shelley thought was a very strong marriage.

As soon as Rebecca was done with her lunch, she asked to leave the table. "Of course, you can," said Shelley. "Anyone with nice manners like you can come and go as she pleases."

"Where are you headed?" asked Karen.

"To the living room," said Rebecca, scooping up her dolls.

"Remember to be quiet," said Karen. "You know who is sleeping." Rebecca gave her mother the thumbs-up sign, something her father did all the time.

"She is adorable," said Shelley, as soon as her granddaughter left the room.

Karen smiled. "She can be."

"And your Robert is wonderful. He uses new words every time I see him."

"*Sesame Street,*" said Karen, getting up and clearing her mother's plate from the table. "Would you like some hot tea?"

"Love some," said Shelley, wiping her mouth with her napkin. "You're doing a wonderful job with these kids, Karen."

Karen filled the kettle with water and set it down on the heating burner. "It's hard sometimes, Mom." She cut the lemon bars and brownies in half and put them on a plate.

"Oh, don't I know that. I almost lost my mind raising you and your brothers, mostly them."

Karen set the plate down on the table then walked back to the counter. She reached into the cupboard for her teapot and mugs. Still facing the cupboard, she said, "You did have a little help though. Your mother certainly came to the rescue."

"She did," said Shelley, "when she was available."

Karen remembered spending most Tuesday and Thursday afternoons at her grandmother's house. Mama, as she and her brothers called her, made them ginger spice cookies and played Parcheesi with them in the winter and, in the summer, took them to the park and treated them to a frozen treat from the Good Humor truck while Shelley ran errands. Mama died suddenly of a stroke when Karen was in high school, her surprise death saddening Karen for weeks. Kevin and Kyle also mourned for Mama. Prompted by their mother, the twins celebrated Mama's July birthday every year with a trip to the local ice-cream parlor. Grampy, Mama's spouse of fifty years, had died a year later. Karen, whose childhood bedroom was across the hall from her parents' room, had heard her mother crying during the night, as well as her father softly speaking what must have been encouraging words. Shelley didn't know what she'd do without the support of her parents, she told her husband in the living room one evening when Karen, at the kitchen table doing homework, overheard. "I don't know if I can do this on my own." Karen wished her mother would support her daughter, much as Shelley's mother had supported her. Karen told her mother that she sometimes felt overwhelmed.

"I know what you mean, honey. Raising young children is exhausting."

"It's hard to do it alone. Bob is so involved in his work."

"As was your father," said Shelley, taking a sip of tea.

"I sometimes think about getting some help, just a couple of afternoons a week."

"Then do that," said Shelley, breaking the lemon bar Karen had cut in half in half again and then taking a nibble.

"I just don't know who to ask."

"Someone in the neighborhood, I would think. That way, you don't have to drive all over creation to get her."

"I guess."

"But don't underestimate your own ability. You do an amazing job with these kids; you keep your house spotless, and you're an excellent cook. I really am proud of the way you've embraced motherhood, Karen. You've done it in the way you do everything else, with complete competence."

They were words she was longing to hear from her husband, but her mother was an adequate substitute for the moment. "Thank you."

"And thank you for lunch. We ought to do this more often."

CHAPTER 7

Karen was physically prepared for her daughter's first day of school. They had shopped for a lunch box, backpack, school supplies, a pair of sneakers, and clothes. They had attended the bus safety seminar together the week before school started. They had even practiced getting Rebecca up and out the door by eight fifteen to catch the bus that would pick her up at the corner four minutes later.

The day started out smoothly enough. Rebecca woke before her alarm, dressed, and ate her breakfast. Karen made waffles as a special weekday treat, and everyone chatted about Rebecca's first day with enthusiasm. Bob told her she would have a new friend by the end of the day. Robert announced that he'd like to go, too. And Karen said she would make Rebecca chocolate cake, her favorite, for dessert that night. At quarter past eight, Rebecca slipped her shiny Barbie backpack, holding the multicolored signed and clipped together forms that gave Rebecca permission to start her new life, onto her shoulders. They all marched out the door and were on the designated curb two minutes later. When the bus rounded the corner, Bob kissed his daughter and then his wife and son good-bye, and jogged across the front lawn to his car in the driveway. Rebecca boarded the bus and then waved to Karen and Robert before facing forward in her seat, as she had been instructed in the safety seminar. Robert waved to his sister's turned head as the bus rolled out of sight. When Karen and Robert were back inside the house, Karen set him down on the couch, turned on the TV, and then walked into the kitchen to call Sarah. She started to cry as soon as she heard her friend's voice. "What's wrong with me?" She wept openly into the phone. "I've been dreaming about this day for years."

Sarah laughed. "So, you *are* a normal mother after all."

"What do you mean?"

"I mean that even though our children drive us crazy, we love them like crazy," said Sarah. "You remember my telling you that I went through the same thing last year with Britney. I couldn't wait until she started at the elementary school, and then I missed her desperately when she did."

Karen grabbed a tissue from the family-size box on the counter. "It's only an hour longer than preschool."

"It's a poignant time, Karen. We want our children to grow up and become independent, but when they do, we realize we have to let go. Time is passing, and they will never be the helpless infants we once held in our arms. They will grow and continue to do so, until they leave us."

"That's not helping," said Karen, using the tissue she had just dried her eyes with to blow her nose.

"I'm not trying to be morbid. This is a big step, for you as well as Rebecca, and it will take some getting used to."

"You've told me this."

"And now you believe me."

"I didn't before." Karen filled a glass of water at the sink and then sat at the kitchen table. "I thought I would be different, that I would be grinning instead of crying when Rebecca got on the bus. This is the first step to my freedom. I have no idea why I'm resisting it."

"It's the first day, Karen. You won't feel this way forever."

"Are you sure?"

"Positive. Now, are you still coming for lunch?"

"Yes, as soon as she gets off the bus, we'll get in the car."

"I'll have the crib set up so Robert can nap here if he wants."

"Either that or we can just put them in front of the TV like last time," said Karen. "Robert slept for a good hour on the floor. And I got him into bed early that night."

"That's always a plus."

Karen, who was looking out the window as she chatted, started when she felt Robert's hand on her knee. "Where's Becca?"

"I've got to go, Sarah. We'll see you by twelve thirty." Karen scooped Robert up off the floor and hung up the phone. "Your sister's at school, honey. She'll be home at lunchtime."

Karen walked into the living room with her son and again set him down on the couch. She walked back into the kitchen and started doing the breakfast dishes. She had just finished putting the juice glasses into the dishwasher when Robert touched the back of her leg. Karen picked him up again and walked him back to the living room. "Mommy has some things to do," she said. "You stay here for a while, and then we'll do something together." Karen hadn't quite finished the waffle iron when Robert showed up again. Karen looked at her watch. "Okay. I'll watch one show with you, just one. But tomorrow you can do it all by yourself, just like when Rebecca went to her other school."

They walked back into the living room and sat on the couch together, side by side. *Barney* was on, one of Robert's favorite shows. Without taking his eyes off the TV, Robert slowly crawled onto Karen's lap. She wrapped her arms around him. Robert responded by leaning back against her chest. In January, Robert would be going to preschool three mornings a week. Karen's kissed the back of his head, breathing in the smell of the baby shampoo she had washed his hair with the night before.

Rebecca was full of news when she got off the bus. Her first day had been, using one of her new favorite words, spectacular. She met two new friends, Martha and Grace, and got to wear a gold star because she knew all her letters and every word on the blue list. Mrs. Taft told her she seemed like a very bright star indeed. "That means I'm smart."

"And that you are." Karen smiled at her daughter, enjoying her enthusiasm, her response to a challenge. "Very smart."

The stories continued on the drive to Sarah's house. They went on a nature walk around the playground, and Rebecca was able to identify two trees, a maple and an oak. They had chocolate graham crackers and apple juice for a snack, which is just what Rebecca wanted to bring when it was her turn. And they did math problems with plastic bears. Three bears plus five bears equals eight bears. As soon as Karen pulled into Sarah's driveway and put the car in park, Rebecca unbuckled herself, opened the car door, and ran up the front walk to find her friend. Britney, who as a first grader didn't start until the following day, greeted Rebecca on the front steps with their usual hug.

"I love school!" Rebecca threw her arms around her friend. "It was just like you told me."

"I go tomorrow," said Britney, taking Rebecca's hand and leading her into the house.

"I'll bet you can't wait."

"My mom says I have to."

Holding Robert's hand, Karen followed the girls into the house. She walked into the kitchen, where she found Sarah putting butterfly-shaped peanut butter and jelly sandwiches onto plastic plates. "How am I going to serve my kids regular-shaped sandwiches ever again?" Karen said, kidding her friend.

"Wait until you see dessert," Sarah said, reaching into the fridge and pulling out a chocolate pudding, brownie, and whipped cream trifle.

"You definitely win the Best Mom prize for today."

"Only because this is a huge day that calls for a serious celebration."

Jeremy walked into the kitchen. He grabbed Robert's free hand, and the boys ran onto the porch together. They sat down next to each other and picked cars out of the red plastic bucket Sarah always had handy. "What can I do?" asked Karen.

"Nothing," said Sarah, taking the plates out to the porch. "I'm going to call the kids to eat, and then you and I can eat our lunch in the kitchen."

As soon as all the children were settled, Sarah pulled two china plates out of the fridge and removed the plastic wrap covering them. Each held a mound of chicken salad, a hard-boiled egg cut in half, two slices of tomato, and six green olives. Sarah then poured two glasses of sparkling water, something Karen consistently forgot to add to her grocery list, and told Karen to sit down. "How do you do all this?" Karen sat as instructed and put the cloth napkin in her lap. Sarah never used the cheap paper alternative, even with her children.

"You forget I'm a morning person."

"I'm a morning person, too, but I'm not making chicken salad."

Sarah shrugged. "You know I like to cook."

"Yes, but do you really? I used to like to cook, before the children were born. But now it seems like such an effort on top of everything else."

"I like it because it gives me control over something," said Sarah, cutting her egg half in half. "I look at a recipe, I combine all the ingredients, I heat it or chill it, and it usually tastes pretty good. Housekeeping is what drives me nuts. I pick up the house, and by the time I get out of the shower, it's trashed again."

"And then your husband comes home and wonders what you've been doing all day."

"He doesn't say it very often, but I know it's on his mind."

"Bob's too," said Karen, chewing a forkful of chicken salad.

Vincent and Bob both worked long hours and were motivated by company competition and the lure of the next step—more territory and a bigger sales team in Bob's case, and clinical trials for Vincent, a PhD in a hepatitis lab. Money, too, was a motivator, but Bob, working for Forester, had the potential to make much more, unless Vincent actually developed a hepatitis C vaccine. Self-confidence was not an issue for either man; smart and dedicated, they had both tasted early success and looked forward to fully satisfying work lives. In annual reviews, their bosses had called them "perceptive," a source of pride for both of them. Yet, their "keen insight" seemed to dissipate on the car ride home. Both Vincent and Bob could be and often were guilty of assuming everything was fine in their family lives because, number one, their wives were competent, and, number two, they looked no deeper than the surface. This refusal to examine their home lives on a level that equaled their investigations at work resulted in a kind of honest deception about the requirements of child rearing and household management.

"They have no idea," said Sarah, spearing an olive, "what it's like to run a household. When I tell Vincent it's not unlike running a laboratory, he can't make the connection."

"I should try that with Bob. Running the house and raising children is a lot like running a company, with a million things going on at once one minute and complete quiet the next. Maybe it's that constant and yet patternless fluctuation that is so hard for me. If it were quiet all the time, I would figure out what to do with the quiet. And if I were flat out all the time, I'd adjust to that, too."

"They must have randomness in their work, too—days that get chewed up by unanticipated events or bad ideas," said Sarah. "But it's still called work. And they are paid, and they are appreciated. When I talk to Vincent about appreciation, he scoffs at what he calls my neediness. But you know what? I *am* needy right now. I give everything I have to my family, and there is not a lot left over for me. Vincent doesn't have to understand that, like I don't understand a lot about what he does in the lab every day, but he can sure enough acknowledge it exists and tell me once in a while—not just on Mother's Day—that I'm doing a good job."

"I need a tape recorder," said Karen, wiping her mouth. "If Bob could hear the same complaints coming out of someone else's mouth, he might begin to wonder if any of it could be true."

Both of their husbands, Karen and Sarah agreed, thought their wives' satisfaction should come from the job. What could be more rewarding than raising children into productive, contributing, successful adults? And both Karen and Sarah agreed that motherhood was, as touted in the women's magazines targeting stay-at-home mothers, a worthwhile and even admirable profession, at least for those mothers who did it well. But the constant lifting, loading, cleaning, picking up, packing up, listening, explaining, admonishing, penalizing, praising, and hurrying were physically and mentally exhausting. "It's like treading water," said Karen. "On some days, I just want to get to the end of the pool." The mental challenge was often even more difficult than the physical. Certainly a college-educated woman could think faster and better than her small children, but could she do it on too little sleep? Could she do it after her two-year-old's third temper tantrum of the morning? Could she do it when her five-year-old announced how bored she was at fifteen-minute intervals? Bored? Karen wanted to tell Rebecca she didn't know the first thing about being bored. "I feel like I use about an eighth of my brain," said Sarah. "The rest of it is dormant, waiting for some kind of stimulation, but receiving none. Vincent tells me this is ridiculous. I can read a good biography. I can learn a foreign language. I can do whatever I want."

"But that's the last thing you want to do after being with the children all day, right? Little motivation sappers are what they are," said Karen. "If I'm going to read a book, it had better be a page-turner and not a literary masterpiece that sends me to the dictionary every three pages."

"I barely make time to read the paper."

"I'll bet you're keeping up on Bill Clinton and Monica Lewinsky," said Karen, smiling.

"I feel sorry for her. I think she had no idea what she was getting into."

"Or who she was confiding in," said Karen. "Who needs a friend like Linda Tripp?"

"Vincent says he'll be impeached."

"For fooling around with a twenty-one-year-old intern?"

"For lying."

Karen scooped more chicken salad into her mouth, chewed, and swallowed. "He's not the first politician guilty of that."

The girls ran into the kitchen and announced they had finished their lunches and were ready for dessert. Britney had told Rebecca about the trifle, and Rebecca, only half believing there could be something that good in an ordinary household refrigerator, wanted to see it. Sarah solemnly rose from the table, reached into the fridge, and pulled out the chocolate creation. Rebecca gasped. "Is that for us?"

"Oh yes," said Sarah, breaking into a smile. "Bring me your lunch dishes and tell the boys to sit down. I'll bring your bowls out as soon as you're ready."

"Britney is such a good helper," said Karen after the girls left.

"Sometimes," said Sarah, scooping the trifle into small plastic bowls. "It helps when she's got some incentive."

"Incentive is the key to everything."

On the way home from Sarah's, Karen thought of an incentive plan for herself. When Bob traveled, which was at least twice a month, Karen could reward herself for making it through the week without losing her temper with Rebecca and Robert. The rules were simple: She could use a stern tone, but she couldn't raise her voice more than she would in everyday conversation. She had to keep the house relatively tidy and get the children to help her. She had to have Friday night's dinner at least underway by the time Bob got home. If he was due home later than six, the children would be fed and ready for bed so Karen and Bob could eat together at eight. If she could do all this, she would do something nice for herself. It could be anything from a night out with Bob to a sweater or new pair of pants. Clothing, she decided as she turned the car into the driveway, was an excellent idea. Buying new clothes would help Karen lose weight. She could only buy things in her old size, a six; nothing in an eight and absolutely nothing in a ten.

Bob thought it was a great idea. He told Karen incentives were an important part of his life, and there was no reason they shouldn't be a part of hers. He was making more money now and would be happy to finance her progress. It was about time she bought some clothes. What a person wore made a statement about who that person was. Clothing had always been important to Bob, but was much more so now than in college or in the early years of their marriage. Until recently, he hadn't spent more than two minutes each morning, most of it devoted to knotting his necktie, in front of the full-length mirror. When they were first married, he had four suits, two for the summer and two for the winter. He had a week's supply of shirts, which he bumped up to a two-week supply when he started traveling, and a dozen or so silk ties, mostly presents from his or Karen's parents. In the last few years, however, Bob had accumulated enough clothing to encroach on Karen's side of the closet. Because she spent most of her time in shapeless garments that could sit in a bureau drawer, Karen had moved most of her work dresses to the attic to make room. He had gone from owning four suits to twenty, two dozen shirts to four dozen, and from twelve ties to more than Karen wanted to count. And his morning routine in the bathroom took twenty minutes instead of ten.

Karen didn't care how long he took in the bathroom, as she had nowhere to go, but she had questioned him a couple of times in the last year or so about his abundance of clothing, which Bob ardently defended. A sharp-looking salesman always has the edge over his frumpy counterpart, he said. Nice suits, crisp shirts, bright but conservative ties, and well-shined shoes made as good a first impression as any opening line or topical joke. They had the money for it; plus, Bob had been able to write a portion of his wardrobe off on their taxes, as a work expense. It was part of being a successful businessman, he told Karen, which was exactly who he had become. And if Karen wanted to be a successful housewife, who took pride in her job and her appearance, she definitely needed a new, updated wardrobe.

As they talked that night, Karen grew more and more excited about the prospect of getting some new things. She hadn't thought much about clothing in years, except in terms of what the children needed and what she could wear that wouldn't require special treatment. Everything got thrown into the washing machine together. Bob had taken a liking to the dry cleaning and laundry services of Image Cleaners downtown, so Karen didn't have to worry about ruining his shirts or separating his black socks from his white T-shirts. She told Bob she would buy just a few things and then use her incentive plan to get more. And he told her he was pleased and looking forward to seeing his wife looking and feeling like a new woman.

Their agreeable dispositions put them in the mood for sex, or rather, put Karen in the mood. Bob was always ready, and if he believed half of what he heard from other salesmen on the road, he was not alone in that category. Getting a piece was all they talked about, chatter that Bob found stimulating at first, until he realized there was no end to pussy and tit talk. Every woman passed in every hallway was a potential conquest to these guys. Bob continued to smile at their lewd suggestions like a good, chameleonic salesman, even though he was soon bored by their sexual banter. He was certainly interested in the real thing though, and wanted to have sex when he got home from a business trip or on a Saturday morning or whenever Karen consented. And her consent came more and more hesitantly and infrequently over the years.

Karen blamed her lack of response on the children. And in truth, they did wear her out. There was always something to be done. There was always something to be cleaned up. There was always something; children were needy from the moment they opened their eyes in the morning until just before and often after they closed them at night. At five, Rebecca could dress, make her bed, and eat without getting food all over herself and the kitchen. But Robert, almost three, was in many ways still a baby who needed constant care and supervision. Karen could leave him in front of the television and get a few things done a room or two away. But she could never be absolutely sure he wouldn't get into something or fall from the couch and open his head on the coffee table. Worrying, while fruitless, took up a lot of Karen's head space. And it was hard for Karen to turn it off and jump into bed with Bob, who had been gone all day or all week, and pretend she wanted nothing more than someone else who needed something from her. And while Bob was a good lover in that he wanted to please her, too, Karen sought a kind of pleasure not found in a seven-second orgasm. She wanted to have what Bob had, freedom. Sex became one more plus in his column and another mess to clean up in hers.

Plus, it wasn't the same as it used to be. When Bob kissed Karen in college, it was just the two of them that mattered. The kisses were sweet, warm, and exhilarating, and the sex was secret and stolen. It didn't happen every day; it didn't happen every weekend. When all of the circumstances were right, when Allison was gone on a weekend that Karen didn't have her period, or when Bob's housemates were elsewhere so the two of them could have some privacy, it did happen, and it was satisfying for both of them. Bob had been romantic back then, often presenting Karen with flowers for the occasion or taking her out for a meal afterward, where they would extend the afterglow by lazily eating and talking about their life together after Karen's graduation. Now, his kisses were sweaty instead of sweet; they were urgent, as if his own mouth was insufficient to sustain his life, as if he needed Karen's mouth to breathe. Karen didn't feel that urgency. Because they had sex at least once a week, she no longer felt the anticipation, the longing she felt in college when three weeks could easily pass before Karen and Bob could count on being alone. Their libido timetable was out of sync.

Nonetheless, Karen usually acquiesced to Bob's desire, more to appease than to please him. If Bob didn't have some kind of sexual release every three to four days, he got grumpy. He was short with the children, if he paid any attention to them at all, and he was extra useless around the house, punishing her with a turned back, with one-word answers. After sex, however, Bob was a new man, a crowned monarch. He would play cars with Robert. He would read a book to Rebecca. He would even do the pots and pans after dinner. It was more agreeable for everyone and worth twenty minutes of Karen's time.

But that night was different. Karen felt a sexual stirring that had been absent for months. Maybe it was because she had a new resolve to lose weight and look better. Maybe it was because Bob was supportive of her new plan. Maybe it was because they were talking pleasantly instead of bickering. Whatever it was, it was working; Karen wanted to take off her clothes as much as Bob did. And sex with him felt almost as good to her as it had in college.

CHAPTER 8

By the end of November, Karen had lost twelve pounds and gained three ribbed turtleneck sweaters, two pairs of wool pants, three pairs of jeans, and brown suede loafers. She had given up wearing sweatpants, replacing them with jeans or corduroys, anything with a fitted waist. She looked as good as she had in college, better even because she had tone and definition from lifting plastic-coated free weights and doing VHS-tape aerobics in the basement three times a week. Bob was newly enamored. When he walked through the back door on a Friday night after a week on the road, he was welcomed by his fit wife, with her shirt tucked in and a belt around her slim waist. And Karen, feeling good about her accomplishments, was happy to see him, too.

Her incentive plan was working better than she expected. Not only did she buy new clothing when she was a patient and kind mother, she bought herself time. She hired their babysitter, Jamie, who had recently announced to Karen that she was more interested in earning money to buy her own car than she was in after-school activities, to come three afternoons a week for two hours each day. So, on Mondays, Wednesdays, and Thursdays, Jamie arrived at four and stayed through what Karen called Whine Time until six.

Sometimes Karen went shopping. Sometimes she went for a long walk or a bike ride. Sometimes she met Sarah (whose new next-door-neighbor was a babysitting ninth grader) at a coffee shop. "I feel like a new person," she said, sitting down at a table with a hot chocolate in her hand.

"You look like a new person."

"It's on the inside more than the outside," said Karen. "I really feel like I've gone through a transformation."

"Me too. It's amazing what a babysitter can do."

"I'm so glad Jamie talked to me."

"And I'm so glad Robin moved in next door." Sarah sipped her tea. "We've become absolute renegades, you and I. We're going to get kicked out of the stay-at-home-mothers club!"

"Not you," said Karen. "Robin comes just one day a week."

"That's all I was able to talk Vincent into. And I was lucky to get that. You know how Vincent thinks. Mothers are supposed to love being mothers. We're supposed to love our children completely and not want to ever leave them."

"Even though sometimes leaving them makes us better mothers."

"Exactly." Sarah rubbed lotion into her hands. "I take it Jamie is working out well."

"She's grown up a lot since she first started watching the kids," said Karen. "She now knows how to say no and sound like she means it. She really knows the kids now, and she seems to legitimately like them. Plus, the house is picked up when I get home."

"Not bad for a fifteen-year-old kid."

"The only thing I worry about is an emergency."

"Me too."

"Wouldn't it would be nice to have someone who drives?"

"Like your mother."

Karen smiled. "I guess I haven't let that go, have I?"

"Hey, I understand. If my mother were still living, I'd expect her to babysit, too."

"I still don't see why she doesn't offer. I still don't get it."

"She's forgotten, Karen. That's all, she's just forgotten."

Karen shifted in her seat, leaning in closer to Sarah. "Even if she's forgotten, even if she has no recollection of how hard it is to raise children, why wouldn't she just offer? She sees how full my hands are."

"Not from what you tell me. You run around like a maniac getting ready for her. She probably thinks you need no help at all."

"Meaning I bring it on myself."

"Well, if she arrived one day without notice and saw the house trashed and the kids crying, she might think differently."

"She wouldn't do that." Karen moved her head from side to side. "The woman lives four towns away and rarely visits. She's way too busy for that."

"Shall I say it again? If you want help from your mother, you're going to have to ask for it."

"I've hinted."

"No hinting. You need to ask for her help."

"And admit I'm a failure."

"That's your trade-off," said Sarah, leaning back in her chair. "Even though you're not a failure." Karen finished her drink. "Try it. Ask her."

"Maybe I will," said Karen, knowing as well as Sarah that she wouldn't.

Sarah looked at her watch and then stood and looped the strap of her purse over her shoulder. "I'll call you."

When Karen got home, Jamie and the kids were doing a puzzle on the kitchen table. As a rule, Jamie was not to turn on the TV when she babysat in the afternoons. Rebecca and Robert didn't seem to mind. At first they missed the shows they had watched regularly before Karen hired Jamie, but they were happy to have Jamie as their new friend. Robert didn't cry anymore when Karen left. He was very happy, though, to see her upon her return and would stop whatever he was doing and scream "Mommy's home!" Then he'd run to her and wrap his arms around her legs. It was one of several endearing things he did, like insisting she kiss him on both cheeks at bedtime and putting his hand on her leg when she read him a book. Rebecca remained seated at the table with Jamie, working another piece into the puzzle border. Now that she was in kindergarten, she liked to do more things for herself. Karen was proud of her daughter's independence, feeling like she had helped foster it. But, she loved the way Robert still needed her, even when she had been away for just two hours.

Karen paid Jamie, sent the children to the living room to watch TV, and started making dinner. When Bob was in town and didn't have a late meeting, he arrived home at six forty-five and liked dinner on the table. Karen made mini meatballs and put them in the oven to bake. She poured a jar of tomato sauce into a pot on the stove and added several spices and a can of tomato paste. She filled a large pot with water and set it on the stove to boil. She cut a loaf of Italian bread in half lengthwise, put butter and a little bit of crushed garlic in the middle, and wrapped it in foil. She set that on the counter next to the oven so she wouldn't forget to put it in. When she bent over to check the meatballs, she noticed her headache. What had been a sensitivity to light for most of the afternoon had turned into something less tolerable. She was tired; the hot chocolate hadn't perked her up at all. She put the back of her hand to her warm forehead. She would get in bed as soon as she got the kids in bed. What she needed was a good night's sleep.

Thirty minutes later, Bob walked into the kitchen. "Something smells good."

"Spaghetti," said Karen, accepting a kiss on the cheek, "and meatballs."

"Great." Bob removed his suit coat and hung it on the back of his chair. "How was your day?"

"Pretty good. Although I don't feel that well now."

"That's too bad."

"I just need some sleep."

"You and me both." Bob walked to the fridge and grabbed a Stella. "Anything for you?"

Karen took the bread out of the oven. "Not tonight."

Bob walked into the living room to see Rebecca and Robert. Karen could hear them talking as she finished making the salad. When Bob returned to the kitchen five minutes later with the children in tow, dinner was ready. Twelve minutes later, dinner was over. Karen, who felt worse than when she sat down, had eaten only three bites. All she could think about was getting to bed. Even Bob noticed. "You don't look very good."

"I don't feel very good."

"We can do the dishes, Mommy," said Rebecca. "Daddy and I can do them."

Karen looked at Bob, who shrugged. "Why not?" he said, smiling at Rebecca.

"Me too!" said Robert.

"You're too little," said Rebecca.

Robert's eyes welled with tears. "We'll find something for you to do," said Bob, patting his son on the head. "You get into bed, Karen. We'll be fine."

"Thank you," said Karen, getting up from the table. "Have the kids come see me before bed."

"Okay." Bob rolled up the sleeves of his custom-made Egyptian cotton button-down.

"Mommy?"

Karen heard the voice, but she couldn't respond. She was in the middle of an art history exam, and if the proctor saw her talking, she would be reported. The university had strict rules about verbal communication during exams—with, as far as Karen had heard, no exceptions. She would just keep her head down and pretend she didn't hear anything. That was the best way to handle it. She needed to focus on the essay question before her, "Why did the Impressionistic painters often skip breakfast?" She had absolutely no idea! There had been nothing in her notes about skipping meals; in fact, there had been nothing about meals at all, unless she counted wine. Maybe it was something about the wine. Maybe, Karen thought, they were too hungover to eat.

"Mommy?"

Don't turn around, Karen told herself. That was the first step to a failing grade. The voice calling her was familiar, however. And it had a tinge of urgency about it that was hard to ignore. Maybe the person had dropped a pen that rolled underneath Karen's chair. Maybe it was just a matter of bending down, picking it up, and handing it back. Surely no one would blame her for that. It was the decent thing to do.

"She's hot, Daddy."

Karen turned around and faced the voice. "Did you drop your pen?" she asked quietly.

"I don't have a pen, Mommy."

Karen felt a hand on her head and knew she was in trouble. That was what the proctors did to excuse students. No words were exchanged, just gestures. The proctor had tapped her on the head; she was excused from the exam. Karen's eyes welled with tears as she handed in her test booklets. It was unfair. She had done nothing wrong. Her sadness quickly turned to resolve. She would go directly to the dean's office and file a complaint. It might take a few days to process, but she would be allowed to retake the exam. And, Karen thought, she would be able to find the answer to the breakfast question. "Karen? Open your eyes, honey."

"I have to see the dean."

"Rebecca, go brush your teeth. Help Robert do the same. I'll be there in a minute."

Karen thought she was going to the dean's office, but she was suddenly in a grocery store. Boxes of macaroni and cheese filled her cart. She needed some fruits and vegetables, but she had no idea where to look for them. There were no staff members in sight. There were no other shoppers. She was alone. She had no idea, then, who or what was lifting her off her feet. "Put me down," she said. "I'm perfectly capable of walking on my own."

"Karen, open your eyes. It's me."

Karen did as the voice said and opened her eyes. She was in her own bed, and Bob was sitting on the edge with his hand on her forehead. "Bob?"

"I think you've got a fever."

"I was dreaming." Karen rubbed her eyes. "I was in a huge grocery store, and no one would help me."

"Have you taken any medicine?"

"No."

"I'm going to get you some Tylenol, and then I'm going to read the kids a story."

"I can do that," said Karen, starting to sit up.

"I'll do it," said Bob, putting his hands on her shoulders. "You're sick, and you need to rest. I need you better by morning."

Karen was not better in the morning. She had a fever of 102 degrees, a sore throat, a headache, and chills that three blankets couldn't ease. Bob was in a mild panic by seven o'clock. Robert needed a diaper change, and Rebecca wanted Bob to do spelling words with her before school. He had a sales meeting at nine.

"Call my mother," said Karen. "Maybe she can help."

Shelley was sorry to hear about Karen's sickness, but had several unbreakable commitments that morning. She would be happy to watch the kids, but she couldn't get there until after two. Bob wanted to ask what kind of commitment a fifty-eight-year-old woman who had never worked a day in her life would perceive as unbreakable, but instead thanked her and told her he would see her that afternoon. "Who else can I call?"

"I don't know," said Karen, her head a hot ball of wax.

"Well, think, Karen. I can't miss this meeting this morning."

"And for the first time in five years, I can't get out of bed, Bob. Your sympathy is overwhelming."

"Hey, I didn't deserve that."

"Oh yes, you did. If you felt lousy, I'd drop everything to take care of you."

"Look what I did last night. I did the dishes. I put the kids to bed."

"Yes, your certificate of heroic behavior should arrive by special messenger this afternoon."

Bob threw up his hands. "I don't have time for this." He walked out of their bedroom.

Several minutes later, Rebecca walked in and climbed onto the bed. "Hi, Mommy. Are you feeling better?"

Karen managed a smile. "Not really, honey."

"Who's going to take care of us?"

"We're working on that."

"Maybe Britney's mom could come over."

"You," said Karen, reaching out to touch her daughter's cheek, "are brilliant. Go tell your father."

"Robert's night diaper needs changing," said Rebecca, plugging her nose with her thumb and index finger. "He's stinky."

"Tell your father that, too," said Karen, closing her eyes.

Sarah took Britney to school and arrived at Karen's house a little before nine. Bob, who left the house at eight thirty, had put Rebecca on the bus and placed a freshly diapered Robert on the couch in front of the television with a bowl of dry cereal in his lap. When Sarah walked in the back door that Bob had kept unlocked for her, Robert was right where Bob said he would be. Jeremy scampered up on the couch with him. Sarah filled another plastic bowl and handed it to Jeremy, took off her coat, and then went upstairs to see her friend. "You look awful."

"Nice to see you, too."

"Where are we on the medications?"

Karen looked at her watch. "I took some Tylenol around seven."

Sarah felt her head. "You're still warm. Why don't you get yourself into a cool bath."

"You think so?"

"I do. Then you can sleep."

Sarah went back downstairs while Karen undressed and got into the tub. She shivered violently as the tepid water level rose. She washed herself and rinsed off, then wrapped herself in a towel. When she walked back into her bedroom, her pillows were fluffed, the blankets were neatly turned down, a clean nightgown lay folded on the coverlet, and a burning candle sat on her bedside table, as did two magazines and a mug of hot tea with lemon. Karen dried herself, slipped the nightgown over her head, and got back into bed. She took three sips of tea, pulled the covers up over her shoulders, and went to sleep. She woke when Sarah, standing over her with a tray, spoke her name. "What time is it?" asked Karen sleepily.

"Almost noon."

"I've been sleeping for three hours?"

"Yup."

"That's amazing." Karen slowly sat up.

"That's terrific." Sarah set the tray down on her lap.

"This looks good," said Karen, eyeing the bowl of chicken soup.

"I keep it in my freezer for times like this."

"I don't want to hear it, you perfect thing."

"Drink the water and take the Tylenol first."

"Yes, Mom."

Bob got home an hour later, telling Sarah how sorry he was for being late. She pooh-poohed his apologies, told him she and Robert had taken Jeremy to school, gave him an update on his wife, and then packed up her stuff and went home. When Bob asked his wife how everything had gone, Karen said she hardly knew Sarah was there. Bob took off his suit coat and hung it in the closet. "I had a great meeting this morning. I'm pretty sure we're going to get this account."

"That's nice." Karen closed her eyes to the stinging light, the boring business talk.

"I'm going to give them the afternoon and the evening to think over our proposal, and call them in the morning. With any luck, I'll have a fat commission check in my pocket at the end of the week."

"Congratulations."

"You don't sound very excited."

"The deal isn't done. Plus, I've got a fever and feel lousy."

Bob kissed Karen's forehead. "You're right, honey. I'm sorry. Did you have a good morning?"

"I slept, which is just what I needed to do."

"Great. Get some more rest. I'm going to go downstairs and check on our little man. Where's Rebecca?"

"Aftercare at school. Sarah will pick her up later."

Bob was back upstairs five minutes later. "Has he eaten?"

"I would guess Sarah gave him some lunch. Ask him."

Five minutes after that Bob was back. "Can he watch television for a while longer?"

"Why not? Unless you want to play with him."

"I've got my work clothes on." He was back in the bedroom ten minutes later. "He's pooped his pants. I don't know if I'm up for dealing with that again."

"Do I look like I'm up for dealing with it?" Karen kept her eyes closed.

In the ninety minutes Bob was home, Karen was able to sleep for thirty minutes. Finally giving up on trying, she sat up in the bed and flipped through *Good Housekeeping,* which is how her mother found her at two thirty.

"Well," said Shelley, walking into her bedroom, "someone's feeling better."

"Not really, Mom. I just can't sleep right now."

"That's the best thing for you, honey. As far as I know, reading magazines has never been a cure for the flu."

Bob poked his head around their doorjamb. "I'm off. I'll be home around nine. I've got a dinner meeting."

Karen looked at her mother. "Can you stay that long?"

"Bob already asked me, and I said fine. Your father's got a card game tonight."

"Dad plays poker?"

"Bridge, dear."

Bob whistled as he walked down the stairs and out to the car. By the time he got home that night, the kids would be in bed, and Karen would be asleep. He could catch the end of the hockey game.

Shelley told her daughter to get some rest before walking back down the stairs to see what Robert was up to. He was still in front of the television. She kissed his cheek and told him they could play a game as soon as she tidied up a bit. In the kitchen, the countertops were covered with open bags of sandwich meats, chips, pretzels, and cookies, and dribbles of mustard, mayonnaise, and butter. Economy-sized jars of peanut butter and grape jelly, with knives standing in their contents like miniature flagpoles, stood guard. A huge box of Cheerios lay on its side on the floor, empty. The table was covered with crumbs. Some very dirty plates, cups, and utensils sat in the sink, inches away from the empty dishwasher. Shelley had never seen her daughter's kitchen in such disarray.

After cleaning up the kitchen, Shelley walked back into the living room. Robert looked like he hadn't moved. She gave him another kiss, told him she was going upstairs to check on his mother. Upstairs, Karen was sleeping, so Shelley walked back down the hallway to Rebecca's and Robert's rooms. Rebecca's was tidy enough, except for several pieces of clothing on the floor. Shelley picked up the clean clothes, refolded them, and stacked them on the bed. Rebecca must have had trouble deciding what to wear to school that morning. Shelley walked across the hall to Robert's room and was immediately aware of the pungent odor of feces. "Good Lord," she said, spying Robert's soiled underwear on the floor.

She picked it up with two fingers and walked it down the hall to the washing machine. She walked back to his room and grabbed the can of deodorizer from the windowsill. Shelley made a face as she sprayed the room. She picked up the other dirty clothes off the floor, walked them down the hall, and started a heavy-duty load, using extra detergent. Robert's room still stank of masked poop when she walked back into it. She cracked a window, then stripped his bed. She had no idea whether his sheets were clean or dirty, but figured they would benefit from a washing either way. Shelley then picked up the toys on the floor and put them into the toy chest in the corner of the room. As she bent down to get the last truck, she noticed the Cheerios. They were all over. How she had not seen them before escaped her; the smell must have overcome all of her senses. She knelt down and began picking them up. There were hundreds of them, it seemed; no wonder the box in the kitchen was empty. Shelley sighed, then stood. She walked back to the laundry closet and grabbed the vacuum cleaner. She plugged it in and sucked up every last Cheerio, from under the bed to the windowsill on the other side of the room. Satisfied, she turned the vacuum off and wound the cord around the handle. As she lifted it, she saw Karen standing in the doorway. "Hello, dear," she said.

"What are you doing?"

"There were Cheerios everywhere," Shelley began. "Too many to pick up, so I grabbed the vacuum. Did I wake you?"

"What do you think?"

"I'm sorry, honey. I was just trying to help."

"If you want to help, Mom, go downstairs and be with Robert. The vacuuming can wait."

"But the dirty underwear couldn't wait, Karen." Shelley launched into the underwear story, which led to the story of the chaotic kitchen, which led into the story of Rebecca's clothing, which Shelley thought was kind of cute. Shivering, Karen folded her arms across her chest and tried to look interested, but all she could focus on was getting back under her warm covers. And as soon as Shelley finished showing Karen the neatly stacked pile of clothing on Rebecca's bed, Karen started back down the hallway toward her room. "I'm not feeling that well, Mom," said Karen by way of explanation.

"Of course you aren't, honey," said Shelley. "I've gone on too long. You get into bed, and I'll go see what Robert's up to downstairs."

Robert had been up to a number of things while Shelley tidied the upstairs. He had taken every toy out of the basket in the living room. He had colored three squares of the living room rug with Rebecca's new (washable, thank God) markers. And, when Shelley found him, he was sitting on the kitchen floor with half a bowl of chocolate pudding between his legs and the other half of the pudding either on or in him. He smiled at his grandmother. "Oh, Robert," Shelley said, wearily. "What are you into now?"

It was a rhetorical question, since anyone with eyes could see exactly what he was into. Shelley stood for a moment looking at him. It wasn't until he started to finger paint with the pudding on the floor that Shelley scooped him up, and, holding him at arm's length, walked him briskly up the stairs and into the bathroom. She set him down firmly in the tub and told him to stand perfectly still while she stripped off his clothes. She put the dirty long-sleeved sweatshirt and miniature jeans into the sink and ran the tub. She gave him a few bath toys from a plastic basket in the corner, then sat down on the toilet lid and watched the water rise. It was all she could do not to walk the pudding-caked clothes down the hall to the laundry. She had to put Robert's sheets in the dryer anyway. But it wasn't safe. And Shelley was proud of herself that she didn't leave her grandson, even for a moment. She washed him, dried him, dressed him, and kept him with her while she emptied the tub, rinsed his clothes, and transferred his sheets from the washer to the dryer. She put his clothes into the washer and started a small load. If she waited until later, the clothes would never come clean. Then, she and Robert went back to the living room to clean up the mess.

Sarah arrived just before six o'clock with Rebecca, who had been in aftercare until three thirty, when Britney's school day was over. They had gone to the bakery for cookies and hot chocolate and then played Barbies at Britney's house. Rebecca was happy to see her grandmother, but surprised her mother was still sick. "Is she going to die?" Rebecca asked, one eye half closed in concern.

"Heavens, no, dear. She's got a flu bug."

"When will she get better?"

"In a day or two. She needs to rest, honey."

"Can I see her?"

"Later, I think. Let's find something to do with Robert."

Rebecca made a face. "I want to watch TV."

"Fine."

Bob called to check in. Shelley was tempted to tell him all about her afternoon, but remembered that sometimes Phil wearied of her lengthy stories. So she spared Bob the details and nobly, she thought, told him everything was going well. She asked him about dinner, and he told her macaroni and cheese and applesauce was their favorite. "If they eat well, they can have the chocolate pudding Robert and I made at lunch."

"Yes," said Shelley.

Bob's meeting was dinner out with Billy. He felt a little guilty about not going home, but was completely unencumbered by the time he parked his car behind Rascals. Karen was in bed and didn't care what he was doing as long as the children were in good hands. Plus, Shelley owed them some babysitting. Inside, Bob found Billy standing at the bar talking with two women. He smiled broadly at Bob's approach and stuck out his hand for a handshake. "Hey,

Bob," he said enthusiastically. "I'd like you to meet two new friends, Donna and Kathy."

"Hi," said Bob, smiling. The women smiled at Bob. Donna studied him with the unchecked gaze of someone almost done with her second glass of Chardonnay.

"The girls don't have any dinner plans. I thought they could join us."

Bob clasped his hands together for a moment. "I tell you what. Let's have a drink with Donna and Kathy and then go our separate ways. I've got some business to talk about with you, which would bore the girls to death."

"Awww," said Donna in a baby-talk voice. She swirled the last swallow of wine around in her glass. "We don't mind your big-boy business talk." Bob looked askance at Billy.

"He's boring, but he's right, ladies," Billy said. "We do have a few things to discuss. But let's get another drink and chat for a while longer before dinner."

Billy signaled the bartender for another round and ordered a draft beer for Bob. They clinked their glasses in a toast to good friends, then listened to Billy's story about the customer who called him from a warehouse filled with sheets of shaved lumber instead of pallets of cardboard. Bob had heard this particular story several times, but had no problem hearing it again, because each time the story was different, continually improved based on its previous audience's reaction. Billy's ability to spin words into pictures, rather than his product knowledge or customer care, was how he earned a paycheck. He could walk into any bar anywhere and have a crowd around him in fifteen minutes.

As Kathy and Donna watched Billy, Bob studied them. Kathy seemed like the sensible one in the pair. She wore a gray wool business suit, albeit with a short skirt, low heels, and wire-frame glasses. She laughed in the appropriate places, and, if she was feeling her Merlot, hid it well. Sultry Donna was what men called an easy mark. She leaned into Billy, who had his arm around her, and looked up at him with large, hooded eyes. She wore a clingy top, accenting her breasts, and tight black pants that hugged her wide hips and soft thick thighs. Her wavy brown hair fell loosely to her shoulders, with bangs that stopped just above her amplified eyelashes. She wore raspberry-colored glossy lipstick on her full lips and had straight white teeth. Would Billy take her home?

Bob hadn't ever taken a woman home. His home had been his parents' home until he was engaged to Karen. He'd had several girlfriends before Karen, but all of them were much like Karen: responsible, intelligent, and attractive in a conservative way. Plus, most of them were high school girlfriends. And while Bob had thought a great deal about sex in high school, the possibility of actually having it with a girl was incredibly slim. First, most respectable girls in high school didn't do it. They did other things, but they didn't have intercourse. And second, the girls who were known to have intercourse were just that, the girls who had intercourse. Any guy who dated a girl like that was known as a guy who was dating a girl who would have intercourse. Those guys got a lot of high-fives in the boys' locker room, but no one took the relationship seriously. Instead, it was a very public joke.

At the community college he attended before transferring to State, he had dated a couple of women, one six years his senior. Page had what Bob called a robust sexual appetite. They had sex on the backseat of his car. They had sex at the beach. They had sex on a blanket in the woods. He did not take her out to dinner; he did not introduce her to his parents. Six weeks into the relationship, she drove him home to her place, where he met her two-year-old son, Donaldson, a product of her failed marriage and a subject never before raised. While Page showered, Bob entertained Donaldson with Lego blocks, all the while acting like a father and wondering what it would be like to be Donaldson's father, to do this all the time. Page emerged from the bathroom with a freshly washed body and an expectant look in her eyes. She put Donaldson in front of a Disney VHS movie and led Bob into her bedroom. But screwing Donaldson's mother in the next room didn't turn out to be all that appealing. Page cried out during sex, which didn't arouse anyone's attention in a parked car, but this time prompted Donaldson to call for her just as Bob was climaxing. Their relationship ended that evening, and put Bob off women for a while. He dated a couple of other fellow students, but felt no lasting attachment. And they, like Bob, lived with their parents, so having sex was a rarity.

Dating, sex in general, looked different now. At thirty, Bob could handle a sexual relationship. He lived in an adult world, in which everyone knew the rules. When a woman and a man who had been strangers until the night they met left a bar together, both of them knew what they were getting into. The plan was not to have coffee or get to know one another better. It was to have sex. If things went well and they were both single, they often spent the night together and shared breakfast in the morning. If things didn't go well or if other commitments got in the way, the encounter was over as soon as one of them got dressed again. People who had sex quickly were often interested in having sex quickly with other people, too.

Bob wondered if he hadn't married Karen and was standing in Rascals as a single man, what he would do. He looked at Donna's chest and decided he would take her home if Billy didn't. And being the kind of guy he was, Billy probably would have passed her off to Bob. And then Bob and Donna would give each other a long look before finishing their drinks and heading for the parking lot. Bob would take her back to his apartment, pour her another glass of wine, then sit next to her on the couch. Ever so slowly, he would lean in and kiss her. She would kiss him back, which would give him the green light to put his hands all over her flesh. She would moan and arch toward him, and the rest would be easy. They would have sex on the couch and, depending on how Bob was feeling afterward, share his bed for the night. "Bob?" Bob looked at Billy. "Where were you, friend?" Bob smiled as he reacclimated himself. Donna giggled. "You ready to eat?"

"Absolutely," said Bob.

"Ladies," Billy said, "thank you for your company. We've had a marvelous time chatting with you. Unfortunately, business calls, and we must leave you." Billy kissed both women on their cheeks. "Have a great evening." He put his arm around Bob and steered him through the bar crowd to the tables in the back. Sandi, the hostess, smiled when she saw Billy. "I've got a booth for you in five minutes, honey."

Billy handed her a twenty-dollar bill. "You are an angel."

As soon as they sat down in the booth, Billy announced that he felt like a burger and then leaned in to study Bob's face. "You look a little shell-shocked there partner. What's up?"

"Nothing, really," said Bob, picking up his menu.

"I think you like my friend Donna." Bob looked at Billy and smiled. "Am I right, or am I right?"

"She is attractive."

"Yes, she is. And I think she thinks the same about you."

Bob put the menu down. "Why do you say that?"

"Chemistry. I can always spot chemistry, and you two have it."

"You had your arm around her. What about that chemistry?"

"That was nothing," said Billy, flicking his hand. "I think she wants to be with you. And I further think I can make that happen for you."

"Billy, I'm married."

"So are most of the guys in here."

"What are you saying?"

"I'm saying being married and spending time with a willing woman are not necessarily mutually exclusive, my friend."

"They are if you want to stay married."

Billy shrugged. "Maybe, maybe not."

Bob studied the menu again and then put it back down. "So where do the married man and the single woman go to have this fun, back to the house with the wife and kids?"

Billy laughed. "To her apartment, Bob. Donna has a nice apartment on Elm Street."

"How would you know that?"

Billy sipped his beer. "I've been told."

Bob and Billy ordered cheeseburgers when their waiter arrived. Billy ordered two more beers. "She's looking at you, Bob. Shall I wave her over?"

"Enough of this," said Bob, shaking his head. "This kind of talk is unproductive."

"I'm not so sure."

"Look. I'm married to Karen. I have two kids. I have a good life, and I want it to stay that way."

"If your life is so good, what are you doing here?"

"Having dinner with a friend. And if you want to remain a friend, you'll support me."

"That's just what I'm trying to do."

Billy told Bob how much he liked and respected Karen, as a wife and as a mother. Billy then told Bob how having an affair can actually strengthen a marriage rather than destroy it. Since most husbands want sex more than their wives, he said, they needed to find another woman willing to have sex. Donna, for example, liked the attention men paid to her before and during sex. Bob wouldn't need to do anything more than tell her how beautiful she was and bring a bouquet of flowers or a nice bottle of wine to her apartment, and he would get what he needed. Donna would get the attention and affection she needed. Everyone would be happy.

"I don't buy it," said Bob, waving off Billy's analysis. "Women are emotional, and they want to be attached. You can't tell me Donna wouldn't put any pressures on me, and you can't tell me she wouldn't get ugly when I called it off."

"You're right. I'm not making any promises. But I sure know it would be fun along the way." The cheeseburgers and beers arrived. Hungry, Bob took a big bite and looked at his watch. It was almost eight. "Feeling a tug from the ball and chain?"

"Let's leave this alone. Tell me about the Greyson account."

They talked about business as they ate their dinners. Billy paid the bill and walked out the back door with Bob. They split in the middle of the parking lot. "Think about what I said," Billy called on the way to his car.

"See you tomorrow," Bob called back.

Bob got in his car and drove home. When he got there, Shelley, who was sweeping the kitchen floor for the second time, told him the kids were in bed, as was Karen. The evening had gone smoothly. Bob thanked her, got her coat out of the closet, and walked her to the front door. He then walked up the stairs to his and Karen's bedroom, where he found Karen asleep. He checked on Robert and Rebecca, also asleep. He walked back to his bedroom and undressed. He got into bed beside Karen and snuggled in next to her. He put his hand on her breast. She rolled over and turned her back on him.

CHAPTER 9

SEPTEMBER 2002

The morning of Robert's first day of first grade was hectic. Karen raced around the house multitasking, but finishing none of the jobs she started. The two vital jobs—loading backpacks with requested lunches and making pancakes with banana slice and chocolate chip faces—she accomplished by bus time. The three of them hustled out the door and stood at the corner; Bob, unfortunately, was out of town on business. Only as Karen looked down the street for the bus's arrival, mimicking Robert, did she think about her son in someone else's care until three thirty that afternoon. She bent down, put her hands on his cheeks and tilted his head. "Are you ready?"

Robert smiled up at her. "Of course, I'm ready, Mom." She wanted to ask him so many things, but knew she could not. Will you miss me? Will you think about me? Will you make new friends? Will you have enough to eat? Will the teacher like you? Instead, she kissed him on the cheek. "I'm not a baby," he said.

"Yes, you are," said Rebecca. "All first graders are babies."

Karen looked at her daughter. "Is that nice?"

Rebecca shrugged. "Sometimes, the truth hurts."

"Especially on the first day of school."

Rebecca put her hand on Robert's shoulder. "I'm sorry," she said. "It's the kindergarteners who are babies."

The bus came around the corner; Robert's eyes grew large as it approached, and Karen gave him one last kiss. Still watching the bus, Robert lifted his hand to his face. "Don't you dare wipe it off," said Karen, with a smile on her face. "That's got to last all day." She watched them get on the bus and sit. Rebecca sat with her good friend, Emily, and Robert sat with Gerald, a boy he knew from his kindergarten class. Karen waved, and Robert waved back. Rebecca was busy talking to Emily. When the bus rolled down the hill and out of sight, Karen jogged back to the house. Instead of grabbing her grocery list, she changed her clothes. She decided to take her bike ride first. Then she could shower for the day and not have to worry about fitting that in before lunch with Sarah.

Michigan's warm August weather had stretched into September, so Karen wore her biking shorts and a T-shirt. She rode her bike to the rail-trail by the river, and then rode west, passing the animal feed warehouse that had recently been converted to new condominiums, past Rascals, the Sleep Inn hotel, the new True Value, and a number of other downtown businesses before reaching the more secluded portion of the trail. In just three minutes, the commercial section of town yielded to the residential, and two minutes later, Karen was riding through marshy grasses and trees. She liked the rural section of the trail best, when she didn't have to worry about traffic at the cross streets, when her brain could switch from analysis mode to casual observation. Six miles out of town was like being in another place, in someone else's life.

On the way back, she thought about Robert; he had been at school for just over an hour. She wondered what he was doing. Math? Social studies? He was sitting in the front row (Bob's request) so he would be more likely to listen and pay attention. He was smart enough, but needed every advantage possible, as he lost interest in everything but Nintendo games quickly, needing reminders and incentives to stay on task. Karen had discussed all of this with his teacher, Ellen O'Donnell, who assured her Robert would be well cared for, as would all the children. He was not like Rebecca, for whom academics came easily. Her teachers praised her intelligence, her work habits, her attitude in the classroom, and her ability to get along with her peers, including those less capable than herself. She was an exceptional girl—they told Karen marking period after marking period in parent-teacher conferences—a natural leader in the classroom who inherently set an excellent example for the other students. Rebecca's attitude was less stellar at home than it was in the classroom, but the pediatrician told Karen that this was to be expected at Rebecca's age. Girls went through puberty earlier, and parents had little choice but to suffer through it.

While Rebecca academically outshone just about everyone, Robert fell into the slow-learners group. And Bob was frustrated with his lack of progress, even though Robert was just six. His kindergarten teacher, Janet Goodwin, had been more focused on Robert's problems than on his successes in parent-teacher conferences, leaving Bob with the impression that his son was an idiot, a loafer, or both. Over the previous Christmas vacation, Bob had worked with him, doing flash cards with simple addition problems and easy words, trying to make a game out of it. But as soon as Robert missed three cards consecutively, Bob quit. Often their sessions lasted just a few minutes. In fact, the tutoring sessions were more aimed at Karen than Robert; Bob wanted her to work with Robert, but Karen refused.

"I don't understand how you can say no to that," Bob said to Karen in bed one night.

"We've gone through this before." She turned out her bedside table lamp.

"Apparently not to my satisfaction."

Karen rolled over to face him, seeing just the shadow of his head by the moonlight coming in through the window. "He's a little boy," she said to the dark. "A lot of the boys in first grade are going through the same thing. They learn at a slower pace than the girls."

"Not my boy. They're not going to put him on the loser track."

"He's not on any track, Bob. He's only six."

"Almost seven. And it's best to start when they're young."

"Start what?" asked Karen. "He's got sixteen years of school ahead of him. We push him now, and we'll have real problems later."

"Or we push him now, and he'll excel later."

"I don't think so."

"Well, I do."

"Then you tutor him," said Karen. "At this point, I think it's ludicrous."

Bob did sit down with Robert several more times, but it often ended badly. Robert would be close to tears, and Bob was angered by his son's shortcomings. Karen insisted Bob stop, saying he was hurting much more than he was helping, and finally Bob acquiesced. It was not because he thought Karen was right. It was not because he didn't think his hard-line approach was in some ways good for his son, still babied by his wife. It was because he got another promotion. He was traveling more and was even busier when he was in town and had no time for tutoring.

Karen rode back through the commercial section of town and through the neighborhood streets to her house. She showered, and then drove her new Grand Voyager minivan to the grocery store, making sure to pick up the ingredients for peanut butter chocolate chip cookies, her children's favorite, for an after-school snack. She stopped at the dry cleaners and the post office on the way home. She hauled the bags into the house and put away the food. It was just after noon, which surprised her. She had purposefully set a later time for lunch because she wanted to accomplish all her errands in the morning. Had she forgotten something? Karen looked at her to-do list on the kitchen counter and saw nothing. She had an ongoing list of house projects, but nothing else scheduled for the first day of school, except lunch with Sarah. Karen decided to make the cookie dough and then bake them just before the children got off the bus, so they would be warm from the oven. The restaurant was crowded, but there was no one in line. Karen, who arrived a few minutes early, stood at the deli counter and looked up at the menu. American Café, with its homemade soups, wraps, and hearty salads, was her favorite place for lunch. Sarah walked in just as Karen was deciding between a sandwich and a salad, her usual warm weather quandary. "How was your morning?" Sarah asked.

"Longer than I thought. I went for a bike ride. I got a ton of groceries. I did a couple of other errands. I showered. And I made cookie dough."

"It's amazing, isn't it? Plus, we'll have another hour or so to ourselves after we eat."

"Should I feel guilty?"

"Why?"

"Because I'm a stay-at-home mother and I've got no kids at home."

"I don't feel guilty," said Sarah. "I feel great."

"Good, because so do I."

They both ordered sandwiches, then sat at a table next to the front window. "When was the last time you were this relaxed?" asked Sarah, momentarily closing her eyes.

"Before the kids were born."

Sarah laughed. "I've been looking at my watch all morning. I keep thinking I have to pick Jeremy up at eleven thirty. Since it's after one, and I'm sitting in a restaurant, that must not be true."

"Sitting in a restaurant, and we're not paying a sitter for the privilege of doing so."

Their sandwiches arrived, and the women chatted as they ate. Sarah was considering taking an economics class at the community college in town and wanted to know if Karen was interested. Karen said she would consider a class second semester, but wanted nothing but freedom for a while.

The word *freedom* sounded foreign to Karen, like she was using a word like *voilà* or *arrivederci,* something in a language other than English. Karen had used it as a weapon over the years, accusing Bob of having it and not appreciating it. He had argued back just how little freedom he had between his job and his family, saying that he was absolutely maxed out. It was, in fact, Karen who had the freedom to do whatever she wanted with her day. And Karen had shot back how little he knew about being maxed out. People like him didn't understand what freedom meant because they'd always had it.

After these heated discussions, when she was calm, Karen acknowledged to herself that Bob's point was valid. Staying home with children afforded her certain luxuries. It was Karen who dictated the day's activities, especially during the summer. She decided when and for how long Rebecca and Robert watched television. She decided when they went to the park. She decided when they had company for lunch or for the afternoon. She decided when she needed a babysitter to relieve her for a few hours. Plus, as Bob pointed out whenever she brought it up, Karen had choices. She could stay home with the children, or she could hire a full-time babysitter and return to work. She could hire a part-time babysitter and return to work part-time. She could do exactly what she wanted to do, but instead of intentionally choosing, she whined. If you don't like it, he said, change it.

Even though Bob was technically correct, he knew and she knew it was more complicated than that. Karen talked about it more with Sarah than with Bob because, as another full-time mother, Sarah understood all the angles. Bob liked to call it a choice, but for Karen and Sarah, it wasn't. When they made the decision to have children, they simultaneously made the decision to raise them. In theory, having a job outside of the home while raising children seemed reasonable, but the practice was miserable. Karen's college roommate, Allison, was a full-time schoolteacher who, as she said, put everything and everyone on hold, emergencies aside, so she could make it through the school year, and then exhausted herself in the summertime trying to catch up. And Sarah had friends in similar situations. They loved their jobs and they loved their children, but they struggled with excelling at managing both. Karen and Sarah agreed that, unless they really needed the money, they couldn't do it, especially when factoring in the guilt. Complain about their self-made predicaments as they often did, they considered themselves stuck.

Being an at-home mother when the children were younger wasn't always difficult or tedious. Karen enjoyed the advantages, like spending the afternoon sipping tea with a friend while the children played in another room, reading while the children took naps, and living in casual clothes instead of suits and stockings and heels, sporting just-right, blow dryer–mandatory hairstyles. Still, the unbreakable, constant attachment to young children was ever present for Karen, whether she was in the house, running errands, out to dinner, or even asleep. Rebecca and Robert were always in and on her mind; her worrying about them appeared to need no rest. She hadn't been free from them since she had expelled them from her swollen body. And yet, having them in school all day afforded Karen the illusion of freedom, the sensation of being able to do exactly as she pleased.

"I never thought this day would come." Sarah sipped a mug of coffee.

"You and me both. Lunch on the first day of school was a great idea. Just think—we could do this every day."

Sarah laughed. "And Vincent would have my head."

"It's not like they don't go out to lunch every day. Bob's not packing a brown bag. It may be just fast food, but that counts in my book."

"Vincent claims to be way too busy for that. He either takes something from home or doesn't eat at all."

"No lunch break?"

"I know; it's crazy. He's says he gets wrapped up in what he's doing, and by the time he looks at a clock, it's midafternoon."

"That's definitely a guy thing. I'm never busy enough that I forget to eat."

Sarah and Karen split the check and walked out to their cars. They promised to call one another in a day or two to make more plans. Karen sang with the car radio on the way home. As she put her car keys on the hook in the kitchen, she realized Sarah was right; she still had another hour before the kids came home. She could go for a walk, but she had just eaten. She could bake the cookies, but she wanted to do that at the last minute. So, she decided to sit under the tree in the backyard and read the newspaper. She changed from a skirt to shorts, and shed her leather sandals in favor of her favorite rubber flip-flops. She poured herself a glass of cold water, took the newspaper from the kitchen table where Bob had looked at it while he ate his cereal, and walked out the back door. She grabbed a beach chair from the shed that housed Bob's lawn mower and Karen's barely touched gardening tools, an illogical Mother's Day gift, and sat in the shade beneath a sugar maple. She had forty-five minutes before cookie time. She skimmed the second section, reading two articles thoroughly. She checked her watch. She had thirty-two minutes left. She drank her water, leaned back in her chair, and closed her eyes. She opened them. She had twenty-seven minutes left. She got out of the chair and walked back into the house, taking the newspaper with her. She refilled her water glass and turned on the oven and then walked upstairs. She took Rebecca's clothes from the dryer to her bedroom, where she folded them before delivering them to Rebecca's room. She walked back down the hall and started another load. Then she walked into Robert's room and unloaded the dirty clothes from his hamper. She walked the armful back down the hall and dropped it into the laundry basket next to the washing machine. She walked back into Robert's room and picked up the cars he had played with before the bus came that morning. She checked her watch; she had another fifteen minutes. She walked down the stairs and into the kitchen, where she scooped the chilled dough onto a cookie sheet. She poured two glasses of milk and put them in the fridge and slid the dough into the oven. As soon as the timer rang, she removed the cookies from the oven and then took the newspaper to the front steps, where she could sit and read and still be ready for the bus. She glanced at a story about free-range chickens, then looked at her watch. With just three minutes left, she walked to the corner to wait for the bus.

Robert descended the bus's metal steps and ran to her. "Mommy!" he said, crashing into her hip.

"Oh my," she said, bending down and hugging him. "I think you've grown while you were at school. You're so big!"

"I am big," he said, smiling at her.

"Hi, honey," said Karen to Rebecca. "How's my fourth grader?"

"Great!" said Rebecca. "My teacher is so nice. She let us have an extra long recess, and she brought in popcorn and juice for reading time."

"That is definitely nice," said Karen, wrapping her arm around her daughter. "Do you have any homework?"

"No," said Rebecca, "but you do. There are a million forms for you to sign by tomorrow."

"Oh boy," said Karen, leading them into the house.

Karen unpacked their backpacks while the children ate their snack. Robert announced that he had been chosen to sit in the front row because that's where all the smart kids sit, and Rebecca talked about Melanie, a new girl in her class, who could jump rope longer than any kid on the playground. Karen listened as she looked at the bundle of colored papers that came out of Rebecca's bag: health forms, school lunch tickets information, an ice-cream social later that week, field trip chaperoning opportunities, room parent criteria, Girl Scouts, after-school care, and a number of others. Robert's papers, while not as numerous, included a half-completed math sheet.

"Can we go to the park today?" asked Rebecca. "I want to tell Britney all about school."

"Let's play here today. Your dad is coming home early tonight for a barbecue."

"Please?" whined Rebecca. "Just for an hour?"

"Call her on the phone," said Karen. "See if they're free tomorrow." Rebecca scooted out of her seat and ran to the wall phone. She pushed the buttons of Britney's phone number, which she had memorized the day the girls met. While they talked, Karen refilled her water glass and sat with Robert at the table. "Tell me more about Mrs. O'Donnell."

Robert put his half-eaten cookie on the table. "She's really smart. She knows all her math facts."

"That is smart."

"I have homework. Most of the kids finished at school."

"How do you know that?"

"They got stickers on their papers."

Karen took Robert's unfinished math sheet from his pile of papers. "Let's get to this now so we won't have to think about it later."

"Can I play first?"

Karen looked at her watch. "For one hour. I've got some things to do to get ready for dinner. After that, we'll hit the books."

Robert finished his cookie while Rebecca wrapped up her conversation with Britney. "They're free tomorrow," she said after she hung up the phone. "Mrs. Keyworth will call you in the morning with the details."

"Perfect. Head outside now and have some fun with your brother. He and I need to do some homework in a little bit."

Rebecca looked at Robert. "You got homework?"

"Only a little bit."

"Your teacher must be insane."

"That's enough," said Karen. "You haven't seen each other all day. Be nice, Rebecca."

"Fine," she said. "Can I make a hopscotch on the driveway?"

"Absolutely. You know where the chalk is."

Karen peeled and boiled potatoes, then chopped celery, onion, and hard-boiled eggs for potato salad. She made hamburger patties and chocolate pudding and decided a green salad would round out the meal. She washed her hands, then called to Robert.

"Oh, Mom," he said, his body already drooping.

"Right now. You've been out there for an hour and a half."

"Go do your homework, baby," said Rebecca to her brother.

Robert stuck out his tongue at her, then threw his stick of purple chalk to the ground. "I hate you," he said.

"Whatever you say bounces off me and sticks onto you," said Rebecca smartly, hands folded across her chest.

"Let's go, Robert." Karen opened the back door wide for him.

Robert walked into the house. "She's so mean."

"Big sisters can be. Let's sit at the table and have a look at that sheet."

Robert sat down, and Karen sat down next to him. He looked at the first problem, then looked at his mother. "Do you have something I can count with? At school, we have little plastic animals. So for four plus five, you make a group of four monkeys and a group of five tigers. Then you count all the animals, and you know the answer."

"That's clever."

"Some kids don't need the animals. They can do it in their heads."

Karen kissed her son's forehead. "I have wagon-wheel noodles," she said getting up from the table. "Will they work?"

"They should."

Karen spilled a few dozen noodles out onto the table and watched Robert group them. He was slow and sometimes lost count, so unlike Rebecca, who was quick to grasp new concepts and even quicker at producing excellent, flawless work. Robert, Karen already knew, was a different kind of student. Being slow didn't mean he wasn't smart—he got all the answers on the first half of the sheet correct—but it was a handicap in a class full of kids. The quicker ones would finish faster and earn the adulation of their peers. The slower ones, like Robert, would lose out on incentives or, worse, be teased. "How many do you have there?"

"Eleven."

"Count again." Methodically, he moved each noodle and mouthed numbers from one to twelve. He erased the second one in eleven and replaced it with a two. On closer inspection of his paper, Karen saw several erasure marks. "You keep working," she said, getting up from the table. "I'm going to do a few more things for dinner, but I'll be right here if you need me."

Karen mixed the potato salad ingredients with mayonnaise, sour cream, mustard, salt, and pepper—just the way Bob liked it. She cut tomatoes and cucumbers for the salad, which she put in the fridge to chill, and then set the table on the porch. She moved a block of Muenster cheese from the fridge to the counter and opened a new box of Ritz crackers. The kids could split a soda, and she and Bob would have a drink to celebrate the first day of school. Karen sat back down at the table and was relieved to find Robert almost done. It had taken him twenty-five minutes to do eight problems. At this pace, he would have homework every night. "All done," he said.

Karen checked the answers. "Excellent." She peeled the backing off the sticker his teacher had paper-clipped to the page and placed the grinning sun next to Robert's name at the top of the sheet. "Go out and find your sister. Daddy will be home soon."

"Daddy's coming home for dinner?"

"He switched his flight to be here."

Robert opened the back door and called out to his sister, who was doing cartwheels. "Daddy's coming home for a special dinner!"

"What are we having?" she called back.

Robert looked at his mother.

"Hamburgers and chocolate pudding."

On his way out the door, Robert called back to his sister, who clapped at the news.

Karen washed all the dishes in the sink, then ran upstairs and switched the laundry. She took her clean clothes from the dryer and folded them on her bed. She changed back into the skirt she had worn to lunch and brushed her hair. She walked back down the stairs to the kitchen and put the tossed salad together. Just as she was slicing the cheese for the hamburgers, she heard Bob in the backyard. She looked out the window. Rebecca was on his back, and Robert was holding his briefcase. When they all walked in the back door, Karen kissed Bob on the lips. "I'm glad you're home."

"I was glad, too, until a bunch of wild monkeys attacked me in a backyard."

"Dad!" said Rebecca, laughing. "You attacked us!"

"That's what monkeys always say."

"Who wants a grape soda?" asked Karen. Robert jumped up and down. "Go out to the porch. Daddy and I will be right out." Karen poured the sodas while Bob poured Karen a glass of wine and himself a beer. "How was your day?"

"Great. I had a meeting with Todd Martin this morning. He's going to retire at the end of the month."

"And?" said Karen, turning to face her husband.

Bob grinned. "I got the job."

Karen covered her open mouth with her hands.

"I can't believe it's really happening. I've thought about this day for years, and it's really here. I'm the youngest vice president in Forester's history."

"I can't believe it either."

"I'll have to do some traveling."

"I know that," said Karen, nodding her head. "You travel now, and that's okay."

"This promotion, counting bonuses, will double my salary as well as my responsibilities. It's incredible."

Karen put her arms around Bob's neck and kissed him on the mouth. "You're incredible. Later, we'll have our own celebration."

Chapter 10

The morning of Bob's first business trip as vice president of sales for Forester Paper, Karen signed up for tennis lessons. Shelley was thrilled, telling her daughter on the phone how much tennis meant to her, both physically and mentally. "My tennis buddies," she said, "are my closest friends." She advised Karen to start slowly, to choose an intermediate group and work her way up if she desired. "The last thing you want is rotator cuff problems from overdoing it," said Shelley, who had done just that and endured shoulder surgery as a result. Karen called the town tennis center as soon as she hung up with her mother and, after listening to her options, joined the Second Time Around Ladies Clinic on Tuesdays and Thursdays. It seemed custom-made for Karen, for women who had played before so they knew the rudiments of the game, but were not quite ready for league play. Karen played as a child, had played well, in fact, until she broke her leg the summer after sixth grade while running along the uneven surface of a public tennis court. She and a friend biked every day it didn't rain to the downtown park that featured two baseball diamonds, several play and picnic areas, and six underused asphalt courts, and were both developing into decent players. Their goal was to make the middle school team the following fall. And Karen knew, even as a child, that she would have made the team easily had she seen and avoided the grass-filled crack behind the court as she was running to return a baseline lob three weeks before tryouts.

She was in a cast for eight weeks, which of course knocked her right out of the running for a spot on the team. Her friend Kelly Brady made the team, which made Karen all the more bitter. She routinely beat Kelly by a margin of more than the required two games. As a member of the team, Kelly was busy with practice after school and had little time to socialize with Karen. She was making new friends while Karen and her crutches rode the bus home every day. By the springtime, when Karen's leg was fully healed and she was as strong physically as she had been before the fall, Kelly no longer wanted to play tennis with her. Kelly had progressed to the point of only wanting to play with opponents who could keep up with her lively game. Karen, who was out of practice, hit too many balls into the net or out of bounds. When Kelly started declining Karen's offers to play and then refusing her phone calls altogether, Karen stopped calling. And since Kelly was her only friend who played tennis, Karen stopped playing. She joined the track team instead—running relays, doing the long jump, making new friends— and forgot about tennis and Kelly. It was as Karen and Bob watched television on Labor Day weekend and he clicked by chance to the women's singles of the U.S. Open that Karen redis-covered her interest in the game.

Sarah helped her shop the day before the clinic started; Karen bought a tennis racket, two tennis skirts, three tops, sneakers, a nylon warm-up suit, and several pairs of short white socks. At the store, Karen again tried to talk Sarah into joining her. She, too, had played tennis as a child. But as an adult, Sarah wasn't interested. She had signed up for an economics class that met twice a week and was considering a pottery class as well. Booking two mornings outside of what she had already scheduled would be too much. Plus, running around the court was no longer Sarah's passion; her life was already hectic. She preferred yoga, which she practiced at home six mornings a week before her children awakened.

Karen felt less confident about her decision the next morning on her way to the tennis center. She was mostly worried about her level of play, but a little anxious about the other women in the group. She wondered if they would be friendly, or if they would already know one another and have no interest in admitting Karen into their inner circle. Karen was finally at a point in her life when friendships would work again. A couple of her high school friends were still within driving distance, but they had infants and toddlers and, consequently, no free time. She had Sarah, of course, but she wanted more than one strong friendship, now that she had time to devote to people and activities outside of her family.

Twelve women gathered around court number one. Four of them, Karen could immediately tell, had come together. They talked and giggled amongst themselves, admiring one another's outfits and barely listening to Ken Doyle, their instructor. Of the other seven, Karen thought two women—Caroline and Ginny, according to their name tags, who were standing together and talking—looked the most accessible. When Ken asked them to divide into three groups of four, Karen approached them, as did Stephanie, a young wife who had played in high school. Caroline and Ginny, like Karen, were mothers of school-age children. Within five minutes, all three of them had used the word *freedom* and laughed about it.

They remained a foursome for the morning and on Thursday morning as well. Karen, Caroline, and Ginny enjoyed swapping child-rearing stories, and Stephanie, married five years and waiting to have children, had no trouble joining the discussion. As the oldest of seven children, she knew almost as much about motherhood as they did. She fed, diapered, and cared for her younger siblings while she was still in elementary school, recalling details with enough clarity for Karen to understand why she was in no hurry to have her own. Stephanie told them she'd feel more like a grandmother than a mother. They had easy conversation as they sipped water on the sidelines between games and even on the court, because they all hit the ball competently. Stephanie, who said playing again was like riding a bike, could hit any ball that came close to her at the net.

During the final court change, Caroline suggested lunch out.

They could all get a bagel or something, nothing fancy, which would mean they could go in their warm-up suits right from the clinic, no showers needed. Ginny, Stephanie, and Karen readily agreed that a bagel and diet soda would hit the spot. At eleven thirty, they thanked Ken for his patience, which made him smile, and headed out to the parking lot. They got into their own cars—everyone had errands to run afterward—and met at World of Bagels near the mall. They chatted as they stood in line to place their orders, then sat at a table for four near the window overlooking an interior courtyard.

It turned out that Ginny, the best tennis player of their foursome, was also an accomplished pianist. She had played the piano as a child and then returned to lessons when her first son was born. She played mostly for her own enjoyment, but also at her church as a fill-in for the aging organist. They paid her fifty dollars a Sunday, which was expected back as a donation to the church. Stephanie had recently quit her job as an accountant and was happy for the moment to have no schedule. She liked the idea of getting into decorating—all of her friends said she had a good eye for color—but had no formal training and was not sure about returning to the classroom to get some. Caroline suggested she could work for one of the three decorating services in the area and get on-the-job training, and Stephanie said she had considered it, but had so far made no inquiring phone calls. At this point, she said, she was more certain about what she didn't want to do than what she did. Cleaning the house, for example, was high on her list of how not to spend her time. In fact, she had booked an interview with a cleaning service that afternoon, which she was hoping would lead to a twice-a-month contract.

Karen thought about employing a cleaning service, but, so far, had been unable to justify it. She was home all day and could therefore dust, vacuum, and scrub the bathtub anytime. When Rebecca and Robert were younger and home with her, she had done her chores while they watched television. A half hour each morning is what she had devoted to cleaning over the years to keep the house presentable. When she had company, she cleaned more thoroughly. She didn't despise cleaning like Stephanie; it was an accomplishment, an easy check mark on her list. And now, with both kids in school, she had more time than ever. But cleaning the house when she was home alone was a poor way to spend her free time. Karen asked Stephanie for the name of the service.

Shine Time Cleaners' representative Barb Ellison arrived the next afternoon. Carrying a clipboard and jotting down numbers, she walked through the house with Karen. At the end of the thirty-minute session, she handed Karen an estimate of eighty dollars per visit and said they could start the following week and come on alternate weeks, as Karen had requested. Karen called Bob that evening, and he okayed the expenditure, joking that one hundred and sixty dollars a month was a reasonable allotment for her happiness. When Shine Time came the following Thursday morning, Karen greeted them at the door in her warm-up suit. She and the girls went to the bagel shop afterward, so Karen didn't get home until almost one. She walked in the back door and was welcomed by the scent of pine cleaner. Wanting to share her good mood, Karen called Sarah.

"How does it feel to be a queen?" she asked.

Karen laughed. "I don't know why I didn't think of this before now."

"You had kids at home. You had all day long to clean your house."

"I still could have had someone cleaning this place."

"True."

"What have you been up to today?"

"You don't want to know."

"I do want to know."

"Okay," said Sarah, cradling the phone on her shoulder while she washed floor cleaner from her hands. "While you were having your house cleaned, I was cleaning mine."

"No."

"A most definite yes."

"Hold on a second, and I'll get you the Shine Time phone number. They're very reasonable."

"That's okay. I don't mind, really. I'm pretty picky about how my house is cleaned."

"That's because you're pretty picky about everything."

"Way too picky if you ask Vincent."

"What are you doing tomorrow?" asked Karen. "Do you want to go shopping?"

"I can't. I'm going on a field trip with Britney's class."

"You are a saint."

"You have no idea. We're going to the nature center to identify trees."

"All day?"

"Eleven to three, with lunch under the giant oak."

"Next week then," said Karen.

But Sarah was busy the next week. She had to study for a test on supply-side economics. Plus, Vincent was going out of town, which meant single parenting. "It always exhausts me," Sarah had said on the phone. "I need a lot of downtime when he's away."

Saying she understood when she really didn't, Karen decided to go shopping anyway. She called her new friend Caroline Miller from tennis, who told her she was in the market for a pair of smart black pants and would love to go.

Karen followed Caroline's directions to the newest subdivision in town. She drove the van into the driveway of Caroline's four-thousand-square foot neocolonial brick house just before nine and instantly felt a twinge of jealousy in her abdomen. How, Karen wondered on her walk along the pristine white cement walkway from the asphalt driveway to the front door, could they afford this? Caroline was Karen's age; was her husband, Rick, older? Karen walked up the three slate steps to the portico, then another five steps to the front door, and rang the bell. Caroline greeted her barefoot, dressed in tight jeans, a tight-fitting white top, and a wide, black leather belt. "Hey, girl," said Caroline. "Come on in. I'm just about ready to go." Karen stepped into the entranceway, bright with sunshine streaming through three large windows several feet above the front door. "You need sunglasses in here today," said Caroline. "We wanted a lot of light throughout the house, and the builder gave us some excellent ideas, but on some days—like today—it's a bit much."

"I love the light." Karen felt like she was in the house of an older, established person, someone her parents' age.

"Have a look around if you'd like." Caroline jogged up the carpeted stairs. "I'll be down in a minute."

A few more steps, and Karen was in the great room, with its cathedral ceiling that must have been twenty-five feet high. A white marble fireplace sat in the middle of the far wall, below a giant flat-screened TV and between floor-to-ceiling windows. The two white leather couches that lined up with the cream walls faced each other, and were separated by a heavy-looking glass and steel coffee table. It was the perfect setting for a cold weather get-together. Karen could picture snow falling outside, a roaring fire inside, and guests mingling with mugs of spicy chili and frothy beer in their hands. Standing in the middle of the room with her arms crossed over her chest, Karen saw herself as the hostess. Like Caroline, she would be wearing form-fitting jeans and cashmere, casual and hip. "We live in this room," said Caroline, descending the stairs. "The girls do their homework at the kitchen table where we can keep an eye on them, while Rick and I lounge in here."

"This is such a beautiful space."

"I wish I could take credit for it." Caroline slipped her pedicured feet into black patent-leather loafers. "I have an awesome decorator."

"Yes," said Karen, wondering whether leather would work in her living room.

Caroline grabbed a lime green denim jacket from her wrought iron coat rack and led Karen out the door. "Indian summer," she said. "Perfect."

They passed the forty minutes to the Oak Run mall easily with conversation about Caroline's house. It had taken a year for her and Rick to agree on the blueprints and another year to build. The list of delays and change orders had caused Caroline many tearful nights. But finally May first, the last in a series of promised completion dates, arrived, and the house was theirs. They were moved in and settled by Memorial Day, after buying six rooms of new furniture. Their open house, on August first, attracted more than a hundred friends, neighbors, and staff members of the hospital, where Rick, the most-sought-after orthopedic surgeon in a large practice, performed what many referred to as miracles.

"No wonder everything looks so clean and fresh. It's all brand new."

"Mostly, yes," said Caroline, reapplying lipstick as Karen parked the car. "Our old stuff was dismal. We'd had it since before we got married."

Karen and Bob had a mishmash of furniture. They had several pieces from their families—Karen's grandmother's dining room table and chairs, two bureaus, and a mahogany desk, and Bob's great-uncle's sofa table, occasional chairs, and love seat—but needed more when they moved into their house. They bought beds, bureaus, and bookcases for the kids' rooms a few years ago, but badly needed a new kitchen table. Plus, Karen's taste was changing; she was especially unhappy with the couch and wing chairs in the living room. However, Bob disliked replacing things that were "perfectly serviceable," and that included the living room furniture.

The mall was populated by women in designer jeans, carrying large shopping bags as they walked briskly from store to store. Caroline fit right in with the other shoppers, as if they all shared the same moving sidewalk at the metropolitan airport. This was not a leisurely pursuit, like Karen's trips to the local mall with Sarah and their daughters. Caroline was on a mission, moving with the speed and determination of a New York City pedestrian. Smart black pants were harder to find than Karen guessed. She peeled off and found two sweaters and a skirt, while Caroline monopolized the sales associates. There was no time for lunch, a cup of coffee, or conversation that strayed from the main topic of where to find the pants. After three hours, Caroline's quest was over, fulfilled in a teeny-bopper shop with gum-chewing associates who looked like they should have been in high school algebra class instead of behind the counter with their chipped lacquered nails. Caroline suggested salads to go; Karen balanced hers on her lap as they drove at seventy-five miles per hour along the expressway. After Karen dropped Caroline at her house, she rushed to the grocery store to pick up a few things for dinner. The rest of her list would have to wait.

When she got home, she had just ten minutes before the bus came. She considered calling Jamie for the afternoon, but resisted. Bob told her she didn't really need Jamie anymore, and he was right. What couldn't she get done in the seven hours her kids were gone? Still, she felt restless. Her day had been more stress-inducing than relaxing, and Karen wanted to chat with Sarah over a cup of tea. She had her hand on the phone when she remembered Sarah was volunteering that afternoon. She would be driving home with her kids, mostly likely making plans in the car. Karen turned from the phone and filled the kettle with water; a cup of Earl Grey at home would have to suffice. Plus, since Bob was coming home early that night, she would have to start dinner preparations.

When Bob walked in at five thirty, the kids had done their homework and were watching television, and dinner was prepared and could be served whenever Bob desired. After he hugged Rebecca, ruffled Robert's hair, and kissed Karen, he poured himself a beer and Karen a glass of wine and suggested they sit on the porch. Karen watched her husband take his first sip. He loosened his tie and undid the top button of his shirt, slightly damp from perspiration. His face was flushed like it always was after airline travel, but it gave him the appearance of good health. His brown hair was beginning ever so slowly to recede at his temples, but not enough for comment or lengthy study in the bathroom mirror. At thirty-four, Bob had lost the extra fat in his cheeks and chin, giving him a rugged, successful businessman's countenance. He had honest eyes. His Roman nose fit his face, as did his moderately sized ears. Karen sipped her wine. She had seen hair growing out of her father's ears and wondered when Bob's first sprigs would sprout. Would he notice one morning while shaving, or would Karen have to tell him? Would he trim them, or would that be her job? "What are you thinking?" he asked.

"Crazy thoughts. Thoughts about getting old."

Bob scrunched up his face. "Sounds like dismal thoughts to me. I'm not getting old."

"What's your secret?"

"I'm going to work myself to death by the time I'm fifty."

"Ah," said Karen, taking a sip of wine. "Tough week?"

"Exhausting." He took a long pull from his beer glass. "When I'm visiting customers, I need to be available to them all the time. Our meetings start early in the morning, often with pastries and strong coffee as breakfast, and continue well into the afternoon, with sandwiches brought in for lunch. Sometimes I get a couple of hours off to catch up on e-mail or get in a run and a hot shower before dinner. And while the dinner conversation can start with where a son or daughter is going to college, or which football or hockey or baseball team is going all the way this season, it always circles back to business. I can have a beer, but that's generally all I have. Business entertaining is very different from regular entertaining; I have to be on all the time because the pressure is constant."

"You're good at it, though, aren't you?"

"I am good at it," said Bob, as if her compliment were obvious. "But that doesn't mean it sometimes doesn't wear me out."

"You need more downtime."

"I do need more downtime, but I don't know where I'm going to get it. I'm traveling more than ever. And when I'm home, Karen, I just need to relax. I know you need help around here sometimes, but it's hard for me to find—or even want to find—that energy when I'm flat-out all the time."

"It's better now." With two kids in school all day, how could it be otherwise? "I have time to myself, which makes me a better mother. I'm less resentful of your ability to walk in and out of the house whenever you choose because I've found some time for myself. It sounds like you need to do the same."

Bob took two swallows of beer. "I've been thinking the same thing myself. A lot of my clients play golf, for business as well as recreation. Instead of meeting in windowless conference rooms, they meet at the first tee. Maybe it's time I learned the game."

"The only place to play golf around here is the River Club."

"Yes."

The River Club sat on the banks of the Joseph River, which ran through town on its journey through three states. The club boasted one of the state's best golf courses, as well as eight clay outdoor tennis courts (a nice complement to the dozen indoor courts at the tennis center), an Olympic-sized swimming pool, and an opulent dining room that splendidly blended the charm of an earlier era with the updated look appropriate for the new century. She and Bob had been there just once, for a wedding reception a couple years ago, and joked about joining. And before Bob's most recent promotion, it had been a joke. The initiation fee and annual dues, Bob had pointed out, would be like another mortgage.

"You think we can afford it?" Karen asked, her eyebrows raised in speculation.

"Because of my new position, I think I can get Forester to take care of the initiation and dues. My boss has a membership there and has encouraged me a number of times to think about it. A couple of weeks ago he intimated that the company would sponsor me."

"And you're just telling me this now?"

"Honey, I haven't been home much in the last two weeks. This has been our first chance to sit down together."

"Forester would pay for everything?"

"For the most part. I think we would be responsible for our monthly food bill."

Rebecca and Robert ran onto the porch, breathless. Karen looked at her watch; one of their favorite shows had just ended. "We're starving!" said Robert, holding his stomach with two hands.

"Me too," said Bob, scooping his son into his arms. "Let's get the shotgun and shoot us some bear for dinner."

"Dad!" said Robert, laughing.

"Yuck!" said Rebecca. "I'd rather starve than eat a poor old bear."

The conversation at the dinner table was livelier than usual. Rebecca and Robert both had a number of school stories to share with their father. Karen, who had already heard their tales that afternoon, listened again, delighting in the sounds of their voices and easy amusement. After dinner, Karen did the dishes while Bob supervised baths and read bedtime stories. Both children were in bed by eight, Karen's goal on a school night. She and Bob sat on the living room couch and watched TV for an hour, then retired to their bedroom, where they read for thirty minutes before having sex.

Bob had always been very complimentary about Karen's body, with a slight dip when she had gained weight after having the children. He routinely told her she was more attractive to him now than she was in college; her body was stronger. She could hold herself above him; she could wrap her legs tightly around his. Karen responded to his compliments. She had worked hard at losing the weight. She exercised four times a week and watched what she ate, and she was pleased with herself. Her health was important to her, but not as much as her image. Successful women with successful husbands were in control of their lives, and that included their appearances. Like Karen, Bob made time for the gym or a run three days a week. His workout was simply built into his day. When he traveled, he used the hotel fitness room. They all had them now. He, too, was as trim as he had been in college. They appreciated the shape and size of their bodies most when they were in bed together.

Afterward, they lay back on the pillows and talked more about the country club. While it was exclusive, Bob would be able to get a membership quickly by virtue of his position at Forester. The company's board members were impressed with Bob and would pave the way. He'd mention something to his boss the next day, and they would be members inside a month. It was after the golf season, of course, but he could book lessons in the spring. Maybe Karen could learn how to play as well. Karen said she liked the idea, but she was more interested in the dining room and social perks. They'd meet new friends. They'd attend great parties. And they'd have somewhere to show off their fabulous bodies. Bob laughed, wrapping his arms around his wife. She took a deep breath, then asked him about replacing their living room furniture. "Go right ahead," Bob said, before kissing her once more on the lips and rolling over to go to sleep.

CHAPTER 1 1

DECEMBER 2002

At three forty-five, Sarah, Britney, and Jeremy walked in the back door. Rebecca, who hadn't seen her friend in weeks, ran to Britney and hugged her. The two girls then hustled up the stairs to Rebecca's room and shut the door. "That's the last we'll see of them for a while," said Sarah, smiling.

"What's in your hands?" Robert asked Sarah, who was holding a cylindrical plastic container.

"A cake!" said Jeremy.

"Hey, it's my turn to do snacks," said Karen, giving her friend a look.

Sarah shrugged. "You know me. I couldn't stop myself."

"Can we have some, Mom?" Robert asked.

"Well, boys, do you want store-bought cookies or homemade cake?"

"Cake!" they shouted in unison.

"Good choice." Karen poured the boys cups of milk, then put the kettle on for tea.

"Shall we call the girls?" asked Sarah.

"You can call all you want," said Karen. "They won't hear a thing over Rebecca's CD player."

"What does she listen to?"

"Teenage girls. It seems anybody can make a record now."

"Yuck!" said Robert. "I hate girls."

"Me too," said Jeremy.

"Except for your sister," said Sarah.

"And you, Mom," said Jeremy.

When the boys finished their chocolate cake, they scooted down from their chairs and headed downstairs to the basement. Robert loved the new playroom and couldn't wait to show his friend. The builders finished the work ten days ago. Since then, the painters had coated the walls with Wow, Orange!; the guys at Flooring, Etc. had laid multicolored striped Berber carpeting; and the brightly colored retro furniture that Karen purchased, after the saleswoman called it indestructible *and* groovy, had arrived. Bob replaced the old television with the better one from the living room (and bought a new flat screen for the den) as the final touch, and Robert had spent almost every hour he was home down there since.

"I'm going down there with them," said Sarah. Karen followed her friend down the stairs, which had also been carpeted. The boys were sitting at the large table in the middle of the room building with Lego blocks. They ignored their mothers' presence. "This looks great." Sarah appraised the room with her hands on her hips. "I love the color. And that couch is fantastic."

"Isn't that fun? I found that first and bought everything else because of it."

"You can't go wrong with lime green. And a piano? I had no idea you were in the market for one."

"I didn't know either. Rebecca wanted to take lessons, so I started reading the classifieds. It's a pretty nice instrument when no one's playing it."

"You're a genius to put it down here. Practice times can be brutal."

"And how silly are those purple swivel chairs?"

"Very silly," said Sarah. The boys hopped into the chairs and immediately began playing the spaceship game Robert had been playing on his own all week. Sarah and Karen walked back up the stairs and into the living room. "I still can't get over what you've done to this room," said Sarah. "It's undergone a complete transformation."

"It felt nice to get rid of that old stuff."

"What did you do with it? I know for a while you were thinking about using it in the basement playroom."

"I was," said Karen. "But it didn't really fit into the theme I have going down there. Bob said he was happy enough to get a charitable receipt from Salvation Army."

"Well, you've done a good job. I would love to have a playroom like that."

"You have your family room," Karen offered, leading Sarah back to the kitchen.

"Which is supposed to be for the whole family. Most days, the kids take that room over, and I'm stuck in the kitchen if I want quiet time to myself."

Karen sat at the kitchen table and poured two mugs of hot tea from the teapot. "Does your basement have potential?"

"Very much so. And I would love to see it become a room for the kids. It's expensive; we have to make choices."

"I understand that. I'd love to do this kitchen, but we're just going to have to wait. At this point, we don't have a lot left over."

"Ummm." Sarah sipped her tea. "This is good. Do you want some cake to go with it?"

"Absolutely," said Karen, reaching for the knife. She cut a generous piece for Sarah and a smaller one for herself.

"Are you trying to make me fat?" Sarah smiled as she accepted the larger piece.

"That would take a lot more than a piece of cake. Although, if you talk to Rebecca, she'll tell you fatness begins in fourth grade."

"Same with Britney. Suddenly she thinks she's fat. She won't have an after-school snack anymore."

"I can't believe this is starting already. I didn't think about my weight until I was in college."

"None of us did. We ate what we wanted and ran off the rest."

But it was a different world now, both women acknowledged. The pressures on children began earlier, curtailing the carefree portion of their childhood. Girls wanted to be thin and pretty, and boys sought intelligence and success. Britney no longer ran around the playground at recess because she didn't want to risk ruining her clothes. Instead, she stood and talked with other like-minded girls. Occasionally, they approached the boys and taunted them into a game of chase, but it was more flirtation than exertion. Britney had not said a word of this to her mother. The news had come to Sarah from Britney's teacher, who was more than a little worried her fifth-grade girls were growing up too quickly. She'd seen an incredible shift over her twenty-year tenure and, socially, didn't like what she saw.

Rebecca was going through a similar stage. She spent an increasing amount of time in her room with the door shut. She teased Robert without mercy, seemingly resenting his mere presence. She'd play with him when she had absolutely nothing else to do, but what used to come naturally, willingly even, was now endured. Fourth grade, according to Rebecca, was the beginning of her adult life. She simply didn't have time for babies anymore. Karen and Bob tried to ignore her dramatic statements because, in some ways, Rebecca, at nine, was more a child than she had been at seven. She pouted when she didn't get what she wanted. She cried easily. She had what Karen described to Bob as meltdowns a couple times a week. Typically, Karen sent her daughter upstairs when she was rude or unreasonable, but it didn't seem to be much of a punishment since Rebecca liked it there. When Karen was really angry, she'd follow Rebecca into her room, where Karen would unplug the CD player and take it with her. Rebecca went berserk when Karen did this, however, so the crime had to be worth the screaming. Bob and Karen had thought about getting Rebecca involved in a service organization like the Girl Scouts, but Rebecca told them she'd rather sleep in a snake pit than join the ultimate nerd club.

"We're bored," announced Rebecca, walking into the kitchen with Britney.

"Have some cake," said Karen.

"Are you kidding? There's about a billion calories in one piece." She looked at Brittney, who nodded.

"Okay, that's more for us," said Karen.

"Well, that's really selfish," said Rebecca, showing off for Britney.

"Hey, I asked."

Rebecca opened the fridge and stood in front of it. "Do we have any Diet Coke?"

"I don't buy Diet Coke."

"Can you put some on your grocery list?"

"We'll see." Karen already knew she was not going to let her daughter start a diet soda habit at nine years old, but hedged her response to avoid a verbal battle.

"There's nothing to eat," said Rebecca, who had moved on to the cupboards.

"There's cake."

Rebecca turned to face her mother and give her the full benefit of her weariness. "We've been through that."

"So we have. Dinner will be at six thirty."

"We'll starve before then."

"Not if you have some cake."

Rebecca glared at her mother, then stomped out of the room. Britney raised her eyebrows at her mother before following her friend. "How did you like the show?" Karen asked Sarah after they left.

"It's a rerun. I live it every day."

Karen poured more tea into their mugs. "Rebecca's changing. While she's always been a precocious child, she was still a child. Now she's a preteen monster."

"She's a monster for you," said Sarah. "She's an incredible student. She's always good at my house. She has simply entered that stage of peer influence."

Karen sipped her tea. "You've been reading again."

"Always. I don't know how to parent without parenting books."

"Maybe I'll read this latest one when you're done. I don't like what I'm seeing."

"I'm seeing the same thing," said Sarah. "Britney can come home with such attitude sometimes that I don't even want to be around her. And yet, when I make the time to be with her, she softens."

"Rebecca softens, too. But only after she's spent some time in her room. She seems to need to unwind after school."

"As does Britney. And that seems crazy for a ten-year-old. What are they going to do to deal with the pressures and stress of life when they're our age?"

"They are growing up way too fast."

"Yeah," said Sarah, taking a sip of her tea. "And it's our impossible job to slow them down."

The more Karen wanted to slow their lives down, the more the world sped things up. Rebecca was busy with piano lessons on Thursday afternoons, modern dance on Mondays and Wednesdays, and Excellent Students First!—an after-school problem-solving and brainstorming session for smart kids—every other Tuesday. Karen offered to spend time with Rebecca in the evenings after dinner. But Rebecca had homework and then usually preferred reading or listening to music than having what Karen called "girl time." The one time Rebecca came to her, wanting her attention, Karen had already committed to attending an evening lecture with Sarah at the library about raising teenage girls. Later that night and for many days afterward, Karen wished she had changed her plans to accommodate her daughter. Karen tried to make up, but Rebecca's intractable nature had become an art form. She was cooler than ever.

Karen's tennis buddies felt the same way about their lives; everyone was too busy, especially the kids. Since Ginny had four, she spent her weekday afternoons in the car. The weekends weren't much better. Her older two boys played soccer and usually had games on Saturdays and Sundays. They hadn't been to church as a family in months. When Ginny had to fill in for the organist, it was a scramble. Caroline's two daughters were doing the same thing Rebecca was doing: music lessons and dance. Only Chelsea and Annie both played two instruments and took two dance classes. They had no free time during the week. Caroline was in a carpool for the dance classes, but for the music lessons, she was on her own.

In spite of their busy lives, Karen and her friends still made time for lunch after tennis. They had tried different restaurants in town, but routinely chose the country club as soon as Karen announced she had become a member. Caroline had been a member for several years, as had Ginny. Stephanie and her husband had joined the previous fall and had both taken golf lessons, but were, in Stephanie's words, worse than awful. Her husband, Patrick, had hit the side of the clubhouse once, barely missing the picture window overlooking the notorious water hazard on the seventeenth hole. The big draw for the women was not the golf course or even the tennis courts; it was the food, gourmet and dazzling at dinner and special events and quick but innovative at lunch. They always ate lunch in the Patio Room, decorated with circular iron tables that had been painted white and covered with glass tops, surrounded by matching chairs cushioned in green and yellow floral fabric. The staff was pleasant and courteous and appeared to know Karen's name after just one introduction. And Karen and her friends didn't have to change for lunch because the dress code in the Patio Room accommodated both weekday and weekend casual athletes.

The chilled white wine was the best thing about eating at the club. Caroline suggested the indulgence one day after a particularly challenging clinic, a substitution for the ibuprofen all of them kept in their car glove box as a means to ease muscle fatigue. Karen was skeptical at first. Alcohol took away her motivation, as well as her energy, and she couldn't afford an afternoon on the couch. Caroline agreed with Karen, but said there was nothing she couldn't accomplish after a glass of wine as long as she drank two glasses of water and a cup of coffee afterward. And that worked really well, until they started drinking two glasses of wine instead of one. It was always fun at the time. They laughed a lot, engaged in the telling, let's-be-honest discussions had by women drinking wine. They complained about their husbands and their children as well as, in lowered voices, the people at the club who let everyone know where they were going for vacation and what renovation was taking entirely too long at their lake houses up north. Karen justified both the wine and the gossip as her downtime, which she told herself she deserved. She, like Caroline and Ginny, had survived the baby years; they were entitled to do whatever they pleased, at least during school hours.

After school was a different story. Most of the time Karen managed to keep it together. She had to, especially when Bob was traveling. Occasionally, however, Caroline's remedy didn't work, and Karen was simply too tired to deal with Rebecca's and Robert's schedules and demands. On those days, she would read magazines on the living room couch, and the children simply missed their activities. They never seemed to mind watching TV, often separately, with Rebecca in the den and Robert in the basement, instead of stuffing a snack in their mouths and running to the car. It worked well for everyone, until the day Bob walked into the house at four o'clock one Thursday afternoon after grabbing the last seat on an early flight home from Boston, and found his wife sleeping under the cashmere throw she had bought for herself, even though Bob had prohibited non-Christmas purchases. "Karen," he said, gently shaking her shoulder. Karen slowly opened her eyes. "Are you okay?"

"Yes." Karen sat up and yawned. "I guess I fell asleep."

Bob looked at his watch. "Doesn't Rebecca have dance on Thursdays? And what's this blanket all about?"

"I got it on sale. You can wrap it up and give it to me for Christmas. And yes, as you well know, Rebecca does have dance today. We both just needed a day off."

Bob sat down on the couch. "A day off from what?"

"A day off from life, Bob," said Karen, her voice serious, an ache developing in her left temple. "You have your days off, too."

"Yeah, on the weekends, when I'm not supposed to be doing something else."

"What, exactly, is it that I'm supposed to be doing that I'm not?"

"For starters, taking your daughter to dance class. You run this house, Karen. And part of running the house is getting the groceries, making dinner, and making sure the kids are where they need to be."

"And I do that ninety-eight percent of the time," she said, getting up from the couch and slipping her sock-covered feet into her loafers. "I can't believe that's not good enough."

Bob stood next to her. "Look, when you're sick or there's some kind of unusual circumstance, I understand that you can't do everything," he said, removing his suit jacket. "But taking a nap when you should be driving your kids to the lessons and activities I pay good money for is ridiculous, Karen. I mean what did you do today that exhausted you to this point?" Karen held his eyes with hers for a moment and then walked into the kitchen. Bob followed her. "Walking away from me isn't going to cancel my question." He was standing in the doorway. "My guess is you played tennis, had lunch at the club, had wine with that lunch, and now can't function."

Karen, who was filling a glass of water at the sink, turned off the faucet. "You don't get to judge what I do because you have no idea what it is. You go off to an office all day, where you swap jokes in conference rooms before treating special clients to expensive lunches."

"And I get paid well for it. When you start making money running errands and playing tennis, I won't give you a hard time."

"Is that what this is about? Money?" asked Karen, reaching into the fridge for a package of raw chicken. She removed its plastic wrap and dumped the six breasts into a large frying pan.

"No," said Bob, pulling a chair out from underneath the kitchen table and sitting in it. "It's about your life, Karen, and what you're doing with it. What are you doing with your life? What's your plan?"

"My plan is to do exactly what I want to do." The fat from the chicken skin sizzled in the pan. "I've been a slave for nine years, and now I'm enjoying my freedom, which I richly deserve."

"A slave?"

"Yes, a slave, Bob. Raising children is an incredibly difficult, tedious, and time-intensive job—not that you'd understand, since you helped about two percent of the time during those years. Now, finally, I have time to myself, and right now I'm happy to spend it doing exactly what I want."

"And that's fine, Karen," said Bob, standing and getting a beer from the fridge. "You can spend the hours the kids are at school in whatever manner you deem suitable. However, when the kids get home from school and need their mother to drive them to classes or help them with their homework, I expect you to be on task. You're on duty from three thirty in the afternoon until eight thirty at night, when Rebecca goes to bed. That's a five-hour day, Karen. That doesn't sound too taxing to me." Bob swallowed a quarter of the can.

Karen lowered the gas flame underneath the chicken, set the wooden spoon in her hand down on the stove top, and then leaned back against the counter, her arms crossed over her chest. Eyebrows raised, she said, "And who makes sure they're up and out of bed? You? No, you're in the shower. And who makes them breakfast? You? Nope, you're being served at the breakfast table right along with them. Who makes them lunches, Bob? Do you know what they like for lunch? Do you even know how to make a peanut butter and banana sandwich? Who keeps track of every detail in their lives, whether they are home or not? You have no concept of what it's like to be on call twenty-four hours a day."

Bob stood and finished his beer. "Who's on call for you when you're drinking at the club?"

Karen transferred the spoon from the stove top to Bob's hand. "I don't know. But you're on call now. The recipe is on the counter." Karen left the room and ran up the stairs. She jogged down the hall to their bedroom and loudly shut the door behind her.

"What's all the noise?" Bob, still standing in the middle of the kitchen holding the wooden spoon, saw Robert standing in the kitchen doorway.

"Hey, pal. Come on over here."

Robert hugged his dad. "Is Mommy okay?"

"She is. She's just tired."

"She's tired a lot."

"Yes, she's busy. Want to help me with this chicken?"

"Why are you cooking?"

"Most of the great chefs in the world are men, my friend."

"Yeah, but you're not one of them." Rebecca had walked into the room. He smiled at her and was met with a blank look.

"How hard can it be?"

Rebecca walked to the counter and looked at the recipe. "This has seventeen ingredients."

Bob turned off the stove. "Let's get takeout."

Karen booked Jamie weeks in advance for the evening of the winter dance at the River Club, as well as salon appointments for her hair and nails the afternoon of the event. Two weeks prior to the dance, she set aside an entire day to shop for a dress. Bob gave her an absolute limit of five hundred dollars; Karen doubled that figure as her true limit. She asked Sarah to shop with her because she didn't want to go alone and she didn't want to go with Caroline, who had no limits. Plus, Sarah knew the difference between divine and disaster. Sarah declined, but told Karen to go for classy over trashy, traditional over trendy, and subtle over ostentatious. Avoid whatever the saleswomen are touting as "the new black." There is no black, she told Karen over the phone, except black.

Karen drove to the Oak Run mall alone, even though her mother offered to clear her calendar to go with her. Karen had seen a lot of Shelley over the holiday weekends, and the memories were still fresh: of being asked to wrap the gifts from Shelley and Phil to her children because her mother had been busy in December with ladies' luncheons and cookie swaps; of hearing several times a day— including right after everyone at the dinner table had just tasted their first forkful of the Christmas trifle Karen had spent hours preparing—how anxious Shelley was to start her post-holiday diet; of watching her leap up from the couch whenever one of Karen's brothers requested another cup of coffee, or, in the evenings, another beer in one of Phil's frosted mugs. Kevin and Kyle were twenty-six and living on their own, but whenever they came home, Shelley treated them like Generation Y sovereigns. Along these lines, Karen suspected her mother would try to dress her like a seventeen-year-old bound for the high school prom rather than the wife of a very successful executive attending a posh adult dinner dance. Women who showed too much cleavage, Shelley had said more than once over the years, had self-esteem issues.

The first boutique Caroline had suggested Karen try was Some Enchanted Evening. Dozens of formal gowns, attractively displayed by color and style on shiny brass racks, greeted Karen as she walked in the door, as did the all-business saleswoman, who promptly instructed Karen to wait for her in the dressing room. There, she took Karen's measurements, told her to wrap herself in the freshly laundered terry-cloth robe that hung on the back of the door, and then disappeared, after promising to return with an assortment of gowns that would fit Karen's specifications. None of the gowns she produced was right—too young, too frilly, too tailored. Discouraged and disappointed that she had set aside just one day to find a dress, Karen asked if there was anything else. The owner of the shop, who had been doing paperwork at the front counter and listening to the exchange between her employee and Karen, approached with three dresses she had just unpacked from a shipment from New York. "Try all three. But I think this one," she said, holding a long black slip dress made of satin, "is the one." When Karen first saw her image in the full-length mirror, her thoughts raced to another era, backward in time. She looked like a singer who had just taken the stage in a crowded nightclub, with everyone's eyes on her, all of them smoking cigarettes and sipping cocktails but otherwise silent, waiting for her to part her lips in song. "We have the right shoes for you," said the owner. "And we have a variety of cashmere shawls. I would suggest a sea green— something to match your eyes and offset your magnificent hair."

Forty minutes later, Karen had spent just under a thousand dollars on everything the owner suggested, including a tiny gold clutch. Once Bob saw her in the dress—and she would not show him until the night of the dance—he would not ask her about the cost. And Karen was right. On the way to the dance, he told her she had never looked more beautiful. At the club, he hopped out and strode around the car proudly to open the door for her. When she emerged, the valet parking attendant grinned broadly. "Good evening, ma'am."

"Easy, pal," said Bob, smiling at the young man and handing him a ten-dollar bill. "She's with me."

"And what a fortunate man you are, sir."

"Yes," said Bob, holding his arm out for Karen. "More than I know."

"You're sweet," said Karen.

Bob kissed her cheek. "You're stunning."

They walked through the heavy glass doors etched with the letters *R* and *C,* down the carpeted hallway, and into the large reception area, alive with conversation between men dressed in tuxedos and women dressed in black, winter white, and every color in between. Everyone talked animatedly, their conversations punctuated with nodding heads and laughter. They were all *on,* like extras in a party scene on a movie set. Karen's heart fluttered with excitement as she and Bob made their way through the crowd. Several men winked at her as she passed by, their approving glances fortifying her knowledge that she looked as good as she felt. She imagined that the dapper club manager, Ron Childs, announced a spontaneous contest for the prettiest woman in the room, and all the men surrounding Karen had just urged her to enter. Deeper in, servers dressed in pressed black pants and crisp white jackets carrying trays of champagne and hot hors d'oeuvres circulated among the guests. Bob took two glasses when offered and handed one to Karen. "To incredible evenings," he said, raising his glass. Karen clinked hers against his and took her first sip. This was often the best part of an event for her, when the evening's festivities were ahead of them, when her anticipation was at a crescendo.

"Karen!" Karen turned and saw Stephanie, wearing a pale pink sequined gown with a white shawl, walking toward her. "Hello," she said in a breathy voice. "This is quite a crowd." Bob smiled at her. "Stephanie Jennings," she said, holding out her hand.

Bob wrapped his hand around hers and shook it gently. "Hi," he said. "I'm Bob. It's nice to finally meet you after hearing so much about the tennis group from Karen."

"And you as well," she said, then turned to the man beside her. "This is my husband, Patrick. Patrick, this is Karen Parsons, my tennis friend, and her husband, Bob."

"Nice to meet you," said Patrick, shaking both of their hands.

"Fabulous dress," said Stephanie. "You look like a naughty nanny."

"Is that good?" asked Karen, smiling.

"Oh yes. On nights like this, naughty is always nice."

Patrick grabbed two champagne glasses from a passing tray.

"How long have you been here?" asked Karen.

"About twenty minutes," said Stephanie, taking a glass from her husband. "Long enough for one of these."

"Have you seen Ginny or Caroline?"

"Not yet," said Stephanie. "Let's head into the dining room. They may be in there. Plus, we can grab a table."

Bob and Karen followed Stephanie and Patrick through the throng and into the spacious dining room, where twenty tables for eight surrounded a section kept clear for dancing. A dozen miniature red roses and sprigs of baby's breath sat in crystal bowls at the center of the tables, which were covered with ironed white linen, royal blue cloth napkins, white china plates rimmed in gold, burnished silverware, and wineglasses.

"We want to be as far away from the band as possible," said Stephanie, leading the others to the far corner of the room. "Last year, once they got going, you couldn't hear yourself think." When they reached table nineteen, Stephanie took eight cards from her tiny evening bag. On each one was printed the word RESERVED. Smiling, Stephanie placed one on each dinner plate. "There," she said. "That ought to do it."

"Where did you get those?" asked Patrick.

"I made them on the computer. Caroline told me this was the only way to hold a table."

Patrick turned to Bob. "Do you golf?"

"I'd like to. But I'll need lessons."

"Burt Sanders, the pro, is excellent," said Patrick. "If he can teach me, he can teach anyone. Word has it he's played with Tiger Woods—and won. Call soon though. The after-work lesson times fill quickly."

"Let's head back to the other room," said Stephanie. "Maybe the others have arrived." The cocktail area was even more crowded than before. At five-foot-seven, Karen couldn't see farther than three people in any direction. Stephanie, two inches taller than Karen, stood on her tiptoes to scan the room. "There they are," she said, pointing, "over by the windows." On the way, Stephanie grabbed another glass of champagne from a server's tray. Karen abstained, knowing that if she didn't put something other than a toast point smeared with caviar in her stomach before having another drink, she might say or do something she'd have to apologize for later.

"Where have you been?" asked Caroline, as soon as they reached her. "We've been looking all over for you."

"In the dining room getting a table," said Stephanie. "You know what a mob scene that is."

"Good thinking, honey," said Caroline, striking a pose.

She was wearing a lacy, flesh-colored dress with a neckline that ran between her breasts and halfway to her belly button, wowing everyone's husband—as well as their wives—except her own, Rick, who must have done his ogling at home. Besides Rick, the only one not looking at her chest was Caroline, who was surveying the crowd with a self-satisfied smile on her face. Bob pulled his gaze up to Caroline's face when Karen introduced them. And he looked at Ginny and Brad Lee and Rick when he shook their hands. But as soon as the introductions were done and the chatter began, he looked back at Caroline's round breasts. Bob found himself wishing for a power failure or a frozen moment in time, when his hands could do what his mind was thinking. Karen put her arm around Bob's back, an unusual gesture. He smiled at her, knowing the point she was making. And he was happy to oblige, for the moment; there would be ample opportunity to look at Caroline throughout the evening. It was what she wanted, after all. Women didn't wear clothing like that to blend in.

When they walked back through the crowd to the dining room, Bob followed Caroline. Her clingy dress showed the curve of her trim waist and the outline of her pear-shaped ass. It was uncanny, really, that a woman could dress this way outside of her home. It was like she was naked, only better, because whatever flaws might exist from bearing children or last night's bowl of ice cream were hidden beneath the stretchy lace. Bob willed her to turn and face him, wished for the rest of the people in the room to disappear. He could see she'd be a willing partner, guiding his hands with hers.

He could tell simply by looking at a woman whether or not she liked it, and Caroline was as hot as her dress. At the table, Karen sat down, and Bob sat next to her. When Caroline sat next to Bob, his groin warmed. He ran his hands through his hair, a nervous habit, then smiled at her. "Tell me about yourself," he said. "What do you do besides play a pretty good game of tennis?"

Caroline laughed. "I do a lot of things." She lifted her champagne glass to her lips and gave him a weighty look over the rim.

"I'll bet."

"And what about you? I hear you're an important person, in addition to being incredibly attractive."

"Important?"

"Word has it you practically run Forester."

Bob laughed. "There are people who would take exception to that."

"Like who?"

"My boss, for one."

"Do you want to dance, honey?" Bob turned and found Karen looking at him. He had been unaware of the music, which was suddenly very obvious.

"Sure," he said, getting up and offering her his hand.

They walked to the dance floor just as the band switched to a slow song. Bob pulled Karen close to him, and, smelling her hair, wrapped his arm around her back and led her in small circles around the dance floor. "Are you having fun?" she asked.

"I am. And you?"

"I am. What do you think of Caroline's dress?" Bob pulled slightly away from his wife and looked at her. "Would you like it as much on a hanger as you do on her?"

"Okay," he said, nodding his head. "I hear you."

"Ginny told me that last year, she fell all over Brad. You seem to be her target this year."

"What do you mean?"

"Apparently Caroline had enough to drink last year that she actually propositioned Brad, who had almost enough drink in him to accept her offer. Ginny didn't talk to Caroline for two months."

Bob felt sweaty. "You don't need to feel foolish. Apparently she does it to all the men, and most of them, like you, are taken in by it."

Bob kissed Karen's forehead. "I'm sorry."

"I'm glad." Bob pulled Karen closer, and she looked up at him. "Because anything she can do I can do better."

Bob's eyes widened. "Let's leave now."

Karen smiled at him. "Later," she said, leading him off the dance floor. "We have all night."

Bob behaved the rest of the evening. He switched to water after dinner and chatted with Caroline's husband, Rick, a surgeon, who had reconstructed three Achilles tendons in the last week, an operation he hadn't performed in more than five years. Injuries, he found, were often cyclical. He did knee surgery most often because it was an injury happening to younger and younger people. Many of his patients were teenagers who blew their knees out skateboarding or playing soccer. They recovered quickly, but he was uncertain about the long-term effects. No one would know the true success rate until the teenagers were forty. And by then, he hoped to be close to retirement and more concerned with his portfolio than his patients. After dinner, all the couples danced. They switched partners several times, and Bob soon enough found himself dancing with Caroline. She hung on him, not so much like a woman on the prowl as a woman who had consumed two or three too many glasses of champagne. She wrapped her arms around his neck and held on as they moved around the floor. At the end of the dance, Bob deposited her into Rick's arms and found his wife. "Let's get out of here," he said. They said good-bye to the others and drove home. Bob quickly drove Jamie to the other end of the street and then rushed back to his wife. He encircled her waist with his arm and led her up the stairs to their bedroom. He locked the door behind them. He slowly removed his jacket and tie and her shawl and draped them over the armchair that routinely hosted a stack of folded laundry instead of someone with a book. Making eye contact with his wife, he unbuttoned his shirt. She stepped closer to him, running her fingers through his chest hair as he unbuttoned her dress. She stepped out of it and stood before him wearing nothing but lacy panties and heels. "Keep the shoes on," he whispered. She laughed, then turned and strutted to their bed. Bob followed closely behind her. They had eager sex; only once did Bob think about Caroline.

CHAPTER 1 2

Right after Memorial Day, Print&Pack, one of Forester's largest customers, declared its intention of switching its business to one of Forester's largest competitors. Tim Reynolds, Forester's president, handed Bob the assignment Tuesday morning and expected him to be on a plane that afternoon. On the way to the airport, Bob was able to book a breakfast meeting with Print&Pack president Carl Hoten, who talked in a constrained manner on the phone, even though he had told Tim he was open to persuasion. Bob spent most of the evening in his hotel room planning his presentation, not an easy task even with a long lead time but especially frustrating since key pieces of information were missing from the Print&Pack paper file, including current orders and price lists. Bob accessed the electronic files on Forester's intranet, but they, too, were spotty. He had met Carl face-to-face twice, but had not talked to him in recent years and was not current with Print&Pack's latest profile and strategy sheets. Billy was their contact—a role that had been questioned several times in meetings that spring—but he was on vacation, inaccessible by e-mail and voice mail, company cell phone turned off. Looking through the paper file, Bob took notes, trying to piece together several possible solutions, ranging from poor to passable. He also made a mental note to talk to Billy. If he didn't straighten up soon, he would lose his job. Then again, if Forester lost Print&Pack's business, Tim would fire Billy *and* Bob without reservation. Tim was neither diplomatic nor apologetic about his policies or his business model. The only reason Billy hadn't been fired already was that Tim had been focused lately on customer growth rather than stewardship.

Bob went to bed late and slept poorly. His first night in a hotel was always that way. When he was younger, he'd have a couple of beers from his mini-fridge before he went to bed. It had become a habit more than a remedy, however, so Bob had in the last year or so switched to Oreos and milk, a comfort snack from his childhood. Because it seemed juvenile, Bob procured his sleep aid at a convenience store outside the hotel rather than order from room service. And it really did help him sleep—unless he faced an especially stressful meeting the next day. He lay awake a good part of the night, thinking about what would convince Carl to reinvest his business in Forester. At the very least, Bob would have to promise him a new sales rep, which could potentially hold the same fate for Billy as the company's losing the Print&Pack account.

The meeting the next morning went smoothly enough for Carl to call a meeting that afternoon with his executive staff. Bob went back to the hotel afterward to work on his presentation to the group. He then went for a run, showered, and was back at Print&Pack's head office twenty minutes ahead of his three o'clock appointment. For two hours, Bob ran through numbers and percentages and answered questions with the clear, crisp PowerPoint slides he made earlier in the day. He guaranteed what he knew Forester could deliver, being careful not to make promises Forester couldn't support. Carl nodded his head throughout Bob's talk, an affirming gesture indicating that if Bob had done the numbers right, Carl couldn't say no. Knowing that customer service was also an issue, Bob said he would personally handle the account for six months.

Carl asked his staff to sleep on it, something he was known for in the industry, and to come to work the next day prepared to make and support a decision. The staff met the following morning and called Bob in that afternoon. Carl asked the additional questions his team compiled; Bob thought he was able to respond to them satisfactorily. Afterward, Bob waited in Carl's office while the staff voted in the board room. Thirty minutes later, Bob was called in: Given the new terms of the contract, Print&Pack would stay with Forester. If, however, Print&Pack was not satisfied at any time during the first three months, a probationary period, the contract would be null and void. Bob shook Carl's hand. "I appreciate this. I will not let you down."

"It's not you I worry about." Carl gave Bob a weak smile. "Keep in touch."

"Absolutely."

On the way back to the hotel, Bob called Tim Reynolds and gave him the details of the contract. Tim said he was impressed, a word he rarely used, and said he would put his appreciation in the form of a commission check. Feeling oddly magnanimous, Bob told him that wasn't necessary, but Tim told him it most assuredly was. "Our business," he said, "is about service, product, and making money. When you take care of the first two as aptly as you did with Print&Pack, the third will always follow, on both corporate and personal levels." Bob finally allowed himself a smile. Karen would be happy with the news.

Bob slept on the flight home. Normally he was too keyed up to close his eyes. But this week he counted as one of the five most intense weeks in his life, in company with final exams his senior year in college, getting married, and closing the Parker deal in 2000. On the drive home from the airport, Bob designed the perfect evening. He wanted to have a drink with Karen. He had some Stella and Karen's favorite Chardonnay in the fridge. Rebecca and Robert would then join them for a quiet family dinner. If Karen had nothing planned, he would simply grill hamburgers from the freezer. Robert could help him. After dinner, they could all watch TV for a while—Bob would even watch a kid movie—and turn in early. Bob was hoping he could persuade Karen to have sex before falling asleep. A quiet, predictable evening was what Bob craved, like a man hungry from physical labor wants red meat after a long shift.

Karen was not home when he walked through the back door into the kitchen. Bob found Rebecca in the den watching TV. She allowed a kiss on her cheek, but didn't take her eyes off the screen when Bob asked her about Karen. Rebecca told him that Karen was at the store picking up a few items for tonight and that she, Rebecca, was the boss of Robert.

"What's for dinner?"

"Company," said Rebecca, clicking through the stations.

"You're kidding."

"I wish. The Jenningses, Millers, and Lees are coming at seven. I have to babysit because Mommy needs some adult time."

"Where is Robert?"

"In the basement, playing with those idiotic cars of his."

"They're metal toys. They have no personalities, Rebecca."

"I think they're stupid."

Bob walked down the stairs and found Robert sitting on the floor in front of the large screen TV. "How's my little man?"

Robert smiled broadly at his father. "Hi, Dad," he said, looking up from the town he had made with Lego blocks. Several Hot Wheels cars were lined up at the dealership, a red rectangular building with yellow windows and a blue roof that he had completed the week before. Robertville had been experiencing an economic boom, and Bob's Cars was the latest addition and the town's largest employer. Robert had recently studied small town economics in social studies class, a nice complement, Bob thought, to the previous unit on manufacturing. "Did you have a good trip?"

"I had an excellent trip. And aren't you nice to ask." Bob heard Karen coming into the house and headed back to the stairs. "I'm off to see your mom," he said as he ascended. When he walked into the kitchen, Karen was unpacking two grocery bags.

Karen turned around and smiled. "Can you do a beef filet on the grill?"

"Do I have to?" asked Bob, walking to her and putting his arms around her shoulders. "Can we just call the whole thing off? I have had a hellish week, and I would like nothing better than to be with my family tonight."

"Honey, we've got six people coming for dinner in forty-five minutes."

"Why? It's a Thursday night." Bob's arms dropped to his sides.

"You said nothing about this last night on the phone, and frankly, Karen, I'm not in the mood to entertain."

"It was an impromptu thing," she said, folding the paper grocery bags, "at tennis this morning."

"Didn't we just see the Millers, Jenningses, and Lees last weekend?"

"Like I said, this was spur of the moment."

"Well, here's an idea. Let's cancel it, spur of the moment."

Karen stashed the bags in food pantry, where she grabbed two boxes of wild rice. "I can't do that."

"I'll do it," said Bob, walking to the phone.

"Bob, that's rude!"

"It's not that rude. I'll take the blame. I'll tell them I'm exhausted. They'll understand."

"They won't understand," said Karen, hands on hips. "I don't understand."

"Karen, we see these people all the time, and that's fine. They're nice enough people. But I, unlike you, can breathe without them. I worked hard all week, and I'd like to spend a quiet evening with my wife and kids."

"Since when do you want to spend time with your kids?"

"Since when do you have to get drunk Thursday nights, in addition to Friday and Saturday?"

Anger flashed in Karen's eyes. "That was mean, Bob Parsons."

"Yeah, well so was your comment."

Karen rubbed her temples. "Can't we just leave the night the way it is? I thought you'd like to come home to a party."

"I don't think that's the way it happened. I think you planned the party without any thought about me whatsoever."

"Please?"

Bob considered his position and knew if he played it just right, he could have at least part of the night go his way. "I want them out of here by nine thirty. It's a Thursday, and everyone ought to understand that. If they don't, I'll explain it to them. And I want you to watch what you drink. I have plans for you later."

"Done," she said. "Now go take a shower while I start this rice."

* * *

When Patrick Jennings walked through the front door with four Cuban cigars in one hand and a bottle of brandy in the other, Bob wanted to immediately usher him out the back door. Instead, he patted him on the shoulder as he always did, kissed Stephanie on the cheek, and made both of them vodka martinis. The Millers and the Lees arrived together, Ginny carrying a lemon meringue pie and Caroline toting two bottles of red wine. Karen put Ginny's dessert in the fridge, while Bob opened both of Caroline's bottles per her instructions. The first martinis were consumed while Patrick told a long story about a lawyer friend who had smuggled the cigars into the country. Apparently, his Gucci loafers attracted airport security's attention. He was frisked twice by custom officials before being led, along with his carry-on luggage, into a small room for questioning. What was his business in Cuba? How long had he been there? Did he plan on returning? How much cash did he have on him? The lawyer counted his cash while the official searched his bag. "Three thousand U.S. dollars," he said. And the official told him that he was in luck, that three thousand dollars was the exact amount needed to exit the country without further interrogation. The cigars, which were in his wife's luggage, were never found. She had been led to a separate room, where she was lightly questioned and allowed to smoke cigarettes while she waited for her husband. Their luggage was sequestered for a week. When it did arrive in the States, the lawyer's bag, taped shut, was missing his other pair of Italian shoes, and the wife's bag was missing her French underwear. But the cigars were inside and intact.

Caroline begged for another round of martinis, and Bob obligingly made them. She followed him into the kitchen, pressed her soft flesh into his, and whispered, "I'd like a large" in his ear. When he stopped the vodka shaker midair and looked at her, she winked and then returned to the porch, where Karen had insisted they move to smoke. Bob lit the grill at seven thirty, but by the time dinner was ready it was almost an hour later, and they had already drunk one of the Millers' bottles of red. Patrick told more lawyer stories, his bailiwick at social gatherings—the best one involving a filthy rich stockbroker who had an insatiable appetite for young women. Night after night he was out, and his wife grew suspicious enough to pay for the installation of listening devices and video cameras in their home and in his cushy Wall Street office. His assignation with a buxom blonde the very next day was recorded and sent to the wife. After she took the evidence to her divorce lawyer, who calculated her settlement, as well as his, to be in the millions of dollars, the wife confronted her husband.

"Do you know what he said?" asked Patrick, buttering a crescent roll.

"What?" asked Karen, already snickering.

"It Wasn't Me!" And then he launched into the refrain of Shaggy's hit from a few years before.

Caroline threw her head back, reveling in her amusement. "That," she said, snapping her head back into its upright position, "is ridiculous!"

"I think it's disgusting."

"Who said that?" asked Karen, turning her head.

"I did." Rebecca was standing in the doorway with her arms across her chest.

"Honey," said Karen, struggling to get out of her chair.

"Careful, Mom. It looks like you might fall down."

Blushing, Karen looked at her guests.

"That's enough, Rebecca," said Bob, also standing.

"I think it's you who's had enough," said Rebecca, turning and walking away. "All of you!"

Karen rushed after her daughter, leaving her friends with no choice but to quickly finish their dinners and proclaim themselves too full for Ginny's pie.

"Well," said Bob a few minutes later. "Let's call it a night then."

"Good thinking," said Patrick, happy to be released from his discomfort and from the silence that had just been broken by Bob's dismissal. "Let's go, Steph."

Ginny helped Bob clear the table before joining the others outside. Bob called good night from the front door and then returned to the kitchen, where he assessed the cleanup process as likely to take forty-five minutes. He thought about joining Karen upstairs, but decided she would rather have his help in the kitchen. She hated a sink full of dishes covered in cold water and congealed fat.

Plus, she had done, as usual, all the prep work, everything but cook the meat. He loaded the dishwasher and then hand washed the crystal glasses they had received as a wedding gift from Bob's parents, carefully inverting them on a tea towel he laid out on the kitchen table. He washed and dried the food-caked pots and pans in the sink, packaged and put away the leftovers, wiped down the counters, and swept the kitchen floor. An hour later, everything was done except grabbing the used table linens on his way to bed. At the top of the stairs, the door to Rebecca's room was closed. Bob knocked and got no answer. He opened the door to find a dark room and his child, who he had lately suspected of faking sleep when he got home late from a business trip and entered her room to say good night, motionless in the center of her bed. She liked to sleep in the very center so whatever monster was hatched underneath her bed in the middle of the night had a longer distance to travel to get her. Often, but not that night, she surrounded herself with stuffed animals in the hopes that the monster's stomach would get full before reaching her. She was very grown-up, but only in the daytime. Bob brushed away her light brown bangs with his fingers and kissed her forehead. He gently closed the door, then walked down the hall to his bedroom, dropping the napkins and tablecloth in the washing machine on his way. Karen was undressing in the closet.

"How did it go?" he asked.

"I thought you were going to come up and help me instead of letting me single-handedly deal with that embarrassing and awful situation," said Karen, focusing on the buttons of her blouse.

"Look," said Bob, sliding out of his shoes. "If you wanted my help, you could have come down and asked for it. I thought you wanted to be alone with Rebecca, so I got rid of our company and did the dishes. You're welcome."

"Next time, I'll do the dishes, like I always do, and you can deal with our rude ten-year-old," said Karen, slipping her new printed cotton nightshirt over her head.

"Fine," said Bob, dropping his khakis.

"Don't even think about it," said Karen, walking past him and into the bathroom to brush her teeth.

"Think about what? How we had a deal and you got drunk instead?"

"You're not exactly sober either, mister."

"It was your party, with your insipid friends," said Bob, removing the folded laundry from their bedroom chair, so he could sit and take his pants off the rest of the way.

"Who forced you to drink, right?" asked Karen, spitting toothpaste foam into the sink.

"In some ways, yes. What are you supposed to say to a blowhard with Cuban cigars and a bottle of brandy and a floozy with a couple of bottles of red?"

"Nice thing to say about your friends." Karen got into bed and pulled the lightweight comforter to her chin, even though the temperature was in the seventies.

"They're not my friends. They're your friends and their husbands. We see them almost every weekend, and now, it appears, we need to be with them during the week, too. I'm sick of them. And I'm sick of how you act when you're with them."

"Oh, and how do I act?" asked Karen, leaning against the two pillows on her side of the bed.

"Like them," said Bob. "Like a woman who has no ambition, nothing better to do in her life than play tennis, lunch at the country club, and drink too much at night."

"Tonight I drank too much, as did you. And yes, I'll do whatever I please. I've paid my dues."

"Is that what raising children is called now, dues paying?" said Bob, pulling his shirt over his head. "Does that mean, now that you've paid your dues, you're released from spending any time with them? Are you now free, Karen?"

"At least one of us has spent time with them," spat Karen. "You were desperate to have them until they were actually born."

"Hey, someone's got to make the money to feed your country club appetite."

"It was your idea to join that club," shouted Karen. "You can't pin everything on me!"

"Then how about this one," yelled Bob back, pants still around his ankles. "What the hell are you doing with your life?"

"Exactly what I want to be doing!"

"And that," said Bob, pointing his right index finger at his wife, "is not the woman I married."

"What the hell is that supposed to mean?"

Bob put his pounding head in his hands. "You used to be a good mother," he said, his voice volume lowered to its normal level, resigned.

"Because I had a ball and chain around my ankle and never left the house? Because I shopped for our food, made our meals, cleaned the house, and spent every moment I had with the children? Is that what made me a good mother?"

"Partly, Karen, yes." Bob lifted his head and looked at his wife. "But it was more than that. You watched over them so carefully. I knew nothing would happen to Rebecca and Robert because you cared so deeply about them."

"And I don't now?"

"I don't know. Do you?"

"I can't believe you even have to ask that."

"You seem to spend time with anyone but them."

"That's because for so many years, I couldn't," said Karen. "I felt like I didn't exist without them next to me, Bob. And now I have this time to myself, and it's unbelievably good."

"Your freedom," said Bob, flatly.

"I know it's a big joke to you, Bob. But that's only because you've never been denied it."

"Karen, you were always free to do what you wanted to do. There's day care. There are babysitters. There's your mother. You chose to stay home because you felt too guilty to leave them."

"Don't you dare disqualify that as a valid emotion."

"Fine," said Bob. "So you finally have this freedom, Karen. What the hell are you going to do with it other than fool around with foolish women? When I talk about your not being the motivated woman I married, that's what I'm talking about."

"And what about the man I married?" asked Karen. "What about the considerate gentleman who put my needs and wants above his? He disappeared at the wedding reception."

"That's not fair."

"It's as fair as you're being with me. Life changes us, and don't for one minute think you're exempt."

Bob removed his pants and stood. He walked to the bed and grabbed his pillow and the blanket folded at the foot. He turned away from his wife.

"Where are you going?"

"Somewhere else."

Karen turned off her bedside light, ending the conversation, ending the night.

Bob left the following week for a ten-day business trip in Ohio and Indiana, so Karen was alone again with Rebecca and Robert, who were lethargic and bored, even though it was the first week of summer. The Keyworths were out of town, spending a week with Vincent's parents on Cape Cod. Caroline and Ginny went to the club pool every day and had several times asked Karen and the kids to join them, but Rebecca each time had declared that she wasn't in the mood for the Millers and the Lees, meaning she was still holding a grudge from the dinner party the week before. Karen suggested they ask school friends to the house, but both Rebecca and Robert declined. They barely wanted to go outside, even though there had been a string of sunny, seventy-five-degree days. Rebecca wanted to hang out in her room, and Robert wanted to play and watch TV in the basement, and Karen quickly realized she hadn't signed them up for enough summer activities. Rebecca was going to an art day camp for two weeks in August, and Robert was scheduled to spend four weeks' worth of July mornings at the club's sports camp, but that was it. Maybe she could find something at the YMCA in town? While Karen rooted through their paper recycling bucket for the Y summer program guide, she wondered if she could find activities for the kids at the same time as her women's doubles group at the club. She had already booked Jamie three afternoons a week, but maybe she could pare it down. While Jamie was a good sitter, Rebecca needed more than Jamie's craft box, neighborhood nature walks, and preteen novels to fill her summer days. Karen found the guide and flipped through it, marking several options. She would ask Rebecca at lunch and then call the Y afterward.

While her languorous children idled away their first week of summer vacation, Karen cleaned out and reorganized her kitchen drawers, and put away the winter hats, boots, mittens, and coats she had been meaning to deal with since the end of April. She sorted the toys, CDs, books, and magazines that lay on the playroom floor, cleaned out Robert's toy box, and reorganized his closet. She cleaned the basement, which she had to do periodically because she didn't want to pay Shine Time another thirty dollars to do it biweekly. She washed and ironed all the curtains in the house. And when Rebecca protested about Karen's tidying up her room, Karen instead baked four-dozen cookies, a coffeecake, and the lemon cheesecake Bob loved. By lunchtime on Friday, she needed a break. She nudged the kids away from their solitary activities with a trip to McDonald's and Dairy Queen. When they got back to the house, there was a message on the answering machine from Sarah, who was back in town. Vincent had stayed on for the weekend at his parents' cottage, and she wondered if Bob was traveling. Karen picked up the phone immediately, inviting them for a late afternoon playtime and dinner. Rebecca and Robert finally showed some enthusiasm.

Weeks had passed since Karen and Sarah had seen each other, which was becoming the new normal. They had run into one another at the local mall, where Karen was looking for a new tennis outfit, and Sarah had just purchased raincoats for her kids. The two women talked, briefly, before Karen broke it off, saying she had to run to Target to get underwear and socks for Rebecca and Robert before rushing home for the bus. In truth, Karen didn't have to get socks and underwear; she just felt guilty about appearing completely focused on herself in the presence of someone who was usually focused on someone else. It had become easier for Karen to talk with Caroline, Ginny, and Stephanie because they used the words *I* and *me* as much as she did. Whenever she did get together with Sarah, Karen was fulfilled by the friendship, but she was also challenged by it, enough so that it was easy to let the weight of it drop. They were both busy, Karen with her new friends, and Sarah at the elementary school and in college classes, handy excuses. But they both knew it was more than that.

Feeling nostalgic for what they had once shared, Karen was pleased Sarah had called. And she was equally pleased that even though it was a weekend, Sarah's request didn't involve the husbands. Karen didn't like Vincent, even though she had only met him once, at a benefit for the hospital almost three years ago. He was well over six feet tall, with dark hair and dark eyes, and long fingers with trimmed nails. When he spoke to Karen, he was condescending in his tone and in his manner, she thought, using his height to further inflate his dominant position. It was his research he talked about, rather than her friendship with his wife, whom he didn't mention. Nonetheless, Karen had decided to push through her initial reaction and invite the Keyworths for dinner, adults only, so they could get to know one another better. And Sarah declined, saying Vincent wasn't social. Karen accepted this explanation, even though it took her a while to understand it. Vincent was unlike most men Karen encountered, who seemed to enjoy, prolong even, their conversations with her. Vincent had been indifferent to Karen's looks and social graces, making it easy for her to dismiss the Keyworths as couple friends. Back then, Karen wasn't doing much entertaining anyway. She had been so busy with Robert and running the household that she rarely hosted anyone other than family. By the time Karen was ready to invite couples to her house for dinner, she and Sarah didn't see as much of each other as they once had.

Sarah, Britney, and Jeremy arrived at four o'clock. Tired of her kids being in the house, Karen told them they had to be outside until dinner. While Rebecca and Robert initially protested, they were all soon settled in the backyard, the boys with giant bubble wands and the girls with beach chairs and drawing pads. Rebecca had taken an interest in drawing after her art teacher at school told her she had potential. And while her sketches of people were somewhat cartoon-like, her still-life drawings were recognizable and realistic. Sarah and Karen parked themselves on the porch with a pitcher of iced tea and a plate of cookies, and caught each other up on what had been going on in their respective lives.

Sarah, having volunteered in both of her kids' classrooms throughout the year, was as happy as Britney and Jeremy that school was out for the summer. And yet she had enjoyed being in the school and experiencing firsthand what was going on in the classrooms. As soon as the teachers discovered she was a reliable and able volunteer, they entrusted her with more responsibility and more interesting work. Photocopying and recess duty were mandatory tasks assigned by most teachers, but Sarah was also often asked to teach a short lesson while the teacher caught up on prep work. Plus, they confided in her. They sought her opinion, as an outsider peeking in. She never would have known otherwise about the school's inefficiencies, both procedural and managerial, or about the inherent strength of the teachers in spite of what came down from the top. The gossip and politics surprised Sarah at first, but then became routine, a source of derision, as happens in offices and business settings everywhere.

When Sarah asked what Karen had been doing to occupy her time, Karen talked briefly about her tennis clinics, lunches at the club, and afternoons reading or napping on the couch. She had immersed herself in this new life, invested everything in her freedom, and yet when she talked about it with Sarah, it sounded much more frivolous than noble. Sarah met Karen's stories with a neutral expression, but Karen got defensive, like she usually did when she felt boxed in. She told Sarah, just like she habitually told Bob, that this year had been a well-deserved reward for taking care of the children. Sarah politely nodded her head in agreement, but Karen's feelings of guilt were not mollified by this gesture. Sarah had, after all, mothered her two children through the difficult years and chosen to spend as much time during the school year as she could with them while Karen had spent the year staying away from hers.

"Bob thinks I have no purpose to my life," Karen said, pouring more tea into their glasses.

Sarah took a cookie from the plate. "Is he right?"

Karen looked through the screen at the kids. "I don't know. Do I need a purpose?"

Sarah took a bite of her cookie. "I don't know. Do you?"

The tears surprised her; Karen had not cried in front of Bob for months. She had been angry enough, certainly, and frustrated enough to cry, but she had refused to do so, thinking he would use it against her. Crying, to him, was a tool women used to soften the resolute hearts of their spouses. He was sympathetic to Karen's crying only when he had deliberately hurt her, by his words or actions. But that sympathy had become jaded by his recent conviction that what he said or did was justified. Plus, if she had cried to Bob—instead of shouted at him—about her need to be freed from the demands of her own children, she would have had to admit her guilt. And she wasn't ready to do that, at least not with him.

Over time, the last school year especially, Karen had conditioned herself to absorb and compartmentalize her emotions, setting them free less spontaneously. She and Bob fought, but they fought less than they could have, each often choosing aloofness over anger. At one point during the year, just after Bob had received another promotion, making him busier than ever, Karen began to deeply rather than hastily question her love for him. It was over the course of a few weeks, when he was more out of town than in, that she had fantasized about being single, made a widow by a plane crash. She chastised herself for allowing these thoughts, but they had been real. Just about every word he said, the few days he was around, was about him: how he felt about something, how his career was going, how he envisioned their future. His words felt like sandpaper on tender skin, irritating, barely tolerable. Through her relationship with Ginny, Caroline, and Stephanie, Karen had been able to slowly discharge some of what she had been holding and hiding. They made it easy because they sometimes felt the same way about their husbands, especially Caroline. She bought things to help her feel better, and Karen had happily taken part. She had willingly made a break from her children and her husband and spent the last nine months convincing herself that she was entitled to her selfish behavior.

Sarah got up from her chair and hugged Karen. "I don't know what's wrong with me," Karen said, blotting her tears with her shirt sleeve.

"The same thing that's wrong with the rest of us," said Sarah, patting Karen's back. "Mothers are incredibly confused people."

Karen drew back from her friend. "You're not confused."

"Oh yes, I am. I may look like I have it together, but there are days I'd give it all up to live with a gorgeous, young French masseuse in Paris."

"You're kidding."

"I couldn't be more serious."

"And leave Vincent, Britney, and Jeremy behind?"

"Without a second look."

Karen took a sip of her tea. "Now that's impressive."

"Yeah," said Sarah, "in a really bad way."

Both women laughed. Karen blew her nose.

"Seriously though," Karen said. "Do you like the way you spend your time?"

"Well," said Sarah, taking another cookie. "I'd better. Starting in September, I'm going to start working in the school system as a teacher's aide."

"In middle school or elementary?"

"I'm going to stay at Butler with Jeremy. They are pretty short staffed, and Jeremy is more amenable to having me in his school than Britney is. She wants to do the middle school thing by herself, and I understand that," said Sarah. "It should be a pretty good job, actually. I'll be in school when the kids are in school, and I'll be home when they're home."

"You'll be there every day?"

"Every day."

Karen poured more tea. "What about your classes?"

"There are Saturday classes."

Karen took a sip from her glass. "What about errands?"

"Vincent and I will split them. If he wants me to work, he's going to have to pull his weight."

"Vincent wants you to work?"

Sarah sipped her tea. "We could use the money, Karen." She

looked out at the children in the yard. "Vincent makes a good salary, but we need to save more money for college, and, if Vincent has his way, graduate school for the children."

It was the first time Sarah had mentioned money. Caroline talked about it all the time, mostly in terms of not having enough. She had to "watch their pennies" because Rick balked at the credit card bills. And whatever expensive clothing Caroline bought she justified by "getting it on sale." It was as if she wanted to convince everyone around her that she did not have the abundance she routinely enjoyed. Stephanie, too, liked to pretend she was frugal and barely interested in material things. She often put down women with more money than she had, calling them the bitchy rich and making fun of their huge houses and expensive cars. And yet, she and Patrick, who planned on remaining childless for another three years, lived in a big four-bedroom house and drove SUVs. (Stephanie referred to her fully loaded Jeep as a truck.) She also downplayed their frequent travel as business trips to burdensome locations, but Karen suspected that six nights and five days in Los Angeles sounded good to anyone not going.

Karen admitted to herself that she, too, had become close friends with her credit cards. She took money out of the bank every week and often forgot to document it in the checkbook log—a habit Bob disdained, saying no one but Bill Gates could afford to ignore his finances. Karen ignored his admonishments. She spent whatever she wanted on whatever she wanted, buying things for herself and her children on a weekly basis. She no longer waited for birthdays, or Christmas, or anniversaries, or holidays, or special events of any kind. They had a lot of money in the bank, and Karen had always thought that there was nothing wrong with spending some of it, especially when Bob kept making more all the time. In the last year or so, she had bought new furniture for the living room, dining room, and playroom. She had a closet full of clothes and shoes and a jewelry box stuffed with silver, gold, and precious gems. And in the fall, she had plans to renovate the kitchen, with new cabinets, a hardwood floor, and taupe granite countertops. She had not once thought about what Sarah might or might not have, because Sarah had not mentioned it until now.

Looking back over the school year, Karen remembered that Sarah had declined a few shopping invites. In return, she had invited Karen to events that didn't cost money and involved the children: trips to the park or lunch at each other's houses. And Karen had put her off, telling her friend it wasn't a good day or that the kids were busy. Why would she sit in Sarah's drab kitchen when she could be grazing on a fresh salad at the club? Sarah had never said a word. "I'm sorry," said Karen, faltering. "I didn't know."

"It's not a big deal."

"It is a big deal. You've put up with me showing you all my new things all year long. I don't think I could have done that."

Sarah smiled. "Sure you could have. When your friends are happy, you're happy."

Karen shrugged. "You're amazing. I have no idea why I'm lucky enough to have you as a friend."

Sarah reached for a cookie. "I love talking with you, Karen. With you, I can express my opinion. I can offer advice. I can be open and honest, most of the time. These are not things I have at home."

"Meaning you cannot talk openly and honestly with Vincent?"

"Yes," said Sarah. "He comes from a very old-fashioned, traditional family. His father's word is the law. His mother does not speak much. And when she does, she is usually corrected. I thought Vincent might be different, more modern. And in some ways he is. But he does not encourage me to express my deep feelings or my opinions to him."

"I'm sorry." Karen was at a loss for what else to say.

Sarah smiled. "I'm used to it; it's okay—not perfect, of course, but okay. So, when I get together with you and can say anything that's on my mind, I'm thankful."

"As am I," said Karen, vowing to herself to spend more time with Sarah. "I would have no idea how to even live my life if it weren't for your sage advice."

Sarah laughed. "I think you'd muddle through."

Karen poured more tea into their glasses. "So, are you excited about your new job?"

"Very much so. It's so nice to use my brain again for something other than making spaghetti pie."

"I know what you mean. Sometimes I question whether I can think at all."

"And it will be good to get out of the house. I've been sitting around too long."

"You, my friend, don't ever sit down."

"I'm sitting now."

"Not for long." Karen stood. "You're on salad detail."

"Another brainless task for Sarah Keyworth."

"That," said Karen, walking into the kitchen, "is the story of my adult life."

CHAPTER 13

Karen checked her reflection in the mirror and decided her recently trimmed hair and freshly waxed eyebrows might help outsiders think she was more confident than she felt. She breathed in deeply and exhaled slowly—a yoga practice Sarah told her relieved surface stress instantly—hoping she could find a way to exude if not feel relaxation. She hadn't been this nervous since her labor with Rebecca, more than eleven years ago. She put the posts of the diamond stud earrings Bob had given her for her thirty-fifth birthday through her pierced earlobes and snapped the watch she had bought herself as a present onto her wrist. Checking it, she had thirty minutes to get downtown, park the car, and walk the three blocks to the brown brick building that held the advertising and administrative offices, newsroom, and printing press of the daily afternoon paper, *The Record.* She looked at herself again and removed a speck of dried mascara from her cheek.

It had been more than a year since her dinner with Sarah and their discussion about working. Sarah had made it through the school year as a teacher's aide and would return to school again in a week, in spite of the dismal pay and what she called *pond scum* status. She loved the hours, but had been wondering if she could find something that paid and made her feel better. She would give herself another year in the school system so she could finish her undergraduate degree. Then, she said, watch out! Every time Sarah talked about working, Karen thought about it. After all, hadn't she complained to Bob for years about not using her brain in a productive manner, about not being compensated and appreciated for her efforts? Yet, she had grown accustomed to her freedom and was reluctant now to relinquish it. If she got a job, even a part-time job, she would have to rearrange her schedule. She already knew she was unwilling to give up tennis, because she liked it, and she was a pretty good player at this point. She was also unwilling to sacrifice her social lunches out. She enjoyed seeing her friends and didn't want to swap the Patio Room with its salads, chilled wine, and linen napkins for an office staff room lit by flickering fluorescent lighting and Tupperware container lunches reheated in a food-splattered microwave.

The biggest reason for Karen's reluctance was that she didn't need, had never needed, financially to work. Bob made a pile of money. They had already put money away for Rebecca's and Robert's college educations, and they still had plenty. And she and Bob had discussed traveling, now that the kids were older and would appreciate it. Disney World over Christmas would be their first official family vacation. They had been here and there for weekend trips, but they agreed to wait until Robert was in third grade to do anything major. Nine-year-olds, Bob and Karen decided, were adequately equipped to stand in line and sleep away from home, to wait for tomorrow to come.

What convinced Karen to think seriously about working again was her experience at Clear Communication, remembering how much she craved the sense of accomplishment that came from finishing an assignment and the praise she often received from her boss and even sometimes from the customer. She remembered, too, the knowing, joking relationship she shared with her coworkers, the common ground they stood upon. In a small office, with everyone working toward the same goal, alliances formed quickly. Karen had a stake in the daily, weekly, and monthly output at Clear and the relevance and timeliness that appeared to fuel it.

And while Bob completely understood a sense of mission, he was surprised when Karen mentioned returning to work. The first words out of his mouth were hers, twisted: "What about your freedom?" Her primary duties, he said, were caring for the children and for the household. He wasn't sure she was capable of playing tennis, lunching out, running errands, getting the kids to activities, planning and preparing the meals, and then working part-time on top of that. She reminded him that he had many times told her that she could do whatever she wanted. And he acknowledged that he had said this—and that he still believed it—but emphasized that Karen was out of practice and wouldn't like some of the choices she might have to make. When she reminded him that Vincent Keyworth, Chauvinist of the Year, now helped with errands and other household chores because Sarah was working, Bob told her that was out of the question because of his travel schedule. She would have to carry the load. Could she commit fifteen hours a week to work and still get everything done? He consented to a probationary period of three months, which Karen thought was juvenile and controlling, but she said nothing. She did not need his blessing, but she also did not need another subject about which they would disagree. So she agreed that if she couldn't handle her household tasks along with those associated with the job, she'd quit.

Bob was hesitant to express too much excitement until the probationary period had come to an end, but he was inwardly pleased that Karen was motivated to work. He remembered when she worked for Jennifer, whose ability to instill self-confidence in young women could have earned her a spot on the local inspirational speakers' tour. Karen had talked Bob through the details of her most interesting projects, like she had talked to him in college about research papers and stimulating professors. That drive, that fascination with pursuing intellectual reward, had gone underground when the children were born. She had been a productive enough mother of babies—always getting the laundry done and dinner on the table—but she hadn't been happy. She viewed young motherhood as a burden rather than a blessing, and her resentment had boiled over into every aspect of their mutual life for many years.

And yet when Karen finally found some time, she wasn't sure what to do with it. Her wanting to work gave Bob hope that their marriage could return to its original state. But he managed his hope like he did his representatives and customers, so that he would remain in control.

Nick Fleming looked up from his computer and smiled when Karen was shown into his small office in the corner of the newsroom. He had thin blond hair that covered the collar of his shirt, warm brown eyes, and a tanned complexion that looked like the product of a week at the beach rather than a summer spent outdoors. Karen guessed he was about her age; the college diploma on the wall told her he was two years younger. Karen started the conversation by asking what a man from Brown University was doing editing a small town daily newspaper in mid-Michigan. He laughed. "I followed my wife," he said. "She grew up here and is now a physician here. We met when she was doing her internship in Providence and got married shortly thereafter. She's the family breadwinner, so I can do what I wish, which is sit in this tiny office every day and try to create a readable, interesting product."

"You do a good job."

They talked for an hour about the newspaper, the part-time feature-writing job Karen was applying for, and their commonalities, which included bike riding and ferrying kids to and from after-school activities. Nick had two jobs, really: newspaper editor from seven until three, and house chief, his words, from the moment he got home until the girls went to bed. Karen told him she was looking for the same setup, only less time at the office. Nick told her he had read her resume and writing samples and would get back to her within the week. Several other writers were applying for the position and, to be fair, he needed to see everyone before making a decision. Karen stood, shook his hand, and thanked him for his time. In the parking lot, she hesitated several minutes before starting her car's engine. What an inspirational man! Even though Karen guessed that Nick and his wife could well afford and provide space for a live-in caregiver, he was a father who liked to spend time with his girls. Dawn, their babysitter, arrived at six thirty each weekday to get Abby, eight, and Emily, six, out of bed, fed, and on the bus for school. She stayed afterward to clean the house and do whatever errands needed to be done, including the family grocery shopping, and clocked out at noon. Nick was home in time to get his daughters off the bus, oversee their afternoon activities, and prepare dinner. While he hated going to the grocery store, he greatly enjoyed creating meals in their kitchen, recently updated to his specifications. He had called it his favorite room in the house. Karen drove her car out of the newspaper parking lot. He worked all day and then cooked dinner!

His wife, Trisha, worked long hours, a phenomenon Karen was overly familiar with in her own spouse. Sometimes Trisha, like Bob, made it home by six thirty for dinner, but more often than not Trisha didn't get home until after seven. Karen had to admit, as she waited at a red light, that Bob had made a good effort over the summer to get home in time for dinner with Rebecca and Robert. Nick said Trisha liked to check the progress of her patients several times a day and it took time, just as Bob liked to keep on top of his sales-people and their customers. Trisha appeared to be unaware of time, which Nick said he found both frustrating and endearing. Whenever he was asked if he knew a good internist, he felt proud to recommend his wife as one of the best in the area.

Karen pulled into a convenience store for a gallon of milk. She, too, was proud of her spouse. Bob had risen quickly through the ranks at work. Of course, this was easier done by a man whose job topped his list of life priorities than by an involved father. Trisha, it seemed, was a member of the same driven tribe. And Karen wondered if this second-fiddle status troubled Nick as much as it bothered her. She could tell he deeply loved Abby and Emily, whose framed school pictures, not Trisha's, sat on his desk. He spoke so enthusiastically about their role in his happiness, yet Karen couldn't help but wonder if he had been resigned to his fate before he embraced it.

As promised, Nick called Karen three days later. They chatted for a few minutes before he offered her the job. If she accepted, she would be working three days a week, from eleven until three. The hard news reporters needed the computers in the morning, but most of them would be packed up by noon, so there would be three or four computers available. On busy days, Karen could do interviews or research for a couple of hours and write her stories afterward. The newsroom was always absolutely dead by one. The pay was terrible, but Nick said he suspected she knew this. He asked for a response in the next day or so, which Karen said she would deliver. As soon as she hung up, she called Bob. "I got the job!"

"No kidding," he said, swiveling his chair away from his computer screen to look out the window. "Tell me more."

"It's perfect," said Karen. "I can start next week. I work on Mondays, Wednesdays, and Fridays, which means I can still play tennis on Tuesdays and Thursdays. And I'll have time before I need to go to work to run errands. I can have school vacations off with the kids, with the exception of summer. So I'll have to work something out, but that's a long way off, and I'm sure by then I'll have thought of something. I'm so excited!"

Bob laughed. "I can hear that in your voice. It sounds like a great job to me, honey. Let's talk about it some more tonight over a drink. I've got to run to a meeting."

Karen hung up the phone and called Sarah. "I knew you'd get it," she said. "It's a perfect fit."

"You think so?"

"I do. Tell me everything."

Karen started with her boss, about how smart he was because he graduated from Brown, and about how wise he seemed because he knew the value of raising children. And because he was wise, he was very generous with vacation time, offering Karen the same days off during the school year as her children. She could even write at home if one of the kids got sick or there was some other reason she couldn't get to the office. She could e-mail her stories to Nick. "The pay stinks," she added.

"Join the club. I take my pay home in a change purse."

"But it's exciting, isn't it?"

"It is exciting," said Sarah. "It feels good to be working, to be engaged. I'm anxious to do more, as you know. But this works for now. And your job sounds like it works for you right now. We'll have to make time to get together after you start, so I can hear all about it."

Caroline was next on Karen's list. While the phone rang, Karen, cradling the phone between her neck and shoulder, took the peanut butter out of the cupboard and the jelly out of the fridge. Caroline, who habitually answered on the fourth ring, couldn't believe Karen's news. "I thought you were joking last week at lunch. You're going to work?"

"It's just three afternoons a week," said Karen, getting bread from the drawer. "You can't beat that."

Caroline laughed. "Sure you can—by not working at all."

Karen spread peanut butter on two slices of bread. "You don't ever want to work?"

"Why in the world would I want to work? I've got too many other things to do."

"Like what?" asked Karen, spreading the jelly on two other slices.

"Like anything I feel like. I wake up each day, lie in bed, and consider my choices. If I want to go shopping, I shop. If I want to play tennis, I play tennis. If I want to pull weeds in the garden, I do that. Plus, my working would drive Rick crazy."

"Why?"

"Because he, like most men, hasn't evolved much further than caveman status, Karen. Seriously? He thinks of himself as a mighty hunter or warrior who goes off to work every day, battles the outside world, wins, and thereby provides amply for his family. It would embarrass him if I wanted to work."

"You're kidding me," said Karen, putting the sandwiches on plastic plates.

"I'm not kidding you. If I wanted to work, it would be like telling him he's not good enough."

"Wow." Karen was surprised that Caroline would put up with anyone giving her directives.

"But it's a moot point anyway. I have no interest in working."

"You'll have to come see me at work, then. My boss is very cute."

"Really?"

She had Caroline's attention now. "Oh yes," Karen said, changing gears, having fun. "He's got gorgeous blond hair and milk chocolate eyes. He has broad shoulders and a wide chest that I'm betting is as smooth as the day he was born. His hands are big, and his palms are soft."

"Ummm," said Caroline. "I love big hands."

Karen laughed. "He's married, Caroline, like you to a doctor."

"I wonder if I know her."

"Trisha. Trisha Fleming."

"It doesn't ring a bell. But tell me more about this delicious Nick."

"He's smart. I think he'll be great to work with."

"Who cares about that? It sounds like he'd be more fun to play with."

"You are so absurd."

"I'm not," said Caroline. "I simply say what everyone else is thinking."

"No. You say what you're thinking."

"Same thing. Hey, let's have lunch next week, a back-to-school celebration. I'll call the others and book a noon table at the club. I've been craving their salmon and goat cheese salad."

"I'm in," said Karen.

The morning of the day before school started, Rebecca, who had emptied her bureau drawers onto her unmade bed, announced she had nothing to wear. Jamie was able to babysit for Robert for a few hours, enough time for Karen and Rebecca to make a trip to the local mall. They ran into Ginny and her twins, Jeffrey and Janet, who were shopping for birthday party gifts. They saw Rebecca's fifth grade teacher, Mrs. Tutt, who again told Rebecca what a wonderful student she had been in her classroom and wished Rebecca luck in sixth grade. They also ran into Sarah and Britney. The girls shrieked when they saw each other and insisted on shopping together. Karen suggested they instead meet for lunch; she wanted to be able to buy Rebecca whatever she wanted without feeling guilty. But Rebecca and Britney begged, Sarah shrugged, and Karen relented. The girls walked ahead, allowing Karen and Sarah to talk freely about them.

"Britney's nervous about middle school," said Sarah. "She won't admit it, but I can tell by the way she's acting."

"You know she'll be fine," said Karen. "Give her a week, and it will be like she's been there forever."

"At this point, I just hope she'll get there on time. She spends so much time in front of the mirror, making sure she looks good from every angle. I've even caught her practicing her smile."

"Rebecca's the same way. Her appearance is suddenly everything to her. She can't walk past a mirror in the house without gazing into it."

"I'm ready to take them all down. Vincent and I know already what we look like, and it's not getting any better."

"And Jeremy couldn't care less, right?"

"I don't think he's ever looked in a mirror."

Rebecca and Britney turned into a store called Young Thing. The mannequins in the windows wore low-rise jeans topped with cotton camisoles and button-down shirts worn open like jackets. The exposed midriff was everywhere, still.

"I'm so tired of seeing everyone's belly button," said Karen, running her hand along a rack of colored T-shirts.

"And I'm so tired of talking about it," said Sarah. "Britney, age twelve, tells me I have no fashion sense. She goes off to school in one outfit, but more than once last year, I found a cropped T-shirt in her backpack. She tells me she wears them just for gym class, but I don't know. The teachers can be pretty lax about the dress code. And I understand that; they've got other things on their minds."

"So how do we control this?" Karen asked, selecting a pale purple and hot pink striped T-shirt for her daughter. "How do you set guidelines and stick with them when everyone else is doing something different and your daughter wants more than anything else in the entire world to fit in?"

"You give and take." Sarah refolded a pair of pants that another customer had draped over the others. "We said no to eye makeup and yes to cropped shirts that touch the top of her jeans. We said no to skintight, spaghetti-strap camisoles unless they are worn underneath something else. We said yes to short skirts as long as the hem is no more than six inches above her knees. But it's a battle. It seems like she's always pushing and we're always pulling."

The girls approached their mothers, smiling and carrying the same outfit: cropped pastel short-sleeved sweaters and madras skirts that looked like, if folded, they could fit in the back pocket of a pair of men's jeans. "That's cute," said Sarah. "Try it on. I want to see where that skirts hits."

Britney glanced askance at Rebecca. "My mother likes my skirts to hit my ankle bones," she said on their way to the dressing rooms.

"See what I mean?" asked Sarah, when the girls were gone.

Karen smiled. "I do. Second verse same as the first, as Bob says. But I'm with you on this. If we stick together, we just may prevail."

At lunch, they talked about their jobs while the girls talked about school. Karen knew Sarah would have very little free time, so she made a mental note to call her in a week or so, and invite her over for afternoon tea. She didn't want to lose touch, now that they were both working.

On her first day of work, Karen stood in front of her closet, feeling a kinship with Rebecca, who still complained, even after a couple of shopping trips, of having nothing to wear. Karen, like Rebecca, had a closet full of clothes; it was choosing the right outfit for a particular day or event that was the continuous issue. And while Karen had guessed and dressed correctly the day of her interview, blending in nicely with the newsroom reporters when she wore khakis and a cotton sweater, on her first day she wanted to wear something that would help her stand out. What she wore, how she looked would form Nick's second and perhaps lasting impression of his new hire, and Karen wanted to get it right without kissing up or being viewed by her new colleagues as a dilettante. She selected a just-above-the-knee denim skirt, which she paired with her brown suede boots. Her new paisley shirt, wide brown suede belt, and light makeup completed the hip, casual look she was hoping to achieve. She was pleased with her reflection in the mirror. Once she was dressed, her thoughts turned to the day ahead and an uneasy feeling churned the bran flakes and strawberries in her stomach. What would Nick expect of her? What about the other reporters—would they accept her or dismiss her for what she was, a stay-at-home mom looking to spice up her life. Was this a mistake? Maybe she, like Caroline, was now wired for friendly competition on the tennis court and socializing with other well-off women rather than the production of something that mattered, something that people outside of her family counted on. This was not her grandmother's chicken pot pie proudly placed on the table for dinner; this was a series of related paragraphs that would routinely run on the front page of the region section—on page one of the front section on slow news days—of *The Record,* delivered to fifteen thousand homes and businesses by four in the afternoon seven days a week.

As it turned out, she made an excellent choice in apparel. Three female reporters complimented her on her outfit, an immediate confidence booster. Everyone was friendly, but busy, especially the reporters close to deadline, so the introductions made by Nick were quick. Karen met two dozen people in the newsroom, the advertising department, and in the front office in ten minutes. As soon as Karen and Nick walked back into the newsroom, Gerry, the sports editor, called Nick to his station.

"Sit here," said Nick, gesturing to an empty desk with a computer and handing Karen a copy of yesterday's newspaper. "I'll be right back."

Karen had been thoroughly reading the paper at home every night as soon as she knew she had the job, a practice she had not made time for since she had children. She glanced down at the familiar headlines and inhaled sharply, as she had the previous night, when she saw the story about the helicopter crashing into the Aegean Sea on the anniversary of 9/11. It was a sharp reminder; something bad happened each anniversary, and Karen suspected the trend would continue until those responsible were held accountable. She turned her attention to the local stories, to what she would be producing: "Reading, Writing, and 'Rithmetic," "Sidewalk Ordinance Challenged," "Mother of 7 Boys Has Daughter." It was this last headline that caught Karen's attention, as it had the night before. She read the article again and thought exactly what she had thought last night: The reporter, Kate Anderson, could have been more thorough. Why did the woman want a daughter badly enough to have eight children? What did the boys think of their baby sister? How did the family support themselves financially? Some of Kate's descriptions felt forced. There was very little transition from paragraph to paragraph, making it a choppy read. She used the word *ecstatic* three times. And Karen would have led the article with a description of the baby followed by her name, rather than the labor story.

"So what do you think?" Karen looked up and saw Nick standing over her. "About the baby story."

"Ah," said Karen. "Well, it's a sweet story, if you like kids."

"I don't know why anyone would want a daughter or a son badly enough to have eight children in that pursuit. I wonder if that was the goal from the beginning or whether it evolved after the birth of the second or third son?"

"I wondered the same thing."

"Kate's young," Nick said. "Her writing is a bit stilted. I'd like you to work with her when you have some extra time. She's one of a rare breed who welcomes constructive criticism."

Karen laughed. "I've never met anyone like that before."

"She's a good kid. All she really needs is a good editor. Sometimes we're just too busy."

"You want me to work with her today?" asked Karen, swallowing air. What would she say to this young woman? What if her counsel disappointed Nick, or what if Nick uncovered in this process that she, too, needed an editor. Was this a test?

Nick smiled. "No," he said, pulling up a chair. "I have other plans for your first day on the job." Karen watched him take a notebook out of his back pocket. He flipped it open and turned several pages before he stopped. "His name is Brendan Pettis," Nick said, reading his notes. "He's eight years old and just took the SATs."

"The college entrance exam?" asked Karen, incredulous.

"Indeed. You have a noon interview with him at Parkdale Elementary School. You'll meet him in the principal's office and talk to him for about thirty minutes during his lunch hour. I'll give you directions. Afterward, I want you to come back here and write the story. We can go over it when you're done." Karen took a deep breath. "It's okay to be nervous. Better questions come to us when we're on edge. Yes, he's really smart, but he is also just a boy. Ask him what he likes to do for fun."

"Should I leave now?" asked Karen, looking at her watch.

"You've got a few minutes before you have to go," said Nick. "Let's get a cup of coffee in the kitchen, and I'll show you around the rest of the building."

Parkdale Elementary School was a seven-minute drive from the newspaper. Karen parked her car in a free visitor space and walked along the wide, white sidewalk, past the giant flagpole just outside the front doors, and into the lobby. Navy blue signs led her down the red brick hallway into the main office, where a cheerful Mrs. Betty Jones greeted her, then phoned the principal. Within a minute, Mrs. Grant walked out of an inner office with a small boy at her side.

"I'm Sophia Grant," said the principal, extending her hand, "and this is Brendan."

Karen shook Sophia's hand and then turned to Brendan. "I'm Mrs. Parsons," she said, looking at him and smiling. "It's very nice to meet you."

"I have to take care of a few things in the building," Sophia said to Karen. "You two can talk in my office while I'm gone." She led them back down the short hallway and into her office, a light airy space with cream-colored walls and sturdy oak furniture. Her bookshelves were filled with neatly stacked textbooks and education paraphernalia, and her desktop was tidy, half covered with stacked manila folders and paper booklets held in place by glass paperweights. "Feel free to sit at my desk, Mrs. Parsons," said Sophia. "Brendan, you may have a seat on the couch."

"Okay," he said, sitting gently down on the front half of one of three tan and cream-striped cushions.

"Buzz Mrs. Jones if you need anything. She's good at just about everything, and that includes making coffee," said Sophia, turning to leave. "I know you two will have a good chat. Brendan's such a nice, polite boy. We're all so proud of him."

"Yes," said Karen, walking around Sophia's desk to the black ergonomic chair behind it. "I'm sure you are." Sophia smiled reassuringly at Brendan and then walked out, leaving the door open behind her. "I've never sat at a principal's desk before," Karen said to him. "It's pretty cool."

"I got to sit there once. Last year, I was the principal for a whole day."

"Was that fun?" Karen broke eye contact for a moment to remove her notebook and mechanical pencil from her leather book tote.

"It was awesome!" he crowed. "I was everyone's boss."

He looked, Karen wrote in the notebook, a little bit like Robert. They were both skinny and wiry, like sprinters, with thick brown hair that refused to stay tamed by a comb or a sweep of their fingers longer than it took to snap a picture. Robert had brown eyes; Brendan had blue eyes. Brendan had freckles; Robert did not. They both had dimples that appeared around their tiny mouths whenever they smiled. Robert struggled in school; Brendan excelled. "Are you smart, Brendan?"

Brendan looked at Karen blankly for a moment before answering. "I guess so," he said finally.

"How do you know that?"

"Well, I get good grades. And my teachers tell me how smart I am all the time, and so do my parents."

"What does it mean to be smart?"

Brendan moved back on the couch cushion, his feet now off the beige carpeting. "It means you know things. You know things other kids your age don't know. It means you can do your work fast and get it right the first time. It means you get a lot of attention."

"Smart kids get a lot of attention?" asked Karen, flipping a page.

"Tons of it. The only people who get more attention than me are the troublemakers and the kids who aren't smart."

"How do you know who's smart and who's not?"

Brendan looked at the ceiling. "The kids who aren't smart can't do three plus five on the blackboard, or they can't spell a word like *tractor*. The teacher helps them all the time, especially Jimmy."

"Who's Jimmy?"

"He's a kid in my class. Some of the kids laugh at him because he's so dumb."

Karen looked at Brendan as she flipped another page. "Do you laugh at him?"

"No."

"Why?"

"Because he can't help it," said Brendan. "He was born the way he was born, and I was born the way I was born. My mother tells me my brain is a gift from God and that it's important I share my gift with others."

Karen sat back in her chair and studied this kid-sized genius for a few moments before she asked her next question. His looks were so typical, like any unremarkable boy, with a fresh chocolate milk stain on his T-Rex T-shirt and new, back-to-school sneakers covering his white-socked, size-five feet. It was his invisible qualities that set him apart. "And do you share your gift?"

"I try to," he said. "I try to help Jimmy. Yesterday, we worked on math problems during recess. He's pretty good when he can count something he can see, like pennies. He's not that great when he has to count it in his head. If he can't see it, he can't do it."

Robert, Karen thought, is a lot like Jimmy. Did his classmates laugh at him? "You didn't mind giving up recess?"

"I'm not big on recess," said Brendan, sitting on his hands. "It's too noisy. Running around that playground is not my idea of fun."

Karen smiled; Robert loved recess. "What is your idea of fun?"

Brendan answered immediately. "Building model airplanes. My dad's a pilot."

"No kidding. That sounds exciting."

"Oh, it is," said Brendan, sliding off the couch so he could put his hand in the front pocket of his pants. A moment later he pulled out a picture and then walked around the desk to show it to Karen. "This is my dad. And this is his plane," said Brendan, pointing at the military jet in the photo background.

"That's some plane."

Brendan's smile grew, then faded. "What he does is dangerous. Since September 11, 2001, he has been busy protecting our country. And he's gone a lot."

"I know he thinks about you all the time when he's away."

"How do you know that?" asked Brendan, his expression hopeful.

"Because dads always think about their sons when they can't be with them," said Karen, knowing she was telling a fib and wondering if Brendan knew. She handed him the picture, which he looked at again before pocketing it. "Tell me about the SATs."

Brendan said the math section was easy and the rest of it was just okay, but he wouldn't know for sure until the results were mailed to him. He said he was interested in how he did, but not half as interested as everyone else seemed to be. He had a hard time being around teenagers when he went to the high school for math classes. Most of them were okay, but some of them called him a geek or a freak. He liked being smart, but it was hard sometimes too. "My mom tells me I'll appreciate it more when I'm older and can do something to change the world. And I know what she means. But on some days, I'd rather be better at kickball than at math."

They talked about changing the world, the Internet, video games, geography bees, and swimming before the principal knocked on the door frame and walked in. "How are we doing?"

"We're just wrapping up," said Karen, standing.

"Thank you, Mrs. Parsons," said Brendan, also standing.

Karen walked around the desk and shook his hand. "Thank you. Tell your mom you don't have to wait until you're older to change the world. Today, you changed mine."

He smiled. "That's our Brendan," said Mrs. Grant.

Karen walked out of the building and then jogged to her car. She drove quickly to the office, anxious to tell Nick about the interview, as if she had been keeping a secret that she was finally allowed to reveal. On the way, her mind spun with ideas for the lead paragraph. There were so many options: the picture of his dad in his pocket; his willingness to help Jimmy; his mother's forecast that he would change the world; taking SATs at the age of eight. Karen pulled the car into the newspaper employees' parking lot and hurried into the building. She walked briskly into the newsroom, which was quiet now that the reporters had filed their stories. Many of them had gone home for a few hours, taking advantage of their midday downtime before sporting events or meetings later that afternoon and evening. The editors were still working—they would until two, finishing their pages and prepping for tomorrow's paper—as were the advertising people in the adjacent office who worked from nine to five.

Karen walked across the room to Nick's tiny office. He was on the phone, with his back to her, so Karen stood in the doorway and waited for him to notice her. Within seconds, he spun around to face her. "I've got to go," he said into the phone. "Yes. Can we talk more about it tonight?" Nick motioned for Karen to sit down in the chair next to his desk. "I understand. Of course you have to make this trip. Well, no. Then go ahead and book the flights." Nick held up one finger to Karen. She smiled indulgently at him. A few seconds later, he hung up the phone. "Tell me everything," he said.

She talked about Brendan's poise and his sensitivity, which were as impressive to Karen as his brilliance. She talked about his compassion for Jimmy. She talked about his occasional discomfort about who he is and what people expect from him, his occasional longings to be regular instead of special. She talked about the surprising depth of his character. He seemed more mature, secure, and sincere than adults Karen knew. Nick raised his eyebrows when Karen stopped. "You got more than I thought."

"Really?"

"I knew this had the potential to be a good story, but, as with all stories, it depends on the reporter as well as the subject."

"Was that a compliment?"

"Yeah," said Nick. "And I'm not in the habit of handing them out on the first day."

They sat for a moment, looking at each other in silence. "What should I do now?"

"Take all the energy you have about this little boy and put it into a page one story."

"Page one?"

"If it's good enough, yes. I want to see your first draft in an hour."

Karen drove home with the windows down and Madonna's *Immaculate Collection* blasting out of her car speakers. She felt as free as a teenager who had just finished her last high school exam and knew she would graduate with honors. *Excellent job,* is what Nick had said about her story; *you did an excellent job.* She could still see his face and hear him praising her for something she had written instead of something she cooked or baked. His words implied she had intelligence, sound reasoning, and insight, all the things she used to hear from professors in college, but had heard rarely since. Jennifer Clear had often praised Karen's work, but it hadn't meant as much as Nick's words today. It had been such a long time since Karen heard words like this about something that mattered. She took her cell phone out of her purse and called Bob. *Hi, this is Bob Parsons. I'm either in a meeting or on the phone at the moment. Leave your name and number, and I'll get back to you as quickly as I can. Thanks for calling.*

"Hi, honey, it's me," Karen told Bob's voice mail. "I had a great day at work, and I can't wait to tell you about it. Call me when you can. I should be home."

At home, Karen plopped her work bag and purse on the kitchen floor, then ran up the stairs to her room to change. Five minutes later, she was in jeans, a T-shirt, and her favorite white tennis sneakers. She bounded back down the stairs and into the kitchen. With fifteen minutes before the kids got off the bus, she grabbed the packaged cookie dough from the fridge, broke it along the precut lines, and placed it on two cookie sheets. She took both of the sheets out of the oven just as Rebecca and Robert came through the front door. "Wow!" said Robert. "Can we have some?"

"Of course you can," said Karen, setting the sheets down on her counter and hugging him.

"You made them for us?" asked Rebecca, looking bored.

"Yes."

"You mean they're not for a luncheon or a friend who got a bad pedicure?" she asked sarcastically.

"Look," said Karen, "if you want me to make cookies for you, I will. But if you're going to be a jerk about it, Rebecca, I won't."

Rebecca glared at her mother. "I don't want your fattening snack anyway," she said, turning and walking out of the kitchen.

Karen watched her go, then looked at Robert, who was sitting at the kitchen table.

"Can I still have your fattening snack?" he asked.

Karen smiled at him and got him a glass of milk. She put two warm cookies on a plate and sat down at the table with him. "How was your day?"

"It was great! We were really good in science, so the teacher gave us double recess. And she can be kind of cranky in science, so I was really surprised."

"Surprises are nice."

Suddenly, Robert's eyes got big. "You went to your job today, didn't you, Mom?"

"I did," said Karen, smiling.

"Did you have a good day?"

She got up from the table and hugged her son from behind. "I had a great day, just like you. Thank you so much for asking."

"What did you do?"

Karen sat back down across the table from him. "I wrote a story about a boy almost your age."

"A story about a kid like me?" asked Robert, taking a bite of his second cookie. "What did he do to get in the newspaper?"

"He's really smart. I think he's going to do something really great for the world."

"I'm going to do that, too. Like do an invention."

"That would be cool."

Robert finished his cookie. "You're the best mom."

Bob called after Robert had his snack and before Karen found out that Rebecca had had a fight with her good friend, Tara, over a boy. Bob had a dinner meeting and would be late. He was on a quick break from a meeting when he called, so he couldn't talk long. He remembered to ask Karen about her job, but appeared too distracted to listen thoughtfully to her answer. Karen was accustomed to this treatment, but that afternoon found it particularly distasteful. He knew how much this new job meant to her; he knew how excited she was. She hung up the phone and dragged herself up the stairs to find Rebecca. She was in her room, lying on her bed with headphones on. She didn't remove them until Karen sat down next to her and folded her arms across her chest. "What?"

"I sense you didn't have a great day."

"You're psychic, Mom," said Rebecca, putting the headphones back on.

Karen stayed put. After several moments, Rebecca again removed them. "What?"

Karen uncrossed her arms. "Do you want to talk about it?"

Rebecca exaggerated a blink. "Do I look like I want to talk about it?"

"Do you want to ask me about my day?"

Rebecca made a face. "Why would I want to do that?"

"Because I started at the newspaper today."

"*The Record?*" asked Rebecca with a forced smile on her face. "Does this mean we have to actually read it before putting it into the recycling bin?"

Parenting Rebecca took a lot of mental energy and anger management. However, instead of getting angry with her this time, Karen lifted herself off the bed and walked out of the room. She felt crappy about what her daughter had said, but pleased that she had remained in control, especially since Rebecca loved to argue. She was a smart enough kid to attack Karen's vulnerabilities, a very good strategy. This afternoon Karen decided she wouldn't give her the chance.

Bob walked through the back door at ten o'clock. Rebecca and Robert were in bed, and Karen was on the living room couch reading the assigned novel for the book group she had recently joined at the library. She looked up when he walked into the room.

"Hi," he said, bending down to kiss her cheek.

She could smell beer on his breath. "How was your meeting?"

"Intense." Bob removed his blazer and loosened his tie. "In the end, we got the account."

"How many beers did it take?"

Bob smirked. "Let's not start, Karen. You know how this works."

"Oh, I am very familiar with how it works." Karen closed her book and turned out the lamp over her head. "It's you who doesn't know how it works."

"What are you talking about?"

"My point, exactly," she said, before walking up the stairs.

Bob slowly followed her, replaying her words in his mind. But they were like a code he couldn't break. He had been busy at work lately, but he was trying to pay more attention to her. After all, he called her today and asked about her job. Hadn't he scored points with that?

CHAPTER 14

Even though he thought it wasn't possible, Bob got busier at work. Forester was doing better than it had in a decade. Its sales of uncoated free-sheet paper and container board looked as though they would continue to soar in the fourth quarter, as they had in the second and third, easily offsetting the high cost of raw materials and energy. Production was smooth and uninterrupted at all of Forester's seven international manufacturing locations, with the exception of a scheduled shutdown at the Alabama plant at the end of September. Management thought a celebration was in order, and Bob was selected to visit each plant to offer congratulations and cash incentives for continued outstanding performance. His visits would coincide with the annual safety reviews, which Bob would attend as well. It was an honor, Bob realized, but it would mean he would be away from home for more than a month.

Karen was far more understanding than he anticipated. In fact, she seemed almost eager for him to leave, telling him again and again that she, Rebecca, and Robert would be fine. When he told her he felt pushed out the door, Karen told him he was being sensitive, a word she seldom used to describe her husband, and that she was just trying to help him feel good about the trip. The night before his departure, Karen arranged for her parents to have the kids for the night. She made Bob's favorite cool-weather meal: roast beef, mashed potatoes, and green beans, and served it with a bottle of Bordeaux that cost well over Bob's fifteen-dollar limit. Afterward, they had sex on the couch in the den, with the Tigers game on the television that Bob had glanced at only once.

When the children were younger, Karen dreaded Bob's extended business trips. The challenges of single parenting managed to outwit her every time, making her cross with Rebecca and Robert as well as herself. She was anxious to see how she'd manage now that her life had turned around. And that's exactly how she felt about her job; it was life altering. She had told Bob and her friends how much working meant to her, but she hadn't been able to measure it until she was faced with this trip and felt relief instead of panic. Without him, she could do exactly as she pleased in the evening as well as during the day.

Karen had recently discovered that, as a working woman, she felt even more entitled to do whatever made her happy on her off hours. She still had Bob and the children to consider, but most of the time, they were manageable considerations. She had to make sure Rebecca and Robert made it to school and to their after-school obligations. She had to shop for food and prepare meals. She had to oversee Robert's homework. And she had to listen to Bob's work stories. That was it, on a day-to-day basis. None of that changed when she started working. What had changed, however, was her attitude about herself and about her leisure time, which was limited again. Gone was any guilt she felt about pleasing herself, replaced by the knowledge that she deserved whatever she wished. And with Bob gone, she had one less person to please before she got to herself.

As soon as Bob told her he was leaving, she started mapping out her five-week plan. She worked Mondays, Wednesdays, and Fridays from eleven to three. She played tennis Tuesday and Thursday mornings. She exercised at the River Club gym on Monday and Friday mornings. She shopped for groceries on Wednesday morning and again on the weekend if needed. She lunched out on Tuesdays with Caroline, Stephanie, and Ginny. That left part of Tuesday afternoon and all of Thursday afternoon free. She decided she'd call her mother and arrange a couple of get-togethers with her in Bob's absence. Maybe she and the kids could go to her parents' house for dinner and a sleepover. And maybe she'd do a little clothes shopping. Since she had started working, she hadn't bought herself a single thing.

The most exciting part for Karen, however, was not the daytime hours; she would be doing what she normally did. It was the evening. Instead of making dinner every night and then eating it while listening to Bob's relentless jabber about work, she'd take the kids out to dinner a few times a week, to Applebee's, Bennigan's, and Taco Bell. When they didn't go out, she'd spend the evening in her bathrobe and slippers after serving boxed macaroni and cheese and applesauce or spaghetti or chicken pot pie for dinner. When she got into bed, she'd read the newspaper and then a novel, instead of fending off Bob's advances. It would be heaven!

Karen felt liberated when Bob drove out the driveway. She convinced herself this was not because she felt any differently about him, loved him any less than she had before. She was simply looking forward to some free time. After all, since she married right out of college, she'd never had any. She moved from her parent's house into a university dorm system, into Bob's apartment, their apartment, and then into their house. She'd never had her own space. Plus, she spent most of her college career attached to him. And at the time, she was grateful. A lot of the women at school had been jealous of Karen because she had been able to land an attentive, attractive boyfriend like Bob. Unlike them, Karen didn't have to wonder at parties if someone would notice her. She wasn't reduced to talking or laughing too loud in the cafeteria or at a campus or downtown bar in a desperate attempt to garner someone's attention, to get someone to pick her out of the crowd. Her future was tidily wrapped up with one guy. Thinking now about the hunt—as her roommate Allison referred to it—Karen wished she'd been more adventuresome. It would have been fun, she guessed, to flirt with one guy on Friday night and another on Saturday night.

During their tennis lunches, when they had two glasses of wine instead of one, Caroline sometimes told stories about her torrid college days, when she dated several guys simultaneously, ignoring what other less attractive and willing women said about her reputation. Reputations, she would often say, are made after college. So, at school, she routinely accepted and evaluated every invitation and then spent the evening with the highest bidder. If one guy offered to simply meet her at a party and take her home to his bed, he was at the bottom of the list, one slot above her opting to stay in. If another boy wanted to take her out to dinner before taking her back to his bed, he was above Bachelor #1. And if another guy was willing to wine and dine her at an expensive restaurant before he took her back to his bed, he trumped Bachelor #2, winning Caroline for the evening. Caroline told Karen and the others that she had had no trouble having casual sex, provided she was attracted to the guy and he used a condom.

Karen thought back to her relationship with Ray McNamara and the kisses they shared that night in the darkened classroom. Objectively, Karen thought, that night was the best kissing session she'd ever had, including the night she and Bob first met and kissed in the street. Ray's kisses were slow and gentle, yet fiery, warming Karen's skin. Karen had been so turned on by his mouth that night that if she hadn't been preoccupied with Bob, she would have unbuttoned her shirt and encouraged Ray to go further.

She couldn't get Ray off her mind all day. She had trained herself not to think about him and had been successful for months, her streak broken when she had seen his picture in the newspaper several weeks before. He was playing for the Boston Red Sox now, making spectacular plays on the field and millions of dollars a year. After the kids were in bed on Bob's third night away, Karen went to the Red Sox website and read his bio. He was married to a woman he had known since childhood. They had three children. Karen typed his name into her computer's search engine and found an official Ray McNamara website. She opened it, and there he was, looking directly at her, looking even better than he had in college. He still wore his hair on the long side. It was kind of like Nick's, Karen realized. They had very similar hair—and eyes. While Nick's were brown and Ray's were an arresting blue, both pairs grabbed and held Karen's attention. Karen sent his fan club address a message, signing it Karen Spears. Two days later, she heard back. He was on the road; could she log on at eleven o'clock that night for an online conversation? Karen hesitated for three seconds before e-mailing the address he sent her: *Yes.*

That day, she played tennis and had lunch with the girls. She ran errands. She helped Robert with his homework, and she and Rebecca painted their fingernails. She took them out to dinner, then let them watch TV. After they went to bed, she read her book group novel and then skimmed the newspaper to pass the time. At ten forty-five, she took her laptop and a glass of wine upstairs to her bedroom and flipped through a magazine while she waited. At exactly eleven o'clock, he wrote:

Hi.

Karen's heart beat in her chest quickened. *Hi back.*

It's so good to hear from you. How are you?

I'm great, wrote Karen, with shaking fingers. *And you?*

Very good. We've had a great season. I can't believe we're headed for the Series.

Because of you, from what I hear, wrote Karen, smiling.

Not really.

You were always humble.

Not humble, honest.

I'm laughing, wrote Karen.

I remember your laugh.

Karen inhaled. *Tell me about your family.*

They're great. Ellen's a terrific mother. We have two girls and a boy. The boy, Carter, loves baseball.

Are you surprised?

No. I love it, too.

I'm glad you still love it.

There was a pause.

I still think about you sometimes.

Oh, Ray.

I think it would have worked between us.

I can't think about that, wrote Karen, thinking about it.

Are you happy?

Yes, wrote Karen before she had time to think.

I'm glad. You deserve to be happy.
So do you.
Can I call you?
Karen thought a moment. *Don't call. I want to remember you as you were in college.*
You always had a good head on your shoulders.
Take good care, Ray, Karen wrote, wanting to talk to him, to see him, to kiss him one more time.
You too.
Instead, Karen turned off her computer, finished her wine, and masturbated.

After a fitful sleep, Karen was slow-moving the next day at work. It took all of her concentration to get through two interviews and write first drafts. When she finished, she was glad they weren't due until the end of the week. Even though she was feeling more awake as the afternoon progressed, the stories needed editing. She was distracted by and regretful of her actions the night before and needed time to sort out what she was feeling. While she was re-solved to quash any impulses to contact Ray again, she was trou-bled by what prompted her to do it. Why now? Just before three o'clock, she packed her bag and shut down the computer. Nick stopped at her desk on his way to the kitchen for more coffee on his way out. "How did everything go this morning?"

"Great." Karen stood next to him. "Mrs. Templeton is ab-solutely hilarious, and her husband is even funnier. If they weren't a husband and wife painting team, they could take their personali-ties out on the road professionally. I've got some great quotes."

"Good. And the Plymouth School playground?"

"They asked me to the ribbon-cutting ceremony next week, which would be a good time to run the story. It will be done before then, but I can add a few inches to make it current."

"I agree. Did you write both of them today?"

"First drafts, yes."

Nick smiled at her. "Since when have you needed a first draft?"

"I'm tired today. Bob's away. Sometimes it takes me several nights to settle into a routine."

"Just in time for him to get back, right?"

"Not this time. He's gone until Thanksgiving."

"That's a long business trip."

"It's a series of trips, really, starting in Alabama and ending in Australia. He's doing what he calls a world victory tour."

Nick laughed. "It must be the season. Trisha's going to Asia for the same thing next week. The area hospitals have sent money and doctors to several small villages in China over the last two years. Trisha and two other doctors are going to spend three weeks checking out the clinics. They have to report to three hospital boards when they get back, and Trisha wants more than anything to be able to deliver good news."

"You should go, too. That could be a great series for the paper."

"Believe me, I've thought about it. I just can't leave the girls that long."

"You can't get someone to take care of them?"

"My mother would fly out in a heartbeat," he said, shaking his head. "But I'd miss them too much. I know, that sounds crazy, doesn't it?"

"Not at all."

Over the weekend, Karen wrote six e-mails to Ray, but didn't send any of them. Even at her loneliest, she didn't think she was truly in love with him, nor, for that matter, had she been in college. Instead, Ray represented an escape from the ordinary. That kiss in college *had* been the best kiss of her life. But if she had broken up with Bob and continued to kiss Ray, the kisses wouldn't have felt that way forever. They, too, would have grown stale and uninspiring. And Karen was smart enough to know that talking to him, even by computer, represented the same thing. It brought adventure and excitement back into her life, and it probably felt the same way for him. Had she gone with him, married him, she could very well be as restless as she was now. Was that what it was, a restlessness? She stopped herself from contacting Ray, but she allowed herself to fantasize about him. And the fantasy, several nights in a row, was the same. They had sex in an empty locker room, with towels still on the floor from his teammates who had showered just minutes beforehand. The steam from the hot water lingered, thickening the air. Bob didn't exist. The children didn't exist. Nothing was real, except for the end of the fantasy, when Ray, night after night, turned into Nick.

Bob called Sunday night from the plant town outside Mobile. He talked to Robert for a few minutes, then spent ten minutes with Karen before he had to go to a dinner celebration. He was energized and encouraged by the workers, who seemed appreciative of management's efforts to thank them. Bob knew the cash meant more than the words, but he was pleasantly surprised to have received a few compliments here and there. Bob asked for Rebecca, but she refused to come out of her room. She'd had another fight with a friend and was, during the phone call, still pouting. Rebecca was becoming even more mercurial and complicated, and Karen was ashamed to admit that she was less stressed out, happier even, when her daughter and her poor moods were elsewhere. At Rebecca's annual physical over the summer, the doctor guessed she would get her period soon. Thinking it could only help, Karen couldn't wait.

Karen's Plymouth School story ran the following week, alongside a story about the town receiving an education grant from the state that would pay for new computers throughout the school system. Nick assigned Karen to follow up with the superintendent of schools; Karen's story, with the headline "Cutting-Edge Education," ran on the front page two days later. Karen next interviewed a twelve-year-old skydiver and sent her draft to Nick, per usual, via e-mail. Fifteen minutes later, he brought a hard copy to her desk. He pulled a chair up next to her and explained exactly why he liked her work. He liked her transitions from one paragraph to another. He liked her consistently parallel construction. He liked her attention to verb tense and sentence length. And he liked her conversational style. Reading her articles, Nick told her, was like listening to a storyteller. Sitting with and listening to him reminded Karen of a favorite childhood memory. When she was ten, she made the birthday cake for her three-year-old twin brothers as a surprise to her mother. Overwhelmed by her daughter's generous spirit, Shelley cried and held Karen in her arms, arms that had been busy with her brothers since the day they came home from the hospital. Her mother lavished her with such praise and attention that Karen continued to make their cakes, as well as just about every other baked good in the house, for years. Shelley told her she was an excellent baker, and that's exactly what she became. And while Karen knew Nick was encouraging her as much as he was complimenting her, she felt appreciated, singled out for her skills.

She was as aware of his presence as she was the sound of his voice. In the tight space behind her desk, he sat close enough to her that their legs occasionally, accidentally touched. His arm bumped against hers when he moved his pencil-holding hand from one side of the paper to the other, underlining, circling her words. She moved her arm whenever his touched it, but it moved back, like a compass to a true setting, her being unaware of its motion until the next touch. When he turned to say something directly to her face, his mouth was no more than twelve, at the most eighteen, inches from hers. His breath smelled vaguely of coffee, but it was sweet too, as if he had recently finished a cinnamon mint. His body smelled but not offensively: no pungent natural odor or overpowering deodorant. Instead, it had the clean scent of someone who had just come inside from a long walk on a sunny, windy April morning. Karen leaned in a little closer. "Great work," said Nick, again facing Karen. "I'm so glad you found us."

"Me too."

"Are you busy this afternoon?"

"Not particularly. Do you want me to do something?"

"Yes," said Nick, leaning back in his chair. "I'd like you to work with Kate for thirty minutes or so. I've made hard copies of a few of her stories, which need some work. Are you up for that?"

"Sure."

"Good," he said, looking at his watch. "Have you eaten lunch?"

"No."

"Walk with me to the deli to get a sandwich."

Over lunch, they talked about writing. Nick started writing as a child, in a journal his mother gave him for his tenth birthday. The mark of an intelligent person, she told him, was not where he worked or how much money he made but rather his ability to put words together clearly and concisely so that everyone who read them could immediately grasp the message and feel rewarded for the effort. "Did she have me pegged or what?" asked Nick, taking a sip of his bottled water. Since then, he had written in a journal every day, almost without exception. Most days he wrote no more than two pages, often about one topic, in the fifteen minutes he allotted for the exercise. But on occasion he wrote four or five pages, ignoring and then silencing the kitchen timer. A shelf in his basement held his more than sixty journals, with their colorful hard covers and lined paper. Sometimes, he thumbed through them, particularly the ones from his childhood. It was his hope, someday, to write a novel—not about himself, but about something universal, something, as his mother said, that would make readers glad they chose it. Nick hesitated for a moment. "I haven't told that to anyone. I have no idea why I've bored you with it."

"I'm anything but bored."

"Tell me about you. When did you first begin writing?"

Karen said she was embarrassed to admit she hadn't thought about it until college. She needed to declare a major and could think of nothing she wanted to specialize in. Her advisor encouraged her to go with communications; its skill set would serve her well no matter what career path she followed. As a result, Karen told Nick, she could speak to anyone with some semblance of confidence, even when she was nervous, and her ability to write had spawned from her desire to communicate with words.

The conversation turned to parenting. Nick said communication was the single most important tool in raising his girls. Like most kids, they wanted things their way and often did whatever it took to ensure that. At first, Nick fought their selfishness with his denial. What he eventually learned, however, was how much better they behaved with clear direction and consistent guidance. Establishing the rules was the easy part, he said. Making sure they were understood and followed is what separated the successful parent of reasonably content children from the unsuccessful prisoner of tyrants. "Can I take notes?" asked Karen, playfully.

Nick laughed. "I talk a good game. I'm not always good at living it."

Nick insisted on paying for lunch, claiming he had done all the talking. On their way back to the office, he raised several story ideas, including Sharon Oriano, a forty-two-year-old who was dying of brain cancer. She had called Nick the other day to request an interview. She wanted to tell the newspaper her story so her children would have the article, something concrete to hold in their hands after her death. Nick at first thought he would do the story, but wondered if Karen wanted to do it instead. She'd have to be attentive without being subservient; she'd have to be compassionate without being emotional. "I think you can do it," he said, opening the front door of *The Record.* "In fact, I think you'd be perfect for it." When Karen didn't immediately answer, he told her to think about it.

Bob sat at the pub down the street from his hotel drinking a pint of Samuel Smith lager at nine o'clock his time, four o'clock Karen's time. It was Thursday, so he hoped she had just dropped Rebecca off at dance, and was on her way with Robert to piano lessons. He had been taking lessons for four or five months and still sounded like a cat on the keys. Nothing came easily to his son. Karen would sit with him at his lesson, wishing, as she had said more than once to Bob, earplugs were acceptable, encouraged even. Then Karen and Robert would run a couple of errands before picking up Rebecca at five thirty, who would announce that she was famished, her word for hunger since her social studies unit on Africa. And if Karen was in the mood, she would head for the McDonald's drive-thru. The children's French fries would be gone by the time they got home.

The Black Swan was a working class pub in a working class town a couple of hours north of London. Most of the patrons were Forester plant workers, with the exception of a table of secretaries celebrating a birthday. They were young women, in their twenties—the birthday girl, Natalie, was twenty-four. Not yet mothers or wives, the women chatted and sipped their lagers and ciders without glancing at their watches, free from the limitations of a babysitter or the nocturnal demands of a husband, nothing to worry about until managing work the next day with a hangover.

With heavily made-up eyes and plump lip-glossed lips on every face around the circular table, the women were aware of their presence in the room, of the effect they had on the plant guys, who openly studied them. Angela, Natalie's self-professed best friend, had been up to the bar several times, for cigarettes, bar snacks, and light conversations with Bob. She had a blond bob haircut, dramatic green eyes, shapely arms that she showed off in a sleeveless turtleneck sweater, and an instant smile. The first time she sidled up to him, she told him she could tell he was a Yank. When he asked why, she laughed and told him it was his accent, even though he hadn't spoken to her until then. The next time she came, she sat on the stool next to him while the bartender got her cigarettes. She asked him where in the States he was from and what he was doing in a place like the Black Swan. He briefly explained he was a businessman, visiting the Forester plant, and she acknowledged his response with a head shake. Both her brother and her father worked there. When Bob asked what she thought of Forester, she shrugged and then said the pay was pretty good, as were the medical benefits. The plant was smelly, however. On some days, there was nowhere in town to go to escape its unmistakable odor from seeping into her pores. Bob told her he'd make a note of it. She turned on her smile as she took a small pad of paper from her purse, writing SMELLY PLANT on a sheet, tore it from the pad, and handed it to Bob.

The secretaries walked out of the pub when it closed at eleven, with the exception of Angela, who lingered at the table looking through her purse. Bob, who had been talking with the second-shift workers, his primary reason for going to the pub, finished his second pint and paid for their ales on his way out the door. Angela followed him. When they got outside, she asked him for a match to light her cigarette. Her flat, she said, was only a short walk away. "Walk me home then?" she asked, after she released a long stream of smoke through pursed lips. When Bob hesitantly agreed, she linked her arm through his and steered him down the alleyway beside the pub. It was poorly lit by low-wattage flood lights attached to the warehouses surrounding them. The rain, which had stopped since Bob walked into the pub, still clung to the brick walls and cobblestones underfoot, making for a slippery stroll. Angela, in heels, seemed either accustomed to the wet surface or oblivious, but Bob was suddenly sober, knowing he'd have some explaining to do if he twisted his ankle while walking an attractive young woman back to her flat when he should have been in his hotel room calling his wife on the phone. At the end of the alleyway, they took two lefts and then a right along narrow streets lined with small, sagging brick houses. One more left and a hundred yards later, they stopped in front of a Tudor-style apartment complex, where she asked him up for a drink. Her roommate, she said, wouldn't be back that night. Her offer surprised and flattered Bob, who hesitated before speaking. "She'll never know," Angela said.

"Who will never know?"

"Your wife."

"How do you know I'm married?"

"Smart, good-looking men like you always are," she said, lighting another cigarette. "Plus, you're wearing a wedding ring."

"Ah," said Bob, looking down at his hand.

Angela moved closer to him and draped her arms over his shoulders. "Come on, then." Bob could feel her breasts against his chest.

"I can't," said Bob, falteringly.

"Baby, you can." She dropped her cigarette and pulled his head down toward hers. Bob didn't resist kissing her. He put his arms around her back, as her smoky tongue explored his mouth. She moaned and moved his hands from her back to her breasts.

"Come upstairs," she whispered, reaching for his crotch.

Bob gently squeezed her breasts as he kissed her. She was right; Karen would never know. He stuck his tongue in her mouth, pushing through a layer of cherry-flavored gloss on her lips. Karen would never know. "Oh God," he said, suddenly releasing her and backing up. "I can't do this."

She pursed her lips into a pout. "I've got so much more to show you."

"Undoubtedly," said Bob, scratching an itchless spot on the back of his neck. "But I've got to go."

He allowed Angela to kiss him on the cheek. "You know where I'll be tomorrow night if you change your mind."

"Yes," said Bob, turning to go. "Okay then."

He watched Angela fish her key out of her bag and open her front door. She gave him a last look over her shoulder, and Bob lifted his hand in a wave. She went inside and closed the door behind her. Bob took a deep breath and walked back through the maze of streets to his hotel. As soon as he got to his room, he called home. He got the machine. He took a shower and went to bed.

When Karen arrived for the interview, Sharon's husband, Louis, greeted her at the door, hung her coat in their small, orderly front hall closet, and told her to ask the important questions first. Sharon had very little energy at this point, he said, and no tolerance for people tiptoeing around her imminent death. They had taken all the videos. They had seen everyone they needed to see. This story in the newspaper was the final step. Sharon had been a journalism major in college and wanted a record of her remarks on newsprint that Louis would have laminated for the girls. It would be the final page in the scrapbooks that Sharon had put together for them over the last six months. Karen, aware of swallowing, nodded her head and then followed him to their living room, to a padded folding chair set up next to Sharon's armchair. She was dressed in jeans and a soft-looking pink sweatshirt. Her feet were covered with fuzzy socks; her head was wrapped in a pink scarf. Her body looked more fit than Karen had pictured, though her pallid face and shriveled mouth announced her illness. "I'm so glad you could come," Sharon said, motioning for Karen to sit down.

"I'm going to get Sharon some water," said Louis. "Do you want some?"

"Yes," said Karen, even though she wanted him to stay in the room.

As soon as he left, there was no place to look but into Sharon's blue eyes. "Did you draw the short straw?" she asked.

Karen smiled, but said nothing. She reached into her bag for a notebook and pencil and started with the question she had rehearsed in the car on the way over. "Why do you want to do this interview?"

Sharon didn't answer, instead looking beyond Karen to the window overlooking the street. A full minute passed, and Karen wondered if Sharon hadn't heard the question or was put off by it and waiting for another one. "Aren't the leaves beautiful?" she finally asked.

Karen turned in her seat and looked at the yellow and red leaves of the large maple tree in their front yard. She had walked under the tree on her way in—in fact, her car was parked beside it—but she hadn't noticed it, even though, now, it was impossible not to notice. Karen turned back to face Sharon. "Yes," Karen said, making a note of the leaves, "they are."

"I rarely took the time to see things like that tree before I got diagnosed with cancer," Sharon said. "I was always too busy with whatever I was doing, lugging in groceries, doing laundry, hurrying the girls into the car, to notice a street lined with trees bursting with color. I know how important that tree is now, and that's why I asked you to come."

Louis returned with two glasses of water. He handed a glass to his wife, who smiled and thanked him, then handed the other to Karen. Sharon took a sip of water before she set the glass on the table next to her chair. She tucked one foot up underneath her. "What I'm going to say is going to sound so trite. It's all been said a million times before. But this is the first time for me, and it's important for me to say it." Karen nodded. "Life is so sweet and so short. There's really no time to do things that don't matter to us. And in saying that, I'm not trying to say that since buying groceries, folding laundry, and running errands don't matter in the grand scheme of things they aren't important. They are all mundane tasks that have their place. Do you have children, Karen?"

"Rebecca is eleven and a half, and Robert is nine."

"Okay," said Sharon, reaching for her glass. "So you know that feeding them nutritious meals is important. You know that taking them to dance class or music lessons or karate after school is important for their growth, both physically and mentally. Running around town in a car after school is no mother's favorite pastime, but most of us—if we stop and look at it objectively—can see the value in it."

"Most days," said Karen, allowing herself a smile.

"Spoken like a true carpool warrior." Sharon paused. "There is value in these tasks because they make the most interesting parts of our lives that much sweeter. They give us perspective, even though we curse their existence. If only we didn't have to do chores; if only we could do exactly what we wanted to do every minute of the day, then we would be happy. Right?" Sharon sipped her water. "Would we? I don't think so. I don't think vacations would mean much if we didn't have to work for them. I don't think a Saturday evening spent with friends would mean as much if we dined with them every day of the week." Sharon closed her eyes and took a quick breath. "That's lesson number one," she said, opening her eyes again. "Work hard for life's rewards, big and small. Lesson number two comes from there." Karen wrote as quickly as she could, writing her observations as well as Sharon's words. "Once you've worked hard, make sure you do what you want with your spare time. Make sure you're spending it with the people who are important to you. If you don't really enjoy your friends, make new ones whose company you do enjoy. If you don't like your marriage, change it or get out of it. If you don't like where you live, move. Whatever it is, make sure you take definitive steps. Don't spend your life wishing for another one."

They talked for another few minutes before Sharon told Karen she'd had enough. Louis, she said, could fill in the rest, which he did with Karen standing next to her car. Sharon had a few weeks to live. She didn't want to leave Louis or her daughters. She had little use for her ex-husband, whom she divorced three years ago for not appreciating her for ten years. His lack of appreciation had eventually manifested itself into something namable, his first affair, with Sharon's best friend, which led to several other affairs and then a string of one-night stands. He was, in Louis's words, an incorrigible lout. Sharon wished she had left him years before she finally had the courage to pack up herself and her children, leaving a good-bye note on their king-size bed. More than anything, she wished she had more time.

Karen drove slowly back to the office, focusing on the road's central yellow lines as a means to control her thoughts in the car. She didn't allow herself to unleash everything Sharon had said until she was back behind her desk. It was when Karen was seated in front of her computer with her fingers on the keyboard, notebook open next to her, that Karen released the rush of Sharon's words, a dammed river set free. Floating on its surface instead of struggling in its depths, Sharon Oriano had mastered life's currents, discovered that the secret of happiness was internal. *The Record* readers, Karen decided as she typed the first sentence of the article, could have the benefit of Sharon's knowledge, her insight for the price of a newspaper subscription, a single newspaper even. *Dressed comfortably in jeans and a clean sweatshirt, Sharon Oriano does not look like a queen. And yet, the wisdom she imparts from the chair in her living room is not unlike an edict from the throne of a sagacious monarch.* Karen wrote the entire story, some sixty-five inches, without stopping. She wrote about Sharon's cancer. She wrote about Sharon's family. She wrote about the tree in front of Sharon's house. As soon as Karen was done, she sent the article to Nick, who, without changing a word, put it on the front page the following day, where it received unprecedented attention. The morning after it appeared, the newsroom phone rang all day with people wanting to talk to Karen. They were calling to tell her that they had clipped the story from the newspaper and put it on their refrigerators, or they had photocopied and mailed it to their friends and relatives in distant cities and states. A few people called in tears. The editors of two newspapers in neighboring towns called Karen with job offers. The praise she valued the most, however, came from Sharon, who said the story was just what she hoped for, and from Nick, who told her it was the best story he'd ever read. "Let's go out tonight and celebrate," he said.

"What?"

"Celebrate your new celebrity. I'll take you out to dinner. That's the least I can do. Can you get a sitter for your kids?"

Nick rang the doorbell at six forty-five. Karen was upstairs changing into a third outfit behind a closed door, so Rebecca responded to the bell. "Hi," he said when she opened the door. "I'm Nick Fleming. You must be Rebecca."

"I am," she said, her head tilted sideways to study him, as if she were trying to comprehend his presence.

He had heard several stories about Rebecca from Karen and knew he needed to choose his words carefully, that she would take in everything. She was older than his oldest by just a few years, but he could see that she was much more mature, poised. "Did you read your mom's story?"

"I did," said Rebecca, still blocking the doorway. "It was quite good."

"You're not the only one who thinks that." He smiled at her. "May I come in?"

"Yes," she said, slowly backing up. And then she inhaled before asking, "As the editor of the local newspaper, what do you think about the results of the presidential election?"

Nick smiled at her. "You have an interest in national politics?"

Rebecca nodded her head. "In an election year, yes."

"Who would you have voted for if you were of age?"

"Kerry," said Rebecca without hesitation. "I think our foreign policy is totally screwed up. My dad says we need to get out of Iraq."

"I agree."

"Too bad he's not here so you could talk about it."

And then she quickly turned and ran up the stairs, calling on her way, "I'll get my mom." Down the hallway and into her parents' bedroom, she found her mother in the bathroom applying lipstick. Rebecca sat on the toilet seat and watched her for a moment without speaking. "Your date's here," she finally said.

Karen reddened. "It's not a date, honey. It's a work dinner."

"Are other people from the newspaper going?"

"No," said Karen, looking back at the mirror and putting her earrings in.

"Then it's a date."

Karen looked at her watch. She bent down and kissed Rebecca on the cheek. "Is Jamie here?"

"Yes. She's in the basement playing with Robert."

"What are you going to do?" Rebecca shrugged. "Well, I'll check on you when I get home. I won't be late."

* * *

Nick and Karen talked easily in the car as they moved from one residential neighborhood to another. Nick talked about "Sharon's Story," telling Karen again how proud he was of her. She complimented him on his editing of the story, a joke between them. After less than ten minutes in the car, Nick drove into the driveway alongside a large Queen Anne Victorian and stopped the car. Karen looked at the giant sage green structure lit by the headlights and then at Nick. She squinted at him. "Where are we?"

"My house," said Nick, turning off the car and opening his door. "I thought it would be fun to make you dinner." He walked around the front of the car and opened the door for Karen, who was making mental connections between the man in the newsroom and the mansion in front of her. "You're disappointed."

"No, no, no." Karen lifted herself out of her seat. "I'm delighted."

"Well, good. My girls are at Dawn's house for dinner and a movie, so we've got the place to ourselves."

Karen followed Nick up the slate pathway to the front door. Inside, they lingered in the carved walnut foyer. On one side, two slim bookcases housing hardcover books with faded spines flanked a window seat with an embroidered cushion. On the other, a large oil painting of a middle-aged man in uniform on a horse hung on the wall in an ornate gilded frame. Nick took Karen's coat and hung it behind the portrait in a hidden closet that appeared from and disappeared into the wall. A grand staircase with Oriental carpeting ran from the far end of the foyer up half a story to a landing before it turned upon itself underneath a leaded stained-glass window and continued up to the second floor. "This is the most wonderful, extraordinary room I've ever seen."

Nick smiled. "You'll like the rest of the house then."

He led her through a narrow passageway that emptied into a large formal dining room. Again, dark wood dominated the space, from the heavy table and chairs to the antique sideboard to the carved china cupboard in the corner. The walls were butter-colored, and the windows at the far end of the room were dressed in lace. A dimly glowing brass chandelier hung above the table, casting a fireplace-like glow throughout the room. They walked through another narrow hallway into the commodious kitchen. Large terra-cotta tiles covered the floor and a light moss green color covered the walls. The cabinets matched the color of the walls, except they were a shade or two darker. Granite and burnished stainless steel were everywhere. A weathered farm table sat in the center of the room. In the back of the kitchen, underneath three large windows, were a variety of planters filled with both flowering plants and herbs. "This," said Nick, washing his hands in the porcelain sink, "is my favorite room."

"I can see why."

"Let me get you something to drink, and I'll start dinner."

Nick poured Karen a glass of white wine and told her she was not to help, either with preparing the dinner or cleaning up afterward. It was a celebration for her, after all. He pulled a chair out from underneath the table for her and then poured himself a glass of wine. They talked about upcoming story ideas while he sautéed, boiled, and baked the contents of several bowls he had retrieved from the fridge. Karen could quickly see that Nick was not a man who made dinner for his wife once a year on Mother's Day. "You're very comfortable with this, aren't you?"

"I love this," he said, turning from the stove to face her. "If I didn't love journalism more, I'd do this for a living." Nick poured Karen another glass, then set the table. He took the plates to the stove, where he portioned out the pasta dish he had been creating for close to an hour, then put them into the oven. He lit the taper candles on the table and turned a dimmer switch until the flame-shaped bulbs of the iron wheel chandelier simulated candlelight. The result was a magical setting more romantic and alluring than the exclusive Coral Club, Karen and Bob's honeymoon destination. The time and attention Nick put into this evening made Karen think differently about their relationship. She thought about several conversations they'd recently had, wondering if her words had indicated what she was beginning to feel. Just before Nick retrieved the plates from the oven, he picked a remote control up from the counter and pushed a button, classical music the result. He set the warmed plates on the table, poured himself more wine, and sat down across from Karen. Like her daughter at the house earlier, she studied him anew, took in his liquid brown eyes, boy-like hair that had been wet when he picked her up but was now dry and straight like soft straw, his smooth-skinned hands with deft, sinuous fingers and clean, trimmed nails. She surprised herself by momentarily imagining those fingers touching her. "To you," said Nick, raising his glass. "Thank you for your incredible writing ability. Thank you for working your way into my life." Karen blushed for the second time that evening. "I mean it. You're the best reporter I've ever had."

CHAPTER 15

For days, Karen didn't tell anyone about her dinner with Nick, and she fervently hoped Rebecca would forget about it by the time Bob got home. The problem was Rebecca had such a good memory, one of the reasons she was so good at spelling and math; Karen knew she would have to lie about her evening to make it seem uneventful. When Rebecca asked about it the next day, Karen told her it was kind of boring, one of Rebecca's favorite words. She told her they went to the restaurant inside the bowling alley, where it was hard to talk over the crash of balls hitting pins twenty yards away. And, as it turned out, Nick, or Mr. Fleming, as Karen referred to him, had asked several reporters to join them, as a surprise. It was sweet of him, Karen explained, but the additional people made for an even noisier evening. In the end, however, she was grateful for the attention and the knowledge that Nick thought enough of her story to submit it for a national journalism award. If the story didn't win, there would be other opportunities. For the most part, she said he told the group, we don't write for awards; we write for our readers and ourselves.

The last part of it was true. Nick had submitted "Sharon's Story" for an award. He told Karen he was going to keep this news a secret, but changed his mind after their evening together. He realized, over the course of their two-hour dinner, what a lovely person she was and that he thought her knowing she was up for an award would be as pleasing for her as winning it. Karen thanked him for his faith in her. At that point, Nick took his eyes off the road for just an instant, to turn his head to her and say, "It's more than faith." Later, Karen played the moment over and over in her mind, ending it with kissing scenarios. While she obviously didn't share this line of thinking with her daughter, who, Karen was satisfied, believed her fabricated story, she did share it with Sarah.

Vincent spent many Saturdays at his lab. Sarah had protested his weekend absences when the kids were younger, when they were in her care all day, every day. But it was easier now. And, as it turned out, their days were often more enjoyable with Vincent somewhere else. He was not the kind of father who wanted to take the kids apple picking, tobogganing, or fishing. When he was home, he was on his laptop anyway. And as the children aged, Sarah had more time to herself. She had been able to leave them for short periods of time since Britney turned ten. Now that Britney was twelve, Sarah left them for a couple of hours on Saturday mornings to get groceries and run other errands. Then, if the children had no other plans, they spent the afternoon doing a group-chosen activity.

Knowing Bob was away for an extended trip, Sarah called Karen the Saturday after her date with Nick and asked if they were free for lunch. Karen eagerly agreed to come at noon and was subsequently treated to homemade chicken salad, cut-up fruit, and frosted brownies. Robert said eating at the Keyworths' house was better than McDonald's. Rebecca, an increasingly grumpy and finicky eater, cleaned her plate. After lunch, the boys built Lego Transformers on the small heated sun porch and the girls went upstairs to Britney's bedroom. Karen and Sarah sat, hands wrapped around warm mugs of tea, in the living room, where, in the afternoon quiet and with the knowledge that the kids were occupied and were not likely to disturb them, Karen shared her story. Sarah listened to her without interruption, without asking a single question. When Karen was done, Sarah lowered her mug to her lap and hesitated a few seconds before asking her friend if she wanted to have an affair. "Of all the things you could ask, why do you ask that?" Karen asked.

"Because that's the question you need to answer first."

"Why?"

"Because that's exactly where this relationship is going."

Karen sipped her tea. "You don't think we can be friends?"

"No."

An *affair:* such a fancy word for what it really was for unsatisfied wives and husbands; it was sex with someone new, someone other than the snoring, heavier than the dating days, or stretch-marked and gas-emitting body that shared the bed. They all started the same way, affairs did, with meaningful, connecting glances and earnest, empathetic conversation, with throbbing chests and unexpected perspiration. But a lot of them ended badly, after the sneaking around, deception, motel rooms, and guilt were no longer worth the effort, after one or both in the partnership lost interest. But what about the affairs that turned out to be the real thing? The people who were meant to be with each other, but didn't meet until after they were married to another? "What if it's more than the typical affair?" Karen asked her friend.

Sarah refilled their mugs from the pot on the side table. "Tell me what you mean."

"What if what Nick and I have is stronger than what I have with Bob? Whenever I am around Nick, I feel smart and worthy of attention. I feel pretty. He makes me feel good about myself," Karen stated. "Do you know how long it's been since I've felt good about myself?"

"About as long as it's been since I've felt good about myself." Sarah sipped her tea. "My job definitely helps with my self-esteem; it proves I can do something other than clean and cook. But I haven't felt really good about myself or my abilities since Vincent and I were first married."

"And why is that?"

"Because back then we were young and in love. Vincent paid attention to me. We didn't have children to distract us from each other, and Vincent didn't work as much as he works now." Sarah bit into a brownie. "Back then, he would occasionally stop on the way home and buy a small gift for me, a cassette tape or my favorite bubble bath. We went out to dinner a couple of times a month. He told me he liked the color of my hair. It's different now."

"It's different in my house, too." Karen took a brownie from the plate between them. "And I don't know why it has to be different. I don't know why we don't treat each other the way we used to."

"So you admit you don't treat Bob with the same love and affection as you did when you were dating?"

"No, I don't. I have a million other things to do—like raising children without a lot of help from him, and now, working. Plus, if he doesn't appreciate me anymore, why should I appreciate him?"

"That's a bad attitude, and both of us know it."

"Why is it so bad?" asked Karen, biting into the brownie.

"Because you can make the first move. Tell Bob how proud you are of him. Tell him how much you love him."

"Yeah, as soon as I do that, he's got my clothes off."

"What I'm trying to say is appreciating each other goes both ways. Bob probably doesn't feel appreciated, even though he gets a paycheck and kudos from his boss. I would guess Vincent is the same way. What they really want is appreciation—and regular sex, of course—from us. But we're so bitter about *their* lack of appreciation that we would rather die than give it to them."

Karen finished her brownie. "Why is it up to us to make the first move? Why can't they make the first move?"

"Because they're like selfish children," Sarah said. "If you want them to share, you're going to have to share first."

As Karen drank her single glass of Chardonnay that evening, she admitted to herself that Sarah made a very good point: Karen had to love Bob in the same way that she wanted him to love her. She had to forget about his promises of taking her on weekend retreats, just the two of them, and the missed parent-teacher conferences or ice-cream socials because he was out of town or working on a big deal, and the hours and hours away from her and the children without a word of regret when he finally did come home. And what about his neediness whenever he was home? Did she have to kowtow to that, too? That's what irked her the most. She could tolerate his work habits, mostly because he was a successful businessman and she knew that came with a price. It was his repeated refusals to help, with anything from sweeping the kitchen floor to picking up a few groceries on the way home to cooking once in a while. Sure, he grilled burgers, steak, and chicken in the summertime, but only because he enjoyed it. Other men, even Caroline's husband, Rick, made pancakes for their children on Sunday mornings. Not Bob. He worked twelve hours a day at his job and saw no reason to help Karen with what he viewed as her job. Instead of doing something to make her life easier, he did nothing, or, more commonly, was interested in her doing something to help him. He wanted sex, or he wanted a back rub, which would lead to sex, or he wanted her to watch a *Cheers* rerun with him when the kids were getting ready for bed. He was a man, and yet he was like a child, as Sarah had pointed out, who couldn't see beyond his own needs. What Sarah was suggesting was that Karen simply disregard his selfishness and pile attention on him. And he, in turn, would pile it on her. Karen didn't buy it. She could shower him with attention for months and, like a dependable vacuum cleaner, he would continue to suck it in. She would give, and he would take.

On laundry day, Karen picked up soiled clothes from Robert's floor and emptied the half-full clothes hamper. She started the washing machine and threw his clothes in. She went into Rebecca's room next and picked up her clothes. The hamper in her closet was empty. Karen walked into the bathroom the children shared, recently enlarged and updated to suit Rebecca's preteen tastes, and grabbed two pairs of pajamas and a wet towel from the floor, along with a washcloth from the countertop and a pair of underwear that was hanging from a drawer pull. As she pulled, the elastic waistband caught and opened the drawer. Inside was a half-used tube of toothpaste, a hairbrush, some tinted lip balm (the only lipstick Karen would let Rebecca wear), gum, and some candy corn with the yellow cones nibbled off. Karen scooped up the candy and threw it away, then opened the drawer completely and saw the latest edition of *Teen People* magazine. When she picked it up to get a better look at the cover photo of Hilary Duff, she saw a package of diet pills underneath. Her stomach dropped. Karen resisted the urge to take the package. Instead, she put the magazine back where it was, shut the drawer, grabbed the rest of Rebecca's dirty clothes, and walked quickly to her bedroom and shut the door. She dropped the clothes on the floor, and then she sat on the bed and called Bob. On the sixth ring, the front desk picked up. "Hotel Carlton."

"Yes, it's Karen Parsons. I'm trying to reach my husband, Bob."

"Very good," said the man. "Let me see if I can locate him." Karen looked at her watch. It was three thirty, meaning it was eight thirty there. "He's apparently out. Shall I tell him you rang?"

"Yes," said Karen. "Please have him call me when he gets in." When Karen went to bed at ten thirty, Bob hadn't called.

When Bob finally did call Sunday afternoon, he was tired and irritable. He talked, briefly, with the children, then spent two minutes with Karen before he said he had to go.

"Where in the world do you have to go," asked Karen, looking at her watch, "at seven o'clock on a Sunday night?"

"Dinner."

"I need to talk to you for five minutes. It's important."

"Five minutes is all I have. I have to be down at the lobby then." Karen told him about finding the diet pills. "What should I do?"

"Take them. Take them and then sit down and talk with her and present them so she can't deny it."

"She'll have a fit, Bob. You know how crazy she's been acting lately."

"And tell her the diet pills are precisely the reason she's been crazy. She's a smart kid. She'll understand."

"I don't think she will, Bob."

"Well, Karen, you won't know if you don't try."

"Easy for you to say."

"Look," he said. "I don't have time for this."

"Of course you don't."

Bob took a moment. "Sit down and talk to her, Karen. You're her mother."

"Thanks for your help," said Karen, sarcastically.

"I've got to go. I'll check in with you later on." The next thing Karen heard was the dial tone.

"You seem distracted today."

Karen looked up and saw Nick standing over her desk. She smiled at him. "Do I?"

"Take a walk around the block with me? I've got an idea."

"Sure," said Karen, standing and getting her wool car coat from the back of her chair.

"Where are you two off to now?" asked the front-page editor, Sam, mid-doughnut, looking up from his computer screen.

"Coffee," said Nick. "Want some?"

"Nah," he said, looking back at his work. "Seven cups a day is my limit." Dave, the sports editor, chuckled.

Nick and Karen walked out of the newsroom and out of the building. "Are we getting coffee? Let me run back in for my wallet."

"No. Coffee sounds less romantic than a walk around the block."

They started down the street. "Do we need to worry about things sounding romantic?"

Nick stopped and looked at her. "We work in a newsroom. Reporters and editors are the nosiest people on earth. People notice I spend time with you."

"Do they think it's wrong?"

Nick started walking again. "I don't know, and I don't much care. I enjoy your company. I enjoy your writing. We work together. There's nothing wrong with our spending time together."

"Good," said Karen, emboldened by his proclamation. "Because I like spending time with you, too."

Nick put his arm around her shoulder, squeezed her to him for a moment, then released her. "Now tell me what's bothering you."

"It's my daughter," she said immediately. "I found diet pills in her bathroom drawer."

Nick took his hands out of his pockets. "I'm sorry," he said. "She's eleven, right?"

"Going on eighteen."

"So she's feeling the pressure to be thin like all of the current female American role models."

"I suppose so, yes. My husband says I should take the pills away and have a good talk with her, but I'm just not sure what to do."

"What do you want to do?" asked Nick, putting his hands back in his pockets. November's chill swirled around them.

"I do want to talk to her, but, lately, we don't seem to be communicating that well." Karen frowned. "She's always sarcastic or angry."

"Is that her personality, or is that the diet pills?"

"I'm not sure at this point."

Nick brushed the hair out of his eyes with his fingers, but the wind pushed it back onto his forehead. "Sometimes, it helps to get an outside opinion."

"That's exactly what I was thinking," she said, brightening. "I was thinking about making an appointment with our family doctor and having her talk to Rebecca."

Nick nodded his head. "I think that's an excellent idea. Let the two of them talk. Rebecca might say things to the doctor that she wouldn't tell you."

Karen smiled. "That's exactly what I'm going to do."

"Good," said Nick. "Now let's get back to the office before my reporters write a story about us."

Dr. Wendy Sonke talked to Rebecca the following week. Keeping some of Rebecca's conversation confidential, the doctor did tell Karen she wasn't overly concerned, at this point. Rebecca was going through what a lot of premenstrual girls experienced. She felt anxious about being a smart kid because she was sometimes teased. And she was worried about growing up; she was torn between wanting the safety and security of her childhood and wanting to explore her preteen notions and fantasies. And, Dr. Sonke said, looking up from her notes, she was concerned about her parents' marriage.

"Really?" asked Karen, eyebrows up, head back.

"She told me you and your husband don't communicate well

and don't seem to love each other anymore." Karen looked at the floor. She tried to shelter the children from their disagreements, but she knew she was not always successful. And if she and Bob fought after they had been out together in the evening, the wine she'd consumed raised her voice and dulled her intuition. "I don't want to begin to try to analyze your marriage, Karen. But if you and your husband are having problems, I can give you the names of a few good counselors," Dr. Sonke said, writing on her prescription pad. "What Rebecca needs most is what every child needs, and that's a stable, loving home environment. There's a lot of stuff to sort through out there in the world, especially during the teenage years. If kids have a safe haven in their homes, they can better handle what's outside of them."

When Karen got home, she looked at the names on the paper Dr. Sonke had given her and then folded it and put it in her bedside drawer.

At lunch later that week, Caroline asked about Karen's job and dreamboat editor. Against her will, Karen blushed. "Excellent," said Caroline, smiling. "Now we're getting somewhere. Will you share your secret with us, or do we have to hold you down and drag it out of you?"

Karen held up her hand. "There's nothing to tell."

"I find that hard to believe. Anyone as scrumptious as he is must attract attention. What's his name, Nick Flannigan?"

"Nick Fleming. And how do you know what he looks like?"

"I dropped an advertisement for our neighborhood garage sale off at the paper. Afterward, I wandered into the newsroom, where he asked me if I needed help. Yeah, I thought to myself, I need help restraining myself!"

Stephanie laughed as she always did whenever Caroline got going on an irreverent or sexual topic. Stephanie's amusement fanned the fire.

"You are such talk," said Karen, buttering a roll she didn't want.

"On the contrary, I'm all action."

"Whatever, Caroline."

"Keep your secrets, Karen, but keep one thing in mind. If you leave that gorgeous, rich husband of yours, there will be a long line of potential replacements." The server arrived with their salads. As Karen took a bite, she glanced across the table at Caroline, who winked at her before asking who in the group would be interested in a shopping trip the following week.

While Caroline liked to kid around, there was usually a serious side to her jesting. In this case, Karen knew that any number of women would, indeed, be happy to find Bob on the other side of the bed in the morning after meeting him in the middle during the night. He provided Karen and the children with everything they needed materially, and he had planned well for the future. Rebecca and Robert would be able to go to any college in the country that accepted them. They could go to boarding school, too, if that's what Karen and Bob decided was best. There were few barriers within reason to what the Parsons family could have or do, and it was all because of Bob's drive to do his very best every day. Over the years, the right people had recognized his potential and rewarded him for it. In the pettiness of every day, Karen knew she often lost sight of what he had done for the financial security of their family.

Perhaps marital counseling was just what they needed. On her hopeful days, Karen was fairly sure that beneath several hardened layers the initial love they had for each other was retrievable. They had enough good history to overshadow the current period of questioning. And a counselor could help them delve into their own psyches, as well as those of one another, to find what they had lost and draw it to the surface. They would discover through their weekly sessions that a relationship like theirs, with a rock-hard foundation, was worth saving. Bob would need to pay more attention to her and to the children, and Karen, in turn, would probably have to give him more sex. Would that be so hard? When Karen got home from lunch, she put the teakettle on to boil, and dialed the phone number of Bob's hotel in Germany. He picked up the phone on the third ring. "Bob Parsons."

"Hi, honey. It's me."

"What's up?" he asked, very businesslike.

"Not much. I just thought it would be nice to talk. We've both been so busy lately."

"I can't right now, Karen. I'm on my way out the door."

Karen looked at her watch. "Where are you going?"

"To a dinner meeting. The Germans work around the clock."

"Ah," said Karen, the resentment she had talked herself out of in the car returning. "Then you must feel right at home."

"I do have to run, Karen. I'll give you a call tomorrow."

"Do you miss me?"

"Honey, I'm late."

"Off you go then," said Karen before she hung up the phone.

Heinz Schroeder was the production leader of Forester's plant in Germany. He was a dedicated, driven employee, like Bob, which the two men instantly recognized, forming a quick bond. They had run through the city's parks on the two mornings before their meetings began, and tonight was the third and final evening out for dinner and drinks. At thirty-six, Bob's age, Heinz had little to tie him down in life. His wife of five years had, citing his work habits, recently left him; they had no children. He was free to work long hours when he wished, or to drink into the night. There was no one to scold him when he finally got home, no disappointed looks. He was a strikingly handsome man, with a hard-set jaw covered by a three-day beard that was a few shades darker than his chin-length blond hair. His hair was the same length sported by many women, a bob, but atop his masculine face and muscular body, there was nothing remotely feminine about it. When he tucked it behind his ears, Bob had noticed a shiny gold stud, which Heinz had recently acquired for no reason other than women liked it. And women did like Heinz; there were young, pretty women who unabashedly approached his table and made their interest in him public.

Bob's last night with Heinz ended up, as the other nights had, at the local bar, The Brauhaus. The safety review had gone better than expected, and the operators had all appeared to enjoy Bob's congratulatory words and cash gifts. Heinz was full of praise for both the company and Bob as a role model. They laughed like old friends as they took two seats at the bar. Within minutes, Ailse and

Bernadette, the two most persistent of the attractive women at hand, were standing next to them. Ailse cozied up to Heinz, and Bernadette, who had announced the previous night a preference for American men, sat on the stool next to Bob. Two beers later, Bob suggested they all go back to his hotel for a nightcap. Even though they all readily agreed, it was just Bernadette who got out of the car with Bob when Heinz pulled his sedan next to the curb. Heinz promised to call Bob before his flight in the morning, waved, and drove away. Bob looked at Bernadette, who smiled at him and said, "The drink?"

"Sure," he said, putting his arm around her and leading her into his hotel. They walked past the bar in the lobby to the elevators, rode in silence to the third floor, and walked hand-in-hand down the hallway to Bob's room. Bob flipped on the light and watched Bernadette take off her coat and toss it casually on the bed. She sat down next to her coat and crossed her trim, shapely legs, all the while looking at Bob. Karen would never know. His heart rate skyrocketed as he thought about his next move. Turning away from Bernadette, he retrieved two beers from the mini fridge, opened them, and handed one to her.

"To you, Bob Parsons," she said, lightly tapping her glass bottle against his.

"And to you," said Bob, taking a sip and loosening the tie that felt very tight around his neck. It wasn't until he sat down on the other queen-size bed that he noticed the blinking red light on his phone. He hesitated just a moment before picking up the handpiece. He pushed the buttons matching his room number followed by the pound key and motioned to Bernadette with his index finger that he would be through in a minute. His hand started a slow descent to his lap when he heard Karen's voice.

"Hi, it's me," she said. "I'm sorry for getting angry before. It's just so hard to talk to you sometimes, especially when you're several time zones away. Call me tomorrow if you get a chance. We all miss you." Bob put the phone down and closed his eyes momentarily. He told himself again that Karen would never know if he had sex with Bernadette. He opened his eyes and looked at Bernadette, who was reclining on one elbow.

"You want to kiss me?" she asked, patting the space on the comforter next to her.

Bob shifted his body from his bed to hers. He leaned down and kissed Bernadette on the mouth, then pulled away. "I do want to kiss you. But I've got to go to sleep."

"I sleep with you." Even though her English was choppy, she was able to get her point across.

Bob ran his hand over his hair. "That would be lovely. But tonight I have to sleep alone."

Bernadette sat up. "No sex?"

Bob shook his head. "No sex, Bernadette. I'm sorry."

Bernadette stood next to the bed. "Because you are married?"

Bob turned his wedding band on his finger. "Yes."

Bernadette opened her purse and took out a wadded tissue. Inside it was a gold ring. She slipped it on her finger. "Me too. My husband travels." Bob guessed she couldn't have been more than twenty-five years old. What the hell happened? He lifted himself and her coat from the bed. He put it around her shoulders and led her to the door. He opened his wallet and took out enough money for a cab to take her anywhere in the city she wanted to go. He kissed her one more time on the mouth and then told her good night. He shut the door behind her. He played Karen's message again before he went to bed, wondering, as from time to time he did, if she would ever fool around on him.

CHAPTER 16

On the plane to Australia, Bob wrote down several personal resolutions on his laptop computer. Number one was to leave the girls
alone. Spending time in bars only led to trouble. He should know
that by now, especially with a friend like Billy. Say what he wanted
about the dissolution of his marriage, Billy spent too much time at
the bar, a problem for him as it had been with his ex. Of course,
Billy wasn't married anymore and could therefore do whatever he
wanted to do in a bar, as well as after he left. But if Bob's marriage
was going to mean anything, he had to leave the girls alone.

Bob knew a couple of married guys through work who regularly
had affairs. They talked about the excitement of sex with different
women. Bud Taylor, a salesman on the East Coast, liked to describe
sex with flavors. His wife was the standard vanilla, or, occasionally,
French vanilla—good but repetitive and predictable. His sex outside his marriage he described as Pink Cotton Candy and Bubble
Gum, Chocolate Rocky Road, and Caramel Fudge. Bud shared his
extramarital activities in detail, making some of the guys envious,
leaving them wondering if Bud made a good point when he justified his randy behavior. He made cheating on his wife sound almost
reasonable. He thought she might know about his dalliances, but

she said nothing, a key factor in what he called the Taylor Theory. His theory stated that men without exception wanted and thought about sex more than women. When women were first married, they put up a good front and had sex with their husbands a couple times a week. After children, however, their interest in their husbands dropped precipitously, as they were swamped with underappreciated child care and housework. The last thing they wanted, he said, was physical contact with something or someone else. This meant the number of nights the wife was open to sexual advances dropped to one or two a month, not nearly enough to satisfy a Forester man. After several years of squabbling about sex, Bud and his wife had agreed that other outlets might work. What he didn't share with his wife was the progression of his digression, when he had made the switch from satisfying himself in the bathroom off their bedroom with a *Playboy* magazine to satisfying himself with a willing partner. He took precautions—always wore a condom— and his wife never questioned him. She was getting sex twice a month. He was getting some kind of release two or three times a week. Their battles over sex had ceased.

Bob's sexual appetite seemed to line up with Bud's. He had physical needs as a man that sometimes surpassed those of a faithful husband. Why couldn't he have a little bit on the side? Why did marriage have to put an end to casual sex? Karen might very well be relieved by not having him climb all over her in the middle of the night. It hadn't always been that way, with the pushing, the blocking, the turning of her back. In college and when they were first married, Karen had seemed as interested as he did. But now she often resented his advances, as if to say, *Again? Didn't we just have sex three days ago?* If he had fresh, exciting sex once a week outside the marriage, perhaps he would be content to have vanilla sex just once a week at home. Bob thought about Angela and Bernadette, about how eager they had been to please him. What was wrong with that?

And yet, he wondered why they were so ready to have sex with him. Angela might have just felt like a romp with a willing foreigner. She could brag about shagging an older man, moaning like Bob in front of her secretary girlfriends at the pub, knowing she would never see him again. But Bernadette was married, just like Bob. Was she looking for another flavor? Did women care about flavors? Or was there some other reason? Had she fought with her husband? Had she discovered he'd been cheating on her and decided to get back at him? Whatever the reason, Bernadette fully intended to follow through and have sex with Bob. She had already made up her mind. It was Bob—the man who ought to have complied, who ought to have had his pants off less than a minute after he closed his hotel room door—who was the one to say no.

Clearly, Karen was behind this behavior. She was his wife, and he felt an allegiance and an obligation to her. But he didn't think it was his wedding vows that stopped him. With Angela, it had been the terrifying notion that Karen would find out. And when she found out, she would divorce him and relieve him of half of his fortune. There would be no marriage counselor, no period of détente. She would leave him if he cheated, just as he would quickly dissolve the marriage if she sought affection elsewhere. While he didn't think Karen would ever cheat on him, he couldn't rule it out. What about her relationship with Ray McNamara in college? Had they been more than friends? Karen was as pretty and confident now, more so actually, than she had been at State. If Bob fooled around on her and she found out, she would do the same, if not for pleasure then for spite. And once that news hit the street, Bob would perish of embarrassment. It's one thing for a man to step out on his woman; infidelity on the man's part surprised no one. But if a husband couldn't satisfy his wife? Bob would rather be anything, a liar, a drunk, a failure, than a cuckold.

That settled, Bob ordered a glass of red wine and put his laptop under his seat. He closed his eyes, and his wife's face appeared in the darkness. He remembered how he felt when he first saw her, sitting next to the window in the student union. It was as if a tiny bolt of lightning pierced his heart. Where had that feeling gone? She was still beautiful, but she had changed. He couldn't put a name to the changes, other than her diminished interest in sex, but, in general he decided, her values, motivation, and her steadfastness had inched their way away from his, a shift in her compositional tectonic plates.

It was the children, he suspected, who were primarily responsible for her change in attitude and behavior, the children he wanted so badly, the children he talked her into having before she was ready. The day Rebecca was born was like an instant, silent coup. Bob was no longer on the throne. And whatever progress Bob had made afterward was swiftly eradicated when Robert was born. Bob slipped from number two to number three on Karen's priority list without incident, without discussion. And yet, she had not been ready for this shift. Two nine-month pregnancies had not prepared Karen for being a mother. She felt like someone had stolen her independence, like a handbag from a shoulder, when she was looking the other way. Plus, she was tired all the time, too tired to go out to a nine o'clock movie on a Friday night, too tired for sex on a Saturday night. It went beyond fatigue in the sex department. She was afraid, too. She was afraid the children would need her, afraid they would be awakened by the thump, thump, thump of the headboard against the wall and walk into their bedroom when she and Bob were naked.

What, Bob thought, not for the first time, had been the rush? Why had he wanted children so urgently? Had it been a means to seal their marriage agreement, establish themselves as a married couple? Had it been expected? And if so, by whom? His parents had moved away from their son and grandchildren, visiting once in ten years. Bob and Karen and the kids stayed with Tucker and Janet in their Florida condominium every February vacation, but, outside of the weather, it wasn't a particularly enjoyable week. Tucker had become increasingly meticulous about his property in his retirement, mowing the lawn every four days, washing his car weekly, and, oddly enough, Bob thought, washing and waxing the kitchen floor. Tucker reminded Bob and Karen every year to encourage the children to not touch the white walls of the condo. Fingerprints could be difficult to remove, and Janet's allergies prevented the use of stringent cleansers. Tucker occasionally played a card game with Rebecca and Robert, or swam with them in the pool. But mostly he watched their movements with a wary eye. When they ate breakfast in the kitchen, Tucker kept the sponge at the table.

And Shelley and Phil? Sure, there had been a lot of excitement, a lot of talk at first about three-generational gatherings, Christmas mornings at Grandma and Grandpa's house, that kind of thing. And for a while Shelley and Phil had been very attentive, driving to Karen and Bob's a couple times a month for a "grandchildren fix." But apparently that itch had been scratched. Phil, who was still working, spent the weekends puttering in his basement workshop, an amateur carpenter who had never made a stick of furniture for his daughter. And Shelley, telling Karen as well as herself that it was good for the nuclear unit to interact without the interference of the larger branches of the family tree, spent time with her female friends, frequenting garage sales and garden tours in the warmer months and getting through winter by listening to lectures at the library and going to the movies. Shelley made no secret of how difficult she had found child rearing and how relieved she was to be on the other side.

What had been the goddamned rush? Bob speared a cherry tomato from a tray hosting a beef filet, garden salad, white dinner roll, and a square of chocolate cake that had been lowered onto the table hovering above his lap. He finished his wine and decided against ordering another. He glanced at the nothingness out his first-class window and let his thoughts drift back to his childhood. He had known his parents loved him, even though they never expressed it verbally, because they cared about what he was thinking and doing. They asked questions. And they made time for him. For a few years, after his older brothers were out of the house, Bob and his father shot hoops in the driveway after dinner, the garage flood-light casting a milky glow on their makeshift court. His mother had been especially attentive when he was younger, reading him bed-time stories and bandaging his frequent cuts and scrapes. They had eaten dinner together, as a family. But there had also been many times that they sent Bob outside or to his room to play with his toys while they pursued their own interests. In the Parsons household, children had been seen and heard, but not nearly as often as they were now.

Before Karen had Rebecca and Robert, she had always been happy. She had a great job. They had a pretty good sex life. And Bob had been the center of her universe. They ate out. They slept in on the weekends. They watched movies and television together. They talked with each other. Then Karen got pregnant. She was nauseous all the time, which evoked Bob's empathy—nobody likes to puke. But she had been negative and tentative, the opposite of what she had been before getting pregnant. And she wouldn't let Bob touch her body until she stopped puking. She was afraid having sex would hurt the baby, if she didn't throw it up first. She was afraid she wouldn't be a good enough mother. She was afraid that having children would change her life. And she had been right.

Bob took the latest school pictures of Rebecca and Robert out of his wallet and studied them. Rebecca had his dark hair and blue eyes, but the delicate nose and chin of her mother. And Robert, again with the dark hair, had Bob's wide forehead and full mouth. Maybe that's what having children was about: reproduction. Progeniture guaranteed a continuation of the family name, the family mission. Was that it? Bob told himself firmly that there was more, that these children of his belonged to him and him to them, that they added value to his life by their presence. Robert, he told everyone, was a really good kid. He was happy, amenable to the wishes of others, a pleaser. Rebecca was more complicated. The fact that she was acting like a jerk at the moment made her more so. Even though their family doctor claimed her behavior was pretty typical for an adolescent girl, Bob knew that he would never have gotten away with some of the things that Rebecca did and said. He'd had his mouth washed out with soap as a child for disrespectful talk. If his parents were in charge of Rebecca, she'd have a cake of soap protruding from her mouth every day by breakfast time. And she was only eleven! Karen coddled, cajoled, ignored, and ignited, but Rebecca's emotions still dictated the moods of those around her.

In spite of her daughter's tantrums, Karen was a more comfortable mother now than she had been when the children were too young for school. Back then, she was miserable. And could Bob honestly blame her? While he had routinely told her she could do or be anything she chose, he knew she was the type of woman who would stay home with her kids. And he was glad; not glad enough to help her, just glad enough to tell others how adept she was at mothering. Back then, Bob had stayed at the office longer than required, mostly to get out of pre- and post-dinner chores. What he enjoyed was swooping in at about seven thirty to read bedtime stories and kiss his children's clean faces. When they were sleeping, he would marvel at their existence, at his part in their creation. But he left everything else to Karen. When the kids were finally old enough for school, Karen finally had some freedom—one of her favorite and most strident words—and Bob finally got some attention, for a while. But now the distance between them had returned. In particular, since she had started working, she had retreated from him again. Was it the job?

When his dinner tray was cleared away, Bob reached under his seat for his laptop. Perhaps he needed to talk to Karen about where they were headed in their separate lives, as well as in their common life as husband and wife and as the father and mother of their children. He didn't talk to her enough about anything but his work. It was something she always brought up in their arguments. It was something he could improve upon.

Karen and Nick often took a ten-minute walk around the block in the afternoon, after the paper was done, as a break from writing and editing. The afternoons were less hectic than the mornings, even though Nick's day didn't end when the reporters had filed their stories. He spent his after-lunch hours writing editorials; negotiating with Joe Harvey, the advertising head, for more news space; meeting with business and government leaders in the community; listening to complaints about what was in yesterday's paper; and hearing suggestions on what should be in tomorrow's edition. Since Karen sat close to his office, she could often hear him on the phone, patiently explaining newspaper procedures, calming irate readers, always keeping his temper in check. Everyone seemed to like him, including Karen, who told herself that what she felt for him was nothing more than a desire to be near him. He was good to her, complimenting her work, featuring her stories prominently in the paper, encouraging her to take advantage of the newspaper's spotty professional development opportunities. He was flirtatious, but in a clean, high school hallways kind of way. Karen sometimes thought he had stronger feelings for her, but he never said anything, until they had lunch together one Friday afternoon.

It was after one; the newsroom was quiet. Nick walked out of his office with papers in his hand and pulled a chair up next to Karen at her desk. He showed her an article he had received by e-mail from a colleague about the previous summer's massive power outage and what was being done to shore up and end speculation about the frailty of the grid. Nick thought it might be interesting to see, three months later, what, if anything, was happening with the local power company. He explained to Karen how local stories can make people understand larger problems. Then he quickly switched gears, asking Karen if she'd had lunch. She said no, even though a tuna, sprouts, and tomato sandwich on whole wheat, one of her favorites, waited for her in the office kitchen fridge. Coats over their arms, they walked out of the newsroom and stopped at the front desk to let Amy, a recent high school graduate who answered the phones and took information for the classifieds, know that they'd be gone an hour. They took his car to Bill's Diner, still busy with the lunch crowd, near the river.

"I love this place," said Nick, following the waitress to an open booth in the back. "The food is better here than at my mother's house. And that's saying something."

Karen sat down, and Nick slid in the seat across from her. She looked out the window to avoid looking at him, thinking he would be able to tell how close she was feeling to him at that very moment. The waitress returned with glasses of ice water and asked them if they knew what they wanted for lunch. Nick ordered two meat-loaf specials and two coffees. "I know that was presumptuous of me," he said, when the waitress had departed. "But you have not had meat loaf until you've eaten it here." Karen smiled at him. "Okay," he said, straightening his cutlery. "I've got something to confess."

"Really?" asked Karen, trying to sound only casually interested.

Nick raised his eyebrows and said, "I've got a bit of a crush on you."

And there it was, out for both of them to hear. His words

floated above Karen's head and then splintered into a thousand pieces and rained down on her; her skin felt prickly, and her ears were hot. Conversations from other tables bumped into their space, but Karen couldn't make out any of the words. His words kept repeating in her head. What she had been telling herself about him, what she had rationalized as nothing more than a desire to be near him, she knew in this moment was laughable. She was, had been for weeks, falling in love with him. A slow smile spread across her warm face. "Throw me a line," he said, laughing, as the waitress set down two mugs of coffee.

"What do you want me to say?" Her smile was full-blown now.

"Anything!"

She counted to five and then said it. "I feel the same way."

Nick sat back and ran his fingers through his hair. "Really?"

"Truly."

"Well," he said, fiddling with his fork, "that's a very good thing and a very bad thing."

"Why?"

"It's good because unrequited love is depressing. And it's bad because we're both already spoken for, aren't we?"

"Yes," said Karen, still focused on his use of the word *love*. Did he love her?

"So," said Nick, moving his water glass so the waitress could set down his plate, "what shall we do about it?"

"Well. We can carry on and pretend we didn't say anything." Nick nodded. "Or, we can carry on like we're not married." She blushed violently as soon as the words left her mouth. Nick laughed out loud. "I can't believe I said that." She covered her mouth with her hand.

"Are you kidding? That was the perfect thing to say, at a perfectly awkward moment."

"I'm embarrassed," said Karen, looking down at her plate.

Nick lifted her chin with his hand until she looked at him. "Don't be. If we can't tell each other everything, then we don't have anything."

"What do we have?" asked Karen in a whisper.

"We have a friendship with the potential for a relationship. We can either stay where we are or we can move forward. If we move forward, however, there's no going back."

Karen took a sip of water. "What do you mean by that?"

"I mean," said Nick, twirling his wedding ring, "that relationships like this move in one direction. If we have a romantic relationship, we will never go back to being just friends."

Karen's heart began to beat faster. "You know this because you've done this before?"

"No. I have never done this before. But I know how it works. If you and I decide to make love, we will either do it until the end of time or it will end badly."

"You sound so serious."

"That's because this is serious."

The waitress walked up to the table and looked at their untouched plates of meat loaf, mashed potatoes, and whole kernel corn. "Is everything okay here?"

"I have no idea," said Karen.

Nick smiled and then, addressing the waitress by her name, asked her to take the plates back to the kitchen and put them under the warmer for a couple of minutes. As soon as she took them and walked away, Nick looked back at Karen. "I've frightened you."

Karen put her hand up. "No, no, you haven't. I just hadn't thought about it in those terms."

Nick nodded his head. "Maybe you haven't thought about us like I've thought about us, in very romantic terms. Karen, I think about being with you, about holding you, all the time. And I've got to do something about it or absolutely forget it. That's the only reason I brought it up today. I was half hoping you'd tell me off."

"Is that what you want?"

"No, but it might be what I need."

The waitress returned with their warm plates, and Nick lifted his fork to show her his eagerness to dig in. When she left, he put down the fork. He looked back at Karen, who lowered her gaze to her plate. "It's probably what I need, too."

Nick inhaled and exhaled. "Okay. Let's say we've talked enough about this today. Let's eat our lunch and talk about newspaper stories and our kids. Let's try to put the awkwardness aside, and we can talk another day."

"I don't know if I can do that."

"And I don't know if I can put your Walmart story in the paper tomorrow unless you change your lead."

Karen narrowed her eyes. "That's a very good lead."

"Yes, it is. Now eat your meat loaf."

When Rebecca got home from school and again announced that she didn't want a snack before walking out of the room, up the stairs, and to her bedroom, Karen decided it was time to do something other than just let it happen. She ascended the stairs a minute or so after her daughter, then knocked on Rebecca's door. Rebecca didn't answer, which Karen chose to interpret as an invitation to walk in. "Mom!" said Rebecca, lying on her bed. "You're invading my space!"

"Actually," said Karen, sitting down on the bed next to her daughter, "this is my space. You're just a tenant."

Rebecca scooted closer to the wall, away from Karen. "Very funny."

Karen waited a moment before saying, "What are we going to do about this eating thing?"

Rebecca focused on her book. "I eat."

"When? You don't eat much at home, and I suspect you're not eating at school."

"You pack me a nutritious lunch every day," said Rebecca in her typical sardonic tone.

"And I'll bet you throw that lunch away. Not only is that unhealthy, it's also wasteful."

"Lecture number 33."

"And 103, and 1,003. This issue is not going to just go away. We need to talk about it. We need to talk about a lot of things."

Rebecca rolled over and faced the wall. "I'd honestly love to, Mom. But I've got a ton of homework."

Karen stood. "Okay, you get to that homework, because you and I are going out to dinner at six, and we'll be gone for a couple of hours."

Rebecca rolled over and faced her mother. "What about Robert?"

"He'll be here with a sitter."

Karen and Rebecca were led to a table for two at Steak Now, Rebecca's favorite restaurant when she was eating. She was a carnivore, just like Bob. Instead of a burger, Rebecca ordered a Cobb salad, with dressing on the side, and a diet soda, duplicating her mother's order. When their meals arrived, Rebecca pushed her plate toward the middle of the table. "I can't eat this. It's loaded with cheese and bacon."

Karen put a forkful of her salad into her mouth. "I know," she said, chewing. "That's what makes it so good."

"If I had known you were going to trick me into eating a salad like this, I wouldn't have come."

"I didn't trick you. You looked at the menu."

"You told me it was good. That it was healthy!" Rebecca's eyes welled up with tears.

"Easy, honey," said Karen, reaching across the table. "Your tears will over-salt your food."

Rebecca frowned and looked out the window at the dark parking lot. "I don't find humor in that kind of remark."

Karen took a sip of her soda. "You don't find humor in much these days."

Rebecca was silent, and then said, "I don't think that's true."

"I do. You seem angry more often than not. What I'd like to do is try to help you with that."

"I'm not angry."

"Then maybe you're just hungry. You've got to eat, Rebecca. To be a healthy person, you have to feed your body. If you don't, it will stop working for you."

"And if I do, my friends will stop talking to me."

Karen put down her fork. "What friends? What are you talking about?"

Rebecca dabbed at her eyes with her napkin. "Clare, Joy, Tina, and Alexandra. They're all a size zero, and if I don't become a zero by the end of the month, I'm out."

Karen sat back against the chair padding. "Why do you want to be friends with these girls?"

"Because they're popular and they like me."

"Only if you're bone thin? What kind of criteria is that for a friendship?"

"You lost weight."

"To get back to a size six, yes," said Karen. "I have no interest in becoming a size zero."

"Well, you're not eleven and trying to fit in," said Rebecca, looking down at her plate.

"Fit in with other, nicer girls, Rebecca. You have so much to offer."

"I don't feel like I do."

"You're smart. You're a talented dancer and actress. And you are the absolute perfect size."

"Says you," said Rebecca, the beginning of a smile on her face.

Karen took another bite of her salad. "Try it," she said. "It's good."

"I'll take it home. Maybe I'll eat some later."

Rebecca held the foam shell of salad on her lap in the car. She told Karen a little more about what she called the pressures of sixth grade, but waited until the car was in the driveway to drop what Karen would refer to later as the bomb. "Are you and Daddy going to get a divorce?"

Karen's heart thumped in her chest as she turned the car off. Perspiration dampened her forehead. "Why do you ask that?"

Rebecca shrugged. "You just don't seem that happy anymore. In fact, the only time you seem really happy is when Daddy's away on business trips."

Karen searched for words. "Do I?"

"Clare's parents are getting divorced. She says it's a good thing because all they ever do is fight about money."

"What does Clare think about that?" asked Karen, unbuckling her seat belt and turning to face Rebecca.

"She's a little sad, I think. But Alexandra told her it's no big deal. Her parents have been divorced for three years. She lives with her mom and goes to her dad's house every Wednesday after school for the night and every other weekend."

"What does she think of that?"

"She says it's okay. Before the divorce, her dad worked all the time, so she said she sees him more now than she used to."

"Is that good?"

"That's how it is with us, Mom. Daddy works all the time, brings home a lot of money, and we get to do what we want." Karen said nothing. "Is that why you're happy when he's gone, Mom? Because you get to do what you want?"

"I am like everyone else; I get to do what I want to do only some of the time, only after other things are done. Having that freedom is important. We need to be able to make choices."

"I'd like to opt out of school. I hate it."

"You might not like the social component right now, but you love learning, and you're a very smart girl," said Karen, reaching over and touching Rebecca's shoulder. "You will figure this friendship stuff out."

Rebecca reached for the door handle. "I hope we both figure it out."

Karen cocked her head in question as Rebecca stepped out of the car, closed the door behind her, and started walking up the driveway toward the house.

Bob opened the door to his hotel room and set his suitcase beside the king-size bed. He left a message on the answering machine at home to let Karen know he had arrived safely, then walked to the window to see the magnificent view of the harbor. On the way to the hotel from the airport, he had decided Australia would be a wonderful destination for a family vacation, even though he had never been before. They could fly down at Christmastime, when it would be freezing at home and warm and sunny "down under." The kids loved wearing shorts and bathing suits in the wintertime, and Karen would welcome a new vacation destination, a change from the sanitized walls of Tucker and Janet's Florida condo. Bob unpacked his bag, then got into a very warm shower to ease his body fatigue from the twenty-two-hour plane ride and to freshen up for his meeting with the production leader that afternoon. He wanted to be sure everything was in place before the safety review and celebrations the following day.

John Simpson was a tall, dark-haired man with a thick accent and a strong handshake. Five minutes into their conversation and plant tour, he invited Bob to his house that night for an early dinner. The workers, Bob could see as they made the rounds, appeared to like their leader, and their latest production numbers were impressive. As part of a non-union shop, the workers were rewarded for their efforts rather than their years of service. Bob was pleased to be able to personally reward their stellar performance this year as Forester's best site. After the tour, John and Bob talked in John's office for another half hour before getting into their cars and driving back toward Sydney.

John's petite wife, Carrie, and their two young boys, Johnny and James, met the men at the door. Bob watched as James jumped up into his father's arms as John was bending down to kiss his wife on the lips. Johnny shouted something about playing ball, and John promised he would as soon as Mr. Parsons was settled. What that meant, Bob quickly discovered, was a seat in a very comfortable lawn chair and a chilled glass holding sixteen ounces of cold beer. "Watch our little game and pretend you're enjoying yourself," John said in a lowered voice as he handed Bob the beer. "I've got to toss the ball for ten minutes, and then I'll be able to join you."

As John threw the first ball to Johnny, Carrie, carrying a glass of wine, sat down in the chair next to Bob's. Bob lifted his glass to her. "Thank you for having me," he said. "Did John give you any notice?"

"About thirty minutes," Carrie said, laughing.

"We can go out, you know."

"No worries. As soon as I was off with John, I called the rib man. He'll be around shortly." They turned their attention back to the game. "This has become a bit of a tradition. John now plays ball with the boys every night when he comes home. When it's bad weather, they build towers with blocks in the basement."

"They seem to enjoy it."

Carrie smiled. "They enjoy anything related to their father. I'm afraid I'm second choice in this family."

Bob decided that if a vote were taken at his house, he'd come in second, too. He knew his children loved him; at least they repeated the words I love you when he said them. But he was suddenly ashamed by how little time he actually spent with them. The notion of playing with them every day was as foreign to him as traveling to Australia. Running around the backyard with Robert was not his idea of relaxing. And what would he do with Rebecca, listen to CDs in her room? Then again, maybe this wasn't John Simpson's idea of relaxing, either. Maybe doing it day after day, week after week had become relaxing. Or maybe he just did it because he had an interest in his children.

"Do you have children?"

"I do. A daughter, Rebecca, who's eleven going on twenty, and a son, Robert, who's nine going on six."

Carrie laughed. "I know what you mean. Sometimes I think Johnny and James will never grow up. Of course, that wouldn't break my heart."

"They're wonderful when they're little," said Bob, looking back at the boys.

"How about your Robert? Does he like to play ball?"

Bob thought for a moment and realized he had no idea whether Robert liked to play ball or not. Did he play at school? Did he play with the neighborhood kid, what's his name? Jason? Did Robert still build with blocks in the basement? Bob did remember that. Robert used to spend hours in the basement building with blocks. Or was it playing with cars?

"Yes, he does," said Bob. "Baseball is his favorite."

"That's what John's going to introduce them to next. They're mad about football, what you call soccer, but John wants them to be well-rounded. He's kind of funny about things like that."

Bob took the last sip of his beer. "I think that's great. Too many parents have their kids specialize these days."

Carrie nodded her head. "Would you like another beer?"

Bob looked at his empty glass. "I'll wait for John."

He didn't have to wait long. Within minutes, John wrapped up the game, scooped up the boys, and put them into the bathtub. Carrie excused herself to bathe them while John poured another beer for Bob and one for himself. Before they finished their glasses, the boys, who were wearing cotton pajamas, reappeared and jubilantly announced they were having a special dinner in the TV room. Bob watched as Carrie popped the frozen meals into the microwave and poured glasses of milk, while John set up two small tables and clicked to what he called one of the best cartoons on television to entertain the boys. Minutes later, the boys were settled and the rib man was at the door. It was a display of efficient teamwork, prodding Bob to think that John ran his home the same way as he ran his successful plant. Bob had very little to do with what happened in his home, which meant being unhappy about it was more his fault than Karen's. Why had he bowed out of everyday involvement? Why had he so fervently drawn the line between what he did and what she did?

On the drive back to his hotel, Bob resolved to spend more time with Karen, to take her out more, and to find an activity he could individually share with each child. He had proven himself many times over at Forester; he didn't need to carry the entire company on his back. The money would still roll in; it wasn't too late to change. He'd start by taking home gifts from Australia, as a kind of peace offering. In the past he hadn't bought his family anything when he was away. His excuse to himself had been that he was too busy. But the true reason was rooted in his self-obsession. He thought about his needs first, at home and on the road. Karen, Rebecca, and Robert became shadows when he was away on business, barely perceptible boats moored in a foggy harbor. Even when he was home, in their midst, he was seldom connected the way John was with his wife and boys. Had Bob's family ever been united?

Bob handed his car keys to the parking attendant and walked into the lobby of the hotel. On the way to the elevators, he stopped, reconsidered, and turned around. With a slight smile on his face, he walked briskly across the lobby to The Mariner for a beer. He could drink to his new resolution: to spend more time with his family. Bob sat on a padded stool at the end of the polished oak bar. He put his back against the wall so he could look out at the harbor through the floor to ceiling windows. The sun was setting, offering a postcard-worthy vista of the Sydney Harbour Bridge and opera house. When his beer arrived, Bob took a sip before returning his head to the wall. He closed his eyes for a moment, allowing himself to be tired. "Buy you a beer, sailor?"

Bob opened his eyes to find a pretty young blonde standing next to him. He smiled at her. "Where did you come from?"

"Melbourne, originally."

"And tonight?"

"Work." She slid on the stool next to him. "I'm a hostess in the dining room."

"Ah."

"You're not from around here, though, are you?"

"No."

"Let me guess," she said, rubbing her chin for effect. "The States; more specifically, the Midwestern states."

Bob raised his eyebrows. "You're very good."

"Not really," she said, shrugging her shoulders. "I asked my friend at the front desk about you."

Bob sipped his beer. "Why would you do that?"

"I guess because I think you're cute."

"Well," Bob began.

"Sheila," she said, holding out her hand. "Sheila Morgan."

Bob took her hand, which was both strong and soft, and shook it once.

"Bob," he said. "Bob Parsons."

"Well, Bob Parsons, how about that beer?"

Bob glanced down at his empty glass and up again at Sheila. She was a knockout. "Sure," he said. "Only I'm buying."

CHAPTER 17

Bob was due home Friday, in two days, and Karen was miserable. She put on a cheery face for Rebecca and Robert, but she wasn't sure she fooled Rebecca, who gave her questioning looks. She did know that Robert believed she was as eager for the homecoming of her husband as he was thrilled about the return of his dad. After dinner, he X'd out another day on the calendar he made when Bob left town. Thirty-five bright red X's stared back at Karen from the wall; two lovely clean, blank squares remained. After the children were asleep, Karen poured herself a glass of wine and took it to her bedroom. She got under the covers and tried to think positive thoughts, but none came without force. She began to cry, but scolded herself for acting foolish. She told herself that she really was glad Bob was coming home, that it was just the change in routine that was upsetting her. She had been so free, so completely able to do whatever she wanted to do, outside of caring for her children. However, at eleven and nine, Rebecca and Robert were fairly independent. She no longer had to hover over them. In fact, Rebecca, in her adolescence, resented anything Karen did that could be mistaken for hovering, including, asking about school, homework, or friends, anything at all. Even Robert, who still loved his mother's attention, enjoyed time to himself. And since she had given him the Nintendo DS for a good report card, Karen had seen and heard from him even less.

Working at the newspaper didn't impinge upon Karen's freedom either; instead it seemed to expand what she sought. She relished the praise she received from her coworkers and from people in the community. And making her own money helped Karen feel like she owned something; Bob had nothing to do with her success as a reporter. Nick, she admitted to herself, was the reason she loved her job and felt free and content. He was at the root of her panic about Bob's return. Karen propped up her pillows and sat back against them. She blew her nose, then sipped her wine. She fully released the thoughts that had been pushing inside her skull to get out, easing the dull ache in her forehead and pulsing at her temples. "Nick," she said his name aloud—handsome, intelligent, caring, good-smelling Nick was the only reason for her tears. She had started to subscribe to her own daydreams that Nick, not Bob, was the one who came through the door at the end of the day. That Nick sat across the table from her at dinner. That Nick was on top of her in their bed. And Bob? In her fantasies, he just didn't exist.

And now he did. For the first time in weeks, Bob's face filled Karen's mind instead of Nick's. She set her empty wineglass down on her bedside table and turned out the light. She had one more night before Bob got home. She could spend it with her children, or she could somehow spend time with Nick. But how? Trish was in town. Maybe just a lunch would do. Maybe they could go back to that diner and discuss their feelings for each other. Karen rolled over in bed, facing Bob's side, willing herself to stop. *You are his wife,* she told herself. *There will be no lunch. There will be no romance. You are married to someone else.*

When Karen got home from tennis the next day, the light on her answering machine was blinking. She played Nick's recorded message four times. "Karen, it's Nick. Call me when you get a chance." She then erased it before picking up the phone and calling the newspaper. Within seconds, she heard his real voice. "Nick Fleming."

"Nick, it's me, Karen."

"Give me a moment, okay?" Karen poured herself a glass of water and sat down on a chair. She took a long drink while she conjured up reasons for his call. He needed her to come in. He needed her to write a story from home and send it to him. He needed to see her. When he got back on the phone, he said, "I miss you today." Karen put her hand over her heart. "Does that sound silly?"

"No, no. I miss you too."

"Listen, I know Bob's coming home tomorrow. . . ."

"Don't."

They were silent for a moment. "Is there any way I can see you tonight?"

"Yes."

"Good. Let's meet at the diner at six."

"I'll see you then."

Karen told Rebecca and Robert she was going to the library to do research for a newspaper article. When Rebecca asked her why she didn't simply use the Internet at home, Karen lied to her daughter, telling her she needed information about the history of their town, something that could be found only in the library's local history room. Rebecca shrugged and retreated to her room. Robert accepted Karen's kiss good-bye just as Jamie was scooping a second helping of macaroni and cheese into his plastic dinner bowl. "I won't be late," said Karen, taking her car keys out of her purse.

"I don't have to be home until ten," said Jamie, hoping Mrs. Parsons would linger at the library until its closing. She was the only mother who paid twelve dollars an hour, especially easy money on a school night.

Karen drove to the diner in silence, rehearsing lines instead of listening to the radio. When she walked in, he was there, sitting in the same booth they'd had lunch in Monday; sitting in the same booth where they had confessed their attraction for each other. Karen walked quickly to the booth and sat down. "Am I late?" she asked, breathless from his presence.

Nick smiled at her. "I've been here all afternoon, trying to figure out what to say to you." Karen looked at him, puzzled. "I'm kidding," he said, reaching across the table and touching her hand. "I just got here."

The waitress poured Karen a glass of water. "What do you want to say to me?" Karen asked. "What do we want to say to each other?"

Nick squinted his eyes. "I don't know," he said. "I only know I wanted to see you."

Karen smiled at him. "I'm here."

The waitress brought menus, which Nick and Karen stared at for thirty seconds before Nick spoke. "Are you hungry?"

"No." Karen put her menu down on the table.

"Me neither. Let's go for a walk." Nick stood and pulled out his wallet. He put a five-dollar bill on the table before buttoning his wool blazer.

Karen watched him button his coat as she buttoned hers. "Will you be warm enough in that?" she asked.

"Are you kidding?" he said, leading her toward the front door. "My internal temperature is about five-hundred degrees right now."

They walked quickly down the sidewalk to the river. Alone with her, Nick wrapped his arm around Karen's shoulder and led her to a bench at the water's edge. They sat, and Karen leaned into him, closing her eyes to the wind and her mind to what was right and proper. He rested his chin on the top of her head briefly and then pulled back just enough to kiss her forehead. She looked up at him. "Tell me," he whispered. "Tell me what you want to do."

Karen put the index finger of her right hand across his lips. He kissed it. She then put both her hands on the sides of his head and pulled his face even closer to hers. "I want you to kiss me." Nick kissed her softly on the lips, then drew back. Karen raised her eyebrows. "You call that a kiss?" He leaned in and covered her mouth with his. She responded, wrapping her arms around his neck and pushing her body into his. She needed to be closer to him; she wanted her body to occupy the same space his did. Her heart felt like liquid in her chest. The only other time she felt like this, felt this good, had been in college when she was kissing Ray McNamara. She vowed not to make the same mistake again.

"You taste good," he said.

"I brushed my teeth before I came," she said, grinning.

"Because you knew I would kiss you?"

"Because I wanted you to kiss me."

They both sat back on the bench. Nick breathed in audibly. "Have you thought about this moment?"

Karen laughed. "About three billion times."

Nick kissed her again. "You have the perfect mouth. I could kiss you all night."

"In a different world, you could." Karen looked down at her hands.

Nick lifted her chin with his fingers. "What kind of world is that?" Karen looked into his eyes, looking for the answer she wouldn't find. They both looked at the river for a moment. "I've got an idea," said Nick, taking Karen's hands and pulling her up off the bench. "Let's go for a drive."

"Perfect."

They walked back to the diner and got into Nick's car. He drove along the river road into town, past the high school their children would attend, past the library where Karen was supposed to be perusing town records, past the storefronts, some of which were still brightly lit with customers milling around inside. "Are you ready for something to eat now?"

"I am a little hungry, yes."

He drove through the next fast-food restaurant, ordered cheeseburgers, fries, and vanilla milkshakes, and handed the food to Karen. He then drove to the newspaper and parked in the lot behind the building. Lit by weak lights, the building looked different, unfamiliar. Frenzied during the day, it was unproductive, serene at night. "You're a romantic, parking here."

"I am a romantic, especially when it comes to you. However, I have another reason for parking here."

Karen set her burger down on its paper wrapper and looked at Nick. He took a sip of his shake. "I got some news today," he began.

"And?"

He reached over and tucked Karen's freshly washed hair behind her ear. "You won the press award for your story about Sharon Oriano." Karen's mouth opened involuntarily. "It was an incredible story because you told it with incredible sensitivity."

"I can't believe it," was all Karen managed to say.

Nick leaned over and kissed her cheek. "I can. You can do anything you want to, Karen."

Karen looked out the window at the empty parking lot, jammed with older model cars during the day. Don't spend your life wishing for another one, Sharon had said in the interview. Karen looked back at Nick. He kissed her lips and said, "I want you so badly."

"You have me already."

Bob walked through the back door just before six o'clock. Rebecca was in her bedroom. Robert was in the basement watching television. And Karen was on the phone with Caroline, who was suggesting dates for a get-together with the Lees and the Jenningses before the holiday rush. Bob gave his wife a warm smile. He set his bag down, crossed the kitchen floor, and wrapped his arms around her shoulders. "I've got to go," Karen told Caroline. "Bob just got home."

"Oh you lucky girl. Tonight's going to be all kinds of fun."

Bob kissed Karen's face. "I'll call you tomorrow." Karen hung up the phone.

She turned to face him and surprised herself by the genuineness of her smile. He had the kind of sheen to his skin that comes from light exercise or long plane rides, and his lips were dry beneath a fresh coating of lip balm. She was taken aback at how handsome he looked, by his masculine jawline covered in brown stubble, by his clear blue eyes. His teeth were white and straight, like coated gum. And he looked at her with such intensity that she drew a deep breath. "Hi," he said, just before kissing her again, deeply this time.

Before she could analyze what she was doing, she was holding him, kissing him longingly, as if she really had missed him. He felt good—the familiarity of his body, the faded smell of aftershave. He had worn the same aftershave since college. Back then, Karen loved smelling like him, when his scent adhered to her skin when they embraced, lingering into the morning after they'd slept in the same bed. Naked they had planned their future. Karen closed her eyes.

"You taste good," said Bob.

Karen blushed. It was exactly what Nick had said after kissing her the night before. "So do you."

"I've got plans for you later."

There it was; old Bob was back. "I'm sure you do," said Karen, now forcing a smile. His plans entailed getting undressed as quickly as possible. He wasn't romantic like Nick, although he had had his moments in college, before his career, before their future became his. Gone, now, was the seduction process, over a shared bottle of wine. Gone were the flowers, the theater tickets, the surprise outings, gone, gone, gone. He hardly complimented her anymore, except in the bedroom, where he would utter something like, *You look so hot, baby,* thirty seconds before he came. Sex was expected rather than treasured now, especially when he had been away. If they didn't have children, he would have hustled her up to the bedroom with his travel bag still in hand.

"Where are the kids?"

Did he want to know because he wanted to see them, or did he want to know because he hoped they were at her mother's house for the night? "Rebecca's in her room, and Robert is downstairs."

"Great," he said. "I'm going to go see them, then have a shower. What's for dinner?"

"Steak."

Bob smiled at his wife. "That's my girl."

Over dinner, they talked about Bob's trip. He entertained them with stories about different customs and cuisine, and the fascinating people he had met in each county he visited. No business talk. No numbers. He gave the children trinkets: foreign coins for Robert and costume jewelry for Rebecca. He presented Karen with a diamond choker, which made her gasp. It looked like a long tennis bracelet, delicate and dazzling. Caroline would be so jealous! She put her fingers to it as Bob fastened it around her neck. He had never bought her anything like this before. It wasn't until after dinner, when Karen was doing the dishes and Bob was sitting at the kitchen table with another beer, that she began to wonder why he had bought her such an extravagant gift. It was not a question of money; it was more a question of timing. Why now? It wasn't Karen's birthday. It wasn't Christmas. It wasn't their anniversary, which they never exchanged gifts for anyway. It was simply the night Bob had walked back into their lives after five weeks away. Was this his new way of thanking her for taking care of the children and the house while he was away, or was it something else?

Caroline had recently told the tennis girls about an article she'd read in a woman's magazine called "Guilt Gifts," about men who habitually cheat on their wives and how they attempt to make up for it. A woman can always spot a wandering husband, the article began, by what he brings home. The first thing he buys his wife is a bouquet of beautiful red roses. After that, he presents spa gift certificates and fine jewelry, especially diamonds. If he doesn't buy something, he may simply ease up on credit card lectures or encourage his wife to shop whenever she feels inclined to do so. He may even take the whole family on a vacation. Bottom line: He spends money on his wife to alleviate his guilt, and he never comes clean. The affair ends only: number one, if he gets caught, or number two, if he gets tired of it.

Karen and her tennis buddies had discussed the article at lunch the week before, after Caroline had announced it was the perfect arrangement. Stephanie, Ginny, and Karen were well versed in Caroline's attention-grabbing remarks, but this one took them by surprise—until she justified her point of view by making several interesting points. One: If your husband is cheating, he and his bad breath are not chasing you around the bedroom as often. Two: If your husband is cheating, chances are he'll feel guilty along the way and, as the article pointed out, present you with expensive gifts. And three: If your husband is cheating, there's no reason why you can't cheat, too. New sex, Caroline said, as everyone knows, is thrilling and satisfying. What Caroline hadn't mentioned, intentionally or otherwise, was the possibility of catching a nasty sexually transmitted disease from a new partner. (This was outlined in another women's magazine, in an article entitled, "The Messy Details of Your Husband's Next Affair." While Karen refused to sub-scribe to what she thought of as journalist trash, she was not above reading it at the salon and in line at the grocery store.) Of course, new lovers could use a condom. But in the heat of untethered pas-sion, many didn't. The wives in the article who were unwilling to leave their philandering spouses often ingested a course of antibi-otics or underwent same-day surgery to deal with whatever their husbands brought home. They didn't want to raise the issue with their men, the article stated, because it would imply a lack of trust. Karen had laughed at that statement. Trust was the least of their problems.

After the children were asleep, Karen and Bob had perfunctory sex. This mechanical intimacy had become normal for them; it had nothing to do, on her part, with her suspicions about his fidelity or, on his part, with his travel fatigue. Their sex life had simply become routine, ordinary. Karen's abstinence for five weeks while Bob was away had neither increased her sexual desire for him nor dimin-ished her indifference. She wondered afterward, as she lay in bed next to her husband, when she had begun to feel apathetic about sex with Bob. Was it one of the side effects of having children? Or was it inevitable, a fallout of every long-term relationship? In col-lege, Karen had been as turned on as Bob when their flesh was free from their clothing. She had been an eager lover, adept at and elec-trified by unbuttoning his shirt, unbuckling his belt, reaching into his boxers. Like water rising in a bathtub, her level of desire had in-creased with each kiss, until her body and mind were fully im-mersed in pleasure. What had happened? When he touched her now, she had no heightened sensation in her breasts, no yearning in her genitals. Yet, when Nick touched her, kissed her, her body came alive. Was this just because Nick's mouth and tongue and hands were new to her?

Karen turned over on her side. She told herself that her feelings for Nick were not the same as what she had once felt for Bob. Her love for Nick was true, pure, everlasting. Plus, she was convinced Bob had cheated on her. He couldn't go three days without grab-bing her ass or rubbing against her in the bathroom. And why else would he have bought her such an extravagant gift? Karen got out of bed and walked into the bathroom, where she turned on the light and looked at herself in the mirror. Had Bob been unfaithful to her? Was she ready to be unfaithful to him? She didn't know the answer to the first question, but she knew the answer to the second.

Over the next couple of weeks, Bob didn't travel. While he made more money for the company when he was away from the office, he was temporarily content to hold internal and Net meetings about finances and policy instead of beating the company drum out on the road. Traveling was exhausting, for one, and his recovery to full capacity after his five-week trip came slowly. He was also newly concerned with Karen and his children. They seemed different to him, as if they didn't need him anymore. Yes, they were happy to see him, Robert in particular, but Bob also noticed a new casualness about his homecoming. *Oh, it's you. Well, welcome home then.*

It hadn't always been this way, or at least Bob didn't remember it being so. When the children were little, they flung themselves at Bob when he returned from a business trip. It didn't matter if the trip lasted for just two days; they squealed and hugged him when he walked through the door. Karen, too, had always seemed glad to see him—not only as her partner, but also as the backup parent. Everyone was so independent now, even Robert in a lot of ways. When he came down to breakfast in the mornings, he was dressed, had a combed head of hair, had made his bed and picked up his room and packed his backpack for school. It wasn't that long ago, Bob thought, that Robert seemed to need help with everything. He couldn't tie his shoes until he was six. Karen alone was responsible for this transformation. And Rebecca, although only eleven, seemed like a young woman. Because she was so smart, she had always appeared older than her age, but it was more noticeable now. She was mentally capable of completing all of her school work unassisted, including research papers with bibliographies; outsmarting her classmates in the seasonal spelling bees and math exams; and thinking up an instant response to any question she was asked. She still needed a lot of affection and guidance, even though she was resistant to it. And she needed to eat more. She was too skinny.

The memory and image of John Simpson playing with his children after work stuck with Bob. It was so natural—a father tossing a ball with his sons. Bob could remember throwing a football with his father and brothers at family picnics, and playing board games on rainy days the few summers they rented a cottage on the lake. It was nothing like what the Simpsons did each night, but it was far more than what Bob offered his children. He was busy making money at work, too busy for Rebecca and Robert. He had been too busy for Karen, as well. He knew he couldn't change the past (and was honest enough to question if he even would if given the chance), but he could do something about the present. He could give his wife the attention she deserved. He could treat her like he had in college, as the woman at the center of his mental and physical world. Fifteen years ago, he had spent almost every moment either with her or thinking about her, and he had spent almost every dollar he had trying to please her. What happened to his devotion? Was some degree of complacency inevitable in all relationships?

On the way home from work the next day, Bob stopped at a florist and bought a very expensive, colorful assortment of fresh flowers. When he presented them to Karen, she seemed more confused than pleased. "My goodness, Bob. What's all this?"

"Nothing, really. I've just been thinking about you."

Karen gave him a slight smile, kissed him on the cheek, and turned her back on him to open the cupboard for a vase. She filled it with cool water and arranged the flowers. "Thank you," she said, setting the vase down on the kitchen table. "They're beautiful."

"You're beautiful."

Karen put her hands on her hips. "A diamond necklace, gorgeous flowers, and personal beauty. I guess I have it all."

Bob looked at Karen quizzically. "What does that mean?"

"I'm not sure what it means. What I do know is you have thrown gifts and compliments at me since you've been home after not paying much attention to me, except for in the bedroom, for years." Karen crossed her arms over her chest. "Two weeks ago, when you were away, you barely had five minutes to talk on the phone."

Bob looked at his feet. "I've been wrong. I've been locked up in my own world and have ignored you and the children."

Karen's eyes widened. "Wow, and you're just coming to this realization now?" Bob shrugged. Karen blinked several times. "After being absent for more than a decade, you're going to run for husband and dad of the year?"

Bob made a face. "I don't think that's the point."

"What is the point, Bob? You can't spend a decade building a wall around yourself and then expect your family to help you knock it down."

"So, there's no going back? Once you've made a mistake, you have to spend the rest of your life paying for it?"

Karen leaned back against the counter. "No. But you can't expect anyone to believe you're serious. Change never happens overnight."

Bob walked to the fridge, retrieving a beer. "So I have to prove myself?"

"Yes," said Karen, immediately. "Not so much to me as to the children. Frankly, they have no idea who you are."

"That's bullshit. They know I'm their father. They know I'm the one who makes the money to buy them whatever the hell they want."

"They need to know you love them," said Karen. "Isn't that what this new Bob Parsons is supposedly all about?"

Bob took a sip of his beer. "I'm sorry I said anything. Obviously you're as set in your ways as I am."

Karen narrowed her eyes. "Don't for one second try to pin this on me. Since college, you have done a complete one-eighty. You used to worship me, and now you barely notice me, except, as I pointed out before, when you want sex. And then it doesn't seem to matter who I am, as long as your needs are satisfied. You work all the time, mostly, I think, because you don't want to spend time with your family. You can say it's about the money, but you're kidding yourself. It's about you. Everything is about you. So don't walk in here with a diamond necklace and a vase full of flowers and expect me to fall at your feet. If anything, your sudden affection makes me question what you were up to when you were on the other side of the world, too busy to talk to your family on the phone."

"So now I'm an adulterer?"

"I don't know—are you?" Bob looked at her and shook his head. "Don't bother to pour me anything," she said, reaching into the fridge for the open bottle of wine in the door. "I can take care of myself."

Bob finished his beer. "Thank you for your understanding," he said, walking out of the room.

"And thank you," Karen called after him, "for absolutely nothing."

They didn't talk much until the ride home from the party at the Millers' house the following night, where they spent the evening drinking and playing Apples to Apples and Balderdash, Caroline's favorites because she was good at them. She was especially animated that evening, flirting with every husband except her own, and Karen wasn't in the mood to play along. Instead, she ignored Caroline's antics. Right after dessert, served in Caroline and Rick's great room, Karen scratched her cheek, the signal Bob had devised for leaving a party early, and Bob stood on cue, announcing both his fatigue and gratitude for the evening. Caroline called them party poopers, standard operating procedure, before wrapping her arms around Bob and kissing him good night on his mouth. Karen accepted kisses from the men on her cheek before wrapping herself in her coat and walking out into the cold night air. Crystals from the snow earlier lingered in the air. Because Bob had had too much to drink, Karen asked him for the car keys, which he refused to surrender. He could find his way home with his eyes closed, he told her. Karen got in the car, made a big deal about buckling her seat belt, and sat silently until Bob spoke. "I had a good time," he said, trying to start a conversation.

"Yes," said Karen, looking out the window.

"Caroline is quite a character."

"She works at it," said Karen, running her hands through her hair. "On some days she's more successful than others. Tonight, she was pretty good."

Bob looked at Karen in the darkened car. "You think she works at it?"

"Oh, did you think she was falling out of her dress and all over you because you're irresistible?"

Bob appeared to concentrate on driving the car. "She wasn't falling all over me," he said, finally.

"Okay."

"Hey. At least she pays attention to me."

"She's a slut, Bob. You can get attention from any slut, anywhere in the world. All you need is money, which, by the way, you've got."

"Is that all I have, Karen?"

Karen looked out the window and said nothing. A few miles later, Bob spoke again. "So, does this discussion mean no sex tonight?"

Karen laughed him. "You are priceless, Bob. Anything can be swept under the rug as long as there's a little hanky-panky."

"Sometimes it's the hanky-panky that can smooth over the rough spots," said Bob, pulling the car into the driveway.

"You're referring to the people—Caroline being one of them—who like to fight so they can make up in bed."

Bob turned off the car. Neither one of them moved. "We don't have to fight all the time, Karen. We can try to change things."

Karen turned in her seat to face him. "I'm happy to try to change things as long as I'm not the only one who's changing."

"You want me to change first."

"Yes. Show me you're really interested in becoming a sensitive husband and a father who matters, and I'll start wearing blouses two sizes too small."

Bob opened the car door. "I've had enough of this conversation."

"I'm sure you have." Karen didn't move.

Bob got out of the car and then turned to face his wife. "Are you coming in?"

"After you fall asleep."

"Caroline wouldn't keep me waiting."

"Then go to her," said Karen. "Maybe you'll hit a tree on the way over."

Bob slammed the car door and walked away. Karen closed her eyes. She was exhausted. She'd had eleven years as a single parent. She'd lost the attention and affection race, coming in a distant second to Bob's career. She'd sacrificed her professional aspirations so that he could pursue his without obstruction. She'd compromised on everything that had once been important to her. And now she had another chance—to be with someone who respected her, loved her, and shared her goals and dreams for the future. It was time, she told herself as she unbuckled her seat belt and opened the car door. She wanted out of her marriage.

CHAPTER 18

Bob parked his car in the lot behind Rascals just after six. He removed his wedding ring for the first time in thirteen years and slid it into his pants pocket. As he rubbed his ring finger, he told himself he just wanted the next couple of hours to himself. He didn't want to belong to anyone. He took a wide-tooth comb out of his suit jacket pocket and pulled it through his hair, making only a psychological difference. When he got out of the car, the cold bit into his nose and chin. Winter had descended fast and hard since Thanksgiving; the parking lot looked like a lunar landscape. He pulled up his coat collar and walked briskly around the building. He hesitated at the condensation-clouded front door and then walked in.

Billy was already there, standing with his back to the bar, a half-filled mug of beer in his hand and a satisfied smirk on his face. Bob didn't see Billy at work much anymore, mostly because Bob traveled two or three times a month. He also had received three promotions over the last two years, while Billy had essentially stayed put. Several years ago, when his affable demeanor still charmed his bosses and when his drinking problem had still been hideable, Billy had moved around a bit, from department to department. Six months had been his longest tenure; six towns was his biggest territory. He was a good salesman because he could tell a good story and find light in a dark situation. But he had become unreliable, missing days and meetings without explanation. In fact, Bob had sat in on more than one meeting during which Billy's future at the company had been questioned. But each time, miraculously, Billy had been able to slide by. His eel-like qualities, in spite of the negative connotations, were his strongest asset. Forester would never fire him. He'd be selling paper to the local school boards well into his fifties. Bob crossed the crowded room and pumped Billy's hand.

"There's my man," Billy said, patting Bob on the shoulder. "How goes the grind?"

"Which one?"

"Now that doesn't sound good." Billy winced for effect. "Let's get you a beer." He turned around and had the attention of the bartender within seconds. Before Bob could dig a twenty out of his wallet, Billy had two full mugs—having chugged the second half of his first one and set it down on the bar—and was moving through the crowd toward the tables next to the newly renovated bay windows that looked out on the street. The tables were all taken, but Billy found an unoccupied section of wall that he and Bob could lean against to survey the scene. "To your mental health," he said, handing Bob a beer.

"And yours." Bob raised his mug and took a long pull.

They were silent for a moment, each man's eyes taking in the surroundings. Rascals was a white-collar, working-professional bar. Most of the guys were in suits, and the women were in dress pants or conservative, knee-length dark skirts and colorful silk blouses. Some of the women wore business dresses. Everyone appeared animated, engaged in loud conversation with their inhibitions drowned in their second drink. It seemed like good therapy to Bob. One of the reasons he was so tense all the time was because he never got to unwind like this. Drinking at home was not the same as drinking in public with other workers who had deadlines, tough bosses, and long hours. Karen hated Rascals for this reason. As a nonworker, she was an outsider there. "I'd forgotten how great this place is."

Billy nodded his head. "I spend a lot of time here."

"That's why you're always so laid-back. You can recalibrate in a place like this."

Billy smiled. "What, you can't recalibrate at home?"

"You know better than to ask that."

Billy shrugged. "You can change that, Bob. Who's wearing the pants?"

"I am," said Bob, "but they're very tight."

Billy laughed just as three pretty women walked in the front door. Bob and Billy watched them as they made their way to the bar. Every guy in their path did the same thing. "One of them could loosen up your pants." Billy gestured toward the women with his mug.

"I have no doubt."

Two young couples at one of the window tables gathered their briefcases, purses, and coats, and stood. "Luck is with us tonight," said Billy. "Let's pounce on this table."

He took three giant steps, landing in the middle of the departing foursome. He wrapped his arm around one of the women. "We didn't chase you out of here, did we?"

The woman laughed. "No, Billy," said one of the men. "We're out of here for some dinner."

"Sally's ribs aren't going to cut it?"

One of the guys looked askance. "The girls want pasta," he said. "Whole wheat pasta."

"You will be rewarded for this one day—not tonight—but some day you will get your greasy burger and fries." Billy shook the man's hand and grinned like a politician running for reelection. This is exactly why, Bob thought, Billy still works for Forester. "Have a good one," Billy said, as they headed for the door.

Bob sat down in a chair. "Who's that?"

"He's a chemist, I think." Billy sat down across the table from Bob. "He works in the research facility on Stellar Road. I sell them a lot of paper."

"Yes, you do." They finished their beers. "One more." Bob stood. "This one's mine."

Billy nodded and handed Bob his mug. He watched as Bob walked to the bar and stood next to the three women they had noticed earlier. He then turned his attention elsewhere and found a wide assortment of activity. The couple at the table next to him was kissing too passionately, some would comment, for a public place. The couple at the table beyond that was fighting. They weren't shouting, or even talking, nothing but sour faces and a heavy, palpable silence. Several young men standing near them had loosened their ties and seemed to be pumped up about something happening on ESPN. Billy shook his head. Sports freaks. He knew a lot of guys who wouldn't even walk into a bar unless it had at least two big screen TVs. When he looked back at the bar, he was surprised to see the three women following Bob back to the table. This was good, Billy thought. He could use a little action tonight. He stood when they approached the table.

"I found some friends," said Bob, with a smile on his face. "They need a place to sit down."

"Welcome to our humble home." Billy pulled out a chair for one of the women.

"Thank you, Billy," said one of the women, giggling.

"Now that's not fair. You know my name, and I don't know yours."

One of the other women said, "Everyone knows your name, Billy."

"My name's Mandy," said the woman who had spoken first.

"And I'm Tanya," said the other one. The third woman, who hadn't yet spoken, was still standing next to Bob. He turned to her and smiled.

"And I'm Denise," she said. "Denise Levy."

Bob shook her hand. "It's nice to meet you."

Bob and Denise sat down with the others, while Billy, as usual, got right down to it. "So, what are three lovely ladies doing without chaperones in a place like this?"

"Looking for chaperones," Mandy said boldly.

"Well, you've come to the right place. But, surely, this isn't your first trip to Rascals."

"We were here a couple of times last summer and had a ball," said Tanya. "So we decided to come back and make an evening of it, you know, dinner and everything."

"We all work and live in River City," explained Mandy, "so we spend most of our time over there."

"Well, that's our loss," said Billy.

"It's not far," Denise said. "Only about thirty minutes on the expressway."

"And worth every one of them. The ribs here are excellent."

"Ooh, I love ribs," said Mandy. "Are they dry or saucy?"

"Saucy, spicy, and sizzling!"

Mandy giggled. "Are you guys here for dinner?"

"I'm not," said Bob, making eye contact with Billy.

"Back to work, is it?" asked Billy, playing along. "That boss of yours is brutal."

Bob shrugged and took a sip of his beer. Denise asked, "Do you have to go now?"

Bob smiled at her; Karen could wait. "Not quite yet."

While Billy gave Mandy and Tanya his Life of a Salesman monologue, Denise and Bob talked quietly. This wasn't easy at Rascals, with the competition from the stereo system, televisions, and everyone else in the room. But it was possible, especially when they leaned their heads into their conversation and ignored everything but the words coming from each other's mouths. Denise told Bob she had grown up in River City and recently graduated from River City College with a degree in business administration. She worked at the credit union and would stay there until something better came along. Her dream job was to own and operate a Curves franchise, maybe two, but that was a long way off. She had some school debt she had to work down, and she had just moved into an apartment near the river. Her parents had encouraged her to stay at home another year to save money, make a real dent in her loans, but she was ready to leave. Her apartment, though costing more than she wanted to spend on rent, was just the right size, with a huge bay window in her living room that, with the leaves off the trees, afforded her a view of the river.

She smiled and blushed when she talked, and Bob could tell she was shy, not at all like her socially forward friends Mandy and Tanya. He liked reticence in a woman, even though he, like a lot of guys, was attracted to the bawdy talk and sexy confidence of long-haired, busty women like Caroline. He had considered cornering Caroline and offering to take her up on her steamy suggestions. What would she do if he arrived at her house in the middle of the day and told her he wanted to have sex on the marbled-surface of her kitchen's center island? That was, after all, one of the places she had confessed to fantasizing about. What would she do then? Bob guessed she probably would have sex with him, and it would be really good sex. But it wouldn't be worth it. Number one, she was Karen's friend, even though it seemed like they feuded more than they bonded. And number two, she was a demanding bitch, a zero on the loyalty scale. It was a good thing Rick made a lot of money as a surgeon and could keep her happy financially, because if he lost his job, or suddenly contracted a terrible disease that would diminish his relative attractiveness or earning power, she would be gone.

If Bob just wanted sex, a raunchy woman would fit nicely into his life. He could get himself off, and buy her whatever she wanted for her services and her silence. It would be risky, of course. Some women grew tired of their on-the-sidelines status, he'd heard, and demanded more. They wanted more than a couple hours in bed with their men. They wanted a dinner out, sappy greeting cards, flowers, promises. Billy had told Bob a number of stories about this kind of woman, who said she was one thing, but turned out to be another. For this and other reasons, Billy avoided relationships. He preferred one-night events that demanded nothing more than a condom and a good mouth rinse with Listerine.

That's what Bob at first thought he wanted. The women who had come on to him on his recent business trip had pushed his interest in other women from a mental state into a physical realm. He could have had sex with any of them. And he would have avoided any consequences by getting on a plane and simply flying away from them. But as he talked quietly with Denise, he began to suspect that he might want more than just sex. She was so attentive. What if he could start over, with a woman who adored him, who loved him more than anything else in her life, with someone like

Denise, who would respect his judgment, follow his word, welcome his authority? In exchange, he would provide her with an upper-class lifestyle. She would be impressed with his money-making abilities, but she would be more impressed with him as a man. The women on his global business trip had approached him because they could see he was successful, yes, but they would have approached, had undoubtedly approached, other men. They wanted a quick, illicit romp. Denise was different. She wouldn't go home with him that night, even if he had a place to take her. She was not the kind of girl who practiced casual sex or the subtle art of entrapment with sex. She would have sex with him eventually out of love rather than pure lust. She would fall in love with him, like Karen had.

Back in college, Karen had loved him like Denise would love him now. Karen's countenance brightened when she saw him. Her breath caught when she talked to him. Her body responded to his touch without embarrassment or weariness or disinterest. Her love was free, unfettered. Whether it was her sickness during her pregnancy with Rebecca or the arrival of the baby itself that changed Karen, Bob didn't know. But he did know that having Rebecca had changed Karen's love for him. She loved him less now than she had before. And gradually, the diluted love that was left had disintegrated altogether until there was nothing but two children, a house, and common history keeping them together.

"I'm talking too much," said Denise, finishing her drink.

"I like listening to you talk. I like the sound of your voice. You have nice inflection."

She tilted her head and narrowed her eyes. "Are you making fun of me?"

"Are you kidding me?"

"Then that's one of the sweetest things I've ever heard."

Bob gave her hand a quick squeeze. "Good. No one ever calls me sweet anymore."

She laughed. "I've told you all about me. Tell me what you do."

"He runs Forester," Billy chimed in from across the table.

"You do?" asked Mandy, eyes wide.

Bob hesitated. "Don't be modest," said Billy. "Tell the girls how important you are."

"Billy and I both work at Forester," said Bob, feeling both proud and awkward.

Denise put her lips to Bob's ear. "Sorry," she whispered.

He turned to her. "It's okay. It's a very legitimate question."

"So, who's hungry?" asked Billy.

"I am," said Mandy and Tanya at the same time. Denise looked at Bob, who stood. "I'm going to be on my way," he said.

Mandy put her lips out in a pout, then said, "Every party has a pooper."

Bob laughed. "I have been called that before."

Denise looked up at him. "I've enjoyed meeting you."

"And I you," said Bob, already knowing he would find her phone number and call her the next day.

Three hours after Bob got to his office in the morning, he was told to return home, pack a bag, and get on a plane. Their biggest customer in California was threatening to break its contract with Forester and sign with a local company that could give them better service. Bob put their paper file in his briefcase, grabbed his laptop, and headed for home. He left a note on the kitchen table for Karen and a voice mail at the newspaper and then went to the airport. He printed his boarding pass, then sat in the lounge to wait for his flight. He took his cell phone from his pocket. As he expected, he got Denise's answering machine. *Hi, you've reached Denise. Please leave a message, and I'll call you back. Thanks, and have a great day.*

"Hi, it's Bob. I had a good time talking with you last night and would like to see you again. I'm at the airport right now, actually, and will be out of town for a few days, but I'll call you when I get back."

Bob put his phone back in his suit coat pocket and sat back. He put his hands behind his head, stretched his legs out in front of him, and looked at the ceiling. Maybe he would take her to a movie and out for a casual dinner. It was easier, he thought, to talk over a burger than it was to get to know one another over filet mignon with béarnaise sauce. Although burgers could be messy. She might be more comfortable eating with a fork and knife. And she would be able to dress up if he took her to a nice place. Plus, she would be impressed with his ability and desire to spend money on her. Women, single women in particular, always measured that. They would not have sex that night. But soon enough, Denise and he would end a date in her little apartment by the river.

As soon as Karen got Bob's message, she walked into Nick's office. He was on the phone, but motioned for her to sit in his corner chair. He swiveled in his chair so he could face her while he wrapped up his conversation. "Hi," he said as he hung up the phone.

She smiled at him. "Bob had to go out of town on business. He'll be gone until the end of the week."

"Now that's interesting information. Trisha's leaving tomorrow for a conference in San Antonio. She'll be gone through the weekend."

"Oh my."

"Do you want to?" asked Nick, suddenly serious.

"Very much," she said, without hesitation.

"Tomorrow night then. I'll pick you up at six and have you home by ten."

"What should I wear?" asked Karen, not knowing what else to say.

"Whatever you want. We'll be eating in."

After standing in her closet and looking at her clothes for ten minutes, Karen chose black wool pants and a royal blue cashmere sweater. She wore silver jewelry and plum lipstick, and spent more time than usual drying her hair and applying mascara. When she was done, she looked in the mirror. This was the new Karen Parsons, the woman who was going to take control of her life and live it exactly as she chose. She was pleased with her reflection as she turned sideways, pleased with the results of her latest fitness plan. She had already lost her holiday weight and had buttoned her pants with ease.

She walked down the stairs and into the kitchen, where Jamie, who had arrived at five thirty, was giving Rebecca and Robert dinner. Karen had told the children she was going out to a community dinner with other newspaper reporters and several editors. In reality, she would drive to the library, where Nick would pick her up at six and drop her off just before ten. It was a perfect plan. Karen jotted down her cell phone number for Jamie, then headed to the front hall closet for her coat. As she put it on, Rebecca approached her, coat in her hand. "I'd like to go to the library."

Karen pushed her arms through the sleeves of her coat. "That's not going to work out tonight, honey. I've got to get to this dinner meeting."

"I know. You can leave me at the library when you go to your meeting and then meet me there afterward."

"Not tonight," said Karen. "I don't mind leaving you alone at the library during the day, but I would prefer to be with you at night. We can go tomorrow night."

Rebecca folded her arms across her chest. "Where are you really going?"

"I told you where I'm going, Rebecca."

"Then why don't I believe you?"

Karen put her hands on her daughter's shoulders. "I'll be home around ten."

Rebecca narrowed her eyes at her mother, then turned her back on her and walked away. Karen hesitated just a moment, wondering if she should pad the lie, before walking out the front door.

When Karen pulled her car into the lot behind the library, Nick was there, standing with his hands in his peacoat pockets and his back against the driver's door. Karen parked next to him. "I wasn't sure you would come."

Karen looked at her watch and smiled. "It's six-oh-two."

"You know how I am about deadlines."

Karen laughed, and Nick kissed her on the cheek. He led her around to the passenger side of his car and opened the door. Never talking his eyes off her, he walked back to the driver's side and got in. Without a word from either of them, Nick drove out of the parking lot and down the street. As soon as he turned the car onto the highway, Karen spoke. "Where are we going?"

"Not far," said Nick, reaching over and taking Karen's hand in his. Karen shifted her body under the seat belt so she was facing him. She raised his hand to her lips and kissed his fingers. "You are so handsome."

Nick laughed. "I guess love really is blind."

They arrived at The Willow Tree Inn fifteen minutes later. It was a newly renovated old country home on an inland lake, with a burgeoning reputation for an exquisite dinner menu and charming guest rooms. Caroline had just mentioned it at tennis the other day, saying it would be the perfect nearby getaway. Nick drove the car through two grand willow trees that stood on both sides of the entrance and down the long drive illuminated by ground lighting to the red brick estate. He parked the car. "Are you ready?"

"Very," said Karen, smiling.

He got out of the car and walked around the back of it to open the door for her. As soon as she was out, he wrapped his arm around her and kissed her temple. She encircled his waist with her arm, and they scurried through the winter wind to the front door. Just before they went inside, Karen said, "I want to feel this good forever."

"If I'm with you, I know I will," he said, ushering her across the threshold and into the small reception area.

"Good evening, Mr. Fleming," said a young man in black pants, pressed white shirt, black jacket, and tie standing beside a podium. "Everything is as you requested. You know where you're going?"

"Yes, I do."

"Very good, sir. Enjoy your stay."

Nick led Karen several more feet to the staircase that wrapped around the wallpapered foyer. She looked at him as they ascended the carpeted stairs. "This is beautiful."

"I thought you'd like it."

"Have you been here before?"

"Yeah. About three hours ago."

Karen didn't understand what he meant, but said nothing. They walked down the narrow hallway to room six. Nick took the key he had received earlier that day from his pocket and opened the door. Karen immediately smelled the roses that filled several vases around the room, and realized he had been there earlier that afternoon, that he had done this for her. Nick closed the door behind them, gently kissed her lips, and then took a book of matches from the table next to the door that was lit by a small lamp. Karen watched as he lit twelve red pillar candles and then drew the heavy striped curtains across the windows. He took off his coat and draped it over the back of a chintz-covered wing chair, then turned and looked at Karen. She crossed the room and stood in front of him, her face just inches from his. She reached up and undid the knot in his tie and the top two buttons of his shirt. "What do you want to do now?" asked Nick, kissing her nose. "I brought a deck of cards."

Karen threw her head back and laughed. "I love you. I love you so much."

Nick unbuttoned her sweater, revealing the lacy bra she had bought on her way home from work. Karen removed her pants, eagerly showing him the matching panties. "You are absolutely gorgeous," he said, putting his hands on her hips and drawing her even closer to him.

Karen unbuttoned his shirt while Nick kissed her. As she peeled it off his shoulders, he kissed the tops of her breasts. She inhaled deeply. A puff of noise emanated from her mouth when she exhaled, a squeak-like sound of barely contained emotion. She wanted to be inside of him as much as she wanted him to be inside her. She caressed his hairless chest, and then kissed it while he removed his pants. He scooped her off the ground and carried her to the four-poster bed. He threw back the covers with his hand and gently lowered Karen onto the bed. "Do you want me?" he asked, already on top of her, entering her. Breathing like a sprinter and unable to speak, Karen pulled his mouth to hers and hungrily sucked his lips. They both came within seconds.

This had never happened with Bob, she thought later, as she and Nick, still sweaty and breathing hard, lay intertwined on the bed. Bob had always come first and then Karen, manually, had come afterward. The fact that she and Nick were in sync, had, in fact become one person, reconfirmed her conviction that they belonged together, to one another. This, Karen told herself, was the difference between having sex and making love. She had always had sex with Bob. She had just made love, for the first time in her life, with Nick. He kissed her mouth and then reached over to the table next to his side of the bed, where he filled two crystal glasses with champagne from a bottle in an ice bucket. He handed her a glass and then tapped his against hers. "To our future."

"Together."

He took a sip before sliding out of bed to retrieve his boxers. He told Karen to lie back on the pillows. He dug her manicured feet out of the covers and began to massage her toes. She closed her eyes and let the feeling of his fingers touching her travel through her body. Slowly, expertly, he kneaded her calves and thighs. He told her to roll over. He gently caressed her back. He lifted her hair and kissed her neck, and Karen rolled back over to face him. She pulled him down to her and removed the cotton boxers he had put on less than twenty minutes before, and they made love again. "You are insatiable," he said, smiling, when they were done.

"Me? I know all about the foot-massage trick."

Nick laughed. They lay side by side, drinking champagne and talking about writing. When they finished their glasses, Nick got off the bed to get the basket that was sitting next to the door. He brought it to the bed and removed its contents: French bread, soft cheeses, nuts, and grapes. He poured her another glass of champagne, then fed her a grape. "Can we stay here all night?" she asked, knowing better.

"Can we stay here for the rest of our lives?"

"I want to be with you, Nick. I want to be with you for the rest of my life."

Nick kissed her lips. "We will be together."

"How do you know?" asked Karen, feeling anxious for the first time that evening.

"Because we are meant to be together. It's written somewhere."

"Like in the stars?" Karen asked skeptically.

"No," said Nick, hopping out of bed, grabbing a notebook

from the pocket of his wool blazer, and scribbling something down.

"What are you doing?" asked Karen, tilting her head in question.

"It's written here." Nick showed Karen the notebook with their names written inside a heart.

Karen laughed. "You are ridiculous."

"Which means you're in love with a ridiculous man. What does that say about you?"

"That I'm ridiculous, too?"

"That's my girl," said Nick, getting back into bed and wrapping his arms around Karen.

Karen looked in the front hall mirror when she got home and could see that her cheeks were red, still burning. She covered them with her hands and felt their warmth. She closed her eyes, picturing Nick kissing her cheeks. She walked into the kitchen, where Jamie was putting books into a backpack. Karen paid her as she heard the report for the evening. Robert had been wonderful. Rebecca had been somewhat less so. She called Karen's cell phone twice, but Karen didn't pick up. Karen swallowed hard, then explained that she had silenced her phone so she wouldn't disturb anyone at the dinner. Was there anything Rebecca needed? Jamie shook her head as she put on her coat and said that Rebecca had just been in a funny mood. She spent most of the night in her room. Karen opened the back door for Jamie, thanked her, and watched her walk across the back lawn to the street, where her dad was waiting for her in their car. When Bob was out of town, Jamie's father chauffeured his daughter to and from the Parsons' house. Karen closed the door and walked up the stairs to Rebecca's room, and found her daughter sleeping in her clothes. Karen gently shook her shoulder. She sat down on her bed. "Hi," she said, as Rebecca opened her eyes. "Are you okay?"

"Where were you tonight?" asked Rebecca, sleepily.

"At the community dinner, honey," said Karen, stroking her daughter's hair.

Rebecca looked up at her mother. "I called, but you didn't answer."

Karen smiled. "That was my mistake. I silenced my phone, so I didn't hear it. I should have checked it afterward."

"I just wanted to know where you were."

Karen reached down and kissed her daughter's forehead. "I'm right here now. Get some sleep, and I'll see you in the morning."

"When does Daddy get home?"

Karen stood. "The day after tomorrow."

"Maybe we can do something as a family this weekend," said Rebecca, rolling over and facing the wall.

Karen hesitated for a moment, looking at her daughter's back. Rebecca hadn't said anything like that in months. Unable to think of anything to say, Karen walked out of the room and closed the door behind her. She walked down the hall to her bedroom and changed into her nightgown. Her skin smelled like the soap she and Nick had used to wash each other with in the shower. She got into bed, sat back against her pillows, and thought about her wonderful night, her future with Nick. She was happy that tomorrow was a work day for her, an opportunity to spend time with the man she loved. She reached over and turned out the light. Just as she lay down, the phone rang.

"Hi," Nick said.

"Hi."

"Are you okay?"

"Are you kidding?"

"Thank you so much for tonight," he said. "I can't stop thinking about you."

"Good."

"I love you so much, Karen."

"And I love you, too."

CHAPTER 19

JANUARY 2005

Bob ran with his travel bag in hand through the sleet, from the driveway, along the slate stepping stones, to the back door. When he got inside, he set the bag down, then took off his raincoat and shook it. He called Karen's name twice before he saw the note on the table. Karen and the kids had gone to the movies and would be back around six. Nice homecoming, thought Bob. Truthfully, he didn't care much. He was tired from the negotiations and wanted a very hot shower and a cold beer.

Under the spray, Bob stood still, letting the water run down his back for several minutes before soaping himself and scrubbing the film of perspiration from his body. He shaved, dressed in jeans and a cotton, button-down shirt, what Karen called his uniform, and went back to the kitchen for the beer that he had been looking forward to since the end of his final meeting. He took it and a small bowl of pretzels to the family room, sat down on the new leather sofa, and turned on the big screen TV. He smiled; the game was only half over. At the first commercial, he muted the sound and reached for the phone in his shirt pocket. He dialed Denise's number and was surprised and pleased when she answered. "It's Bob."

"Hi," she said warmly. "Are you home?"

"I am."

"You must be exhausted."

He smiled at her sweetness. "I'm okay. A hot shower can work wonders."

"Did you have a good trip?"

"Yes," said Bob, wondering when Karen had last asked him about a business trip. "They're going to keep their business with Forester."

"Because of you."

"I guess my willingness to fly out there and talk with them helped."

Denise laughed. "You don't have to be modest. I know how good you are."

"You do?"

"You radiate success," she said.

"Can I see you soon?"

"Yes. I'd love to spend some time with you."

"Good. How about dinner Tuesday night? I'll pick you up about seven?"

"That sounds great. I live in the Glen Dale Apartments."

"I know where you live. I'll see you Tuesday night."

When Karen and the kids got home, Bob walked into the kitchen to greet his family. Robert was the only one who seemed glad to see him. Rebecca, who was still upset her mother dragged her to a dumb G movie, glanced at her father's face and then went directly to her room. Karen gave Bob a peck on the cheek before quickly turning her attention to the basket of take-out menus on the kitchen counter. She'd been having cravings lately, for savory foods, as if she were again in the final stage of her pregnancies, when the food finally stayed put in her stomach and she snacked all day long. She was not pregnant, she knew, because she took birth control pills. Bob had years ago volunteered to get a vasectomy after their last child was born, telling Karen that since she would have to carry and birth the children, this would be his contribution to the effort. After Robert emerged, however, Bob told Karen he'd had second thoughts. Karen flipped through the menus until she found what she was looking for: pizza for Rebecca and Robert, hot wings for her and Bob, and a ready-made Caesar salad. As she called in the order, Robert followed his dad back into the den, where they both plopped down on the couch. Bob offered the last pretzel in the bowl to his son. "Just the guys," Bob said, as Robert popped the tiny knot into his mouth. "Just the way I like it."

When the food arrived, they all sat around the kitchen table, the sound of forks scooping up the Caesar salad and slurped milk filling in for conversation. "I want a cell phone," said Rebecca, breaking the silence as she often did with a request.

"I don't think so," said Karen, dipping her wing into the plastic container of blue-cheese dressing the restaurant provided.

"Why not?"

"Because you spend enough time in your room on the phone already."

"Like you care."

"Pardon me?" asked Bob, who stopped chewing.

Rebecca put down her fork and looked at her father. "It's not like either of you want to spend any time with me, or Robert, or each other for that matter. If we're going to be a dysfunctional family, I might as well have all the accessories."

"What's *dysfunctional* mean?" asked Robert.

"We're not dysfunctional," Bob told him.

"Oh no?" asked Rebecca. "Then what do you call this dinner? We have the family gathered here for a meal for the first time in days, and no one has anything to say to each other."

Karen glanced at Bob, who leaned back in his chair. "I'm tired," he said. "I've had a long week."

"So what else is new, Dad? When aren't your weeks long?"

Bob put his fork down. "So what I'm hearing, Rebecca, is that you'd like to spend more time with me? That I'm letting you down?" Rebecca made a face. "Maybe, if you moved on from your sullen, life-is-so-hard-for-an-eleven-year-old-girl phase, we'd be able to exchange pleasantries instead of barbs." Rebecca's eyes welled with tears. Bob tore the flesh off a chicken wing with his teeth. "You can dish it out, honey, but you sure can't take it."

Rebecca stood. "Most fathers wouldn't ask their daughters to take it!" she loudly proclaimed as she left the room.

"Robert," said Karen, "why don't you take your plate downstairs and finish your dinner in front of the TV. You can use the cool new table." Robert, who was old and experienced enough to know when his parents wanted him elsewhere, put another slice of pizza on his plate and walked out of the room.

"What is her problem?" Bob asked Karen.

"She's hormonal."

"She's a monster, a spoiled brat. She needs some discipline."

Karen took a sip of wine. "You're saying I don't discipline her?"

"Well, do you? Do you ever say no?"

"Look around you, Bob. Does it look like we live in a house full of nos?"

Bob finished his beer. "I can think of a number of nos that I've heard recently."

Karen shook her head slowly. "That's what we need right now, to turn this conversation into an argument about sex. You've got a daughter who can't stand you, and all you can think about is sex."

"First of all, Rebecca does not hate me; I give her everything she asks for. And second, if we had sex with any regularity, we wouldn't have to argue about it."

"Get over it!" Karen said, venom in her voice. "You are not an eighteen-year-old boy! You cannot have everything you want when you want it!"

Bob stood. "Oh yes, I can," he said calmly. "Having everything I want goes hand in hand with fulfilling my business ambitions. I can, indeed, have it all."

Karen was shaking. "You are the most selfish person I've ever met."

"And you," said Bob, throwing his napkin onto the table, "are just like me."

Karen watched him walk out of the room. She sat for just a minute before eating three more wings, so that Bob would not be able to have them before he went to bed.

* * *

Bob called Karen Tuesday afternoon and told her he had a dinner meeting with clients in River City and would not be home until
ten. As soon as she hung up the phone, she called Nick. He said he
doubted Trisha would be home before nine anyway and that he
could ask his caregiver to come back for the evening. That would
give them a couple of hours. "Let's go to the diner," said Karen,
"and then park by the river."

Nick laughed. "You want to go parking? It's freezing outside."

"I think we can find some heat."

"There goes my concentration for the afternoon." Karen smiled
at the phone. "I'll meet you in the library parking lot at six."

"I love you," she said.

Bob worked until six, then jogged down two flights in the stair-
well at the end of the hall to the basement locker room. It was
quiet, with just a couple of guys changing into running clothes for
their evening workout. He opened his locker and took his shaving
kit off the metal shelf. At one of three sinks, he washed his face,
shaved, and brushed his teeth. He took off the shirt he had put on
that morning and changed into a clean one. He chose a new tie
from the several he stored in his locker. Having extra clothes at
work was something Bob had found essential in the last couple of
years. High-powered meetings were called without warning; a fresh
shirt and a washed face gave the right impression. He made it to
River City in twenty-three minutes and decided to stop by the
restaurant to check the reservation he made that afternoon. As requested, a table in the City Room, overlooking the river, was waiting for them. Bob gave the maître d' a twenty-dollar bill and told
him to take good care of them. Dinner, he said, would take two
hours instead of the standard ninety minutes. He would not be
rushed.

Bob drove to the Glen Dale Apartments and parked near
Denise's unit. He walked up the outdoor staircase and down the
short indoor hallway to the end. A vase of fresh flowers stood on a
small table in the corner, next to a powder blue door with the
bronze numbers one and six attached to its surface. He checked his

watch. It was exactly seven. He rang her doorbell. Seconds later, wearing a short black dress with a pale pink shawl wrapped around her shoulders, Denise opened the door and smiled at him. "You are incredibly punctual."

"And you are incredibly lovely."

Denise backed up a few steps, inviting Bob into her apartment. "I'll be right back," she said. "I've just got to grab my purse from my bedroom."

"Take your time."

Her living area was decorated with inexpensive but tasteful furniture. The sitting area featured a wicker love seat and matching chairs topped with comfortable-looking pastel-print cushions. Beyond that, next to a bay window, stood a wood dining table, surrounded by four ladder-back chairs. Remembering what Denise said about her view, Bob crossed the room. It had been dark outside for a couple of hours, but he could see by the streetlights that she had a decent winter view of the river. His thoughts jumped for a moment to the tree service that had raked and bagged their leaves while he was away. He made a mental note to ask Karen if she had paid them in cash or with a check. Denise walked out of the bedroom with a small black purse and a fresh coat of pink lipstick on her full, soft-looking lips. "Ready?" asked Bob, resisting the urge to kiss those lips.

"I am," she said, wrapping her shawl tightly around her.

Bob put his hand on the small of her back and gently guided her out the door. He watched as she took a set of keys attached to a silver *D* from her purse and locked her door. They walked through the door at the end of the hall and down the staircase.

"Oh, it's colder than I thought," she said.

Bob wrapped his arm around her shoulders and pulled her close. They walked briskly to the car. Bob opened the door for her, then walked around the back to the driver's side. Inside, Bob started the car and flipped the switch to heat the seats. He could feel the warmth on his legs immediately. "Better?"

"Wonderful. You have a beautiful car. I love BMWs."

"It gets me from A to B," said Bob, pulling out of the parking space.

Denise laughed. "I'd guess it does a lot more than that. My Buick gets me from A to B."

"You have a Buick?"

"My father is a safety freak." She buckled her seat belt. "He doesn't want me driving a tin can no matter what people say about gas mileage."

"Safety is important. At Forester, we are always thinking about how we can improve our record," said Bob, turning the corner onto the main road.

On their way to the restaurant, Bob asked Denise about her family. She was the oldest of three girls. Her sisters were both still in high school, and the juvenile arguments over clothes and curling irons started at six in the morning. Diane, the middle daughter, who would graduate from high school in June, swore she was going to move to Texas, just to get as far away from Nancy, the baby, as possible. Denise's father was an accountant, which Denise said she knew sounded boring, but he wasn't as bad as what those who made snap judgments about accountants thought. Sure, he liked reliable cars, but he also liked skydiving. Denise's parents tried it for their twenty-fifth wedding anniversary several years before and had been doing it a couple times a year since.

"From this day forward, I will never think about accountants in the same way," said Bob. Denise laughed as he drove the car into the parking lot of the City Room.

"Oh, I love this restaurant. I've been here just twice, both times feeling like I've left River City behind in favor of a glamorous city like New York or San Francisco."

Bob, who had been to both cities, said, "The restaurants there don't get much better than this." He got out of the car and jogged around the front to open Denise's door.

"Have you been to a lot of big cities?" she asked, as he offered her his hand.

"I travel a lot for business."

"The only traveling I do for business is to Office Depot."

Bob laughed hard. "That's the best one I've heard all day."

They walked hand in hand into the restaurant and were seated at the table Bob requested. They drank wine and shared their meals, as well as more stories about their jobs, families, and dreams. Bob listened more than he talked. He was touched by, arguments about hair product aside, how close Denise was to her sisters, in spite of their age difference. He had lost touch with his older brothers, Jonathan and Mark, who were as committed to living in California as Bob was to living and working in Michigan. They had made their fortunes, several times over, yet were still too busy to come home. Not that Bob would see them if they did, since Tucker and Janet had moved from their family home to Florida. Had it been twelve years already? His parents spent their days on the golf course and playing bridge with a close group of friends. They sent checks for the children's birthdays and at Christmas and received dutiful thank-you notes in return, and that seemed to be the extent of the relationship outside of Bob and his family's annual trip in February. Karen had long ago stopped asking about holiday plans with Tucker and Janet.

Of course, Bob said nothing to Denise about his immediate family, about Rebecca, Robert, or Karen. He knew if he told her he was a married man with a family, she wouldn't finish her dinner. What woman with any self-respect would? He would have to say something if they kept seeing each other, but he didn't want to confess prematurely. If the evening didn't go well, there would be no reason to say anything. If the evening did go well—and he had a feeling it would—he would eventually have to tell Denise about his family. He had recently considered separating from Karen; perhaps he would do it sooner rather than later. Then he could tell Denise that he was separated instead of married. She couldn't fault him for that.

After dinner, they ordered coffee. Denise asked Bob about his job. She wanted to know all about how he had been able to achieve such success. Bob explained that he was an incredibly focused person at work. If he had a task to accomplish, he did little else until it was done. He put in long hours whenever necessary; he sacrificed his personal life for the good of Forester. And in return, he had been rewarded. It was his drive, his single focus. If Denise wanted to own and operate a Curves franchise, she had to want it more than anything else. Denise opened her mouth to speak.

"What?" asked Bob.

"I do want it." She stirred a packet of Equal into her coffee. "But I want other things, too."

Bob sipped his coffee. "What else do you want?"

Denise blushed. "It will sound silly to you."

"I'm a businessman. Nothing sounds silly to me."

"I want to be in love with someone," she said, breaking eye contact for the first time since they had sat down. "I want to be successful in business, but I don't want to spend my life alone." Bob reached across the table and covered her hand with his. She looked up at him. "You work so hard. Do you ever feel lonely?"

Bob swallowed hard. "Not tonight. I haven't felt this content in a long time."

Bob took Denise home after dinner. She asked him in, which he declined. He was resolved not to cheapen the evening by ending it in bed. Denise opened the door with her key, then lingered. She turned to face Bob. "Thank you," she said with her back to the door. "I had a wonderful evening."

"So did I. I'll call you in a couple of days."

"That sounds good." She put her hands on his shoulders, stood on her toes, and kissed his cheek. "You're pretty nice, for a businessman."

Bob put his hands on Denise's cheeks, drew her face toward his, and gently kissed her lips.

"And you're pretty nice period."

He kissed her again before releasing her. She thanked him again, then went into her apartment and closed the door behind her. Bob walked down the hall and jogged down the steps to his car, humming as he went. When he got home, the house was dark and Karen was in bed. He didn't know if she was asleep or pretending to be asleep, but he made no attempt to wake her. He had no interest, oddly, in having sex with her. The only one he wanted to touch at the moment was Denise, and he knew he couldn't do that until he was free from Karen. He would tell her tomorrow, he thought as he undressed. He would tell her he wanted a separation. She would not argue. It would be amicable. It would be easy. And it would allow him to be with Denise.

Only he didn't tell Karen the next day. He had a long day at the office and then had real clients to entertain for dinner. The last thing he wanted to do at ten at night when he was exhausted and cranky was start a discussion about the dissolution of their marriage. Plus, twenty-four hours after being sure he wanted to do it, he was less sure. He wanted to be with Denise, but he also knew divorcing Karen would not come without pain. After all, he had once loved her deeply. In college, she had either been by his side or on his mind. Sixteen years ago, she had been at the center of his individual universe, a human sun. Everything he did or thought revolved around her. And now he was going to swap universes, just like that?

Even if he did, Karen would not go away, and neither would Rebecca and Robert, who would become divorce offspring and live out of suitcases. Every other weekend, they would pack their precious belongings (Nintendo DS for Robert, iPod and earbuds for Rebecca) along with their clothing into overnight bags, then ride from their home with Karen to Bob's new home, where he would live alone for a while, and then, perhaps, with Denise. Rebecca and Robert would pretend to be happy to see him, at least Robert would. But, in time, they would resent their uprooting. They would want to spend their weekends at home, near their friends. Bob could entice them, of course, with gifts and trips to restaurants, movie theaters, and amusement parks. Often the best way to solve a problem, whether at home or at work, was to throw money at it. Did he care if his children were more interested in his money than his company, advice, or love? Bob ran his fingers through his hair. Maybe that's what it was all about anyway.

Karen was in bed reading a magazine when Bob walked into their bedroom. She looked up at him briefly, then returned her gaze to the article.

"How was your night?" he asked.

Karen looked up again. "I can't remember the last time you asked me that."

Bob shrugged. "I think about asking it. I guess my thoughts don't always work their way into words."

Karen looked back at the magazine and flipped a page. "It was uneventful. Rebecca spent most of the night in her room. Robert and I worked on homework and then read together."

Bob took off his suit coat and hung it on a hanger. "Should we be more worried about Rebecca?"

Karen put the magazine down next to her. "I don't know. The doctor tells me her behavior is normal, that girls her age have a sudden and overwhelming need for privacy. It becomes a concern when she chooses it all the time, when she shuns her family, us, altogether."

Bob hung his pants on another hanger. "We're not there yet?"

Karen hesitated. "I don't think so. Although on some days we're close."

Bob nodded his head. "Well, she looks better anyway, not as skinny."

"You're right about that. She has begun to take more of an interest in eating. I think she's growing. And I am trying to give her what she wants. I'd rather have her eat take-out pizza than not eat at all."

"Good thinking. And don't worry about me. I'll never get sick of pizza."

Karen raised her eyebrows. Where had this conversation come from? Bob emerged from the closet in flannel pajama pants and a clean T-shirt. He got into bed beside Karen. "I am exhausted," he said, kissing her on the forehead, then turning his back to her. "Sleep well."

Karen looked at the back of his head, waiting for it to flip so she would be looking as his face, waiting for his eyebrows to rise in appeal. When nothing happened, she reached over and turned out her light.

As soon as Jeremy followed Robert to the basement playroom, and Britney and Rebecca disappeared up the stairs, Karen and Sarah settled in at the kitchen table. They made small talk while the water in the kettle slowly came to a boil. Karen set her new china mugs, milk, sugar, spoons, and a plate with four cookies on a tray, while Sarah placed four cookies each on two other plates and then carried them upstairs to the girls and downstairs to the boys. Now that the children were older and able to be careful, Karen allowed them to eat outside of the kitchen and living room. When Sarah returned to the kitchen, Karen was pouring the steaming tea into their mugs. Sarah continued with her list of what was wrong with the school system. Number one had been the administrators, and number two was the superintendent. Lousy leadership does not a good system make. It was disheartening because the people at the top were the hardest to get rid of, Sarah said, wrapping her hands around the mug Karen handed her. Plus, lately, she had been spending too much time at school in an effort to help the overworked teachers, and, consequently, had lost the sense of balance in her life that she had struggled for months to establish. She had less and less time to herself. Vincent wasn't as understanding as he had been when she first started working. One of his favorite lines now was, *Welcome to my world.* She felt that she had fallen into this new pattern and didn't know how to break it. "Blah, blah, blah," she said. "I'm boring myself to death. Tell me about you. How's your job going?"

Karen finished her tea and poured herself more. Telling Sarah was one of the reasons she'd invited her for tea. With part-time jobs and busy children, they hadn't seen each other in more than a month. And the last couple of times, Karen had not talked about Nick, and Sarah had not asked. It had been three months since the day Karen had confided in Sarah, three months since Karen and Nick had gone out to dinner for the first time. Was that just ninety days ago? Had she fallen in love with another man, had sex with him, and decided to dissolve her thirteen-year marriage in ninety days? *Impulsive* was the first word that came to Karen's mind. What would a marriage counselor say about a decision like that? Karen could feel her facial furnace kick in. She sipped her tea, silently convincing herself that time didn't matter. What she had been feeling about Bob, about her marriage, had been building for years. It wasn't a decision she made over three months; it had been coming since Rebecca was born.

"Do you want to tell me something?"

"Yes," said Karen, pouring more tea into Sarah's mug. "I'm just not sure how to do it."

"It's about Nick Fleming. Your relationship, I'm guessing, has progressed."

Karen set her mug down on the table. "I want to leave my husband to be with him. I'm in love with him."

Sarah reached for a cookie she was not hungry for. "Have you had sex with him?"

Karen looked down at her trembling hands. She couldn't meet Sarah's eyes. "Yes."

Sarah broke the cookie in half and bit into one of the pieces in her hands. Because it was unwelcome, its hard edges scraped the roof of her mouth. She chewed and forced a swallow, pushing down the gagging reflex brought on by Karen's confession. She shifted her gaze from the plate of cookies to the heavy gray sky out the window; it looked as if it was just about to open and shower the earth with snow. Sarah sipped her tea, and then said, "You can still save your marriage. People survive affairs. Sometimes, they make marriages stronger."

"I don't want to save my marriage. I want to get out of my marriage."

"How do you know? How do you know this isn't just a passing thing and that six months from now, Nick Fleming will be a name you can barely remember."

Karen shook her head. "I have more of a chance of forgetting Bob's name than I do Nick's name."

Sarah's eyebrows shot up. "Tell me. Tell me how you know this."

It was a familiar story to Sarah, who had been confided in before. It was the story of attention and affection, when the two people involved have been searching for something, never thinking they would find it, and then miraculously doing just that. This new relationship, they believe, is like no other. No one can ever or will ever share love the way they do. The man is kind, gentle, and, uncharacteristically for his gender, unselfish. The woman is childlike in her devotion, euphoric. Their love for one another consumes and deludes them; quickly they are barely able to be without one another. Their love is stronger than any obstacle the world can present. There are no words to adequately describe their feelings for one another. And yet Sarah knew what Karen was feeling for Nick was not unlike what she had felt about Bob, or what Sarah had felt about Vincent many years ago. The idea that this love between Karen and Nick was any different from any other love, illicit or otherwise, was utterly foolish and equally undeniable. Sarah listened without interruption. When Karen was done explaining why she had no choice but to leave her husband, Sarah closed her eyes and shook her head. "There is always a choice, Karen. Love isn't everything."

Karen's eyes widened. "Are you kidding me? Love is *everything.* If you don't have love, what do you have that matters?"

Sarah refilled her mug. "You have security. You have familiarity. You have a past and a future. You have a family. Karen, have you considered what this will do to your children?"

Karen bit into a cookie. "Some," she said. "Rebecca is going to be impossible. But she is impossible about everything anyway. Eventually, she will see the good in this arrangement. She knows how bad it's been. And Robert will adjust quickly. And they'll see Bob all the time. I know we can work out something that will work for everyone."

"Do you really believe that?"

"Yes." Karen was resolved. "I know there will be some difficult times. But I will go through them with someone I love rather than with someone I no longer know. Bob and I have grown apart; he'll readily admit that. In fact, it may very well be Bob who gives me the least trouble of the three. He's out at these business dinners or on the other side of the world; who really knows what's going on, Sarah. Maybe he's in love with someone else, too."

"And that wouldn't make you the least bit sad?"

"I've been sad for a long time." They were silent for a several moments. "Do you hate me for this?"

"No," said Sarah. "Perhaps a small part of me is even envious. In some ways, you are right. If your marriage is no good and you don't see it getting better, why not get out? I just don't want you to regret your decision."

Karen shook her head. "I won't."

"And you've considered counseling?"

"Counseling is for people who want to make their marriage work. I'm done working on mine."

"And Nick is ready, too?"

Karen smiled shyly. "Yes. He loves me."

CHAPTER 20

Days passed, and Karen had still not discussed a separation with Bob, nor had Nick talked to Trisha. And yet Karen and Nick talked about talking about it, breaking the news they called it, all the time. They repeatedly reconfirmed their determination, yet admitted their reluctance about dissolving marriages and splitting families. When she was being truthful with herself, Karen was very concerned about the effect a breakup might have on her children. And, although she and Nick calculated that they would be okay financially, she was worried about money. She had been comfortable for so long. She suspected Bob would be willing to throw money at the children, but she knew he would be stingy with her. And Nick's money came from his wife, which meant he was facing the same prospect of financial setback. Their new life together would come at many costs.

After Bob and Denise's third date, Bob accepted her invitation into her apartment. They drank port on the couch, kissing and fondling one another, and then had sex in her bedroom. Afterward, Bob told her he had an early meeting the next day and had to get home. They showered together before Bob left, promising the next time he would stay the entire night. On the way home, he thought about sex with Denise. Her body was so different from Karen's. While Denise was far from what men would describe as fat, she was soft and fleshy. Women in an uncharitable mood might call her solid. Her body reminded Bob of the young secretary in the English pub—what was her name?—Angela, with her ample chest, full ass, and pudgy fingers. Denise was as ripe and ready as Angela had been outside her flat, where Bob had kissed her plump lips and held her breasts. And Denise was a good lover, naïve but willing. That was the biggest difference between having sex with his wife and having sex with someone new: Denise wanted him. Bob's cock stiffened as he thought about having sex with her again. When he stayed the night, they would have sex that night and again in the morning. His hard-on softened when Bob realized his blunder. How could he spend the night with Denise? A minute later the answer came to him: He could simply tell Karen he was going out of town on business. He could tell her he had to entertain clients in another city. Dinner would go late, and it would be better if he stayed the night in a highway hotel and drove home the next day. She would understand. In fact, she would welcome his absence.

Bob called Denise the next day at work and asked her out for dinner Friday night. He told her he could spend the night at her apartment; she told him she was thrilled. He next called Karen, who told him to do whatever he needed to do, that she would be fine with the kids. As soon as Karen hung up with Bob, she called Nick and told him they could be together Friday night, and that instead of talking about being trapped in their marriages they should focus on the positive, on their happy future together. Nick told her he loved her, their new way to end phone calls, and would find a way to be with her. As soon as they hung up, Nick called the hospital and left a message for Trisha. He was going to attend, last minute, an all-day seminar on the survival of the small-town newspaper. He would be gone all day Friday, getting home late Friday night. He would ask their caregiver to take care of the girls. If Dawn couldn't do it, he would find other arrangements. He hung up, made one more call, then sat back in his chair with a smile on his face. Three more days, he thought, just three more days until he would again hold his lover. They would explore each other's bodies by candlelight. They would eat sensual food. They would make concrete, feasible plans to leave their spouses.

It was a big-blue-sky day on Friday, warm for the middle of February. Hardened snow sat in the tree Vs, creating that Winter Wonderland effect his elderly neighbor was so fond of pronouncing whenever Nick used his snowblower to clear her driveway. He drove to the library with his driver's side window cracked an inch to let in some fresh air, listening on and off to an interview on the radio and thinking about the evening ahead of him. Karen had arranged for her sitter to stay until eleven; they would have six hours together. He had never been with her for six hours, even at the office, and was full of expectations about what it would be like to have her for that long. They would not run out of things to say to one another, like he and Trisha often did, even when they hadn't seen one another all day. He vowed not to look at his watch until he knew it was getting late. Instead, he wanted to spend the time looking at her, at her auburn hair that she had recently lightened as a manifestation that she was a new person, that she was starting a new life with the right man. Her skin was pure white, except for the smattering of freckles along the ridge of her nose, and so soft to the touch. She had laughed at this, when he first told her, telling him that with the amount she spent on skin care products, her skin should feel like velvet. He would be able to touch her for six hours. He would be able to unguardedly gaze at her without worrying what others might think. At work, he was careful, too careful probably. But he knew people talked about them, so he had been more cavalier in his interactions with her, paying less attention to her than the other reporters. In some ways, it was easy. She was the best writer by far and needed his attention less than everyone else at the office. But it was also difficult not being able to give her his attention because he was so much in love.

Karen spent part of the hour before she met Nick in the tub. She sat with her eyes closed in a landscape of caramel-scented bubbles. Karen pictured Nick in her mind, the intensity in his eyes and the firmness of his arms and legs. She could hear his voice, talking to her on the phone, and she could picture him in his office, amid the disorderly piles of stacked newspapers and the clipped articles, wire reports, and pink "urgent message" slips on his desk. She sank lower in the water, allowing the bubbles to surround her neck and crackle in her ears. Where would he take her tonight, she wondered. Would they return to the inn? Karen hoped not; it would be impossible to duplicate or surpass that magical night. Karen opened her eyes to check the clock on the bathroom shelf. With just thirty minutes to get ready, she washed and shaved her legs before getting out of the tub. She changed into a short black dress, black heels, and gold jewelry, and then kissed her children good-bye—telling Rebecca she was excited about her fancy girls' night out with the other female reporters in the office—and walked out the door.

As Nick and Karen each drove toward the library, Bob sat in a weekly sales meeting. While the figures for the week were below target, Bob was having a hard time concentrating on numbers and projections. Soon, he would be standing at Denise's door, and he was anticipating how beautiful she would look and how satisfying their night together would be. He longed to touch her, to taste her; her skin was ever so slightly salty. Her oval face showed all of her emotions the moment she felt them. He particularly liked the look of pleasant surprise punctuated by her eyes and brows when he had entered her. She had whispered encouragements in her playful voice. He looked at his watch and breathed in deeply. He had made the dinner reservation for eight at Denise's request, but was scheduled to be at her place at six. She thought having a drink at her apartment first would be fun, as she put it. Bob hoped her idea of fun matched his.

Denise took a half-day vacation Friday to get ready. First, she went to the mall and bought new underwear and sleepwear and six white taper candles. She then went to the grocery store and bought cashews, large green olives, and grape tomatoes—foods they could feed each other. She bought eggs, cinnamon crumble coffeecake, real orange juice, and freshly ground coffee for the morning. On the way home, she stopped at the florist for a colorful assortment of cut flowers. In her apartment, she arranged the flowers in a large glass vase and set them down on the coffee table she had dusted the night before. She placed two candles in the living room, one in the kitchen, one in the bathroom, and two in the bedroom. She took a long, hot shower and washed and conditioned her hair. Naked in the bathroom, Denise rubbed sesame oil into her arms, legs, and abdomen. She wrapped herself in a terry-cloth robe, and walked into her closet to retrieve the chocolate-brown silk pants suit she had picked up at the dry cleaners and matching heels. When Bob rang the doorbell an hour later, she was ready for him.

Just before six, when Bob was parking his car outside Denise's apartment building, Karen and Nick were making love in a large feather bed in a one-room log cabin in the woods. It was the work space of a best-selling author friend of Nick's who was out of town on a book tour and had given Nick permission to use it. It held very little: the bed; a large, single-drawer pine desk; a miniature stove, sink, and refrigerator; and a toilet, sink, and shower, separated from the rest of the room by walls that reached three-quarters of the way to the ceiling. The bed faced a large stone fireplace, in which the last log slowly burned. A bearskin rug sat on the hearth, and next to it, two champagne flutes Karen and Nick had drunk from before they removed each other's clothes. In bed, they laughed and smiled as they touched each other. Afterward, they talked about their future, about their new resolve to tell their spouses. They would do it at the same time—Sunday afternoon. They would get sitters to take their children to the movies, so they could quietly ask for divorces at home. Neither of them expected a fight. In six months or so, they could be together legally.

Denise loved that Bob was punctual. She opened her door to find him in a dark gray suit, holding a dozen red roses, and looking like someone from the pages of a magazine. She couldn't believe he was here to be with her, to take her out, and to spend the night in her bed. He smiled when she opened the door, and took a step forward to kiss her on the cheek. He told her she was beautiful, like he always did, and she slowly backed up to let him in. She put the flowers in a white china vase and took them to the bedroom, so they could see and smell them later on. When she walked back into the living room, she found Bob standing where she had left him and laughed. "Would you like something to drink?"

"I would." Bob followed her to the kitchen. "Let me make you something."

"I've got champagne."

"Perfect."

Denise took two freshly washed and hand-dried flutes down from her cupboard and set them on the counter. She'd had them out earlier, but put them away in case Bob wanted a beer instead of the champagne. She watched him open the bottle, admiring his ability to keep the contents from shooting across the room. They took their drinks to the couch and drank to their relationship. Denise took a cashew from its pottery dish and slipped it through Bob's lips. He responded by kissing her immediately; she could taste the salt. He took an olive, bit it, and fed Denise half of it. She closed her eyes and let Bob take the glass from her hand. Seconds later, he was gently unbuttoning the top of her pants suit. She opened her eyes and watched him. He inhaled when he saw her brown silk bra. She stood, letting her shirt fall to the floor, took his hand, and led him into the bedroom. She lit the candles and then slowly undressed him. Naked, he watched her remove her pants, revealing the thong that matched her bra. Seconds later, they were on the bed.

At seven thirty, both couples were showered and dressed again. Karen helped Nick strip the bed of its sheets and replace them with clean ones. He put the soiled laundry in a bag and dropped it next to the door. Together, they washed the few dishes they had used and made sure the embers were well contained within the fireplace. Just before they walked out, Nick pulled Karen to him. "We can do this. We can be together every night, just like tonight."

Karen kissed him gently on the lips. "I can't wait."

Nick lifted the bag of laundry onto his shoulder, and they walked to the car. As always, he opened the passenger side door for Karen, who slid in, buckling the seat belt over her camel-hair coat. "So, where are we going for dinner? For some reason, I'm starving."

Nick smiled at her. "Recreational sports will do that."

Karen leaned over and kissed his cheek. "Do we have time for more?"

"You are nothing if not insatiable."

"Only with you."

Nick started the car. "We're going to the new Italian place, just outside River City."

"Oh great! I hear it's wonderful."

Afterward, when they were both dressed again, Bob watched Denise strip the sheets from her bed. As she stooped to pick them up from the floor, Bob enjoyed a full view of her rear end. She had a rounded, perfectly shaped pear bottom. It was feminine and inviting, unlike the hard asses of women who spent their mornings in high-impact aerobics classes. Men he knew preferred women who looked and felt like women; most guys were more turned off than on by the toned female, with her taut thighs and sinewy biceps. He followed Denise, as she walked out of the room and into the tiny laundry room next to her kitchen. She put the sheets in the washing machine and turned to face him. "You're like a puppy," she said, smiling.

He took her in his arms. "I'd follow you anywhere."

She kissed him. "Well, you can follow me back into the bedroom and help me remake the bed, or you can relax on the living room couch."

Bob hesitated. "Do you want me to help?"

"I want you to do whatever makes you happy."

"Okay," said Bob, who hadn't made a bed since his children were very young. "I'll stay here. I'll put the hors d'oeuvres in the fridge and wash the glasses."

"That sounds good. I'll be back in five minutes."

Bob looked at his watch. "Perfect. We need just ten minutes to get to the restaurant."

"Where are we going?" called Denise over her shoulder as she walked away.

"Villa Cesare. It's the new restaurant on Route 10."

"Oh, I've been wanting to go there. I hear it's wonderful."

Denise grabbed the set of satin sheets she had bought the previous weekend from her bedroom closet. As she smoothed them over the mattress, she realized she was glad Bob was not helping her. She wanted the regal comfort of her bed to be a surprise. She had not put these sheets on the bed that afternoon because she suspected what had happened would happen. Instead, she saved them, so they could linger in the morning in the midst of satin. One of her coworkers had told her that nothing, except another human body, felt as good on skin.

On the way to the restaurant, they talked about business. Denise wanted to hear about Bob's career, about how he had started as a salesman and made it to the top. Bob laughed at the notion of being at the top. "The president has that job," he said, smiling.

Denise reached over and touched his shoulder. "Temporarily. I have all the faith in the world that you will and can do anything you want."

"You're so sweet."

When Bob and Denise arrived at the restaurant, Nick and Karen were already seated. Bob didn't see them as he escorted Denise through the dining room. It was a large room with busy carpeting and perhaps seventy-five tables, and Bob was focused on two things: Denise, and the table they were being led to. He had asked for a nice table, by a window or in a corner, as far away from the kitchen as possible, and he was hoping the hostess would honor that request. It wasn't until Bob knew that she had and they were seated at a table in a bay window that he took a casual look around and saw, on the far side of the room, a woman who looked very much like his wife. Feeling suddenly very warm, Bob looked at Denise, who was already reading the menu. He reached into his suit pocket for the glasses he had picked up last week to correct his diminishing distance vision and looked back at the woman across the room. It was Karen. She was laughing, and her left arm was stretched across the table so she could touch her date: Nick Fleming, her editor. Bob picked up his menu as he gathered his thoughts, his heart pumping double-time. He held the menu in front of his face and glanced back at Karen's table. This time, she was looking back at him. Bob put his menu down on the table. "Excuse me, honey," he said to Denise. "I've got to run to the men's room. Would you please order me a martini?"

Denise smiled at him. "Of course I will. Hurry back."

Bob walked down the staircase behind their table, following the sign for the restrooms. He paced and ran his hands over his hair. That bitch, he thought. She's been fucking Nick Fleming all along! Less than a minute later, Karen appeared at the base of the other staircase, accusation in her eyes, anger on her contorted face. "How's your business trip?" she spat.

"Don't start with me, you tramp," Bob shot back. "How long, Karen? How long have you been lying to me?"

"And I might ask you the same question," she said, hands on her hips. "Or do you expect me to believe that's a business colleague on the other side of your romantic, candlelit table for two?"

"You can believe whatever the hell you want because I don't give a fuck what you do anymore."

"Well, join the club, because I haven't cared about you for years."

Bob stepped back, as if Karen had pushed him. "What do you mean?" His tone was softer, defeated. "What do you mean you haven't cared about me in years?"

Karen turned away and walked to the chintz couch against the wall. She sat down heavily and draped her arms along her legs. "Look at us. We've both been caught with someone else and we're trying to justify our anger with each other. It's over, Bob. I don't want to scream at you, especially not here. I just want to start another life."

"You want a divorce?" asked Bob, incredulous, even though the word had been running through his mind for several weeks.

"And you don't? You want to continue pretending we still love each other?"

Bob closed his eyes. "I don't know, Karen. In some ways, I do still love you."

"Don't," said Karen, standing and holding up her hand. "Don't say that. You may be in love with the idea of still loving me. But you haven't loved me for a long time. You love your job, and you love yourself."

Bob took a step toward his wife. "Now that's not fair."

"I'm sorry," Karen said, putting her hands on his shirtfront. "It doesn't matter, Bob. Whatever mattered once is long gone." They were both silent for a moment. "I'm going back upstairs. I'm going to tell Nick I don't feel well, and I'm going to go home."

"I'll do the same thing. We can talk more at home."

Karen looked at Bob's watery eyes. "What are we going to say to each other?"

Bob reached out and put his hands on her cheeks, seeing her face as if for the first time. "We're going to work things out."

Karen closed her eyes. "I don't want to work things out. I can't, Bob. I need to start a new life."

"That's what I mean. We're going to work out the details of separate lives."

Karen swallowed, which wasn't enough to clear the constriction in her throat. "You go first. I'll give you a couple of minutes to leave."

Bob headed for the stairs, then turned to face Karen. "I'll see you at home."

By the time Karen made her way to the top of the stairs, she was crying. She couldn't understand why she wasn't laughing, absolutely jubilant, skipping back to the table to tell Nick the good news. Instead, she walked back slowly. Seeing her, Nick rushed to her. "Are you okay? I've been worried about you."

"I don't feel well," said Karen, holding her stomach. "Can we go home?"

"Absolutely, darling. Let me get you into the car, and then I'll settle things in here."

On the way home, Karen closed her eyes and pretended to

sleep. She didn't trust herself to keep quiet about everything that had just happened, about everything that had happened since the day she met Bob Parsons in the student center at State. She held her stomach, which truly did ache. She let the tears that filled her eyes fall down her cheeks. How could exactly what she wanted to happen hurt so badly?

CHAPTER 21

MAY 2007

Karen opened her eyes and slowly adjusted to her surroundings. She and Nick had moved into their new house three months ago, but she still expected to see her old bedroom, the one she shared with Bob before she shared it with Nick. She rolled over in bed and, for several seconds, watched Nick sleeping. Then, she kissed him on the cheek, got out of bed, and wrapped her bathrobe around her body. Rebecca would be up soon, and Karen needed a cup of coffee before she could balance the highs and lows her fourteen-year-old experienced hourly.

The kitchen was already light. The large windows and double-glass doors that led onto the deck coaxed the morning sun into the room. Karen started the coffeemaker, then walked to the doors and looked out. The sky was already clear, promising delivery on a sunny forecast. It had been an excruciatingly long, and at times, difficult winter, weather-wise and otherwise. Bright sunshine was the best cure Karen knew for the blues, for the days when doubt and frustration pulled at her. While she and Robert had soldiered through the toughest hours, Rebecca had been a wreck. Crying jags, sarcasm, painful words—even more than normal—indicated her vulnerabilities. Some of the things Rebecca said made sense, the talk about whether this new relationship was worth the destruction, the questions, the compromising, and the resentment. In the occasional moments when Karen saw Rebecca's point of view, she, too, wondered if being with Nick was worth everything it took. Because on those days—when Rebecca was particularly emotional—it had taken more than Karen's reservoir had to offer, temporarily depleting her optimism and her convictions.

The divorce, itself, had gone well, her lawyer said, as divorces go. Bob had been extremely generous, both with his time and his money. He and Denise agreed to having Rebecca and Robert every other weekend and on one night during the week when it worked out. This had taken some time to iron out, since Denise hadn't talked to Bob for a full month after she found out he was married. She expected him to woo her all over again, which Karen had found amusing. Eventually, he did win her, as only Bob Parsons could. And when he did and announced their plans to marry, Karen had felt the squeeze of jealousy, even though she knew she had no right to such feelings.

Bob still traveled a great deal, so more often than not the kids spent their weeks with Karen and Nick. They were not yet ready—Rebecca had announced she would never be ready—to spend the night with just Denise and their stepsister, Melody, who was three months old.

Nick's wife, too, had given Nick very little trouble. Trisha still worked constantly, meaning Nick had his girls most of the time. Karen had worked hard at establishing a warm relationship with Abby, ten, and Emily, eight, and they were usually receptive. However, she was sometimes surprised by their presence, as if they had been dropped off for a sleepover at the wrong house.

The strangest, hardest part for Karen had been the adjustment to living with and marrying a man who had been her lover. She realized how ludicrous that sounded—she had gone through the same process with Bob—but her marriage to Nick was different from her fantasies about their union. Before, when she had imagined them together, their common lives were like their romantic dates. Nick was showered and sweet smelling. He was cooking for her, feeding her, laughing with her, and telling her how much he adored her. They made passionate love, insatiable for each other's nakedness. The best part of Karen's dream world, however, was Nick's constant attention. When he and Karen were in the same room, he was completely focused on her needs, powerless to pursue anything but that single goal.

Karen poured a cup of coffee and sat down at the kitchen table, knowing how foolish she had been. She had pictured her new life much like a teenage girl thinks of marriage rather than a thirty-eight-year-old woman who knows better. After all, she had been married for almost fourteen years to Bob. She knew what it was like to raise children and run a household. She knew how busy and tedious the days could be, and she knew how unappreciated she felt for steering everyone in the house through those days, those weeks, those years. After all, it was that lack of appreciation that had made Karen turn in another direction, wasn't it? And here she was again. It wasn't exactly the same. Nick was a caring and loving and wonderful man; that hadn't changed. What had changed was this: Nick was now a father, a husband, and a constant presence rather than a secret lover.

Setting up house had been exhilarating. Karen loved having Nick's clothes in their walk-in closet, his toiletries around the other sink in the master bathroom. They would look at each other in the morning and laugh, as if they'd gotten away with something while the rest of the world was looking the other way. The children, except for Rebecca, had been on their best behavior, not quite knowing what to say or how to act in the presence of someone new. Behind closed doors, Rebecca had screamed at her mother and cried until her red, swollen eyes could no longer expel water. But that was only at first. Six months into the new arrangement, Rebecca had grown to tolerate Nick, who had enough sense to give her the space she needed at the beginning. She complained to Karen about the difficulties of being a child of divorce, but Karen knew the divorce also had its benefits. Rebecca saw her father about as much as she used to, considering his travel schedule. And when she did see him, he lavished her with gifts—every teenager appreciated the latest technology gadget—and his attention. In fact, he paid more attention to Rebecca and Robert now than he had ever paid to them as their live-in father.

Robert sometimes missed Bob. He had always been the one to enthusiastically greet his father when Bob came home from work, especially after a business trip, and to eagerly listen at the dinner table to Bob's stories while Rebecca begged to be excused and Karen's brain had shut down. He loved his dad, and not for any obvious reason. Bob hadn't paid extra attention to Robert. He hadn't, even once that Karen could remember, sat down on the floor with him to build Lego houses and play with Robert's large collection of toy cars. He hadn't even talked much to his son. But Robert adored him. And so Robert, like his sister, sometimes cried at night. When he did, Karen went to him and lay down beside him until he fell back asleep. She had mentioned it to Bob several times, and he dutifully promised to spend more time with Robert. But as soon as another business trip surfaced, Bob was gone. Work still came first.

Yet, Bob was different, too. He seemed happier than he had before, and somehow more relaxed. When he picked up the children, he was pleasant and appeared to look forward to the weekend. He chatted with Karen in her kitchen while Rebecca and Robert, who were more eager to go with their father than Karen had predicted, packed their things in the colorful duffels Bob had bought for this purpose. On one occasion, Karen and Bob even split a beer, Karen keenly aware of the fact that both of them had drunk from the same bottle.

Karen sipped her coffee and smiled. And had he always been that good-looking? Nick was handsome, in a very youthful way. His fine, sandy-blond hair (that he had grown even longer during the divorce) took flight when he walked. His face looked clean-shaven, even after skipping a day. His cheeks had a little bit of color, as if he had just come in from outdoors. His soft brown eyes exuded compassion. And he was surrounded by an inexplicable aura of paternity. Most of the young reporters and editors in the newsroom considered Nick a father figure as well as a boss.

The opposite, Bob was rugged looking. He had thick brown hair that barely moved, even in a strong wind. He had a thick beard that he shaved every morning—even on the weekends—only to appear like he needed another shave by dinnertime. It was a manly look, Karen decided. Something she'd seen a thousand times on television commercials for razors and shaving cream. And his eyes were the same blue, with a touch of gray, as the sky sometimes looked after a rainstorm. Their bodies, too, were different, Nick's and Bob's. Nick was thin and toned, like a long-distance runner. For someone who loved food, Nick had no visible fat. There would be no paunch in the years to come. There would be no shopping trips for pants in bigger sizes. Bob was more solid and muscular. He ran three or four times a week, but looked more like a wrestler. He had a broad chest and thick thighs and a stomach that had the potential to hang over his belt in his fifties. He looked like he was made of rock, while Nick appeared to have been constructed of thick twigs.

That they were different, even physically, made sense to Karen. After all, she left Bob because of all the things she didn't like about him. Nick was everything Bob was not: empathetic, sensitive, unselfish, and completely in love with his children. Bob was pigheaded, overly driven, obtuse when it came to family matters, and often unavailable to anyone other than his boss. However, since Karen was not living with Bob anymore, she didn't see those characteristics as closely and consistently as she once had. The sharpness of his personality flaws had dulled, now that their relationship had changed from husband and wife to the separated parents of Rebecca and Robert. The bitterness of the months and years leading up to the divorce, too, had subsided in Karen's mind, the bad taste gone. Once in a while—and it was usually just after she and Bob had talked and even laughed together while he waited for Rebecca and Robert to get their things ready for the weekend—she wondered what all the fighting had been about, wondered why they hadn't been able to work it all out. She told herself such thoughts were misguided and unproductive. She was with Nick now. Bob was with Denise. They were happy in their new arrangements. It was her current happiness, Karen concluded, that enabled her to have charitable thoughts about her ex-husband. She started when she felt a tap on her shoulder.

"Earth to Mother," said Rebecca, who walked to the fridge and opened it.

Karen smiled. "Good morning, honey. How did you sleep?"

Rebecca took the orange juice from the top shelf. "Why do you feel compelled to ask me that every morning?"

Karen shrugged. "Because my mother asked me, I guess. It's a good question." Rebecca poured herself some juice and sat down at the table with her mother. "What time is your rehearsal today?"

"Six to ten." Rebecca took a tablet from the bottle of multivitamins on the table and swallowed it with the juice. "I can't believe this is my last one. The play is this weekend you know."

"No. Really?" asked Karen, kidding her daughter.

"Daddy and Denise are going Friday night."

"And Nick, Robert, the girls, and I are going Saturday night. What a large fan club you have."

"Not really," said Rebecca, taking her juice glass to the sink. "All the CDs have the same arrangement."

CD was Rebecca's acronym for children of divorce. It was a term she coined just after the separation, and Karen had heard it dozens of times since. But it still bothered her. She walked into the mudroom, where Rebecca was slipping her feet into her shoes. She watched as Rebecca heaved her heavy pack onto her back. "What?" asked Rebecca, looking at Karen.

"Nothing. I'm just so excited for the play this weekend."

Rebecca smiled for the first time that morning. "Yeah, me too. It's going to be awesome."

"You're going to be awesome. I'm so proud of you." Rebecca lifted her eyes to the ceiling. "I really am." Rebecca tilted her face toward Karen, who kissed her cheek. While Rebecca didn't kiss her mother, she allowed Karen to kiss her. "I'll see you after school." Facing forward, Rebecca offered her mother a limp-wristed wave as she walked out the door.

Bob hadn't seen Billy more than in passing in months, so he eagerly accepted his old friend's invitation to meet him for a beer after work. When Bob called home to tell Denise (a practice she had lovingly insisted on and Bob had agreed to), she offered to get a sitter for their baby and join them. "I haven't been to Rascals in the longest time," she said. "That's where we met, honey."

"I know, sweetheart. And I think we should spend an evening there soon. Tonight, I think it's best if it's just Billy and me. You know Billy. He'd love to see you, but he can be such a guy's guy, too."

Denise laughed. "Actually, he's more of a ladies' guy. But I know what you mean."

"Two beers. I'll be home by seven thirty."

"I'll wait to make dinner. I'll put the baby to bed, and we can have some time together."

"Sounds good," said Bob, hoping Denise's reference included some quiet time. She could talk and talk.

Rascals was crowded, as usual, which Bob attributed to the fact that it was the only decent bar in town. There was Harry's, but that was mostly for the beer-guzzling, pool-playing crowd. And there was Moonlight, the bar in the Grand Hotel. But that was a typical first-date location: low lights, soft music, an extensive wine list, and soft-speaking servers. Bob and Karen had gone there a couple of times—just to do something different—but it was not a place where people had fun, which is what Bob was looking for when he went out. Rascals was the opposite. Walk through the door in a bad mood; twenty minutes later feel like a celebrity. It was the jovial atmosphere that made people genuinely feel good. Billy was standing with his back against the bar when Bob walked in. They waved at each other before Bob started his journey through and around the amiable mob to meet his friend, shaking his hand when he did. Billy patted Bob on the back. "I took the liberty of ordering you a pint of Samuel Adams," said Billy, knowing Bob was always on time.

"You are a true friend. I'll get the next one."

Billy peeled a ten-dollar bill off the wad of money he kept in his front pocket and laid it on the bar. He lifted the glass of freshly poured ale from its coaster and handed it to Bob. "To men," he said, lifting his half-empty glass. Bob laughed and touched his glass to Billy's. They both took a long drink. "Ah," he said. "There's no finer ale in all the kingdom."

"You are in fine form tonight."

"Me?" asked Billy, looking surprised.

"Who is she?"

"Who's who?"

"The woman who's got your number."

Billy took another drink. "Let me tell you," he said with a grin. "She had a lot more than my number last night."

Bob laughed. "Oh, here we go."

"No, no, no," said Billy, dismissive of Bob's suggestion. "There's nothing new to report. It's the same old thing."

Bob lifted his eyebrows. "Still resolved to remain a bachelor forever?"

"Until death do me part. But enough about me; let's hear about you. I see you're wearing your wedding ring this evening, which tells me everything is copacetic in the Parsons' household."

"Absolutely," said Bob, more enthusiastically than was warranted.

"Happy as a pig in shit, are you?"

"Happier." Bob shifted his eyes to his beer.

Billy leaned in close to his friend. "You wouldn't lie to your Uncle Billy, would you?"

"You are such a pain in the ass."

"Which is precisely why you're here with me instead of home with the wife."

"Denise. Her name is Denise."

"Of course it is. And how is Denise? Everything you could ask for and more?"

"She is."

"That's good," said Billy, again patting Bob on the back. "I hear the second time around is always better than the first."

"It's different. You go in with your eyes wide open."

"There's an innocence about the first one though, isn't there? It's the two of you against the world, especially when you're young. I mean, I was twenty-two when I married Stacy, and you were about the same age when you married Karen, weren't you?"

Bob's heart thumped at his ex-wife's name. On some mornings, he woke up thinking they were still together. "Twenty-three," he said. "Karen was twenty-two."

Both men finished their beers. Bob turned around and ordered two more drafts. This would be his last, he told himself. Billy would undoubtedly try to talk him into a third—after all, he had no one to go home to—but Bob would be firm in his resolve. Three beers always led to four. The bartender placed two brimming glasses down on the bar and took the twenty Bob had set down. Bob turned around and handed a beer to Billy. They nodded their heads at each other somberly, then took their first sips.

"I think the people who wait to get married have a better chance of making it," said Billy, looking around the room. "Take that couple over there. They're both in their early-to-mid-thirties with no wedding bands on their fingers. They're talking and laughing with each other and looking like they're having a good time. He's not trying to grope her underneath the table, and she's not trying to put her unshod foot in his crotch. There's a dignity, a maturity about them that men and women in their twenties just don't have."

Bob laughed. "You're in your early forties and still groping women every chance you get."

Billy shook his head. "I'm a different sort of person. I'm not your typical Joe—simply because I don't want to get married. But if I did want to get married, I sure as hell wouldn't be standing here with you. In fact, I wouldn't come to this trendy pick-up joint at all."

"How can you say that about your second home?" said Bob, teasing his friend.

Billy made a face. "It's a bar, Bob. Drunks like bars." Bob sipped his beer. A moment later, Billy clapped him on the shoulder. "Enough of the doom and gloom." He forced a smile.

"Look, you can get out of this place, this life, if you want to," said Bob, seriously. "Just because you've told everyone you're a confirmed bachelor doesn't mean you have to be one."

Billy shook off Bob's remark. "I don't have what it takes to make a good husband. I don't have the commitment level. I don't have the energy."

"The energy for what?"

"The energy to sustain the level of care and concern that every marriage needs," said Billy. "It's easy in the beginning. The husband and wife are madly in love, as well as having great sex constantly. It's very easy to be married at that point. Now, when the children come along, and the pressures of your job escalate, and your wife shuts down, and your next-door neighbor is looking pretty good in her short skirts and heels, and life closes in—these are the kinds of things that test wedding vows. An ordinary marriage can't survive it. Because when the going gets tough, the tough usually aren't as tough as they thought."

Bob nodded his head and then finished his beer, not wanting to get caught up in Billy's melancholy. "I'm going to take off," he said, putting his empty glass on the bar. "Come with me for some dinner. I know Denise would love to see you."

"Nah. I'm going to hang a little bit longer. Thanks though."

"You okay?"

"Absolutely. Listen, stop by the florist on your way home and get Denise some flowers."

"I will. You take care." Bob shook his friend's hand.

"I always do."

Bob walked out into the warm evening air, but Billy's words followed him, making him think about his marriage to Karen, making him admit that even though she had been the one to have an affair first that he had been more guilty than she had.

The next day, Bob called Karen from his office and asked her if she was free for lunch. Karen's stomach lurched. "Is everything okay?"

"Yes. Everything's great. I just thought it would be nice to get together for more than ten minutes. When I pick up and drop off the kids, it's always so hectic. So, can you meet me at the downtown deli at one?"

Karen thought for a moment. "Yes. I can do that."

When Karen walked into the deli, Bob was already sitting at a table by the window. He smiled and stood when he saw her. As soon as she reached the table, he leaned in and kissed her on the cheek. "Hi."

She cocked her head back, startled. "What was that for?"

Bob shrugged. "I don't know. Thirteen years, I guess." Karen gave him a questioning look. "Okay, enough of that. Why don't you stay here while I get us something to eat. Roast beef, Swiss, lettuce, tomato, and lots of mayonnaise on whole wheat?"

Karen laughed. "Yes. Grilled ham, cheddar, and tomato on rye for you?"

Bob smiled. "I'll be right back."

As Bob stood in line, he looked back at his former wife. She was sitting with her back to the large window behind her. The sun shone through the glass, surrounding her in soft, cream-colored light. She held a dessert menu in her lap and was looking down at it, her face in light shadow. Her coppery hair, shorter now than it had been in college, but every bit as vibrant, framed her face. And in an instant, Bob was back in the bustling student center at State, working his way through the crowded hallway and seeing Karen Spears for the first time. She was an angelic vision, aglow in heavenly serenity. Bob had been able to think of nothing else that day. And when he met her, he worked as hard as he had at anything in his life to win her love.

"Can I help you, sir?" Bob looked at the woman behind the deli counter.

"What?"

"What can I get you for lunch?" Bob frowned. What happened to that love? He ordered their sandwiches and walked back to the table. Karen looked up at him as he approached.

"Save room for dessert," she said brightly. "This caramel cheesecake looks amazing."

Bob sat down. "What happened to us?" Karen's smile faded as he reached across the table and covered her hand with his. "What was so bad that we couldn't work it out?"

Karen looked out the window. "It's different looking back on it than it was going through it."

"It was horrible going through it?"

Karen tilted her head. "Sometimes."

"The fighting was horrible. But it's hard, now, to remember what brought on the fighting."

Karen sighed. "We were living different lives, Bob. You were caught up in work and traveling, and I was bogged down with stay-at-home motherhood. Our worlds were so far apart. . . ."

"That there was no way to get them back together?"

Julie, a perky blonde in her twenties wearing an apron and a pin-on name tag, arrived at their table with a tray holding their sandwiches and tall glasses of ice water. She set the glasses down, then held a green plastic basket in the air. "Roast beef?"

"Right here," said Karen.

Julie set the basket down in front of Karen. "You're going to love this," she said. "The roast beef arrived this morning. And the grilled ham and cheese for you, sir." Bob nodded, and Julie placed his basket down. "Enjoy your lunch," she sang as she walked away.

"Sure," said Karen, returning to their conversation, "there are ways to get back together, but both people have to want to. Other things—women like Denise—get in the way."

"Men like Nick get in the way, too."

Karen shook her head. "If this is where this conversation is going, then I don't want to have it. Let's try not to lay blame at each other's feet, because both of us were at fault. Instead of turning to each other for love and support, we started to look elsewhere."

Bob took a bite of his sandwich. "I don't know why we did that." After he swallowed, he said, "I'm sorry, Karen."

Karen looked down at her roast beef sandwich. "I'm sorry, too." She took a bite of her sandwich, hoping that swallowing food would ease the ache in her throat.

"We did have some good times," he said. "Remember the time the power went out and we drank warm white wine by candlelight in the bathtub?"

Karen smiled. "And remember when we decided to go on a family picnic and Robert ate all of the devilled eggs in the car and then threw up when we got there?"

Bob laughed. "Rebecca was asleep, or she definitely would have squealed on him."

"She still sleeps in the car. I can't drive to Rite Aid without her taking a nap. I don't know how she's ever going to drive on her own."

"Trust me. She'll figure it out. She's one smart girl."

"Yes, she is. She takes after you."

Bob held up his hand. "No, no. She's absolutely your daughter, from her brainy head to her well-shaped feet."

Karen smiled. "She does have gorgeous feet."

"As do you."

And so the conversation went for the next hour: an exchange of compliments, bursts of laughter, smiles of recognition, and tinges of regret. Bob and Karen finally stood, long after their lunches were gone, and walked out of the deli together. Bob walked Karen to her car, where they kissed each other on the lips before saying good-bye.

That afternoon Bob was distracted at work, his normal focus on strategies and percentages subverted by attention to the conversations he'd had with both Billy and Karen. He was stuck, a skipping record album, on the thought that if he and Karen had worked harder at their marriage, they would still be together. It was a futile line of thinking because nothing could be done about it. He was married to Denise, the woman he had left his marriage for and the mother of his baby. Karen, too, was no longer available, no longer his, now that she was with her *soul mate,* as she had once described Nick. Bob glanced at the spreadsheets covering his desk. Whatever the hell that meant; he thought he and Karen had been soul mates.

Karen looked at the kitchen clock; she had just over an hour before Robert came home. She looked in the cupboards and the fridge and, finding all the ingredients, decided to make turkey sausage lasagna for dinner, one of Nick's favorites and a meal tolerated by everyone else at the table. She took a whole-wheat baguette out of the freezer as the meat browned. She sliced the goat cheese, his suggestion for turning a plebian dish into a gourmet meal. Bob's favorite meal was steak, Caesar salad, and white garlic bread, a man's meal for a man's man. She didn't blame him anymore for who he was because, when she was honest with herself, she admitted that he had always been that way. He had always worked hard, even in college, which then was something Karen had admired about him. Unlike some of the other boys, who appeared to do little outside of drinking past capacity on the weekends and skipping afternoon classes in favor of playing touch football on the green, Bob had always been driven. He worked hard enough to eliminate his competition, both in the classroom and on the social scene. Hadn't he wooed Karen away from other suitors, including Ray McNamara, who had been ready to marry her and make her the very wealthy wife of a baseball legend? Karen looked out the windows into the backyard. Where would she be now if she had taken Ray up on his offer? St. Louis?

Karen sometimes wondered if Bob had proposed to her more out of the fear of losing her rather than out of an overwhelming desire to be her husband. It didn't really matter, she thought, as she layered the lasagna noodles in the pan. What mattered was that she had accepted his proposal, that she had agreed to marry him because she wanted to be with him for the rest of her life. She placed the goat cheese on top of the noodles and then ladled on a layer of sausage sauce, and then repeated the pattern, topping the final layer with mozzarella cheese and then covering the pan with aluminum foil. Rebecca and Robert ensured that she and Bob would continue to be together as parents, even though they were no longer life partners. Karen split the loaf of bread with a serrated knife. She couldn't look at her son without seeing her husband. And her daughter was just as smart and motivated as her dad. Once Rebecca shook her teenage angst, she would be every bit as successful as her father. Rebecca and Robert were Karen and Bob's children. Nick wasn't a part of that equation, just like she was outside the Venn diagram of Nick's relationship with Trisha and their girls, Abby and Emily. They were adorable girls, but they looked and acted nothing like Karen. Nick was visibly in love with his daughters, which Karen found both endearing and annoying. She wondered how and why he loved them so much, questioning her love for Rebecca and Robert. Her resentment of the trappings of motherhood had formed a wedge between her and her children, between her and her husband. Why hadn't she done something to temper that? Why wasn't she the type of mother, like Sarah, who could give up everything for her children? She put the lasagna in the oven. She had been as selfish as Bob. If both of them had been able to, had wanted to put their own interests and their innate stubbornness to the side, they should have been able to work it out.

When the phone rang, Karen was not surprised that it was Bob, even though he rarely called. "Hi. It's me." She sat down in a kitchen chair. "I've been thinking about you all afternoon."

Karen inhaled. "And I've been thinking about you."

"Why are we thinking about each other like this?"

"I don't know. We're questioning our decisions, I guess."

They were quiet for a moment. "Did we have a good marriage, Karen?"

"Yes," she said immediately. "For a while, we had a good marriage."

"Did we have something other marriages didn't, or was our marriage like everyone else's?"

Karen filled the teakettle with water. "We had a good marriage, Bob."

"So we blew it."

Karen smiled. Bob sounded like a little boy whose gym-class team had just lost a playground baseball game. "Yes. We blew it."

"I wish we had another chance." Karen put her hand to her chest. "Look," he said, in response to her silence. "I've got to run. I'll talk to you soon."

Bob walked through the door of the house he and Denise had bought several months ago. While everything was put away— Denise was incredibly organized and tidy—it still didn't feel like home. He set his heavy briefcase down and then draped his coat on one of the gold-tone hangers that hung in the front hall closet. "Hello!" Denise called. "We're in the kitchen."

Bob walked down the long hallway from the front of the house to the back and found Denise, his wife, sitting on the pristine white floor with Melody, his daughter. Denise stood when he entered the room, deftly scooping up Melody and kissing her cheek before she kissed Bob. "It's Daddy," Denise said, beaming at her daughter. "Daddy's home! How was your day, honey?"

"Good," said Bob, loosening his tie. "And yours?"

"Melody and I went grocery shopping so we could make you a nice dinner. How does lasagna sound?"

"Wonderful," said Bob, who hoped she'd put meat instead of spinach into it.

"Great." She kissed him on the lips. "I'm going to change her, and then we can sit down and talk. There's some red wine on the counter."

Bob uncorked the wine bottle. He poured two generous glasses and carried them back down the hall to the living room. He sat in one of the matching armchairs Denise called their thrones and took a sip from his glass. He closed his eyes. When he opened them, Denise was hovering over him with their daughter. She put Melody down in Bob's lap, and he put his arm around the daughter who didn't feel like Rebecca had, who didn't feel like his.

Across town, Karen took her first bite of lasagna as Robert talked about playing Little League baseball, and Emily made a face at the tangy Italian dressing Karen had put on the salad. "This is so good," said Nick, chewing.

Karen smiled at her new husband. Putting a piece of garlic bread into her mouth, she willed herself to focus on her family and the chatter at the table. When she looked at Robert's animated face, she saw Bob, and let the afternoon's conversation run again through her mind.

A CHANGING MARRIAGE

Susan Kietzman

About This Guide

The suggested questions are included
to enhance your group's
reading of Susan Kietzman's
A Changing Marriage!

DISCUSSION QUESTIONS

1. Within minutes of seeing Karen for the first time, Bob knows he is going to marry her. What is the difference between love at first sight and lust?

2. Bob is the youngest child in his family, and Karen is the oldest of her siblings. How does their birth order affect them as children and as adults?

3. If Karen and Bob have "a completely honest relationship, one that friends described as extraordinary," why is she attracted to Ray McNamara? What is it about Ray that continues to haunt Karen long into her married life?

4. Bob loves Rascals, the downtown bar that caters to young professionals, almost as much as his coworker Billy Townsend does. What is Bob attracted to? How does Rascals define his friendship with Billy?

5. Bob talks Karen into getting pregnant before she is ready, presumably because he wants children. Why does he spend so little time with Rebecca and Robert? Is this a conscious decision?

6. Karen has a meaningful, genuine friendship with Sarah Keyworth, and a more superficial, convenient friendship with her tennis buddies. Explain how these relationships shape Karen's views and attitudes.

7. Is Karen a good mother? How do her conflicted views about motherhood affect her parenting abilities? How does her frustration with her situation cross over into her relationship with Bob? Would Karen and Bob's relationship be different if they had chosen to not have children?

8. What does Karen's job at the local newspaper represent to her? Is her editor, Nick Fleming, a grown-up version of Ray McNamara?

9. Bob's global business trip presents him with opportunities that challenge his marital vows—yet he comes home resolved to be a better husband and father. What happens to his resolutions?

10. What does Denise Levy represent to Bob? Do Bob and Karen ever feel guilty about their relationships with Denise and Nick?

11. When Bob and Karen run into each other at Villa Cesare, their argument is short. Are they more sad than angry?

12. At the end of the novel, Bob and Karen have lunch together. What happens—and does it signal a new beginning?